PHANTOMS OF BRESLAU

PHANTOMS OF BRESLAU

Marek Krajewski

Translated from the Polish by
Danusia Stok

MACLEHOSE PRESS
QUERCUS · LONDON

First published in Great Britain in 2010 by

MacLehose Press
an imprint of Quercus
21 Bloomsbury Square
London WC1A 2NS

Originally published in Poland as *Widma w mieście Breslau*
by Wydawnictwo W.A.B. Co Ltd, 2005

A CIP catalogue reference for this book
is available from the British Library

ISBN (HB) 978 1 906694 73 9
ISBN (TPB) 978 1 906694 74 6

2   4   6   8   10   9   7   5   3   1

Designed and typeset in Octavian by Patty Rennie

Printed and bound in England by Clays Ltd, St Ives plc

Truth is like a sentence.
How did I deserve it?
STEVEN SAYLOR

BRESLAU, WEDNESDAY, OCTOBER 2ND, 1919
A QUARTER PAST EIGHT IN THE MORNING

Criminal Commissioner Heinrich Mühlhaus slowly climbed the stairs to the second floor of the Police Praesidium building at Schuhbrücke 49. Placing his foot on each step in turn, he pressed down with his full weight, to check whether the eighteenth-century sandstone would crack beneath the heels of his shining brogues. He would have liked to crumble the old stone to bits, scattering dust, and then retrace his steps to draw the caretaker's attention to the mess. He would then be able to delay going into his office. He would not have to see the pained expression on the face of his secretary, von Gallasen, nor look at the wall calendar, filled with important deadlines, with its picture of the recently constructed Technische Hochschule, or the framed photograph of his son, Jakob Mühlhaus, taken at his confirmation. Above all, he could avoid the troubling and unpleasant presence of the pathologist, Doctor Siegfried Lasarius, whom the police messenger had announced a moment earlier. This information had spoiled the Commissioner's mood. He did not like Lasarius, a man who considered the dead to be the best partners in conversation. And the dead appreciated him, too, even if they did not laugh at his jokes, lying as they were in the concrete troughs of the

1

Institute of Forensic Medicine, bathed in the icy water that streamed from a shuddering rubber hosepipe. Every one of Lasarius' visits heralded at best difficult questions, at worst serious problems. Nothing less than an interesting conceptual problem or a threat could induce Charon to leave his holdings. The Commissioner wanted to believe it was the former. He looked about him. He could see nothing that would give him an excuse to delay meeting the taciturn physician. Once again, he pressed his foot down on a stair. The lacquered leather of his shoes, reflecting the metallic leaves entwined around the bars of the banister and the colossal elevation of the stairs, creaked a little. A din and a loud cursing drifted up from the courtyard. Mühlhaus peered over a neglected fern, whose abominable condition was noticed by every woman who entered this male world. Although not a woman himself, he noted the gnarled twigs begging for water and, with an enraged expression, turned and ran downstairs towards the duty room. He did not reach it, however.

"Commissioner, sir!" he heard Lasarius' stentorian voice from above. He stopped and caught sight of the dark spread of a hat and the damp pattern formed by sparse wisps of hair on a skull. Lasarius was descending majestically. "I couldn't wait to see you."

"It's only five to nine," Mühlhaus said, pulling out a silver fob watch from his waistcoat. "Can't you wait a few seconds, Doctor? Is your business so urgent that we have to discuss it on the stairs?"

"There's nothing to discuss." Lasarius opened his leather briefcase and handed Mühlhaus two pages headed "Post-mortem Report", then stared out at the courtyard where the caretaker and a carter were clanking cans of paraffin about. "We're not going to say anything at all. Not a word. To anybody."

"Especially not to Mock," Mühlhaus rounded off after quickly reading the report. He observed the bewhiskered carter who was passing the cans to the caretaker and was so puffed up his waistcoat buttons seemed about

2

to shoot across the courtyard in all directions. "Doctor Lasarius, don't your stiffs have names? Why are these two anonymous? If you don't know their names, you should give them some. Even farm cattle have names."

"In my book, Commissioner Mühlhaus," the physician murmured, "there's no difference between cattle and humans, apart from the size of their heart or liver. What is it like in your profession?"

"We'll call them . . ." the police officer passed over the question and glanced at the paraffin cart which bore the logo: "Lighting Articles – Salomon Beyer". ". . . we'll call them Alfred Salomon and Catarina Beyer."

"I baptize you in the name of the Father and of the Son and of the Holy Ghost," said Lasarius. He rested his briefcase on the banister, jotted down the names in the relevant spaces and made a sign of the cross over the pages.

"Not a word to anybody . . . especially Mock," repeated Mühlhaus, lost in thought, and he shook the physician's hand. "There's no distinction between men and animals in my profession either. But it's hard to keep files without names."

BRESLAU, THAT SAME OCTOBER 2ND, 1919
NINE O'CLOCK IN THE MORNING

Criminal Assistant Eberhard Mock staggered out of Affert's tobacconists in a dark gateway on the north side of Ring. The October sun dazzled his cloudy irises over which, every now and again, his swollen eyelids drooped. Swaying on his feet, he leaned on the gate to the Ring Theatre and slipped a pince-nez with vivid yellow lenses onto his nose. Now, thanks to the skill of Jena Opticians, everything around him was drenched in a bright glow. Acrid cigarette smoke found its way between the lenses and the whites of Mock's eyes, which were scored with red veins. Mock gasped and blew out the smoke, instinctively covering his eyes with his hands. He hissed in pain: his eyelids were a mass of neuron endings, and hard nodules drifted beneath the clammy skin. Holding on to the wall with one hand, he proceeded like a blind man and turned into Schmiedebrücke. His palm glided over the glazed shopfront of Proskauer's Menswear. Glare reflecting off the golden watches laid out in the window of Kühnel's pierced his eyes. He scraped along the rough walls of the building occupied by the German Fisheries Company until he eventually crossed Nadlerstrasse and hit upon the glass door of Heymann's Coffee House.

Mock staggered inside. At this time of day the coffee house was still empty and quiet. In the main room, a boy in a stiff white apron was busy stacking tables and chairs into pyramids, breaking up the activity from time to time with skilful swipes of a damp cloth to gather dust and cigarette ash from the surfaces of the tables and tablecloths. Seeing Mock trip and fly straight towards the fragile pyramid of furniture, he unintentionally swung his cloth and whipped the face of this early customer. The bright-yellow pince-nez danced on its chain, Mock lost his centre of gravity, and the tables and chairs their stability. The boy watched aghast as the well-built, dark-haired man landed on the chairs' jutting legs and curved back-supports, breaking some of them with a terrible crash while starched tablecloths tumbled onto his head. Particles of dust flickered in the October morning sun. An open salt cellar fell into Mock's thick hair and salt trickled down his cheeks with a faint rustle. The Criminal Assistant closed his eyes in defence and the stinging intensified. He was pleased – the pain would prevent him from falling asleep, would work better than the six cups of strong coffee which he had already managed to consume since five o'clock that morning. Contrary to the young waiter's assumption, there was not a milligram of alcohol in Mock's veins. Mock had not slept for four days; Mock was doing everything he could so as not to sleep.

4

Although Heymann's Coffee House was not yet open, two men sat there raising cups of steaming black coffee to their lips. One of them was smoking cigarette after cigarette, the other — ivory stem of his pipe clenched between his teeth — expelled small columns of smoke from the corner of his mouth into the thicket of his beard. The young waiter did everything he could to make the dark-haired man — a police officer, as it turned out — forget the recent incident. He cleared away the broken furniture, brought coffee and milk, had the famous Friedrichshof biscuits delivered from S. Brunies, the nearby patisserie, twisted cigarettes into his little pipe-shaped cigarette-holder for him, and listened attentively to the conversation in order to read every wish of the man he had so severely mistreated. At one point the victim of his cleaning manoeuvres took a few sheets of folded paper from the inside pocket of his jacket and handed them to the bearded man. The latter read them, puffing out squat mushrooms of smoke from his pipe. His companion brought a small phial to his nose and the pungent smell of urine drifted across the table. The boy escaped behind the bar in disgust. The bearded man read carefully, his features and folds of skin forming a question mark.

"Mock, why have you written this absurd statement to the press? And why are you showing it to me?"

"Commissioner, sir, I am . . ." — Mock pondered his next words, as if speaking a language he was not in full command of — "a loyal subordinate. I know that if . . . if a newspaper were to print this, then I'm finished. Yes, finished. Dismissed from the police force. Without a job. That's why I'm telling you about it."

"And what?" In a shaft of sunlight which cut through the clouds of smoke, tiny droplets of spittle could be clearly seen settling on Mühlhaus' beard. "You want me to save you from being thrown out?"

5

"I don't know what I want," Mock whispered, afraid he might close his eyes at any moment and be transported to the land of his childhood: to the Heuscheuergebirge, covered in dry leaves and warmed by the autumn sun, where he used to go with his father. "I'm like a soldier, informing my commanding officer of my resignation."

"You're one of the men I want for my new murder commission." The bowl of Mühlhaus' pipe gurgled. "I don't want idiots who trample over evidence left at crime scenes, whose only assets are exemplary military service. I don't want former informers who work for both sides. And I don't want to lose you because of this absurd statement of yours which will make a laughing stock of the entire Police Praesidium. You've been holding back from sleep for several days now. If you've gone clean out of your mind, as both this statement and your behaviour seem to indicate, then you won't be much use to me anyway. So you have to tell me everything. If you remain silent, I'll take you for a lunatic and leave. If you talk nonsense, I'll also leave."

"Commissioner, sir," Mock said, placing the phial of smelling salts on the table. "Please hold this under my nose if I start to fall asleep. I'm glad you don't mind the stench of ammonia. Hey, you," he called to the boy. "What time do you open? We've enough time, Commissioner," he said when he heard the answer. "And you, boy, I want you out of my sight. Come back just before opening time."

The boy ran out, happy to relieve his nostrils of the unpleasant smell. Mock rested his elbows on the table, slipped on his world-brightening pince-nez, and turned his face towards the sunlight pouring through the lace curtains on the front window. He rubbed his eyes, hissed in pain and then slapped them with open palms. Fireworks exploded beneath his eyelids. The corners of his eyes stung. His cigarette burned down in the ashtray.

"I'm fine now," Mock said, taking a few breaths. "I won't fall asleep.

I can tell you now. As you might have gathered, it's all to do with that investigation of ours, the Four Sailors case . . ."

BRESLAU, MONDAY, SEPTEMBER 1ST, 1919
HALF PAST SEVEN IN THE MORNING

Mock opened the heavy two-winged door and found himself in a flagstoned hallway in near darkness. He made his way forward slowly, without bothering to muffle the ringing of his spurs. Suddenly he came across a velvet curtain, and drawing it aside he entered another hallway, a waiting room with doors leading to several rooms. One of them was open but another curtain hung from its lintel, which made Mock hesitate for a moment. In one of the waiting-room walls, instead of a door, there was a window that gave, so Mock assumed, on to the ventilation pit. On its outside sill stood a paraffin lamp whose feeble glow barely penetrated the dusty windowpane. In this meagre twilight, Mock could make out several figures sitting in the waiting room. He did not, however, manage to get a closer look at them since his attention was drawn to the curtain hanging at the door of the room. It moved abruptly, and from behind it came a sigh. Mock made towards it but a tall man in a top hat barred his way. When Mock tried to move him aside, the man took off his headwear. In the pale semi-darkness, knots of scar tissue were clearly visible as they refracted the light. Instead of eyes, the man had a tangle of criss-crossing and interweaving scars.

Mock looked at their thick lines, at the dark patches that stood out on the wall next to his bed. He rubbed his eyes and turned away from the wall. The curtain isolating his bed alcove was bathed in sunlight.

From beyond the curtain came the sound of his father's bustling. Mugs clattered, stove lids rattled, fire crackled and bread crunched beneath the weight of a knife. Mock reached for the metal jug beside his bed and sat up so as not to spill the water as he drank. He tilted the jug and liquid poured into his dried-up orifice of a mouth and over his rough, swollen tongue. It flowed in a broad stream and soaked his nightshirt, which was tied at the neck with stiffly starched straps. Rusty rings squeaked along the metal rail, the curtain parted and let a bright band of light into the stuffy alcove.

"You look like the seven plagues of Egypt," said a short, stocky man holding a chipped mug in his gnarled fingers.

His facial features, which had absorbed the fumes of boiling shoe-glue, his brown liver spots and stern, grey eyes had combined to make Willibald Mock the bogeyman of local children. Eberhard Mock was not afraid of his father, as he had long since ceased to be a child. He was thirty-six years old and had a piece of metal in his thigh, as well as rheumatism, bad memories, and a weakness for alcohol and red-headed women. Now, above all else, he had a hangover. He stowed the jug under his bed, side-stepped his father and entered the sun-drenched room which served as both kitchen and his father's bedroom. Uncle Eduard, who had died several months earlier, had once jointed beef carcasses here, flattened tender pieces of pork and pounded sticky chunks of liver. It was here that he had stuffed intestines smelling of Riesengebirge bonfires, and then hung rings of sausages above the stove where Willibald Mock had set milk to warm for his hungover son.

"Don't drink so much," his father said as he left the alcove. Grey whiskers bristled above his thin lips. "I never neglected my work. I always sat down to my shoes at the same time each day. My hammering in the workshop was like the cuckoo of a clock."

"I'll never match up to you, Father," said Mock a touch too loudly as he went over to the basin by the window and splashed his face with water. He opened the window and hung a razor-sharpening strap onto a nail. "Besides, I'm on duty a little later today."

8

"What kind of duty is that?" Willibald Mock struggled with small bottles of medicine. "Booking whores and pimps. You should be out on the beat helping people."

"Let it be, old man," Mock said as he sharpened his razor and rubbed soap onto the thick bristles of a shaving brush. "You, on the other hand, spent your life breathing in the odour of other people's smelly feet."

"What did you say?" His father cracked eggs into a cast-iron frying pan. "What did you say? You're talking quietly on purpose because I'm deaf."

"Nothing. I'm talking to myself." Mock scraped the foam off his cheeks with the razor.

His father sat down at the table, breathing heavily. He stood the frying pan with its yellowy mush on the bread board from which he had first carefully removed all crumbs. Then he spread slices of bread with dripping and arranged them one on top of the other to form a rectangular stack, evening out the edges so that none protruded at the sides. Eberhard Mock wiped the foam from his face, rubbed his cheeks and chin with a shaving stick, pulled on his vest and sat down at the table.

"How can you knock back so much?" With a pair of scissors, his father snipped the stalks of an onion growing in a flower pot and sprinkled them over the scrambled eggs. He separated the slices of bread he had already stuck together and scattered a tiny amount of chives between each one, and then stuck them back together and wrapped them in greased parchment. "I never got so drunk. But you do almost every day. Remember to bring the paper home – I'll use it again tomorrow."

Mock ate the semi-liquid egg garnished with its thatch of chives with relish, then got to his feet, slid the frying pan into a tub of water by the washbasin, put on his shirt, fastened a square collar to it and knotted his tie. On his head he placed a bowler hat, then he walked to the corner of the room and opened a hatch in the floor. He descended the steps to the former butcher's shop and stopped to glance at the row of hooks from which pigs' carcasses had once hung, at the polished counter, at the gleaming shop window and stone slabs that slanted slightly towards a drain covered with an iron grille. Uncle Eduard had once poured warm animal blood into this grille.

Mock heard the wheeze of his father's breathing and violent coughing coming from overhead. He smelled coffee being poured into a thermos. The coffee's steam had momentarily taken his father's breath away, he thought, or rather whatever had not already been taken away by the bone-glue fumes. Mock stepped outside, tinkling the brass bell on the doorframe.

From the window Willibald Mock watched his son as he walked through the back door and into the yard. Bowing to the caretaker, Mrs Bauert, Eberhard Mock glimpsed the friendly smile bestowed on him by the maid of Pastor Gerds — the tenant of a four-roomed apartment at the front of the house — who was standing by the pump. Snorting at a stray cat, he accelerated his step, jumped over a puddle and, unfastening his trousers and swearing at the excessive number of buttons, forced the rusty padlock and entered the privy in the corner of the yard.

His father closed the window and returned to his chores. He washed the frying pan, plate and milk pan, and wiped the oilcloth that was fastened to the table with drawing pins. He took his medicines and sat in the old rocking chair for a moment in silence. He stepped into his son's alcove and stared at the tangled sheets on the bed. As he leaned over to fold them, his foot kicked the jug containing what remained of the water. It overturned and water ran into one of his leather slippers.

"Damn it!" he yelled, shaking his leg; the slipper flew straight into Mock's face as he closed the hatch in the floor. His father sank onto his son's bed and quickly unfastened the straps holding up his sock, which he removed and smelled.

"Don't get worked up," smiled Mock. "I don't use a chamber pot any more, and even if I did I wouldn't hide it under my bed. It's only water."

"Alright, alright . . ." muttered his father, pulling his sock back on with difficulty. He was still on his son's bed. "Why do you need water under your bed? Oh, I know. It's there ready for your hangover. You're always knocking it back, knocking it back . . . If you got married, you'd stop drinking . . ."

"Did you know, Father" – Mock handed his father the slipper, sat down at the table and sprinkled a few pinches of blond tobacco onto the oilcloth – "that schnapps actually helps me?"

"Do what?" his father asked, taken aback by the friendly tone. His reproaches about alcohol and bachelorhood usually incensed his son.

"Sleep through the night." Eberhard lit a cigarette and arranged on the table the objects which would soon find themselves in his briefcase: the packet with bread and dripping, a tobacco pouch and an oilcloth file containing reports. "I've told you a hundred times – if I go to bed sober, I get terrible nightmares; I wake up and can't get back to sleep! I prefer hangovers to nightmares."

"You know what's better for helping you sleep?" The father began to make his son's bed. "Chamomile and hot milk." He straightened the sheet and suddenly looked up at him. "Do you always have nightmares when you're sober?"

"Not always," Eberhard smiled, closing the steel fastenings on his briefcase. "Sometimes I dream of the nurse in Königsberg. Red-headed and very pretty."

"You've been to Königsberg? You never told me." The father held up a jacket as his son slipped his arms and broad shoulders into the sleeves.

"I was there during the war." Eberhard fanned himself with his bowler hat and reached for his watch. "There's nothing else to say. Goodbye, Father."

11

He made his way towards the hatch in the floor, hearing his father muttering behind his back: "He'd better not drink so much. Only chamomile and hot milk. Chamomile and hot milk."

In the Hospital of Divine Mercy in Königsberg, a cadet officer of one year's standing used to be given chamomile before he went to sleep. The beautiful, red-headed nurse gazed with admiration at the polished boots fitted with spurs that stood by his bed. She had called him "Officer", not realizing that every scout from the artillery regiment wore spurs since they rode on horseback. Addressing him thus, she had poured spoonfuls of the infusion into his mouth. Twice-wounded Cadet Officer Mock did not have the strength to protest that he was not an officer, and was ashamed to admit that he had not passed his exams or undergone the appropriate training, but had found himself in the war simply through conscription. He was too shy to ask his angel her name, and he did not have the strength to turn his head to watch her go. In an attempt to broaden his field of vision, he had traced burning circles with his eyes. All they took in, unfortunately, was the neo-Gothic vaulting of the hospital. They did not see either the soldiers lying next to him or Cornelius Rühtgard, the greying, slender orderly to whom Mock owed his life; and the red-headed nurse did not fall within the wounded cadet officer's field of vision ever again. Much later, when his broken limbs had set and he could move around on crutches; when finally he learned that his injuries indicated that he must have fallen from a great height, that the orderly Rühtgard – until recently a doctor in Cameroon – had, on his way to work, found him abandoned on Litauer Wallstrasse, and had quickly taken him to the hospital to treat his ribs and his lungs, which had been punctured by splintered rib bone; when Cadet Officer Mock knew all of this, he began his search for the red-headed nurse. Limping along, he rapped his crutches on the sandstone flags, but everywhere he met with a lack of understanding. The nurses grew impatient when the convalescent produced yet another description of their supposed red-headed colleague, looked them in the eyes for the hundredth time and tried to catch the scent of their bodies. The caretakers and ward attendants shook their heads, some tapping their brows when he spoke of steaming cups of chamomile, until finally the former doctor Rühtgard, demoted to the rank of orderly, explained to the patient that the red-headed nurse may have been a figment of his imagination. Hallucinations were not unknown in people in similar states to that of Cadet Officer Mock on his arrival at the Hospital of Divine Mercy in Königsberg. For he had been totally unconscious. Not because he had fallen from a great height, but from alcohol.

Now Eberhard Mock went down the stairs to his Uncle Eduard's old butcher shop.

"Chamomile and hot milk. Gets drunk, so he gets what's coming to him," came the voice of his father from overhead; he had remedies for all his son's ailments.

Eberhard heard a hard hammering on the windowsill. "Must be that moron Dosche with his foul dog," he thought. "That mongrel's going to be shitting all over the polished stairs again while Dosche and my father play chess all day."

The scrambled eggs and chives made him gag like a hair stuck in his throat. "Chamomile and hot milk. He knocks it back, always knocking it back." Mock turned and went back up the stairs. His head appeared above the floor. The sill rattled again. His father was at the window, hopping on one foot; on his other hung a darned sock.

"Can you not understand, Father," yelled Eberhard, "that chamomile and milk don't bloody well work on me? I don't have a problem falling asleep, it's the dreaming!"

Willibald Mock stared at his son, understanding nothing. The torso above the hatch. Clenched fists. Hangover gushing in his head like the sea. Chamomile and hot milk. The father grew pale and did not say a word.

13

"And tell that shitty chessplayer, Dosche, not to come here with his mongrel and not to thump on the windowsill so hard, or he'll be sorry."

Eberhard's legs were now in the room too. Without looking at his father, he went to the basin, knelt beside it, removed his bowler hat and poured a few ladles of water over his wavy hair. He heard his father's voice through the stream of water that gushed over his ears: "It's not Dosche hammering on the sill, it's somebody for you."

Eberhard leaned towards the old man and slipped the sock over his foot.

BRESLAU, THAT SAME SEPTEMBER 1ST, 1919
EIGHT O'CLOCK IN THE MORNING

Kurt Smolorz had not been working under Mock in Vice Department IIIb of Breslau's Police Praesidium for long. He had landed there straight off the streets of Kleinburg, where he had walked the beat without knowing why; in truth, this beautiful villa district adjacent to South Park had about as much in common with crime as Constable Smolorz had with poetry. Yet on one warm day in 1918, it was precisely there that some dangerous criminals, sought by all the police in Europe, had crossed the constable's path. And it was a happy day for him. Criminal Assistant Mock had been doing a routine check in a plush house of ill repute on Akazienallee. He had a habit of combining pleasure with work. After checking the income ledger and the health records, and when he had quizzed the madam about her more eccentric clients, he had begun to look around for his favourite lady who, as it turned out, was busy, along with two other employees, pleasuring two – and here the madam sighed – very rich gentlemen.

Intrigued by the configuration of two to three, Mock had peeped through a concealed window into the so-called pink room and received a shock. He had run out into the street and immediately bumped into the red-headed constable, who was clanging his sword threateningly and tugging at the collar of a rascal he had apprehended a moment earlier for firing a catapult at passing droschkas. On Mock's orders, Constable Smolorz had punished the rascal with a hefty clout and let him go. Then, together with Mock, he had burst into the pink room of Madame Blaschke's establishment and – rubbing his eyes in astonishment at such a complicated arrangement of bodies as he had never seen before – arrested the two men, who had turned out to be none other than Kurt Wirth and his mute bodyguard Hans Zupitza, pioneers of European coercion and extortion. That day a great deal changed in the lives of the protagonists of this event, and they all became permanently linked: Wirth collaborated with Mock and was rewarded when the latter turned a blind eye to his extortion of smugglers who floated arms from Austria, coffee from Turkey and tobacco down the River Oder. Mock had become a rich and influential man in the criminal underworld, and this was to prove extremely useful to him. Smolorz, meanwhile, had gone from being a district constable to an employee at the Police Praesidium. Like all the *dramatis personae*, he held a sizeable bank account of dollars paid by Europe's most wanted criminals in return for their freedom. Mock soon recognized Smolorz's assets as a colleague, and one of the most valuable of these was his reticence.

Smolorz was silent even now as he sat next to Mock in a river-police motorboat steered by a uniformed boatswain. They navigated the shallow flood waters of the River Ohlau among sparse trees and partially submerged fields. The motorboat moored at a temporary landing stage not far from a paved road.

"New House!" shouted the boatswain, as he helped Smolorz and Mock to disembark.

A droschka was waiting for them on the road. Mock recognized the cabby, whose services the police had often found indispensable. He shook his hand and threw himself onto the settle, rocking the carriage. Smolorz took the seat up on the box and the droschka moved off. Mock, attempting to forget the thirst which tormented him, studied the outbuildings of New House. The lowing of cattle could be heard from Swiątniki Farm, two kilometres away. The smell of damp air from the Oder wafted through the sunlight. After a while they came to a lock where they climbed out of the droschka and crossed over to the island, Ottwitzer Werder.

At Ottwitzer Dam, among blackthorn bushes, Mock spied the destination of his morning's travels across the flood waters of the Oder and the Ohlau tributary. A dangerous cascade of water spurting from the base of the dam kept at bay the gawpers who were standing on the embankment by the hamlet of Bischofswal, trying to see what the police had discovered on the island on which only the previous day they had enjoyed their picnics and beer. They were prevented from stepping onto the dam by the strong arms and fierce glares of three sword-bearing gendarmes who wore shakos adorned with a blue star and on their chests sported badges that gleamed with the words "Gendarme Station Schwoitsch". Mock gazed with nostalgia at the elegant pseudo-Gothic building in the vicinity of Landungsbrücke and remembered the nocturnal pleasures to which he had so recently surrendered. Now duties of a different nature had summoned him to this distant corner of Breslau. He turned to the river-bank fringed with thorn bushes and to the pile of four – so Mock guessed – human bodies. They were covered with the Institute of Forensic Medicine's grey sheets, which were always carried in the carriages and first cars to arrive from the Police Praesidium. Seven detectives were already there, five of whom were examining the ground immediately surrounding the bodies; squatting, they searched centimetre by centimetre the wet grass and rich earth which clung to their heels. Having examined a chosen square of ground, they grunted as they shifted the weight of their bodies from one foot to the other and, still squatting,

16

continued their search. Despite the coolness of the morning, none of them wore a jacket. Sweat trickled from beneath their bowler hats down to their moustaches. One of the men, not believing in the accuracy of photography, was drawing a shoe print he had found in the damp soil. Two policemen wearing jackets stood on a police barge moored to the bank and questioned two teenage boys in school uniform who were trembling as much from nerves as from the cold. One of the policemen waved to Smolorz and Mock, indicating a square of land marked out with little flags where the corpses lay covered with sheets. This man was their boss, Criminal Councillor Josef Ilssheimer, head of Vice Department IIIb, and the area he was pointing to had already been examined.

Mock and Smolorz entered the marked-out plot and took off their bowler hats. Ilssheimer came over to join them, lifting his feet high and moving swiftly. It seemed to Mock that their chief was about to perform a high jump and fall heavily on the sheets, but instead he stopped beside the bodies. He leaned over and tugged at the cloth. At first Mock could not make head nor tail of the stiff, blue limbs, frozen in rigor mortis. Stretched out before his eyes was a most peculiar sight, as if someone had arranged a pyre for a large bonfire. But instead of dry twigs and branches there were four human torsos from which heads, legs and arms protruded at various angles. Furthermore, all these limbs were connected to each other in some way or other: here a foot protruded from an armpit, there a knee grew from a collarbone, while a shoulder emerged from between a pair of shins. In many places, the skin of the deceased was pierced by sharp shards of bone, jutting through and disappearing among blue swellings. So as to set the twisted human limbs on a "top-bottom" or "right-left" axis, Mock's eyes searched for a head. He soon found one, and thanks to a thick beard, he identified its gender as male. From beneath a sailor's hat, long, pomaded strands of hair tumbled over the dead man's face while curly, stiff bristles propagated over his jaw and on his upper lip. All this hair was stuck together with reddish-brown clots of dried blood mixed with a watery fluid. The source of all this gore was two eye-sockets – two dead lakes filled with blood and shreds of membrane from perforated eyes.

When he suffered from a hangover, Mock was tormented by various sensitivities. After eating fried onion, the delicate smell of burning would not leave him for the entire day; the keen odour of a horse – or even worse, that of a sweating man – would evoke associations of sewage and cause convulsions in his bowels; spittle meandering down a window grille would hasten his mistreated stomach's reflexes . . . In order to function in any way, a hungover Mock should be left to himself in the lair of his bedding, isolated from all stimuli. But today the world did not protect him. Mock glanced at the wisps of hair, stiff with blood, that fell from beneath the sailor's hat, at the curled growth of the beard, at the sparse hair on the torso and the pubic hair that poked out from beneath the leather pouch covering the victim's genitals. He felt all this hair in his throat and started to take deep breaths. He gazed up at the bright, September sky and through his mouth released the sour stench of his hangover, the onion-like reek of chives, the insipid smell of scrambled eggs. He kept his head tilted back and inhaled rapidly. He felt he was losing his balance and gave himself a violent jolt, almost toppling Smolorz who was standing behind him on one leg wiping a mud-covered shoe with his handkerchief. Smolorz stepped aside and Mock sat down on the damp grass. Still busy with the dirty toe of his shoe, Smolorz did not help him to his feet. The world did not favour Mock today; it was not protecting him.

Ilssheimer nodded and stared at the Landungsbrücke from where a small steam boat was departing. The investigative police had already gathered the evidence. They rolled down their shirtsleeves, donned their jackets and exhaled clouds of smoke into the dew-scented air. A huge van

18

stopped on the opposite bank and eight stretcher-bearers in leather aprons emerged. A man in his forties hopped down after them wearing a doctor's gown tied at the neck and a top hat which barely covered his skull. In a voice hoarse from tobacco, he began to give out orders. The stretcher-bearers penetrated the crowd, clearing a way for their boss, their folded stretchers serving as pikes to break up the dense throng. A moment later, the dam was swarming with employees from the Institute of Forensic Medicine who were making their way forward carefully, holding on to the taut rope. The unsecured far side of the dam still spurted water, whipping up cones of thick froth. The police officer who had been questioning the two schoolboys with Ilssheimer now shut his notebook and called everybody's attention with an authoritative glance. Waving his left hand he dismissed those giving evidence towards the moored barge and extended his right to the man in the top hat who was now making his way down the dam.

"A good day to you, Doctor Lasarius!" he called, then he raised both arms and boomed at the policemen: "Gentlemen, silence, please!"

The detectives stamped their cigarettes into the ground; the schoolboys soon disappeared, squeezing past the knees of the stretcher-bearers; Doctor Lasarius removed his top hat and began to inspect the bodies, tossing the broken limbs about; his men rested on their stretchers as if they were spears; Smolorz shook the mud off his trousers and Mock leaned towards Ilssheimer and asked:

"Councillor sir, who is that?"

"My name is Criminal Commissioner Heinrich Mühlhaus," said the police officer giving the orders, as if he had heard Mock's question, "and I'm the new chief of the Murder Commission. I've come from Hamburg, where my duties were similar. And now, *ad rem*. Two schoolboys from Green Oak Community School came to the dam at half past seven this morning for a cigarette. They found the bodies of four men; two lying on

19

the ground, the other two on top of them." The police officer approached the bodies and used his walking stick as a pointer. "As you see, gentlemen, the deceased are lying in a very irregular configuration. Where one has his head, another has his legs. All are practically naked." The walking stick spun pirouettes. "All they are wearing are sailor's hats on their heads and leather pouches over their genitals. This peculiar outfit is why I've invited Vice Department IIIb of the Police Praesidium to work with us. We have here its chief, Criminal Councillor Ilssheimer." Mühlhaus glanced respectfully at his colleague. "With his best men, Criminal Assistant Eberhard Mock and Criminal Sergeant Kurt Smolorz." Mühlhaus' tone as he uttered the adjective "best" expressed at least a shadow of doubt. "Briefing in my office at midday sharp, after the post-mortem examination. That's all from me. Over to you, Doctor."

Doctor Lasarius completed his perfunctory examination. He removed his top hat, wiped his forehead with fingers that had touched the corpses, reached into his gown and, after some time, extracted a cigar stump. He accepted a light from one of the stretcher-bearers and said with deliberate irony:

"Thank you, Commissioner Mühlhaus, for so accurately specifying the time of the post-mortem. I was not aware until now that I was your subordinate." His voice became serious. "I've ascertained that the four men have been dead for approximately eight hours. Their eyes have been gouged out and their arms and legs broken. Here and there contusions are visible on their limbs which would indicate imprints made by the sole of a shoe. That's all I can say for now." He turned to his men: "And now we can remove them from here."

Doctor Lasarius fell silent and watched as the stretcher-bearers grabbed the corpses by their arms and legs and gave them a mighty swing. The bodies landed on the stretchers, leather suspensories protruding from between their spread legs, and then came the dull thump of the

20

remains as they hit the deck of the police barge. On Lasarius' orders, the schoolboys standing on deck turned their heads from the macabre sight. The doctor set off towards the car, but before he had gone far he stopped in his tracks.

"That's all I can say for now, gentlemen," he repeated in a hoarse voice. "But I have something else to show you."

He looked around and extracted a thick, dry branch from the bushes. He rested it on a stone and jumped on it with both legs. A brittle crack resounded.

"Everything points to the fact that this is how the murderer broke their limbs." Lasarius flicked his cigar stump into the thorn bushes beside the Oder. The cigar caught on one of the bushes and hung there, wet with spittle, torn from lips a moment earlier by fingers sullied by the touch of a corpse.

Mock felt hair in his throat once more and squatted. Seeing his convulsions, the police officers moved away in disgust. Nobody held his sweating temples; nobody pressed his stomach to hasten its work. Today, the world was not looking after Mock.

BRESLAU, THAT SAME SEPTEMBER 1ST, 1919
NINE O'CLOCK IN THE MORNING

The large motorboat in which the six plain-clothes police officers sat had not seen a war; it came from Breslau's river police surplus. Steering it was First Mate Martin Garbe, who studied the men from beneath the peak of his hat. When their broken conversation began to bore him, he looked out at the unfamiliar river banks overgrown with trees and lined with formidable buildings. Although he had lived in Breslau for a couple of years, he had only been working for the river police for a few weeks and the city as seen from the Oder fascinated him. Every now and then he leaned towards the police officer nearest to him, a slim man with Semitic features, to make sure he was correctly identifying the places they passed.

"Is that the zoo?" he asked, pointing to a high wall behind which could be heard the roar of predators being fed their daily ration of mutton.

The banks of the Oder passed slowly. Occasional anglers, mostly retired men, were returning home with nets full of perch. The trees dripped with foliage; nature was refusing to recognize the approach of autumn.

"That's the water tower, isn't it?" Garbe whispered, pointing to a square brick building on their left. The police officer nodded and addressed a colleague sitting opposite him clutching a locked hold-all marked MATERIAL EVIDENCE:

"Look how fast we're going, Reinert. I told you we'd get there quicker by river."

"You're always right, Kleinfeld," muttered the other man. "Your Talmudic mind is never mistaken."

First Mate Garbe looked up at Kaiserbrücke spanning the river on its steel web and accelerated. The air was hot and muggy. The police officers on the motorboat fell silent. Garbe focussed his attention on the rivets in the bridge, and once they had cleared it, on the faces of his passengers. Four of them sported moustaches, one a beard, and another was clean-shaven. The bearded man blew smoke rings from his pipe which then trailed over the water, and talked in a whisper to the fair-haired moustachioed man sitting next to him. Both men were trying to make it clear with every word and gesture that it was they who gave the orders around here. Kleinfeld and Reinert wore small moustaches, and red whiskers bristled on the top lip of the stout and taciturn police officer. Next to him sat a stocky, clean-shaven, dark-haired man. He looked exhausted. He leaned over the water, breathing in the damp air, and then a cough would tear at his lungs, persistent and dry, as if something was irritating his throat. He rested his arm on the boat's machine-gun and stared down at the water.

First Mate Garbe soon tired of scrutinizing the six silent men and looked up at the underside of Lessingbrücke, which they were now approaching. From its girders dripped water or horse urine. Garbe navigated in such a way that not a single drop fell onto his motorboat. When they had passed under the bridge, Garbe caught a very interesting snippet of conversation:

"I still do not understand, Excellency" – barely suppressed irritation could be heard in the dark-haired man's voice – "why my man and I have been summoned to this crime. Would you, as my immediate superior, care to explain it to me? Has our duty remit been extended?"

"Of course, Mock," the fair-haired, moustachioed man said in a shrill voice. "But let us first get one thing straight. I don't have to explain anything to you. Have you never heard of 'orders'? Police work is founded on issuing orders and often calls for a strong stomach. And subordinates are to execute these orders, even if it means throwing up a hundred times a day. Do we understand each other, Mock? And do not address me as Excellency unless you're attempting to be extremely ironic."

"Yes sir, Criminal Councillor sir," the dark-haired man said.

"I'm glad you've understood." The blond moustache curved into a smile. "And now, think about it yourself and answer me: why do you think you and I are both here? Why has Criminal Commissioner Mühlhaus asked us for help?"

"Naked corpses with leather pouches on their balls," came a muttering from beneath the red moustache. "They could be queers. Those of us in IIIb have come across men like that before."

"Good, Smolorz. I didn't actually ask you, but you're right. Four murdered queers. That's a case for Commissioner Mühlhaus and the men in IIIb. As of today, you and Mock are to be transferred, for the duration of this investigation, to the Murder Commission under the direction of Commissioner Mühlhaus."

The dark-haired man stood up so abruptly that the boat rocked: "But of our men Lembcke and Maraun are much more sure of themselves in the homosexual demi-monde than we are; they're the ones best acquainted with it. Smolorz and I book girls and sometimes raid illegal clubs. So why . . ."

"First of all, Mock," said the man with the pipe and thick beard, "Councillor Ilssheimer has already explained the meaning of an order. Secondly, we don't know whether or not these four sailors *were* homosexuals. We'd like you to tell us who else might wear leather suspensories. Third, and finally, my respected colleague Ilssheimer has told me a great deal about you, and I know I wouldn't be able to stop you conducting your own private investigation into this case. But why would you conduct your own investigation when you can do so under my command?"

"I don't understand." The dark-haired man spoke slowly and huskily. "What private investigation? Why should I want to conduct any sort of investigation into the case of a few murdered queers?"

"Here's why." From the greying beard puffed a cloud of Badia tobacco smoke. "Read this. This card was stuck in the belt of one of the dead men's underpants. Be so kind as to read it. Out loud."

First Mate Garbe did not pay the slightest attention to the Regier-ungsbezirk Schlesien building which they were just passing on the left, or to St Joseph's Hospital built of white clinker bricks on their right. He was listening to the cryptic message being read slowly from the card:

"'Blessed are those who have not seen and yet have believed. Mock, admit your mistake, admit you have come to believe. If you do not want to see more gouged eyes, admit your mistake.'"

"What?" shouted the man with the red moustache. "Are you talking to yourself?"

"Listen to me, Smolorz, use that thick brain of yours," the dark-haired man said quietly and deliberately. "No, that's too much of an effort for you. Read it yourself. Read the card yourself. Well, go on, read it, damn you!"

"'Blessed are those who have not seen and yet have believed. Mock, admit your mistake, admit you have come to believe. If you do not want to . . .'"

"Commissioner, sir, Councillor Ilssheimer was right . . . I'd have conducted a private investigation into this case." The dark-haired man now coughed as violently as if it were splinters stuck in his throat, not hair.

BRESLAU, THAT SAME SEPTEMBER 1ST, 1919
NOON

Thick clouds floated across the sky and obscured the sun. Ten men were present in the briefing room on the second floor of the Police Praesidium at Schuhbrücke 49. Doctor Lasarius held a thick, brown cardboard box full of handwritten documents. Next to him sat three police officers with short names: Holst, Pragst and Rohs. They had searched the scene of the crime and then, on Mühlhaus' orders, had been present at the post-mortem and taken down minutes of the proceedings. Smolorz and Mock settled on either side of their chief, Councillor Ilssheimer, while to the right and left of Mühlhaus sat his own most trusted colleagues: Kleinfeld and Reinert. Tea in Moabit porcelain was set out in front of the men.

"This is what happened, gentlemen," Lasarius began as he extracted a cigar from a tin carrying the logo of Dutschmann tobacconist's. "At about midnight, what was probably a horse's dose of drugs entered the bodies of these four sailors, all aged between twenty and twenty-five. This is indicated by traces of opium on their fingers. There was so much it could have put them to sleep for a good many hours. As a result it acted as an anaesthetic while their limbs were being broken. Let us add that all

25

these men were, most likely, drug addicts, as demonstrated by their emaciated bodies and numerous scars along their veins. One of them had even injected morphine into his penis . . . So nobody would have had much trouble persuading them to smoke a pipe containing a large quantity of opium."

"Were they homosexuals?" Kleinfeld asked.

"An examination of their anuses does not support this theory." Lasarius did not like to be interrupted. "We can be certain that none of them had anal intercourse over the past few days. Returning to my interrupted train of thought . . . At about midnight, while they were under the influence of the drug, their eyes were gouged out and their arms and legs broken. The perpetrator broke sixteen limbs, all more or less in the same place, at the knee joint and the elbow joint." Lasarius passed the police officers an anatomical atlas and pointed to the elbows and knees on an ink drawing of a skeleton. "I've already mentioned that the contusions are the imprints of a shoe . . ."

"Could it be a shoe with a print like this?" This time it was Reinert who had interrupted. "I made this drawing at the scene of crime."

"Yes, it's possible," Lasarius said without bridling at the policeman. "These contusions are the result of significant pressure, conceivably applied by somebody wearing shoes jumping on their limbs. Gentlemen" – he drew on his cigar and extinguished it in an ashtray, scattering sparks – "it is as if the murderer jumped onto their arms and legs while they were propped on a bench, stone or some other object . . ."

"But surely that was not the cause of their death?" Mock asked.

"No, I'm just going to read you my findings," Lasarius sighed with evident annoyance. He began: "The cause of death was stab wounds to both lungs as well as a haemorrhage of the left pulmonary cavity and a clot in that same cavity." Lasarius looked at Mock and said in a hoarse voice: "The murderer stuck a long, sharp instrument between their ribs and then practically pierced the lungs all the way through. They would have been in agony for several hours. Now, please ask your questions."

"What kind of instrument could that have been, Doctor?" Mühlhaus asked.

"A long, sharp, straight knife," the pathologist replied. "Although there is another instrument which seems even more likely to me . . ." He passed his hands – their skin devoured by chemicals – over his bald pate. "No, that would be absurd . . ."

"Go on, Doctor!" Mock and Mühlhaus shouted almost simultaneously.

"Those men's lungs were pierced with needles."

"What sort of needles?" Kleinfeld leaped from his chair. "Needles for knitting socks?"

"Exactly." Lasarius hesitated briefly, then formed an elaborate conditional sentence: "Were I to examine these remains in the context of a medical error, I would say that some quack had made a bad job of tapping their lungs." Lasarius slipped his cigar stump into his waistcoat pocket. "That's exactly what I'd say."

Silence descended. The steady, powerful voice of an interrogating police officer reached them from the next room: "Listen, you and your men have to try harder . . . What are we paying you for, you shits? We want to know everything that's going on in your area, understand?" Drops of rain rapped against the windows. The officers sat in silence, frantically racking their brains for intelligent questions. Mock stretched his hands out in front of him and studied his knuckles which were lost in folds of skin.

"One more question." Mock lifted his hands, then dropped them on the table again. "You inspected the scene where the bodies were found very carefully, Doctor. Could that also be where the crime was committed?"

27

"I found no traces of blood from the eye sockets on the ground or grass around the victims' heads, which means that their eyes were gouged out elsewhere. The remaining injuries led only to internal haemorrhaging, and from those we can deduce nothing as to where the crime was committed. But I'll still carry out an Uhlenhuth blood test, as a formality. Can I go now?" Lasarius got to his feet and made towards the exit without waiting for a response. "Some of us have work to do."

"Commissioner, sir," Mock's hands rose once more and fell with a slap on the table top. "The murderer wrote a message on a card for me. I'm to admit to some mistake, I'm supposed to believe in something, or we're threatened with more murders. Let's read it again. 'Blessed are those who have not seen and yet have believed. Mock, admit your mistake, admit you have come to believe. If you do not want to see more gouged eyes, admit your mistake.'" Mock lit a cigarette and immediately regretted it when he realized that all those assembled had noticed his hands were shaking. "I assure you I don't know what mistake he's referring to, or what I am to admit to. But there is also this Biblical quotation. Let us pursue that. Unless I'm mistaken it refers to doubting Thomas, who came to believe only when he had seen the risen Christ with his own eyes."

Mock approached the revolving board in the corner of the briefing room, wedged it still and wrote in even, beautiful script: "doubting Thomas = Mock, Christ = murderer, murdered sailors = warning for Mock."

"The first two equations are clear," Mock said, angrily shaking the chalk dust from his sleeve. "The murderer is a religious fanatic who has sent a message to an unbeliever – me. When I discover what 'mistake' I am being punished for, I'll also discover the murderer and my 'mistake' will become evident to everyone. Because everyone is going to ask: 'Why did that swine kill four young men?' The answer is: because he wanted to punish Mock for something. 'And what did Mock do?' everyone is going

28

to ask. And I don't know the response to that at this stage. Everyone will find out how Mock once harmed the murderer, everyone will find out what Mock has been punished for. And that's what the murderer is aiming at. If that pig had killed some old woman, it would have blown over without a murmur. A week ago, in Morgenau, two old women were killed by P.O.W. soldiers freed by the Russians. They stole twelve marks from them. Imagine – the equivalent of two theatre tickets! Did that shake public opinion? Not in the least! Who cares about some murdered old women?"

"I know what you're saying," interrupted Mühlhaus. "The murder has to be spectacular because only in this way will the murderer draw people's attention to your alleged guilt. And what could be more spectacular than gouging out the eyes of four young men in leather underpants?"

"You know," Mock said slowly, "I've got a terrible feeling . . . I don't know what I'm supposed to be admitting to so I can't say anything . . . I'm not going to say anything and the world's not going to find out a thing from me . . . And he . . ."

"He's going to get more and more frustrated," said Lasarius, who was standing in the doorway listening attentively to Mock's deductions. "He's going to wait and wait for you to admit to your guilt . . . Until, until . . ." Lasarius searched for the appropriate word.

"Until he gets truly pissed off . . ." Smolorz came to his aid.

BRESLAU, THAT SAME SEPTEMBER 1ST, 1919
TWO O'CLOCK IN THE AFTERNOON

Above the entrance gate to Cäsar Wollheim, River Shipyard and Navigation Company at the river port of Cosel, hung enormous banners with the slogans: "Strike – Unite with our Comrades in Berlin" and "Long Live the Revolution in the Soviet Union and Germany". In the gateway stood workers wearing armbands; some wielded Mauser rifles in their calloused hands. On the other side of the street, with West Park at their backs, soldiers from the *Freikorps* were arranged in battle formation, staring starkly at their adversaries' red-starred banners.

The droschka carrying Mock and Smolorz stopped a fair distance from the entrance to the shipyard. The passengers climbed out and the cabby pulled slowly to the side, unhitched his horse and gave it some fodder. Mock contemplated the ideological conflict before him and decided that, as a state functionary, he rather sided with the opponents of proletarian revolution. Not wanting to hear the whistle of flying bullets in the square, which was on the verge of becoming a battleground, he and Smolorz hurriedly approached the commander of the *Freikorps*. Mock showed his identification and, silently rueing his rough tongue swollen with yesterday's alcohol and tobacco, forced himself to ask questions. He did not need an explanation of the present situation; all he needed was one piece of information: the location of the port's director. Company Commander Horst Engel immediately summoned an old sailor whom he introduced to Mock as his informer. Mock thanked Engel and, stooping beneath a non-existent yet possibly imminent hail of bullets, led the informer Ollenborg to the droschka. The old sailor told him that the grand launching of a small passenger ship, the *Wodan*, which was to cruise the Oppeln-Stettin line, was taking place at that very moment. Julius Wohsedt, the director of the port, was sure to be there. Ollenborg then showed Mock a side gate which was not blockaded by revolutionaries.

"Oh, he's a very hard-working man, Wohsedt," replied Ollenborg in answer to Mock's question about whether the strike was not interfering with the port director's grand launching. "He's got to sell the new ship, but he can afford the odd strike. Haven't you heard of strike insurance, Officer?"

"And tell me, my good man," Mock said, looking in bewilderment at the shipyard's ivy-patterned side gate guarded by several *Freikorps* soldiers, above which hung the non-revolutionary banner "Welcome". "Who's going to launch his new ship for him when everyone's out on strike?"

"Everyone, my foot!" the old sailor said with a toothless grin. "Have you not heard, Officer sir, of non-striking workers? Old Wohsedt has considerable influence over both strikers and scabs. Besides, he persuades them both with the same . . ."

They had arrived in a square where tables laden with bottles, joints of poultry and rings of sausages had been arranged in a horseshoe. At one table sat a priest with a stoup and around him perched shy port officials, as well as proud-looking businessmen in black suits and top hats. But in the faces of the ladies who accompanied them Mock read nothing other than anticipation of a sign that they could throw themselves upon the victuals. Nobody was eating yet; everybody was waiting for something. The man standing beneath a magnificent parasol selling ice creams and lemonade, however, was not waiting for anyone. He did not have to. Customers weary of the sun stood in a long queue at his cart. Smolorz, Mock and Ollenborg climbed down from the droschka and mingled with the large crowd on the shore where a small passenger ship was moored, carrying the Danzig flag with its two crosses and a crown. Ollenborg started talking to an acquaintance whom he addressed as Klaus, while Mock and Smolorz listened attentively. It soon became clear that the director of the river port and his wife, who was to be the ship's godmother, had not yet arrived; it was for them that everybody was waiting.

"Maybe old Wohsedt is irrigating his wife before launching the ship," Klaus laughed, and he used his rotten teeth to lever a porcelain cap off a bottle of beer bearing the seal of Nitschke's tavern, which was nearby. On seeing the frothy drink, Mock felt alcohol upset the balance of liquids in his body. "It's an old custom, irrigating the wife or lady friend. Besides, the buyer might even have requested it. I've heard of a similar custom when carts are sold. Before sealing a deal, the seller uses the cart to transport whatever the buyer's going to carry in it. It's supposed to be good luck . . ."

"You're right" said Ollenborg, who could only dream of using his teeth. "Irrigation, in this case, is a must. It's like baptizing a brothel. After all, that's what this new ship's going to be used for . . ."

"What's that rubbish you're saying, old man?" A sailor with a strong Austrian accent had turned to Ollenborg. "What's this ship supposed to be used for? A brothel? Am I to sail a brothel? Me, Horst Scherelick, a sailor on S.M.S. *Breslau?* Say that again, old man."

Klaus reassured the sailor: "Oh, come, it was a slip of the tongue. My friend meant to say 'initiate', not 'irrigate'. And you, Ollenborg," he said more quietly, "stop jabbering or somebody's going to stick a knife in your ribs."

For a few minutes Mock looked on intently as Scherelick was pacified. Then he shifted his gaze to the huge magnum of champagne carried by a small boy in a sailor's outfit. As he wondered whether the champagne was cold or warm, he once again felt a pang in his stomach and dry splinters in his throat. He beckoned to Smolorz and Ollenborg.

"I've a favour to ask of you, Smolorz," he whispered. "Find that port director and bring him to the droschka. Discreetly. I'll question him there. And you, Ollenborg, I'd like to talk to you now."

Smolorz pressed his way through the throng and went off in search of the head of the river port. Mock distanced himself a little from the crowd, sat down on an old lemon crate and pulled out his cigarette case. Ollenborg squatted down next to him and willingly accepted a cigarette. The march "Under Full Sail" resounded on the quay, and an orchestra approached the ship in step with the music. When the musicians came into view, many of the sailors started cheering and throwing their hats in the air. The priest got to his feet, the businessmen looked about for the master of ceremonies and the ladies waited for the first daredevil to help themselves, uninvited, to the food and drink.

"Listen, sailor," Mock said. "The moment director Wohsedt appears, you're to point him out to me."

"Yes, Officer sir," Ollenborg replied.

"One more thing." Mock knew he had to formulate his question skilfully. He did not, however, want to have to think. He wanted to drink. "Do you know, or have you heard of four young men, twenty, twenty-five years of age? Good-looking, bearded sailors? Maybe they came looking for work here? You might have seen them wandering around the port? They wore leather underpants. Here are their photographs – dead."

"I don't peer down people's trousers, Officer sir," Ollenborg said indignantly as he studied the pictures. "I don't know what sort of underpants anyone wears. And how do you know they were sailors?"

"Who's asking the questions here?" Mock said in a raised voice, arousing the interest of a blonde woman in a blue dress who was walking past.

"I haven't seen them and I haven't heard of them," Ollenborg smiled. "But allow me, Officer sir, to give you one piece of advice. *Barba non facit philosophum*.† Why are you looking at me like that? Because I've studied Latin? Once, on a voyage to Africa, I avidly read Georg Büchmann's *Geflügelte Worte*;‡ I practically know it by heart."

Mock said nothing. He did not feel like talking. Today it seemed hard to find the right words. Lost in thought, he watched the young blonde woman in the long blue dress and veil. She was on her way to the table

---

† A beard does not make a philosopher. (Latin)
‡ Loosely translated as "Winged Words" and subtitled "A Treasury of German Quotations", first published in 1864.

but suddenly changed direction, approached the ice-cream and lemonade vendor and smiled at him. As she did so, she stuck out her neck which had been hidden by a high lace collar held in place with hooks; it was covered with dark, scaly patches. The vendor handed the woman some lemonade without her having to queue. "Where have I seen that girl before?" Mock asked himself. "In some brothel, no doubt," was his own response. Trapped in a tedious existence, between booking prostitutes, alcoholic delirium and the superhuman effort it took to continue to show his father respect, Mock realized that he saw a harlot in every woman. But this is not what horrified him. He was already used to unhappy thoughts and his own partially feigned cynicism, and he was well acquainted with his own demons. But all of a sudden he was afraid for his future. What would he do if he had a wife who, faithful up to now, suddenly started coming home late at night, her lips concealing alcohol fumes, deceit lurking in her eyes, satiation slumbering in her body, and on her breasts the marks of passionate bites? What would this brave conquerer of indifferent prostitutes and venereal pimps do then? Mock did not know how he would behave. How much easier it would be if the entire female kind was made up of harlots! Then nothing would surprise him.

Sergeant Smolorz interrupted these dismal thoughts.

"The port's director was in his office," he said loudly, trying to shout above the orchestra which was now playing "Der Präsentiermarsch", a tune from the time of East African colonization.

"And what, was he irrigating his wife?" Ollenborg said, spitting out his cigarette butt.

"Probably," Smolorz muttered and pointed to the blonde who was drinking lemonade from a thick glass. Her scaly blotches were not visible. "She looks quite happy, doesn't she?"

"That's the port director's wife?" asked Mock.

"I found his office. Went in. He and that woman were there. I

34

introduced myself. He said goodbye to her nervously: 'Bye, my little wifey. I'll be there in a minute.'"

"Take me to his office," Mock said, springing to his feet and talking more fluently now. "Now that he's irrigated his wife, and before he launches the ship, the port director has some questions to answer."

"I've already asked them," Smolorz said as he pulled out a notebook. "And I showed him the photographs. He didn't recognize the murdered men. But he gave me a list of all the agents in Breslau who recruit riverboat sailors."

"How did you know I wanted to ask that?" Mock secretly admired the terseness and love of hard facts which distinguished his colleague.

"Ah well, I just guessed. I do know you a little." Smolorz reached into his pocket and pulled out a bottle of dark beer with the Biernoth Tavern label. "I guessed this too. I do know you a little."

"You're irreplaceable," Mock said as he spontaneously squeezed Smolorz's hand.

The orchestra began to play "Marsch der freiwilliger Jäger". From behind the building strode a red-faced, fifty-year-old man in a top hat. His cheeks looked fit to burst with a surplus of blood, and the buttons on his waistcoat strained under the pressure of excess fat. He approached the table, picked up a glass of champagne with his plump fingers, and raised it in a toast.

"That's Wohsedt, the director of Wollheim's shipyard," Ollenborg informed them.

The buzzing in Mock's ears — intensified by the bubbles in the beer — drowned out Wohsedt's speech. The police officer heard only the words "godmother" and "my wife". Whereupon a buxom, short, fifty-year-old woman who had previously been sitting next to the priest made her way to the table where the magnum of champagne stood. She smashed the bottle against the hull of the ship and gave it its mythological Germanic name. The blonde in the blue dress put down her glass of lemonade and watched the ceremony. Mock sipped his beer slowly, straight from the bottle. Unlike Smolorz, who no longer knew which was the wife and which the mistress, he was not surprised by anything. To his satisfaction he was able to confirm that the world was returning to its old ways.

BRESLAU, THAT SAME SEPTEMBER 1ST, 1919
FOUR O'CLOCK IN THE AFTERNOON

Cabby Helmut Warschkow, who for several years now had been working solely for the Police Praesidium, was riding up on the box in a most uncomfortable position, forced as he was to share the seat with Sergeant Kurt Smolorz, the size of whose body was inversely proportional to the economy of his speech. Pressed into the iron frame by Smolorz's hefty shoulders, he lashed his whip, deep down beside himself with indignation that his carriage was being used for ignoble purposes by Eberhard Mock from Vice Department IIIb. Mock had closed the roof and, having thus isolated himself from prying eyes, was subjecting an innocent girl in a blue dress – whom he had none too courteously invited into the droschka during the ship-launching ceremony – to a ritual as old as the hills. Warschkow's suspicions, however, were wrong. The rocking of the carriage was not caused by the movement of Mock's loins but by the bumpiness of the alley in South Park along which they were travelling. The otherwise lecherous Mock, looking at the scales on the girl's neck, thought of everything but the mating dance and its consequences. The girl herself was in no way innocent; on the contrary, she was highly amenable to the kinds of requests made by men that no virgin could satisfy. Now she was reacting with equal submission to Mock's demands, beating her shapely breast and swearing to "sir" that, whatever the consequences, she would confirm that she had been kept by Wohsedt for several months now, especially since it was he who had infected her with "this filth".

"I beg of you, don't lock me up . . . I have to work . . . I have a small child . . . No doctor's going to stamp my book . . ."

"You have two options," Mock said, feeling disgust towards the sick girl, and disgusted with himself for revelling in her consternation. "Either I bring you in for having an out-of-date health record or I don't. In which case you have only one way out: to work with me. Agreed?"

"Yes, agreed, honourable sir."

"Now you're addressing me as you should."

"Yes, honourable sir. And that's how I'm going to address you from now on, honourable sir."

"So you're Wohsedt's kept woman. Do you have other clients as well?"

"Sometimes, honourable sir. He keeps me, but he's too miserly to have exclusivity."

"Are you sure he's the one who infected you?"

"Yes, honourable sir. He had it already the first time I was with him. He liked biting my neck. He infected me like a rabid dog."

Mock studied the girl. She was shaking. Tears glistened in her cornflower-blue eyes. He touched her cold, wet hand. She was moulting, layers of skin flaked from her neck. Mock felt sick; he was revolted by all kinds of things when he had a hangover. With a hangover he could never be a dermatologist.

"What's your name?" he said, swallowing.

"Johanna, and my three-year-old daughter's name is Charlotte." The girl smiled, pulling her high collar further up over her neck. "My husband died in the war. We've also got a little boxer. We love her . . . She's called . . ."

When he was young Mock had a boxer at his family home in

Waldenburg. The dog would lie on its side and little Ebi would snuggle his head into its short fur. In the winter, the dog was happiest lying beneath the stove. Dog-catcher Femersche also lived in Waldenburg. The dogs he disliked most were Alsatians and boxers.

"I don't give a damn what your mongrel is called!" Mock roared and pulled out his wallet. "I don't give a damn about your bastard child!" He took out wads of banknotes and threw them into the girl's lap. "I'm interested in one thing only: that you get rid of that fungus! There's enough money for you to live off for a month. The doctor won't take anything from you, he's a friend of mine: Doctor Cornelius Rühtgard, Landsbergstrasse 8. You're to come and see me in a month, when you're cured! If you don't, I'll track you down and destroy you! You don't believe me? Ask your friends! Do you know who I am?"

"I do, honourable sir. You paid me a visit when I was working in the Prinz Blücher cabaret, Reuscherstrasse 11/12."

"Ah, that's interesting . . ." Mock tried to remember the circumstances. "Was I a client of yours? And what? How did I behave? What did I say?"

"You were . . ." she hesitated, "after some alcohol . . ."

"And what did I say?" Mock felt increasingly tense. Often, after nights of heavy drinking, he would hide his head in the sand like an ostrich. To his companions in these nocturnal escapades he would say: "Don't remind me of it. Don't talk about it. Not a word. Not a single word." But now he wanted to know. May it fall on him like a sentence.

"You told me, honourable sir . . . that I look like your beloved . . . nurse . . . Except that she was ginger . . ."

"One says 'red-headed' or 'flame-haired'. And what else?"

"That of all dogs, honourable sir, boxers are your favourite . . ."

BRESLAU, THAT SAME SEPTEMBER 1ST, 1919
FIVE O'CLOCK IN THE AFTERNOON

Cabby Warschkow stopped once more at the wharf of the Wollheim ship-yard, alongside the *Wodan* which had been launched that day. The guests were just boarding the ship, where the rest of the festivities were to take place. Blood-like stains of wine remained on the tablecloths alongside yellowy spillages of beer. Chewed duck and goose bones were being swept into a bowl to form a crumpled skeleton, a funeral pyre of poultry. Mashed potatoes and beetroot — which only moments earlier had encir-cled ducks' breasts, but now looked more like tubercular spittle — were being scraped off plates with a spoon. The September sun casting its benevolent light on this culinary battlefield revealed nothing, but did add radiance. The last of the revellers, unwilling to part with their *bratwurst*, were stepping onto the ship which was to sail up the Oder. Just as they were about to raise the gangway, one final passenger appeared: Eberhard Mock. Nobody asked for his invitation, nor was anyone surprised by his somewhat staggering gait.

Dancing couples occupied the upper deck as the orchestra played a foxtrot that was very much in vogue. Women wearing low-cut dresses, many decorated with strips of fabric slung low across their hips, leaned on the shoulders of their partners, moving swiftly with the dance. Elderly ladies stared through opera glasses; elderly gentlemen smoked, played skat or did both; younger men crowded around the gleaming bar and poured liquids of various colours down their fathomless throats from glasses, some of which — so Mock thought — had the coarse charm of cut prism, others the questionable refinement of a cone. Mock ordered a cognac and, without taking a sip, looked out at the iron spans of Posenerbrücke. Against its backdrop he caught sight of the man he had come to see — the river port director, Julius Wohsedt. Under what Mock was convinced was a fungal arm, he sheltered his wife and the ship's godmother, the short and exceptionally corpulent Mrs Eleonore Wohsedt. Her husband was flushed with alcohol and dressed to the nines. He carried himself stiffly and formally, but had foregone his top hat. Mock burst out laughing at the sight of his sparse hair, which pomade had fashioned into an elaborate curl. He knocked back his cognac and silently toasted well-matched married couples.

The director felt alcohol-spiced breath on the triple folds of his neck. He turned to bestow a broad and sincere smile upon what he imagined would be one of his guests, and instead saw a dark-haired man he did not know. The man, who was of medium height and slightly overweight, was clenching his jaw and holding out a business card in gnarled fingers: CRIMINAL ASSISTANT EBERHARD MOCK, POLICE PRAESIDIUM, VICE DEPARTMENT IIIB. Wohsedt glanced at his wife, and Eleonore, registering the words "Vice Department" with a flicker of her eyes, moved away with a polite smile.

"One of your men," said Wohsedt, reading the words on the business card, "has already been to see me today. Have you also come about those murdered sailors?"

"Yes, I'm leading the investigation," Mock said, resting his hands on the polished railings. "I have to establish the identities of the victims." He took a large envelope from his jacket pocket and handed it to Wohsedt. "Take another good look at them."

Wohsedt flicked through the photographs carelessly. As he was sliding them back into the envelope, one of them caught his attention. He pulled them out again and considered every detail, turning them upside down and even examining the reverse sides. At length he sighed and returned the photographs to Mock.

"I don't know them," he said and wiped his sweaty head with a handkerchief. "I really don't know them."

"You don't know them, sir," Mock said quietly and clearly, "but maybe those working under you, your managers, your foremen, your caretakers – maybe they know them. Maybe the agents who recruit crews for river lines know something?"

"Do I have to ask all of them?" Wohsedt smiled at an elderly lady and lowered his voice. "Perhaps you'd like me to interrupt my negotiations with the striking workers, stop repairing ships and walk into my office every morning asking the question: 'Does anybody know anything about the murdered sailors yet?' Is that what I'm supposed to do?"

"Yes," Mock said even more softly.

"Very well then," Wohsedt said, yet again baring acrylic teeth. "That is what I shall do. When would you like me to report back to you?"

"In a week at the latest, sir." Mock slipped the photographs into an envelope on which he had neatly written: "Tuberculosis of the skin after being bitten by someone with tuberculosis".

BRESLAU, THAT SAME SEPTEMBER 1ST, 1919
SEVEN O'CLOCK IN THE EVENING

The cruise ship *Wodan*, having safely navigated the Bürgerwerder and Sand locks, ploughed its way to the small landing stage opposite Sandinsel, at the foot of Holteihöhe. Several passengers disembarked to climb the steep embankment, leaving behind the bright, dancing deck where brogues thumped and high heels clattered. Mock was among those leaving, tormented by a keen thirst and chaotic thoughts. His throat cried out for crystalline liquids, his mind for a clear breeze which would disperse the trails of mist and fog that shrouded his capacity for cause-and-effect analysis. He found relief in the garden of the Steamboat Landing Stage Restaurant near Sandbrücke. Admiring the edifice of the modern market hall, he relished a chilled glass of schnapps, which cut the taste of the Bismarck herrings whose silver skins were slashed with black criss-crosses. He divided a hot potato with his fork and slathered half of it with the soured cream coating the herrings. The fork impaled a piece of potato, then speared a slice of onion with a crunch before finally piercing a chunk of apple. In ecstasy Mock slid all these specialities into his mouth and chased them down with some more cold schnapps to stimulate his digestion. Next, he sucked down a long draught of Kulmbacher beer, then sprawled himself comfortably with his legs apart. Threads of gossamer brushed his cheeks and neck. He welcomed imminent drowsiness with warm hospitality. A tall, handsome man approached his table and sat down opposite him. He covered his ears with outstretched fingers through which the yellowish-red fluid began to flow; his ears were bleeding, his eyes were pouring out onto his sailor's collar. Mock sprang to his feet, knocking into a waiter who was making his way towards two distinguished-looking ladies with some apple cake and glasses of brown liqueur. The waiter neatly tossed the tray from one hand to the other, spilling only a few drops which ran down the glasses' slim stems.

Mock raised his bowler hat and apologized to the waiter and the two ladies, then turned to confront the spectre which had disturbed his sleep. In its place, a little sparrow was hopping around on the table, picking at what remained of the potato on his plate. Mock did not shoo it away. He rolled a cigarette of Georgian blond tobacco and lit it, listening to the chimes of the school chapel's bells. Moments later the frightened bird flapping its wings in his heart had also calmed down. Mock's thoughts and chain of logic became clearer: "The murderer commits a spectacular crime to force me to admit to some past mistake. Here one has to consider two things," he explained to the sparrow hopping across the starched tablecloth. "Firstly, the singularity of the crime; secondly, my past mistake. The singularity of the crime might have gone unnoticed if the corpses had been discovered only later, in a decomposed state, after several months, for example. In that case, it would only have been noticeable to Doctor Lasarius and his men, who would find gouged eyes and broken bones even in a jelly of corpses. So why does the murderer count on his luck? But is it luck? Every day a large number of people cross Ottwitzer lock to the island and then continue on to Klein Tschansch. The bodies would certainly have been discovered, and news of the four murdered men would have gone round the whole district and then the entire city. Then there's my past error, if one is to presume that the victims are there to illustrate the gravity of this error, accusing me through their very absurdity, then none of their characteristics have anything in common with me. The crime is little more than ostentation, form without content."

The sparrow flew away and Mock noticed with some surprise and satisfaction that his thoughts were not only mere associations, not only a stream of chaotic images, but were acquiring the form of a small treatise, dictated in perfect, elaborate sentences. The more inebriated he became, the more sober were his thoughts. He forgot about the spectre with lymphatic fluid pouring from his ears, quickly pulled out a notebook and began to write feverishly: "The dead men have two characteristics that have been deliberately emphasized by the murderer. These are the only characteristics we have that can lead us to identify the victims. They were sailors, and their genitals were adorned with leather thongs. Wohsedt will take care of the first aspect; I will deal with the second. Wohsedt is dealing with sailors, and I with lechers. To whom would genitalia be displayed in such a dissolute manner?"

Here Mock interrupted himself and recalled a certain illegal brothel in the centre of Ring, which he and Smolorz had come to know about via an informer. The stool pigeon had been trying to destroy the competition and at the same time distract the police from his own establishment, which was fronted by a kind of photographic studio. Mock and Smolorz swept both places off the face of the metropolis. In both they had discovered an

43

assortment of outfits and straps, and no shortage of leather underwear consisting of nothing but a belt and suspensoria.

"It matters not to whom one displays one's genitalia," Mock wrote. "More important is where this is done. The answer is: in brothels. Another question springs to mind: what might the victims have had to do with brothels? There are two possible answers: they could either have worked in one, or they could have made use of the pleasures on offer. Unfortunately, *utrum possible est*. If they were clients at some brothel and wanted to enhance their arousal by wearing suspensoria, then our investigation should begin with an interrogation of all the prostitutes in Breslau."

Mock was surprised to note how paper and a pencil appeared to ennoble his morals. If he had been relating his train of thought to someone in speech, he would have said "whores in Breslau".

"If, on the other hand, they worked in a brothel to arouse guests of the female sex (after all, Lasarius had ascertained that they were not homosexuals), we have but to delve into the memory of Breslau's brothel specialist and ask him: where would a four-man crew serve to enthral female clients?"

And here Breslau's most accomplished bawdy-house specialist fell into hopeless reflection which yet another cigarette failed to enlighten. It could only be an illegal brothel, kept strictly secret and intended solely for trusted members. It dawned on Mock that, in fifteen years of working for the police Vice Department, or in his numerous official and unofficial wanderings through the temples of the goddess Ishtar, he had never come across a club where women were not employees, or where men were anything other than clients, or guards there to keep an eye on the clients.

"And on top of all that, these sailor's hats!" Mock muttered to himself, forgetting that he was venturing into territory allocated to Wohsedt. "It would have to be an exclusive and secret brothel for society ladies! A Chinaman in one room, a sailor in another, and a soldier in a third!"

The waiter serving Mock a third glass of schnapps listened to this monologue with surprise and interest, as did the two women of a certain age who were drinking cocoa liqueur at the next table. Mock looked at them intently and set his imagination to work – one of them approaches and asks him: "Kind sir, I would like a sailor . . . where can I find one?" He glanced again at the ladies nearby and realized how inauthentic such a hypothetical scene sounded. In fact the inauthenticity was so acute that he tasted its bitterness in his mouth. He decided to rinse it out with rowanberry schnapps.

BRESLAU, THAT SAME SEPTEMBER 1ST, 1919
A QUARTER TO MIDNIGHT

Mock sat at a table in the dance hall of the Hungarian King Hotel and, holding a square bottle of gin to his eye, observed three couples dancing on an area marked out with coloured lights. The surrounding tables were occupied by a few lone men, all of whom were leaning on the railings encircling the floor, puffing out clouds of smoke, occasionally drinking from their glasses and watching the movements of the dancers. Beyond the tables and up a few steps were alcoves, some with cherry-coloured velvet curtains drawn across them, some with the curtains pulled back. The open alcoves shone with emptiness, and those that were closed resounded with women's high-pitched laughter. Whenever the head waiter discreetly struck his little hammer against one of the iron curtain rods, Mock pricked up his ears and strained his eyes. The waiter would then draw the curtains aside, and the ladies would adjust their hair and run slender fingers over their velvety nostrils. There were not many men in the alcoves. Mock smelled sweat and face powder, as well as the scent

45

of perfume. The haughtiness with which they addressed the waiters made it apparent that the ladies belonged to high society. Their laughter, on the other hand, was quite plebeian, and greatly aroused the plebeian in Mock.

The orchestra played a shimmy in the rhythm of a funeral march and it was obvious that the musicians would have liked most of all to return to their former occupation, namely that of immersing their moustaches into enormous tankards of beer. The dance hostesses displayed a typical Monday-morning willingness to work as they turned with studied elegance in the arms of three merry dancers, while their eyes – which Mock could see quite clearly through the magnifying lens of the gin bottle – betrayed reluctance and indifference.

This observation made Mock think of women of ill repute, who – like dance hostesses tired out after a working Sunday – also concealed smooth apathy in their eyes. Eyes that would usually come to life three times in a session: once when the girl approached her client, once when she feigned pleasure and once when she took his money. In the first two situations, she was generally a poor actress; in the last, an efficient calculator. He remembered his reasoning: the dead men were clients, not employees of a brothel. The thought had been prompted when he had imagined one of the ladies sitting next to him in Michael's restaurant asking for a sailor-stud, and the image had not rung true. Sensing this inauthenticity at the time, he had resolved to take the difficult and long road which he was going to describe at the briefing the following day in Mühlhaus' office. He was going to question all the prostitutes in town, starting now. He poured his first glass of gin and conceded that he was going to stop at the one. He did not want to fall asleep. There was no way he wanted to fall asleep. Dreams were not his allies, either in this investigation or in life.

Mock the rationalist intended to begin his questioning at this very venue. He would fire the prostitutes with questions concerning clients who had a penchant for leather underwear. If, however, someone had asked him why he had begun his explorations at the Hungarian King on Bischofstrasse, he would not have known what to say. Had he been sober, his answer would have been: "Because the lighting is good and the venue is made up of three ascending circles – the dance floor, the tables and the alcoves – so it has the best view. I need to start in a place like this before I bury myself in the dark corners of those forbidden dives near Blücherplatz." Had he been drunk, he would have retorted: "Because the prettiest whores are here, and I want them – all at the same time." Mock the rationalist did not want to permit the thought that something might be controlling him; he did not want to admit, with his petty bourgeois conscience, that his trousers concealed a ruthless and capricious demon. Right then it reminded him of its existence.

Mock removed the cold bottle from his burning cheek and acknowledged that the statement about the beauty of the girls working there was indeed true. He got up and made towards the steps leading down to the dance floor. As he walked by one of the alcoves, he heard a woman say to a waiter in a slurred voice: "Call me a cabby!" He passed, followed by the woman's persistent: "I want a carter! Now! Immediately!" and the waiter's reply: "Right this minute, at your service, my lady." Mock stepped onto the dance floor and sensed the eyes of the men at the railings turn to him; the opera glasses and pince-nez belonging to the ladies in the alcoves burned into him; and the eyes of the female dancers enticed him. He asked one of them to dance, a petite, slim, red-headed girl with Jewish looks. He held her tight, and beneath the thin material of her dress he could feel the hooks of her brassiere. After a few wrong steps the girl helped him catch the rhythm. Not for long. Mock had no talent for dancing. After a while he realized that his partner's dancing skills were not up to much either. Fortunately, the orchestra took a break and the weary musicians sank their noses into their frothy beer. The girl stood helplessly in the middle of the dance floor, not knowing what to do with herself. Mock kissed her on the hand and offered his arm, aware of the ironic smiles of the lone drinkers and the astonishment of the ladies in the alcoves. "He kissed a whore on the hand," he could almost hear them whisper.

The girl held him gently by the arm and allowed herself to be led to his table. She was very docile and devoured the snacks and drinks Mock bought for her with relish. She agreed with everything he said, which was not hard since he did not say much, nor did he ask for her opinion. She nodded automatically. But she did not consent when he proposed they spend the night together in a hotel. Instead she invited him to a room she rented in the house next door.

I.IX.1919

An ordinary school day. I was woken by the cries of children hurrying to school. I tried to get back to sleep. Despite tremendous tiredness, I did not succeed. This happens sometimes. You are dead tired, yet are not able to fall asleep. Maybe it is your daimon which prevents you from doing so.

It is noon. I am going to the Municipal Library.

Evening. Today I translated a number of pages from Augsteiner's work. It is written in difficult Latin. It is as if some spirit is speaking through the author. Sentences are broken and unclear. Often there are no predicates. Yet one can look at them from a different angle: they are the notes of a scholar, lacking grammatical brilliance, yet abounding in the brilliance of truth. Augsteiner fascinates me more and more. According to him, Platonic notions are nothing other than souls. This is not, however, a primitive animism of reality. Augsteiner makes precise distinctions between souls. He divides them into active and passive on the one hand,

and potential and actual on the other. Objects have a passive soul, meaning they are ordinary reflections of the ideal, while human beings have an active soul, meaning they are independent reflections of the ideal. Independent in the sense that they possess the possibility of abstraction. This may take place actually or potentially. The author poses the question: How can a subject, that is, a human being, abstract the active soul? But unfortunately he does not offer an answer. His complex epistemological system, saturated with the ideals of Christian Rosenkreuz (not surprising, they lived at the same time!), lacks even the slightest nod towards spiritualism. There are no instructions whatsoever: How is one to set about it? How is one to abstract a man's soul from him? This past night, I followed Gregorius Blockhus' instructions and tried to perceive the souls leaving these four bodies at the moment of their deaths. I proceeded according to Blockhus' writings. I opened up the energy channels in their bodies, did away with the blockages in their joints and arranged them just as he advised. By puncturing them at precise points, I took away their breath. According to Blockhus one cannot help but perceive such concentrated energy. I did not sense this energy. I failed. I do not know whether I understood Augsteiner's difficult Latin correctly, or Blockhus' instructions, which smack of superstition. Tomorrow I shall get down to Augsteiner's work again. Maybe there will be other passages with instructions on how to proceed. Maybe Augsteiner will finally drop his haughty philosopher's mask and assume the attitude of a classical spiritualist?

BRESLAU, TUESDAY, SEPTEMBER 2ND, 1919
SEVEN O'CLOCK IN THE MORNING

The small yard at Plesserstrasse 24, in the Breslau suburb of Tschansch, was full of the the usual morning bustle. Pastor Gerds' maid was hanging bedlinen over the balustrade, while the concierge, Mrs Bauert, scrubbed away at the wooden stairs that lead to the locksmith's workshop at the back of the small building. Konrad Dosche, the retired postman, emerged from the lavatory, and a small ginger mongrel leaped at his feet with unrestrained joy. Streams of sunlight cut through the yard, and as the pump squeaked and tiny particles of dust soared above the linen recently thrashed by the strong hands of the pastor's maid, an elderly man walked out into the yard. The skin on his face and hands was deeply furrowed, his eyes were bloodshot, and his breathing wheezy. He sat down heavily on a bench and whistled to the ginger dog, which raced up and began to fawn at his feet, all the while glancing at its master. Dosche approached the elderly man and shook his hand.

"And a very good day to you, Mr Mock." Dosche's face radiated delight. "How did you sleep?"

"Badly," Willibald Mock said shortly. "Something stopped me getting to sleep . . ."

"A bad conscience, no doubt," Dosche laughed, "gnawing away at you after yesterday's game of chess . . ."

"What do I have to do" – Willibald Mock rubbed his eyes edged with crusts of pus – "to make you believe that I didn't move that bishop when you were in the toilet?"

"Alright, alright," Dosche reassured his friend, still smiling. "And how is your son? Had enough sleep yet? Got up, has he?"

"He's just coming." Relief registered on the old man's face.

Eberhard Mock marched briskly across the yard. He walked up to his father and kissed him on the cheek. The old man did not detect a strong smell of alcohol and drew a long breath. Eberhard shook Dosche's hand and an uncomfortable silence descended.

"I'm just on my way to the pharmacy," Dosche said, to break it. "My dog's got diarrhoea. Terrible diarrhoea. Can I get you anything?"

"If you'd be so kind, Mr Dosche," replied the old man, "as to buy us a loaf of bread from Malguth's on your way. It has to be from Malguth's".

"I know, I know, Mr Mock," Dosche nodded and told his dog: "You stay here, Rot. Mr Mock will look after you. You can crap in the yard but not under the bench!"

Dosche set off in the direction of Rybnikerstrasse. The old man played with Rot. Murmuring, he tickled him lightly on the neck while the dog growled and squirmed, catching the old man's hand gently in its teeth. Eberhard sat down next to his father and lit his first cigarette of the day. He smiled at the events of the night. He realized he had not got around to asking the girl about any clients in leather underpants. "Never mind," he thought, "yesterday I was there outside working hours. As of today, the actual investigation starts. I'll ask her today."

"It's so early and you're already awake, Father." He blew smoke straight at the sun.

"Old people get up early. They don't wander around in the night and they sleep in their own beds."

"I didn't drink that much yesterday. I'm conducting a very difficult case over the next few weeks. I've been seconded to the Murder Commission, and I'm no longer booking whores. You ought to be pleased, Father."

"You're always knocking it back and mixing with whores." The old man's stale morning breath engulfed Mock like a cloud. "You ought to get married. A man ought to have a son to hand him a tankard of beer when he comes home from work."

Mock placed an arm on his father's bony shoulder and rested his head against the wall. He imagined this idyllic scene: his future son, Herbert Mock, handing him a tankard of beer and with a smile turning to his mother at the kitchen stove. The woman nods approvingly, praises Herbert: "You're a good boy, you've given your papa some beer", and stirs the large pot on the hob. She is tall and handsome, her generous breasts

51

pressing tight against her clean apron, her skirt touching the pale, scrubbed floorboards. Mock strokes little Herbert's hair, then walks up to his wife and holds her by the waist. Red hair frames her delicate face, the apron is a nurse's apron, an appetizing smell emanates from the pot where syringes are being boiled. Mock lifts the lid and sees a decoction of bones. "Bones for shoe glue," he hears his father say. Large globules float to the surface – human eyes.

Mock felt his lips burning, then shook his head and spat out the cigarette butt. A trickle of sweat flowed down from beneath his bowler hat. He looked about him. He was still sitting on the bench by the wall. His father was just disappearing through the gate. Mock got to his feet, picked up the cigarette butt – much to the concierge's satisfaction – and hurried after his father. Willibald Mock had wanted to get home, but feeling tired he had sat down on a bench by the butcher's shop. He was breathing heavily. Rot lay down beside him and hung his pink tongue out. Mock hurried over to his father, touched him on the hand and said:

"Let's move out. I'm plagued by nightmares here. Right from the start, ever since we inherited this apartment after Uncle Eduard's death, I've been plagued by phantoms in my dreams, right from the very first night in this foul butcher's shop . . . That's why I drink, do you understand? When I'm dead drunk, I don't dream . . ."

"Every drunkard has some sort of excuse . . ."

"This isn't some twisted explanation. I didn't sleep at home last night and I didn't have any bad dreams, not one. And now, I only just got here, I nodded off for a moment and had another bad dream . . .

"Chamomile and hot milk. That does the trick," his father muttered. He began to breathe more easily and returned to his favourite pastime other than chess, that of amicably teasing Rot.

"I'll buy a dog," said Mock quietly. "We'll move to the centre and you'll be able to take the dog for a walk in the park."

"And what else!" The old man caught the dog by its front paws and listened with pleasure to his growl. "He'd have diarrhoea like Rot. He'd be bound to soil the house . . . Anyway, stop talking nonsense. Get yourself to work. Be on time. Somebody's always having to come to get you, always having to remind you it's time for work . . . Look, here they are again."

Mock turned to see Smolorz climbing out of a droschka. He did not expect to hear good news, and his intuition did not fail him.

BRESLAU, THAT SAME SEPTEMBER 2ND, 1919
EIGHT O'CLOCK IN THE MORNING

No noise from the street reached the mortuary on Auenstrasse; the rays of the strong September sun did not penetrate; the smoke and smell of the bonfires burning on the nearby banks of the Oder near Passbrücke did not float in on the air. In Doctor Lasarius' kingdom reigned a silence that was broken only by the grating of trolleys bringing in more bodies. There was an odour hanging in the air like that of overboiled carrots, but nobody was cooking vegetables here. All that could bring a kitchen to mind was the sharpening of knives.

And so it was now. Doctor Lasarius' assistant sharpened a knife, approached the corpse lying on the stone table and made an incision from the collar bone down to the pubic hair. The grey skin fell aside to reveal a layer of orange fat. Mühlhaus snorted violently; Smolorz rushed out of the mortuary, and when outside the building opened his mouth wide to take in as much air as he could. Mock stood on the viewing platform intended for medical students and fixed his eyes on the open body, absorbing the information the pathologist was passing on to his assistant.

"Male, aged about sixty-five." Mock saw the assistant note the information beneath the name "Hermann Ollenborg". "Height one hundred and sixty centimetres, weight seventy kilograms. Water on the lungs."

53

With a quiet crunch of the knife, Lasarius cut away the bloated, hard lobes of the lungs and made incisions with a pair of small scissors. "There, you see?" – he showed Mock the pulp and water that ran from the bronchi – "That's typical of death by drowning."

Lasarius' assistant lifted the dead man's skull a little, inserted the tip of his knife behind one ear and made another incision. He then got hold of the scored skin of the occiput and a whitish membrane and drew both layers across eyes which were no longer there. They had been gouged out.

"Write this down," Lasarius said, turning to him. Blood was slowly filling the cavity in the body. "Internal bleeding into the right lung cavity. Perforations on the lungs made by a sharp instrument . . ."

The legs and arms of the corpse began to jerk. Lasarius' assistant was sawing into the skull, causing the body to move. Mock swallowed and went outside. Mühlhaus and Smolorz were standing bare-headed in the morning sunshine, staring at the brick buildings of the university's Department of Medicine and at the yellowing leaves on the old plane tree. Mock removed his bowler hat, loosened his buttoned collar and approached them.

"An angler found the body under the Scheitniger sluice," Mühlhaus said. He extracted a pipe from the pocket of his frock coat, an anachronistic garment that was the object of much teasing in the entire Police Praesidium.

"Was a note about me, or to me, found on him?" asked Mock.

"'Blessed are those who have not seen and yet have believed.'" Mühlhaus extended his hand, holding in a pair of tweezers an ordinary sheet of paper torn from a squared exercise book. He pressed his pince-nez to his nose, brought the note closer to his eyes and read: "'Mock, admit your mistake, admit you have come to believe. If you do not want to see more gouged eyes, admit your mistake'." He handed the page to Mock. "Did you know this man, Mock?"

"Yes, he was a police informer, a man by the name of Ollenborg." Mock slipped on a glove and scrutinized the scrap of paper. The writing was crooked and uneven, as if traced by somebody who was illiterate. "He was well acquainted with the people and the goings on in the port. I questioned him yesterday in connection with the Four Sailors case."

"The writing is different," Smolorz said. "Different to yesterday's."

"You're right," Mock looked at Smolorz with approval. "The piece of paper found on the four sailors was written in a neat hand by someone who went to school. The one on Ollenborg was written unevenly, messily and . . ."

"Which could mean they were written by the victims themselves. One of the 'sailors' went to secondary school . . . Explain something to me, Mock" – Mühlhaus filled all his respiratory passages with tobacco so as to kill off the odour of the mortuary – "How is it you're here? I was informed by Duty Officer Pragst and I forbade him to tell anyone else about it. Only the angler, Pragst and myself know of the murder. Most strange." He pondered for a few moments. "Yesterday the bodies were found several hours after the murder. The same thing today. Perhaps those boys yesterday and now the angler were somehow directed by the murderer . . . We ought to question them more closely . . ."

"Smolorz, show the Commissioner" – Mock made way for a hefty orderly who was pushing through another body on a squeaking trolley – "what I received today . . ."

"A letter was found in the Police Praesidium letterbox," Smolorz stuttered. "Somebody dropped it in last night. Addressed to Criminal Assistant Mock. This was in the envelope." He held a page from a maths exercise book under Mühlhaus' nose.

"Don't bother to read it to me," Mühlhaus said, furiously sucking air into his pipe, which was going out. "I know what it says."

"The same words are on the piece of paper in the envelope as were found on Ollenborg's remains," Mock said. "And there's a short footnote: 'Location of body – Scheitniger sluice'. He's telling us where he's leaving the corpses."

BRESLAU, THAT SAME SEPTEMBER 2ND, 1919
TEN TO NINE IN THE MORNING

The hot September sun broke into the Murder Commission's briefing room at the Police Praesidium. The clatter of horses' hooves, the grating of trams and the parping of automobiles rose up from the traffic on Schuhbrücke into the cloudless sky. Schoolchildren drifted along the narrow pavements, each with a briefcase under his arm or a belt holding a pile of exercise books slung over his shoulder. They were hurrying towards Matthiasgymnasium to be on time for their second lesson. Some of them dawdled, standing beneath the statue of St John Nepomuk to throw stones at the bursting husks of chestnuts. A coachman shouted in annoyance at some supplicants who were leaving the High Court and swarming into the road. An elderly man in a bowler hat approached the schoolboys and reprimanded them fiercely. "The schoolmaster, no doubt," thought Mühlhaus. He closed the window and regretfully returned from the land of school memories. He looked at the gloomy, tired and irritated faces of his employees and felt a wave of despondency. He did not want to talk to these thick, hungover mugs; he did not know how to begin.

"Commissioner, sir." Mock saved him the trouble of opening the discussion. "You can relieve all these men from the Four Sailors case, sir. They're not needed . . ."

"I," Mühlhaus said slowly, "am the one to decide who is going to work with me on this case."

"Yes, Commissioner, sir."

"And, just as a matter of interest" – the Commissioner approached the window once more, but this time did not open it — "why do you say 'all these men' are not needed? And what does 'all' mean? All except you? Is that what you had in mind, Mock?"

"Yes, that's what I had in mind."

"Explain yourself!"

"The murderer, as we have already established, wants me to admit to some mistake. So he murders four lads with pouches over their balls. It's supposed to be a spectacular murder, one that the whole town will be talking about, and is to prevent me from ever sleeping peacefully again. The image of the murdered boys with gouged eyes is to forever work its way into my head."

"We already know that, Mock," said Reinert, sounding bored.

"Shut up, my friend. It's not your name that swine's putting in his notes."

"Reinert, don't interrupt Criminal Assistant Mock," Mühlhaus snarled. "Let him continue."

"Smolorz has observed quite rightly" — Mock gazed in concentration at Reinert's face as waves of anger passed over it — "that the murderer is going to carry on killing unless I admit to my mistake. And, unfortunately, he's proved himself a good prophet. Gentlemen, the victims have nothing in common with each other . . ."

"Oh, but they do," Kleinfeld spoke for the first time. "They're somehow connected with water. The first four were sailors, or pseudo-sailors. They were, as Mr Mock has suggested, debauched regulars at brothels. It's not for no reason that they were wearing sailors' hats and leather pouches on their balls. The next victim is an old sailor and a police collaborator. All sailors, some inauthentic, one authentic."

"I do not know, Mock," Mühlhaus said, ignoring Kleinfeld's statement, "how you intend to justify your peculiar suggestion that everyone except yourself should leave the investigative team. Besides, I'm not

57

interested in your justification. I'm not going to dismiss anyone or dispatch them to other cases. Gentlemen, there are now eight of us." He looked around at his men and counted them out loud. "Holst, Pragst, Rohs, Reinert, Kleinfeld, Smolorz and Mock. Eight, and that's how it's going to stay. And now, down to business . . ." He went to the revolving board and below the words "doubting Thomas = Mock, Christ = murderer, murdered sailors = warning for Mock" written by Mock the previous day, he added: "In which brothel did the murderer meet the four sailors?" "Smolorz is going to look into that. As an employee of the Vice Commission he knows every brothel in the city. You'll be assisted by my trusted men, Holst, Pragst and Rohs." Below this the Commissioner wrote: "Ollenborg's last moments". "Kleinfeld and Reinert will take care of this. I want to see you all here, in this room, on Friday at nine in the morning. That's all for today."

"What about me?" Mock asked. "What I am to do?"

"Let's go, Mock," Mühlhaus said. "I'm going to introduce you to somebody."

BRESLAU, THAT SAME SEPTEMBER 2ND, 1919
NINE O'CLOCK IN THE EVENING

Doctor Kaznicz was Professor Hoenigswald's assistant. He specialized in experimental psychology and described himself as a disciple of Freud and Wernicke. He held lectures and classes in psychoanalysis at the University of Breslau which took the form of experimentation on students. From these experiments he drew generalized conclusions which led the more malicious academics to state that "the psychology practised by Doctor Kaznicz is no more than a study of students". His probing questions, which frequently touched on personal behaviour, initially annoyed Mock a great deal. Later, realizing he could not allow there to be any more victims, he lowered his guard and told all he knew about the people he had met or been in contact with in as much as this contact may have inspired in somebody a desire for revenge. He did not mention Wirth, Zupitza or the nurse in Königsberg's Hospital of Divine Mercy. Kaznicz's assistant noted everything down carefully in a thick copybook and looked imploringly at his master for at least one nod of approval. The master, however, barely acknowledged his helper and merely nodded when Mock offered him ever bolder confessions from his childhood and youth. He would then smile encouragingly and repeat the same thing each time: "I understand."

Mock heard these words clearly even as he lay in his bedroom alcove kissing a bottle of cognac. He cradled it in his arms, bestowing it with a tenderness no woman had yet received from him apart from those in his imagination and dreams – apart from the nurse in Königsberg, who may not even have existed. Behind the curtain, Mock's father settled himself to sleep on his rickety bed, while in the alcove his son caressed his mistress Booze. "I understand," Mock heard, and recalled the more inter-esting fragments of the psychological interview conducted over eight hours by Doctor Kaznicz. He pictured the psychologist's wise eyes, and his faint smile through the thicket of his black beard when Mock recounted how he had tormented fat Erich Huhmann in the yard of their Waldenburg primary school. Twelve-year-old Mock, along with some other children, had poked his finger into Huhmann's stomach and chest. The latter had cowered, struggled, squirmed; brick-red patches spread across the skin of his cheeks, blood ran from his nose and stained his buttoned collar, neatly ironed by his mother. Erich Huhmann fell to his knees among the bushes surrounding the yard; Erich Huhmann begged for mercy; Erich Huhmann begged heaven for the fiery sword of vengeance; Erich Huhmann dug a long needle into the bodies of the murdered sailors.

59

Mock acknowledged that this thought — that fat Erich Huhmann, taking revenge on him for past humiliations, could transport the bodies of the murdered men and break their bones — was absurd. "People change," he thought, "grow up, grow strong, cultivate past hatreds." Paying no attention to his father's grumblings that he could not get to sleep because of his son's creaking bed, Mock reached for his jacket which was hanging over the chair and pulled out a notebook. He took a large swig from his bottle and wrote down Huhmann's name.

"I understand," Mock heard Doctor Kaznicz say again and recalled another confidence he had shared that day. Schoolboy Eberhard Mock washed out a flask and test tube, then sat at a stone table in the chemistry laboratory. He had got the highest mark for proving that the salts of certain heavy metals do not dissolve in water to produce precipitation. Envious looks from the other boys. His body found no support, his arms flapped at his sides, his shoes slid forward along the floor, his hand grabbed the tray that held the chemicals, glass cracked, a pungent liquid spilled, his head hit the edge of the chair that Karl Giencke had pulled out from under him as a joke. Then Mock sees himself striking blindly with the tray; its pointed edge digging into Giencke's head; a trickle of blood appearing on the spiteful schoolboy's neck. Giencke losing consciousness; Giencke in hospital; Giencke in a wheelchair; Giencke walking again — "That Giencke has a funny way of walking!"

"He walked in a funny way before," Mock thought as he slid into his leather slippers, "nothing changed." He emerged from the alcove in his nightshirt, over which he had thrown a quilted dressing gown. In his hand was the bottle of cognac. He raised the hatch in the corner of the room and went down into the butcher's shop. He squatted next to the heavy metal grille that covered the drain and listened for the squeaking of rats. He heard nothing. He sat on the counter and put the bottle to his lips. After a few swigs he tied some string around its neck, hid it in the drain and replaced the grille. Now his father would not find the bottle and pour it out. He went back upstairs and lowered the hatch, thinking about the rats he occasionally saw on the ground floor. Sitting heavily on his bed, he extinguished the candle and was sure he would soon be overcome by the sleep of a drunkard: heavy, thick, and free of nightmares. "It's a good thing I didn't tell him about my dreams." He did not think kindly of Doctor Kaznicz's wise eyes as he drifted off. His suppositions were correct: he did not dream of anything.

2.IX.1919

Eureka! I think I have found the clue that will enable me to continue, after all my endless searching. Today I came across a very interesting passage in Augsteiner, a quotation from a letter by Pliny the Younger. We read one of his letters in secondary school – trivial, charming holiday reading. This was towards the end of the school year, after a whole year of read the cripplingly difficult and dull-as-ditchwater Livy. That letter was light relief for us, if any Latin text can be considered light relief and not merely a superhuman exercise for the brain. It was a beautiful story about a boy swimming on a dolphin. I had not known that this same Pliny also wrote about ghosts. I quote the most important fragments of this letter in my clumsy translation:

"In Athens there was a house which was large and spacious, yet sinister and and surrounded by ill fame. In the night's silence, at first as if from a distance and then ever closer, the clanking of iron would be heard, and if one listened carefully, the rattling of chains. Shortly afterwards a phantom would appear: a thin old man, dirty and emaciated, with a matted beard and his hair standing on end. There were chains on his hands and manacles on his feet. He shook them as he walked.

61

"The terrified inhabitants passed long sleepless nights of horror and gloom. Sleeplessness was followed by sickness, ever-increasing fear by death. Even by day, though the ghost had withdrawn, the memory of it tormented the household. It seemed to them that the spectre still glided before their eyes – fear tormented them for longer than what had caused it. So the house was uninhabited and condemned to being deserted; and all that it contained seemed to belong to this horror.

"The building was put up for sale – should someone ignorant of such great misfortune wish to buy or rent it.

"There arrived in Athens at this time a philosopher named Atenodor, who read the announcement about this sale or rental. Intrigued by the low price, he enquired about everything in great detail and when he learned the whole truth he nevertheless – or all the more so – rented the mysterious house.

"As dusk fell he ordered his bed to be made up in the front part of the house and asked for some tablets on which to write, as well as a graver and a candle. His family, on the other hand, he settled in the inner rooms. He tried to occupy his mind, eyes and hands solely with writing, so that none of the phantoms he had heard about and no unnecessary fears would arise in his idle mind.

To begin with there was nothing but silence, but a short time later the rattle of chains and clanging of manacles could be heard. The philosopher did not look up, did not set down his graver and remained deaf to the noise. The noise, on the other hand, grew louder and could already be heard on the threshold, already in the room . . .

He looked up and recognized the apparition that had been described to him. The spectre stood wagging its finger as if beckoning Atenodor. Atenodor, however, reached once again for his graver and wax tablets. Meanwhile the ghost continued to rattle its manacles, now almost above the philosopher's head. Atenodor looked at it again, and the ghost made

the same sign as before. So he stood, picked up the candle and followed the phantom. It moved slowly, dragging its heavy chains. As it turned
into the courtyard of the building, it suddenly dissolved into thin air.
Atenodor remained alone. He picked up some leaves and grass and used
them to mark out the spot where the spectre had disappeared.

"The following day he went to the administration and asked that the
yard be dug up at that exact spot. Bones, bare and gnawed, were found
bound by chains. Only they remained; the body had, over the years,
perished in the soil. These remains were gathered up and officially buried.
Ever since then ghosts have, fortunately, ceased to torment the household."

What conclusion can be drawn from Pliny's text? Man's spiritual
element can be abstracted, and then perceived through its urge to return,
which must be appropriately contrived. Maybe this is a way of activating
clusters of spiritual energy. We shall see. I have conducted an experiment;
time will verify its results. How did I do it? I isolated the man and forced
him to confess to his adultery in writing. It was a terrible confession for
him to have to make since he was permeated to the bone with middle-class
morality. I brought this man to a certain place late at night. He was bound
and gagged. I freed his right hand, tied him to a chair and then asked him
once again to deny what he had written previously, promising him that if
he obeyed I would give this second letter to his wife. He feverishly scribbled something down. I took the second letter, the denial, and slipped it
down the drain. I witnessed his fury and his pain. "I'm going to come
back here," his eyes told me. Then I took the man out to the carriage and
drove away. Later I killed him, leaving him where he was sure to be found.
His ghost will return and draw the attention of the inhabitants of that
place to the drain.

Doctor Cornelius Rühtgard, specialist in sexually transmitted diseases, received patients in his five-room apartment at Landsbergstrasse 8, near South Park, on Wednesdays. The apartment occupied the entire first floor of the detached tenement building, so its windows looked out in all four directions. From one of the bathrooms stretched a view of the park, which was now being admired by a young woman pulling on a long-legged undergarment after her thorough examination. Doctor Rühtgard sat in his surgery writing out a prescription for Salvarsal. He smiled as he thought of her earnest protestations that over the past year, that is, ever since the death of her husband in the war, she had not had intercourse. The state of her health clearly indicated otherwise, and the time she last surrendered to the above-mentioned act – with all its consequences – could be established to within a few days. Pretending to take her at her word, he walked her to the door, then returned to his surgery and gazed out of the window. His patient approached a smart Daimler parked by a lamp post. She did not get into the car but, clearly upset, explained something to the person inside. Rühtgard knew what would happen next; he could almost hear the infected man yelling with fury and the tyres squealing as the automobile violently pulled away.

He would certainly have heard the shouts had it not been for the racket and piano cacophony coming from the parlour adjacent to the surgery. He wrenched open the door and a singular sight met his eyes: two young men were sitting at the piano, their four hands thumping the delicate keyboard on which his wife, who had died a few years earlier, had once painted the crystalline landscapes of the *Goldberg Variations* and executed the precise strophes of *Das wohltemperierte Klavier*. Clasped around the waist by some scoundrel, Doctor Rühtgard's daughter, nineteen-year-old Christel,

64

was prancing beside the piano. Both she and her partner were pulling silly faces, evidence that these barbaric chords were giving them unutterable pleasure.

Rühtgard smelled sweat, an odour he loathed almost as much as the lice which had tormented him only a year earlier on the Eastern Front, or the pathogens of syphilis which devastated the bodies of his patients. The odour was strong, and he swiftly discovered its source: dark stains beneath the arms of one of the men at the piano. Both players noticed the doctor at once and leaped to their feet, bowing politely. The dancer stopped his prancing, bowed and clicked his heels. Christel stood still, smiling and flushed from movements which only a blind man would have called dancing. But Doctor Rühtgard was neither blind nor deprived of the sense of smell. And so his reaction was violent.

"What are all these savage dances?" he yelled. "What's all this roaring like wild animals? Goodbye, gentlemen! Leave at once!"

"We're sorry, Papa," Christel said, frightened by his outburst. "We were just fooling around a bit . . ."

"Quiet, please" – the doctor was short of breath – "Go to your room. And to you, gentlemen, I bid farewell! Do I have to repeat myself?"

The young men quickly vanished, unlike the odour emanating from them. Rühtgard opened a window and with relief drew in the fresh air suffused with the scent of late summer. He sat down in an armchair and looked at Christel. She was so unlike his wife. His daughter did not have the warmth, softness and fragility he had so loved. Christel was rebellious, sporty, angular, strong and independent. "Probably deflowered already." The thought pained him as he imagining her lying beneath the male with the sour smell.

"Christel," he said as gently as he could. "The parlour is not a circus. How could you allow those stinking Hereros to demolish the piano on which your mother played?"

"And what would you say, Papa," she snorted, "if one of those savages was to become your son-in-law?"

Without waiting for an answer, she went to her room; Rühtgard frowned and lit a cigar. He cast an eye around the parlour to seek solace in the beauty of the apartment he had been renting fully furnished for a year now, for the considerable sum of a thousand marks a month. Five rooms and two bathrooms. Tomes over a hundred years old. Eighteenth-century paintings. Turkish rugs and Arabian carpets. And amongst these works of art his sporty, baby daughter, with a dull-witted bull who knew nothing but how to thrust himself between her open legs. Rühtgard smoked his cigar and paced the apartment. He had to talk to somebody. Then he remembered that, apart from his daughter, his servant and himself there was someone else in the apartment. Someone he trusted completely. He knocked on the door of the second bathroom and, hearing a strident "Come in!", he entered. In the bath spread with a sheet, lay a well-built, dark-haired man with a cigarette between his teeth. Criminal Assistant Eberhard Mock.

BRESLAU, THAT SAME SEPTEMBER 3RD, 1919
THREE O'CLOCK IN THE AFTERNOON

Mock and Rühtgard sat at the chessboard devising clever strategies for the opening. Mock picked up a pawn from e2 and placed it on e4.

"You've got it made, Ebi," muttered Rühtgard as he moved a pawn from b7 to b5. "You didn't go to work after yesterday's drinking binge . . . Nothing's going to happen to you . . ."

"I did go to work, but not for as long as usual. Apart from talking to the psychologist I did nothing for five hours. It's to do with the case I'm working on." Mock looked miserable. "I'm not going to talk about it. Tell me" he said, suddenly coming to life, "is the thing I came to see you about serious? Did I catch anything from that girl?"

"Itching with no other symptoms" — the doctor smiled — "doesn't mean anything. It might be nothing more than a desperate appeal for hygiene."

"If you lived where I do" — Mock brought his knight into action — "you wouldn't be making daily offerings to Hygiea either."

"Well said. And what about your offerings to Hypnos?"

"I'm not sleeping." Mock lost the desire to juggle with mythology. "I'm having nightmares. That's why I drink or take up with harlots. When I'm pissed, I don't dream at all. When I'm with a whore, I don't sleep at home. And I only get nightmares at home. Unfortunately, I can't move out because my father doesn't want to. The only two friends he has live there: a retired postman and his dog."

"Sorry for poking my nose into something that's not my business, but why don't you ask Franz to take your father in, at least for a while?"

"My father's difficult. Irmgard, Franz's wife, is even more difficult . . . But I don't need to tell you that. Quietly and gracefully, she's sucking away at my brother's blood. Franz drinks and my ten-year-old nephew, Erwin, is constantly ill. That explains everything."

"Yes, that's clear enough." Rühtgard attacked the knight with his bishop. "You know what, Ebi? I've been thinking about your nightmares and a simple solution occurred to me. Don't eat supper and abstain from women for a time. I stick to a vegetarian diet, I don't eat anything at night and I abstain from sex. Does that surprise you? It's not difficult in my profession. I've seen my fair share of syphilitic pubes. Apart from that, I'm seven years older than you. We'll see whether you're such a stud at forty-three . . . If I do have dreams, they're only pleasantly erotic ones. And another thing . . . You wouldn't have to worry about any itching, or spend your time soaking in my bath. Do you know how much I have to pay the caretaker to heat the water?" He smiled. "Now, tell me honestly: how much did you eat last night?"

"A lot." Mock threatened the bishop with a pawn. "A huge amount. But I can't get to sleep if I'm hungry."

"Then don't sleep. And you won't have nightmares." The physician was deep in thought. "Either way, you'd get rid of the nightmares if you changed your way of life."

"I don't believe my nightmares have anything to do with over-eating . . ." Mock said. He felt uneasy about his knight.

"It's not a matter of what you believe," Rühtgard said, then remained silent for a long while, pondering a winning move. "I'll prove to you what a proper diet can do. But first of all, you yourself have to believe that the nightmares stem from your overloaded and overworked bowels. I'll prove it to you, if you do as I say." He struck a decisive and powerful blow. "Give up, or still struggling?"

"Are you talking about chess or my hunger therapy?"

"Both."

Mock no longer felt like playing and as a sign of surrender laid his king on the chessboard.

BRESLAU, THAT SAME SEPTEMBER 3RD, 1919
TEN O'CLOCK AT NIGHT

In one of the discreet alcoves beside the dance floor at the Hungarian King Hotel, the head waiter was taking down an enormous order. The slim figure of the distinguished, greying man who was giving it might have suggested a completely different taste in food than what was being jotted down on the order pad.

Another man, a few years younger, was nodding in agreement at his companion's culinary decisions, but remained silent.

"Yes, as I said, Eberhard," said the first man as he dismissed the waiter with a perfunctory gesture. "First comes the painful part of the therapy. Do you know how young smokers are encouraged to give up their addiction? They're told to inhale the smoke and cough. Try it, go on try . . ."

Eberhard took a drag of his cigarette and coughed. He felt pain in his lungs and bitter bile rose to his mouth. For some time he breathed in the smoky air as the cigarette burned down in the huge ashtray. The orchestra was playing a foxtrot and two shapely dance-hostesses were dancing alone, illuminated by bulbs that flickered all around the dance floor, while single, ageing men drank glass after glass to give themselves the courage to dance and debauch. Giggling and snorting could be heard from behind the drawn curtains of the alcoves. "Probably some ladies snorting white powder," said one waiter to another. A wheezing reverberated in Mock's alcove. "Probably some asthmatic choking," the other waiter retorted.

"Come on, Cornelius," Mock groaned. "Look what you've done to me . . ."

"So now you've experienced the hideous taste of tobacco," Cornelius said, staring at the dance-hostesses. "But that's not the addiction we want to destroy in you . . . We want you to eliminate your addiction to supper, to devouring mountains of meat in the evenings . . . This evening you're going to experience the awful consequences of overeating on your own skin, or rather your own liver. Your brain is going to pick up signals from your burdened bowels, and it's going to respond in a way that will punish you – with nightmares. . . Mock, are you hungry now?"

"I'm starving." Mock reached into the ashtray and ground his cigarette butt into the powdered ash. "I did as you told me. I haven't eaten a single thing since coffee and cakes this afternoon at your place."

"So now eat to your heart's content, until you're full." Cornelius watched the waiter lay out the hors d'oeuvres on the table. "Think of our conversations in the trenches at Dünaburg. That's all we talked about, nothing but food . . . We didn't have the courage to talk about women . . .

69

We didn't know each other well enough then." Cornelius grasped the slender neck of the litre carafe of schnapps and filled their glasses. "You could talk about Silesian meatloaves for hours, while I responded with the characteristics of plaice à la Teutonic Knights, which the medieval knights liked so much."

Mock poured a burning stream of Krsinsik's lemon schnapps down his throat and plunged his knife into the thick cube of butter garnished with a spring of parsley. He spread some onto a slice of wheat bread and then with his fork broke into the delicate insides of pigs' trotters in aspic. The cubes and oblongs of aspic, in which wedges of eggs, cloves of garlic and strips of pork had been set, disappeared into Mock's mouth. As he swallowed he touched the rim of both empty glasses with his fork, creating a pure sound.

"Zack, zack," Mock said, looking at the oily consistency of the chilled lemon schnapps he was pouring. "Here's to you, Rühtgard. To the health of the one who's paying."

He then emptied his glass, holding it by its fragile stem, and started on the fried herrings which lay on a long dish in a puddle of vinegar marinade. He crushed flakes of the fish joyfully between his teeth, delighted that the bones, softened by the vinegar, were pliable and harmless.

"That's how it was." The two large shots of schnapps were evident in Rühtgard's voice. "We talked about women much later. When we were no longer ashamed of our feelings. When . . ."

"When we had got to know what friendship is." Mock scraped his fork across the empty dish and sprawled out comfortably on the couch. "When we had grasped that, in a world of shrapnel, splinters and vermin, it was the only thing that made sense. Not the Fatherland, not conquering yet another *barbaricum* bridge-head, but friendship . . ."

"Don't be so pompous, Mock, old comrade." Rühtgard smiled at the sight of two waiters laying the table with silver dishes whose dome covers were embellished with the two-headed Austrian eagle. "Look" — he lifted a cover as if to sit it on his head — "This is what our helmets looked like . . ."

Mock laughed out loud as a drop of hot fat rolled off the cover and landed on Rühtgard's neck. While the doctor whacked himself violently, as if stung by a mosquito, Mock filled the empty glasses, gradually increasing the distance between bottle and glass. The last drops fell from a height little short of ten centimetres.

"Pathos was a poor background to what we experienced during those two years." Rühtgard got to his feet and drew the curtains of their alcove. "The wrong background. Friendship and comradeship aren't born in the face of death. There are no friends then. Everyone faces death alone, and stinks of fear. Our comradeship was sealed by the daily humiliation, the daily contempt we experienced. Do you know when I realized that?"

"When?" Mock asked, lifting the covers off the dishes.

"When we had to crap on command." Rühtgard broke off to clink glasses with Mock and swallow the burning liquid. His throat barely accepted it. "Captain Mantzelmann would come along and order the entire platoon to crap at the same time. Even me, a medical orderly. When he decided it was time to crap, we'd squat in the trenches with the icy wind lashing our backsides. Mantzelmann marked out the time for us to crap. Pity he didn't mark out the time to die. Mock, damn it!" he yelled. "There's only the two of us in this world! You and I!"

"Be quiet, and stop drinking." Mock tied a starched napkin around his neck. "You're not having supper, so you shouldn't drink so much. Three large shots are more than enough."

Four browned goose necks landed on Mock's plate. He cut this delicacy into strips and arranged them on round, crunchy slices of potato. Enclosed in a sheath of goose skin was a stuffing made from onion, liver and goose fat. Mock placed soft, braised onion rings on top of these

71

pyramids and began a concentrated assault. He ate slowly and methodically. First he plunged his cutlery into a dish where hunks of roast pork swam in a thick sauce of flour and cream. On top of a piece of meat now speared on his fork, he balanced a mound of potato and goose. When he had devoured this complicated formation he slid a layer of fried cabbage with crackling onto his fork as if it were a shovel. The plates gradually emptied.

"We spoke about women later," Rühtgard said, lighting a cigarette, "when the Russians started singing their dumkas.† We'd stare at the starry sky and each one of us would think about warm bodies, soft breasts, smooth thighs . . ."

"Cornelius, stop making things up." Mock pushed aside the empty plates, lit a cigarette and poured another two shots from the carafe. "We didn't talk about *women*, but about one woman. Each one of us spoke about one woman. I told you about my romantic ideal, about the mysterious, red-headed, unknown Lorelei from the hospital in Königsberg, while you only talked about . . ."

"My daughter, Christel." Rühtgard drank without waiting for Mock. "About my little princess Christel who now flirts with men, who smells of rutting . . ."

"Let it go." Mock was suddenly very thirsty. He pulled the curtain aside to summon a waiter with a frothy tankard. "Your little princess is now a grown-up young lady and ought to be getting married."

Rühtgard threw off his jacket and began to unbutton his waistcoat.

"Mock, my brother!" he shouted. "Our friendship is like that of Patroclus and Achilles! Let's exchange waistcoats, as Homer's heroes exchanged their armour!"

As he said this Rühtgard threw off his waistcoat and sat down heavily. A moment later black sleep, brother of death, descended over him. Mock

† Melancholic Ukrainian folk songs.

72

left the alcove to look for a waiter, but instead caught sight of the drunken smile of the Jewish-looking girl who was swaying on the dance floor, alone, her handbag slung over her neck. He also saw spilled schnapps, stained tablecloths and the white dust of cocaine; he saw a soldier hiding pamphlets under his greatcoat; he saw his friend, Doctor Rühtgard, who had once saved his life in a town on the Pregolya. He clicked his fingers and a young waiter appeared.

"Be so kind," Mock could scarely pronounce the syllables as he went through the notes in his wallet, "as to call a droschka for me and my friend . . . And then help me carry him to it . . ."

"I can't do that, sir," said the lad, putting the ten-mark note in his pocket, "because our manager, Mr Bilkowsky, doesn't allow the hiring of fiacres. Their horses foul the pavement in front of the hotel. For important patrons such as yourself, sir – I saw you here yesterday, and again today – and your friend, we provide our own automobile. The chauffeur has just arrived outside, and he's probably still free. "

The young waiter disappeared. Mock returned to his alcove, paid the head waiter for his supper, and then spent a long time tying his laces, a task much hindered by a belly bloated with the heavy delicacies. Puffing and panting, he helped Doctor Rühtgard to the beautiful Opel whose roof was adorned with a flag bearing the Austrian eagle and the name of the hotel. The automobile made its way through the city. The night was warm. The people of Breslau were preparing for sleep. Only one man was preparing himself for a meeting with phantoms.

BRESLAU, THURSDAY, SEPTEMBER 4TH, 1919
TWO O'CLOCK IN THE MORNING

The net curtain billowed at the open window. Mock sat at the table, listening to his father's snoring. Beyond the window, a shaft of light from the gas lamp in the square yard illuminated the pump where Pastor Gerds' maid stood stretching lazily and gazing at Mock's window with a smile. She stroked the arm of the pump and wrapped her whole body around it. The pump played a rusty tune into the night. Water poured into a bucket while the pastor's maid, swinging on the lever, kept on smiling up at Mock's window. Once the bucket was full, she slid lower and squatted, holding on to the upper part of the lever. Her nightdress strained across her buttocks, the pump lever protruding between them. Smiling, she glanced one more time at Mock's window, picked up the bucket and made towards the gate. Mock listened intently. The bucket clanked against the window of what used to be the butcher's shop. The bell tinkled gently. He heard light footsteps on the stairs. Mock got up and looked closely at his father, fast asleep. Then he crept to his bedroom alcove, lay on his bed and pulled his nightshirt up to his chest. He waited, tense. The hatch in the floor squeaked. He waited. A window casement blew against the wall. Crash. The trapdoor in the corner of the room hit the floor with a dull thud. His father muttered something in his sleep. Mock got up to close the window and, at that very moment, heard what he had feared. The tin bucket tumbled down the stairs. Every stair forced from it an ear-piercing racket. The empty bucket rasped against the sandstone slabs and landed in a puddle.

"Do you have to make such a noise, damn it?" said his father, opening his eyes and immediately closing them again. He turned over and began to snore.

Mock doubled over to conceal his arousal, then covered himself with his nightshirt and tiptoed to approach the hatch. He knew how to open it without it squeaking; he had done so many a time when he returned drunk and did not want to hear his father say: "You're always knocking it back". He half-opened the hatch and peered into the depths of the butcher's shop. Light footsteps on the stairs. From the square of darkness loomed a head

74

and neck. Wisps of pomaded hair were arranged in an intricate curl; the neck was covered with flaking eczema. The head tipped back to reveal congealed red lava flowing from its eyes. The mouth opened and spat a bubble of blood. More appeared, bursting without a sound. Director Julius Wohsedt looked far less handsome than he had at the launching of the ship Wodan.

Mock quickly backed away from the trapdoor and tripped over a basket of logs. Flapping his arms, he knocked down a large bottle of paraffin.

"Ebi, wake up, damn it!" His father was shaking his arm. "Look what you've done!"

Sitting amongst the shards of glass, he felt the burning of small cuts on his legs and buttocks. Threads of his blood meandered over the surface of the paraffin. The hatch was closed.

"I must be a lunatic, Father," he croaked, his breath reeking of four large shots of schnapps.

"Knocking it back, always knocking it back." The old man waved him aside and shuffled over to his bed. "Clean it up — it stinks and it'll stop me sleeping. We'll have to air the room." He opened the window and looked at the sky. "You're a drunkard, not a lunatic. There's no moon tonight, you idiot." He yawned and clambered into the warm refuge of his quilt.

Mock took the first-aid kit which hung on the wall. His father had put it together himself when they moved in: "So that no inspector picks on us. Every workshop ought to have a first-aid kit. That's what the labour law says." Hammering little nails into the pale planks, he had did not want to hear the fact that the apartment was not a craftsman's workshop and that he himself had not been a shoemaker for some time.

Mock gathered up the shards, removed his nightshirt and used it to wipe the floor. He felt the cold instantly. "Not surprising," he thought.

"After all, I'm naked." He threw over his shoulders an old coat which served him in winter for his trips to the toilet, took an iron candlestick from the kitchen and opened the hatch. His back prickled. In the weak glow of the street lamp outside the shop, he looked down the stairs. Empty and dark. Cursing his own fear under his breath, he lit his way with the candle. There was no bucket below, nor any trace of spilled water. Mock squatted to study the drain in the floor, listening for sqeaking rats. Nothing. Silence. A shadow glided across the wall. Mock felt a rush of adrenaline, his hair stood on end and he began to sweat. Postman Dosche and his dog with its upset bowels had crossed Plesserstrasse. Mock felt a gust of cold wind. All of a sudden he remembered his grandmother, Hildegard, who considered a downy duvet a remedy for everything. In her well-scrubbed kitchen in Waldenburg, she would wrap the duvet around little Franz and little Eberhard, saying: "Hide your heads in the duvet. The room's cold. And where it is cold there are evil spirits. It's a sign from them."

Mock sat on the counter and opened the first-aid box. He moistened a piece of cotton wool with hydrogen peroxide and by the feeble light of the candle dabbed at the three small wounds on his thigh and buttock. Then he approached the drainage grille. He levered it up with his fingernail and moved it aside to reveal a square hole. Mock knew the remedy for everything – for evil spirits and the cold. It was hidden beneath the grille. He felt the familiar shape of the flat bottle in his hand and pulled it out without using the candle, which was burning down on the counter. This was a task he could accomplish even in the dark. He heard a rustling in the hole. A rat? He held the candlestick aloft. A crumpled piece of paper lay embedded in the depths. A squared sheet, torn from a maths exercise book. He held it up to the flame and began to read. There were things in this world for which Mock did not have a remedy.

Mock sat next to Smolorz in a covered two-person gig manufactured years
ago for the police at Hermann Lewin's carriage factory, and blessed the
skill of the builders who had laid the cobblestones on Kaiser-Wilhelm-
Strasse. Thanks to their good work he no longer had to hold his stomach
and curse his gluttony as he had for an hour, from the moment he had
found Julius Wohsedt's letter in the drain of Eduard Mock's former shop
and rushed out into the street, half-naked, to catch a droschka. The four
large shots of schnapps he had drunk in the night had been offset by a
mountain of fat-ridden food, and should not have seethed and surged in
Mock's body as he was well trained in battling with alcohol. And yet they
had made themselves felt as the droschka sped along the bumpy streets
of Klein Tschansch, turned abruptly, braked and finally came to a stand-
still when the old hack slipped on a cobble and broke a shaft in the fall.
Despite suffering digestive agonies, Mock finally made it to the XV
District police station at Ofenerstrasse 30 and telephoned the lawyer
Max Grötzschl who, inveighing against night-time calls, had descended
several floors to pass the information on to his neighbour, Kurt Smolorz.
Mock had then borrowed a police bicycle and transported his leaden
stomach to the Police Praesidium on Schuhbrücke. There in the yard,
coachman Kurt Smolorz was waiting for him on the box of a fast, two-
person gig.

During those two nocturnal hours, Mock did not have the opportunity
to re-read the letter he had found in the sewers of his house. His hands
had been occupied either with his quivering stomach or with the handle-
bars of the bicycle. Now, with Smolorz driving skilfully along cobbles
damp with warm rain, Mock could read the peculiar text once more.

"To Eleonore Wohsedt, Schenkendorfstrasse 3. The swine is wearing
an executioner's hood." Mock held the note up to his eyes and read the

77

scribbles with some difficulty. The task was not made any easier by the streaks of light and shadow gliding across the page as the carriage passed the street lamps surrounding Kaiser-Wilhelm-Platz. "I wouldn't be able to recognize him. He tortured me, forced me to admit that I'm an adulterer. It isn't true Eleonore, my dear wife. I was forced to write the letter you're going to get from him. I do not have, nor ever have had a mistress. I love only you. Julius Wohsedt."

They were approaching the crossroads at Kürassierstrasse. Broad avenues ran on either side, and between them a pavement planted with maples and plane trees. This sort of road planning had been hatched by the militarized brains of German architects, who had designed the green belt with cavalry officers in mind. Just one such powerfully built soldier in cuirassier's uniform was now riding across the street that had been dedicated to his unit. Clearly angry, he allowed the speeding gig to pass, throwing Mock a hostile look. Mock did not notice, however, being too busy observing a group of drunks who had poured out of a taproom hidden in the yard behind Kelling's dye-works. A few men were watching two women as they fought and whacked each other with their handbags. Mock asked Smolorz to pull up. The women stopped fighting and looked at the police officers, ironically and provocatively. Through the layer of powder on the face of one of them, prickles of morning stubble were beginning to appear. Mock waved them away and told Smolorz to move on and pull up after turning right into Schenkendorfstrasse. Smolorz tied the reins to a lamp post and rang the bell. Unnecessarily. Nobody was asleep in the huge house where all lights were ablaze. Mrs Eleonora Wohsedt would certainly not be asleep. Wrapped in a checked blanket, she stood with two servants at the entrance door and stared helplessly at the police officers coming up the stairs. The butlers were ready to fend off the attack, their eyes betraying the friendliness of a cobra. Mrs Wohsedt was shaking. In the woollen blanket, and without her false teeth, she looked like a street vendor who might stamp her feet to chase away the cold. The September morning was cool and crystal-clear.

"Criminal police." Mock held his identification under Mrs Wohsedt's nose, and for a few moments fixed his eyes on the butlers as their faces softened. "Criminal Assistant Mock and Sergeant Smolorz."

"That's what I thought. I knew you'd come. I've been standing like this for two days waiting for him," said Mrs Wohsedt, starting to cry. The tears fell silently and profusely. Her huge, soft body shook as she wept. Sniffing, she brushed aside the tears, rubbing them into her temples. A thought struck Mock which was so hideous and absurd that even he was disgusted by it. Swiftly he pushed it aside.

"Why didn't you report your husband's disappearance if he vanished two days ago? Where could he have gone?" The hideous thought would not leave Mock in peace.

"Sometimes he doesn't come home. He takes our little bitch out for a walk in the evenings and goes down to the shipyards. He works in his office through the night and only comes home for dinner the next day. The day before yesterday he took the dog for a walk" – her alto voice lowered to a whisper – "at about six o'clock in the evening. And he didn't come back for dinner . . ."

"What breed is the dog?" Smolorz asked.

"A boxer." Mrs Wohsedt wiped away the last of her tears.

Mock imagined the scene: a little girl playing with two boxer bitches, while on an iron bed behind a partition two people covered in eczema are cavorting, Wohsedt's fat, triple chin resting between Johanna's shapely breasts.

"Is this your husband's writing?" Mock showed her the piece of paper he had found in the drain, now protected by two sheets of transparent tracing paper. "Read it, but please handle it only through the tracing paper."

79

Mrs Wohsedt put on her glasses and began to read, moving her sunken lips. Her face lit up:

"Yes, it's his writing," she said quietly, and then suddenly she shouted with joy: "I trusted him! I trusted him and he didn't let me down! So what he wrote in that other letter isn't true . . ."

"What other letter?" Mock asked.

"The one I got today," Mrs Wohsedt said, turning in circles. "It's not true, it's not true . . ."

"Calm down, please." Mock grabbed her by the shoulders and glared at the butlers who were ready to pounce.

"This one, this one." She pulled out an envelope from under her blanket, tore herself away from Mock's grasp and carried on spinning in a joyful dance. Mock noticed flaking skin on her neck.

"You've got a pair of gloves, Smolorz," Mock said as he lit his first cigarette of the day. "Take the letter from Mrs Wohsedt and read it out loud."

"'My dear wife,'" Smolorz obeyed. "'I keep a mistress. She lives on Reuscherstrasse . . .'"

"'I was forced to write the letter you're going to get from him,'" Mrs Wohsedt's voice sang. "'I do not have, nor ever have had a mistress. I love only you. Julius Wohsedt.'"

"'. . . You can easily check,'" Smolorz continued reading. "'She has the same eczema as I do. Julius Wohsedt.'"

"When did you get this letter?" Mock asked.

"At about eight." Mrs Wohsedt's lips turned into a horseshoe. She had clearly got to the part about the torture. "I was waiting for Julius on the terrace. I was worried he hadn't come home yet."

"The postman came and handed you the letter?"

"No, some scruff on a bicycle came to the fence, threw the envelope on the path, then quickly rode away."

"Mock, sir," Smolorz said before his chief could ask about the "scruff's" appearance. "There's something else . . ."

Mock looked at the squared sheet of paper. He ran the tip of his tongue over his rough palate and felt extremely thirsty. Faint fumes of alcohol emanated from his body, and his head was absorbing the heavy acids of a hangover.

"Lost your tongue, Smolorz?" hissed Mock. "Why the hell are you showing me this? You've just read it."

"Not all of it." Smolorz's pale and freckled face turned pink. "There's something else on the back . . ."

"Then read it, damn it!"

"'Blessed are those who have not seen and yet have believed. Mock, admit your mistake, admit you have come to believe. If you do not want to see any more gouged eyes, admit your mistake.'" Smolorz turned purple. "There's a postscript too: 'South Park.'"

"Didn't I tell you, didn't I tell you," Mrs Wohsedt said in a high singsong. "I told you he went to South Park with the dog . . ."

"A long walk," muttered Smolorz as Mock tried hard to force from his mind the hideous thought that had occurred to him.

They left the port director's house and climbed into the gig. As they set off towards Kaiser-Wilhelm-Strasse, Smolorz said to Mock:

"This might be silly, Mock, sir, but it's no wonder the director had another woman."

Mock did not say anything. He did not want to admit even to himself that the hideous thought which had tormented him from the moment he set eyes on Mrs Wohsedt had now been put into words.

81

South Park was completely empty at this hour. In the alleyway leading from Kaiser-Wilhelm-Strasse appeared the figure of a woman in a long dress. Next to her, tugging her from side to side, trotted a large dog. The cold, pale-pink glow of the goddess Eos sharpened the image: the woman wore a bonnet, and on her body was not a dress, but a coat from beneath which trailed the straps of a nightgown. She was walking briskly, not allowing the dog to stop for any length of time to do what a dog sets out to do on its morning walk. She passed the pond and skipped along the footbridge, hastened by the sight of a man in a peaked cap standing beneath a tree. She ran to him and threw herself into his arms. Now left to its own devices, the giant schnauzer bucked up at its mistress' decision. The man twisted his moustache, turned the woman around and pulled up her nightdress. The woman bent over, supported her hands on the tree and noted with relief that no lights were burning in the enormous edifice of the Hungarian King Hotel and Restaurant. All of a sudden the dog growled. The man in the peaked cap stopped unbuttoning his trousers and looked round.

Some fifty metres from them two men were forcing their way through the bushes. Both wore bowler hats and had cigarettes between their teeth. The shorter one kept stopping, grasping his stomach and groaning loudly.

"Quiet, Bert," the woman whispered as she stroked the dog. Bert growled softly and watched the two men shake thick drops of dew from their clothes.

The shorter man removed his bowler and wiped the sweat from his brow, and the two of them continued on their way towards the pond where some fat swans had now appeared. Suddenly the shorter of the two stopped and said something loudly, which the woman understood as: "Oh, damn it!" and her partner as: "Oh, fuck!" The groaning man handed his bowler and coat to his taller companion and, pressing his thighs together, he pushed his way into the bushes and squatted. The unfulfilled lover decided to carry on with humankind's eternal act, but his consort had a different idea. She tied the dog to a tree and hid behind it. Leaning out a little, she watched anxiously as the squatting man ran his fingers over his cheek, looked at them carefully, then looked up. Once again he blurted out the words which the maid and her lover had understood so differently, but now his voice was amplified by horror. At the crown of the old plane tree swung a man hanging by his legs. The dog yelped, the woman screamed and her lover saw a freckled hand covered in red hair with a gun aimed at his nose. The early morning tryst had ended in total disaster.

BRESLAU, THAT SAME SEPTEMBER 4TH, 1919 HALF PAST FIVE IN THE MORNING

Mock was familiar with the right wing of South Park Restaurant. There was a hotel in the wing where two rooms were forever reserved. Just under a year earlier, when he and Cornelius Rühtgard had been sent, much to their delight, on a Polish train to Warsaw, where the Poles disarmed them, both had sensed a favourable wind at their backs. They had passed through Łódź and Posen on their way to the Silesian metropolis which, as Mock assured his friend, was to Königsberg like fat carp to dry cod. On arriving in Breslau they had lodged with Franz, Mock's brother, and that same day they had gone to South Park Restaurant. Their table had been next to the pond, by the stone steps leading down to the water, and the autumn sun had been exceptionally strong that day. Conversation had flagged because Mock's eight-year-old nephew Erwin, bored by his uncle's wartime stories and fed up with feeding indifferent swans, had kept on interrupting. Everyone had feigned distress at losing the war, when in fact all had been thinking about their own affairs: Franz about his frigid wife; Irmgard about little Erwin's tendency to tears and melancholy; Erwin about the gun which he believed must be hidden in his uncle's backpack; Rühtgard about his daughter Christel, who was taking her final exams that year at a Hamburg boarding school for well-born young ladies, and whom he was to bring to Breslau; and Eberhard Mock about his dying mother in Waldenburg, with the old shoemaker Willibald Mock sitting at her side, trying to hide the tears that ran down the furrows on his face. When Franz's family had hurriedly said their farewells and set off for the nearby tram terminus, Mock and Rühtgard sat in silence. The festive mood which accompanied them through the elegant restaurants of Warsaw, the dens of Łódź that smelled of onions, and the steamed-up restaurants of Posen, had somehow evaporated into thin air. As they were knocking back their second tankard of beer that day, they had been approached by a head waiter endowed with impressive whiskers. As he changed their ashtray, he had smacked his lips and winked. Mock knew what that meant. Without a moment's hesitation they had paid and gone up to the first floor of the hotel where, in the company of two young ladies, they had celebrated the end of the war.

That same head waiter was now sitting on reception. He did not wink or smack his lips; his eyelids and lips were glued together with sleep. Mock did not need to show his identification. Over the course of the year, head waiter Bielick had become well acquainted with Criminal Assistant Mock from the Vice Department of the Police Praesidium, and he did not feel like laughing.

"How many members of staff are there in the hotel, and how many guests?" Mock said with no introduction.

"I'm the only member of staff. The caretaker, the cooks and the chambermaid come at six," Bielick said.

"And how many guests?"

"Two."

"Are they alone?"

"No. The one in number four is with Kitty, the other in six with August."

"What time did they get here?"

"Kitty's one at midnight, the other – yesterday afternoon. August, the poor thing," Bielick giggled, "he won't be able to sit down."

"Why did you lie to me by saying you're the only member of staff?" Mock spoke softly, but his voice shook. "Kitty and August are here too." He lit a cigarette and remembered the existence of a malady called drinking too much. "I've not been here for a long time, Bielick," he muttered. "I didn't know you were running a brothel for queers."

"I informed Councillor Ilssheimer about it directly," Bielick said, a little embarrassed. "And he gave his assent."

"I'm going to pay Kitty and August a visit. Give me the keys!"

Jangling the keys, Mock climbed the stairs to the first floor. As he mounted the crimson carpet, he did not notice Bielick reach for the telephone. He paused on the mezzanine and glanced out of the window. The boughs of the plane trees swayed. The policeman cutting down the corpse was out of sight, whereas Smolorz was perfectly in view, questioning the unfulfilled lovers. He could see Mühlhaus too, as Smolorz pointed out the hotel to him. And now he could also see the body coming down – fat, and with a red, bloated neck. From that distance the eczema was not visible.

Mock arrived on the first floor and opened the door marked number four. The room was fitted out like an elegant, eighteenth-century boudoir. Mirrors set in gilt frames hung on the walls, and syringes containing powder stood in front of them. There was an enormous four-poster bed and the immense spider of a still-burning chandelier. Next to the bed stood a dress. It stood because it was supported by a whalebone frame

85

from which flowed the skirt. There were two people in the bed: a small, slight man lay cuddled up to a pair of generous breasts squeezed into a corset. The breasts belonged to a woman who was snoring heavily, opening lips accentuated by a charcoal beauty spot. Wearing an abundantly powdered and tiered wig, she looked as if she had been transported from the days of Louis XIV.

Mock turned off the light, walked up to the chair where the man's clothes hung and pulled out his wallet. He sat down heavily at the coffee table, pushed the woman's lingerie off the marble surface with his elbow and noted down the man's details. "Horst Salena, forwarding agent, Marthastrasse 23, two children." Then he got up, yanked the eiderdown off the bed and scrutinized the man who was lying on his back, his ribs protruding above his long johns. He was very thin and ordinary. He could have done anything but haul Wohsedt's hundred-kilogram body up a high tree. They both awoke. The woman cursed under her breath and covered herself again with the eiderdown.

Mock studied the forwarding agent's frightened face.

"Beat it, Salena. Right now!"

Salena got dressed without a sound and quickly left, hardly daring to breathe. Mock stepped into the corridor, locking Kitty in her room, and pushed at the door to August's room. The key did not fit. Mock swore at Bielick under his breath and with a furious expression went downstairs to reception. He looked so fierce that the receptionist slid the correct key across the counter without a word. Mock grabbed it and ran back upstairs. From the corridor he heard a window slam, and then the dull thud of someone landing heavily. He drew his Mauser and rushed to the window. Criminal Councillor Josef Ilssheimer was running, limping, across the lawn. His bowler hat was missing and his coat was thrown carelessly over his shoulders. Mock rubbed his eyes in astonishment and burst into August's room. The young man in a dressing gown was not in the least frightened and gazed at the intruder with a smile. Mock looked around the room and saw a bowler hanging on a peg. He took it down and examined it. On the sweat-stained ribbon inside he found the embroidered initials "J.I." – Josef Ilssheimer had jumped from August's window! Now Mock knew why he had not been informed by Bielick about the modification to the service offered by South Park Hotel. Mock swallowed acrid saliva and felt it scratch at his throat. He dropped the bowler on the floor and dug his heel into it several times before throwing it into a corner. From that day nothing could surprise him any more. Nothing would have surprised him after having found Wohsedt's letter in a drain at his very own home, and then discovering the man's body hanging in a tree in South Park – even finding Councillor Ilssheimer, father of four, in August's arms. But he could not understand why August was still smiling. He approached him and watched as his open palm struck August's cheek, leaving a burning red mark.

"What the fuck are you smiling at?" Mock asked, and without waiting for an answer left the room.

Kitty's little salon was already tidy and she herself was dressed; she had forgotten only to remove her tiered wig. Sitting at the table she lowered her eyes modestly. Mock sat opposite her and drummed his fingers on the marble slab set in the silver tabletop. "Not a bad imitation of an eighteenth-century table," he thought. "Everything in here's from the eighteenth century."

"From what time were you with him, Kitty?"

"Who, Criminal Assistant, sir?"

"The man I just threw out."

"Six, I think. That's when he arrived. He paid for the whole night up front. He's a good client. Bought a carafe of cherry schnapps and paid for dinner, too. A good client. He used to live not far from here . . ."

"A good client." That's what they had called Mock when he used to drink away his wages in the Hungarian King. That's what they called him when he used to take two girls to a room and paid them generously, although in his drunkenness he could not move his hands or legs, let alone anything else. They used to bow to him when he walked into his favourite Jewish taverns on Antonienstrasse and stood for hours at the bar, silent, furious and glum. That whore, she too would have bowed to him from afar in the days when he used to go for walks with his father in South Park. That was only a few months ago. Then Mock's bad dreams had begun, as had his father's apathy, broken only by his games with postman Dosche's dog. A good client in taverns and brothels. A good client with whom nobody had any sympathy – no innkeeper and no whore. And why should they sympathize with him? After all, how were they to know that some monster was slaying people and writing him letters! They weren't interested; they were too busy looking after their own affairs. They had their own problems. Mock banished these unpleasant thoughts and asked Kitty mechanically:

"So, he lived not far from here?"

"Yes. He once came with his dog, for a quickie."

"A dog?"

"He took his dog for a walk and came to see me. The dog lay beside the bed, while on the bed we . . ."

"Well, I should hope the dog wasn't in there with you . . . And has a fat man called Julius ever been to see you? He had nasty eczema on his neck . . ."

"My clients don't introduce themselves . . . And I don't recall anyone with eczema . . . No . . . There hasn't been anyone like that . . . Besides, I wouldn't take anyone like that on . . ."

"You're demanding, Kitty." Mock got to his feet. "And would you take me on?" He went to the window and watched Mühlhaus questioning the would-be lovers while Lasarius squatted beside the corpse. Mühlhaus asked Smolorz something, and the latter pointed to the hotel. The commissioner strode briskly towards the building, as if he had seen Mock standing at the net curtain.

"Any time, Mr Mock," Kitty smiled flirtatiously. It pained Mock to think that this beautiful woman in a crooked wig had once been a child, cuddled and kissed by her parents. "Naked or dressed up? I've got a Roman outfit too . . . And all sorts of lingerie accessories . . . For the clients, too . . ."

Mock studied the girl in silence. In his head thundered the words: "Dressed up . . .", "outfit . . ."

"Listen Käthe," he said, addressing her by her rightful name. "I've not been here for a long time. I didn't know queers came here. I didn't know anything about dressing up . . . Who thought all that up? Your new boss?"

"Yes, Mr Nagel."

"And August, does he dress up for his clients, too?"

"Rarely." Käthe smirked. "But some do ask."

"And what does August dress up as?"

"A gladiator, a worker," she mused. "Oh, I don't know what else . . . Usually it's a gladiator . . . There was one client who yelled" – and here Kitty shouted, imitating a drunkard's gibberish – "I want a gladiator!"

Mock believed in the promptings of intuition and in the automatism of thought – a recent fashion in avant-garde art – and he appreciated the notion of a chain of even the most extraordinary associations. He believed in the prophetic value of a sequence of images, and he did not consider Duchamp's manifestos to be inauthentic or degenerate. He believed in premonitions and in a policeman's superstitions. He knew that now, too, it was intuition which had prompted him to ask about August dressing up. He closed his eyes and tried to conjure up associations. Nothing. Thirst. A hangover. Tiredness. A sleepless night. Kitty imitating a drunk and shouting: "I want a gladiator!" A lady in an alcove yelling, in a voice distorted by alcohol: "I want a carter! Now! Immediately!" Mock heard the sounds of a foxtrot. A few days ago, heavy with gin, he had wrapped his arms round the waist of a slim dance-hostess. In the Hungarian King. A young waiter, who was helping him carry Rühtgard, had explained to him: "Our manager, Mr Bilkowsky, doesn't allow the hiring of fiacres. The horses foul the pavement in front of the hotel." The lady had shouted: "I want a carter!" The waiter had then replied . . . What had he replied? Yes, he had replied: "Right this minute, at your service, my lady."

"Tell me, Käthe," – Mock could sense the trail he was going to follow – "does August dress up as a carter? Or a sailor, perhaps?"

Kitty shook her head and watched in surprise as Mock, despite her negative reply, smiled gleefully and ran from the room, almost breaking the high mirror sprinkled with powder.

BRESLAU, THAT SAME SEPTEMBER 4TH, 1919
SIX O'CLOCK IN THE MORNING

Mock bumped into Mühlhaus in the hotel entrance. The new chief of the Murder Commission was crushing the mouthpiece of his pipe in his teeth and twirling his grey beard in his fingers. He took Mock by the arm and very slowly led him to where the corpse had been found. The birds, lost in song, announced another hot September day. Above the plane trees rose the yellow circle of the sun.

"Let's take a little walk, Mock. Do you like taking early-morning walks in the park?"

"Only when there are no corpses hanging from the trees."

"I see you're in a good mood, Mock. Nothing like gallows humour." Mühlhaus took the pipe from his mouth and squirted brown saliva into the bushes. "Tell me, are we dealing with a serial killer?"

"I'm not well up on criminal theory, and anyway, I don't know whether such a thing exists, or how serial killings are defined . . ."

"And according to you . . ."

"I think we are."

"Victims of serial killings have something in common with each other. Firstly, the murderer leaves them in a place where they're bound to be found. The sailors' corpses at the dam, a body hanging from a tree in a popular walking spot . . . And secondly, what do these victims of 'Mock's enemy', as the perpetrator is widely known, have in common?"

"'Widely' meaning where?"

"For the time being where we work, in the Police Praesidium . . . Before long in the Breslau newspapers and across the whole of Germany. Despite the secrecy of the operation, sooner or later there's going to be a leak to the press. We can't hold everybody in quarantine, like that maid in the park and her lover. You're going to be famous . . ."

"What was it you asked me?" Mock wanted to slap Mühlhaus as he had August, and then to run, fly to where pimps offer up male prostitutes dressed in sailors' outfits; instead of which he had to traipse along beside Mühlhaus with the acrid, smoky aroma of Badia tobacco in his nostrils. His fingers and his back itched; he knew that no amount of scratching would relieve him. The sensation overwhelmed him quite frequently, and he could never find quite the right word for it. A fragment from Livy came to mind in which a Latin adjective perfectly expressed the present state of his spirit: *impotens* – out of one's mind with impotence.

"I asked you what the victims of 'Mock's enemy' have in common with each other?"

"That singular name given to the perpetrator is an answer in itself. Why are you asking something we've already known for so long?"

"I could give you the cutting answer that I'm the one asking questions here, Mock, but I won't. I'll play at being Socrates and you'll arrive at the truth yourself . . ."

91

"I haven't got time . . ." said Mock, leaving Mühlhaus abruptly and walking resolutely alongside the pond.

"Halt!" shouted Mühlhaus. "That's an order!" Mock stopped short, turned towards the pond, knelt on the grassy bank and scooped some water into his hands. "No time, eh? Well then, as from today you'll have plenty of time. There isn't much going on in the Vice Department. You don't work for me any more. You're going back to Ilssheimer."

"Why?" Trickles of water ran down Mock's face, and through them he could see the slits of Mühlhaus' squinting eyes. He conjured up his future in the Vice Department: bisexual Ilssheimer sacking the man who had exposed him, giving as his reason "dereliction of duty due to alcohol abuse".

"I took you on for two reasons. Firstly, the murderer wants something from you. I thought you knew what he wanted; I thought you would make after him like a rabid dog avenging the death of innocent people . . ."

"The rabid dog of vengeance." Mock wiped the water from his cheeks. "Are you acquainted with Auweiler's poetry?"

"Whereas you have no idea what the murderer wants. The psychotherapy session with Doctor Kaznicz certainly hasn't moved the investigation . . ."

"And that's why you're dismissing me?" Mock saw columns of magnesium shoot into the sky several metres away, where the body had been discovered. Smolorz had just left the spot and, carrying the notes he had taken when questioning the unfulfilled lovers, was making his way over to Mock and Mühlhaus. "The rabid dog of vengeance no longer proved necessary, right?"

"That's not the reason, Mock." Mühlhaus took him once again by the arm. "That's not the reason. You haven't answered me. I'm not going to play at being Socrates and you're not going to be my Alcibiades . . ."

"No, especially as the latter came to a sticky end . . ."

"Secondly, what do the victims have in common? Their murderer's hatred of Mock. That's what all six have in common. But what do the last two victims have in common?" Mühlhaus raised his voice and glanced at Smolorz as he approached. "Well, tell me, damn it, what do the last two victims have in common? The old sailor Ollenborg and Wohsedt, the river port director?"

"They were both questioned by Criminal Assistant Mock," Smolorz said.

"Correct, Sergeant." Mühlhaus looked approvingly at Smolorz. "That swine wants to tell us: 'I'm going to kill everyone you question, Mock. So don't question anyone. Don't conduct the investigation.' Now do you understand why I'm taking you off the case? Who else did you question, Mock? Who have you poisoned? Who else is going to die in this city?"

BRESLAU, THAT SAME SEPTEMBER 4TH, 1919
A QUARTER PAST SIX IN THE MORNING

A prison wagon pulled up outside South Park Hotel. Two uniformed policemen climbed out and ran briskly into the building, swords clanking at their sides. A moment later they emerged holding Kitty by the arms as she thrashed about and tried to bite them in an attempt to break free. One of the men's shakos was knocked askew. Mühlhaus, Mock and Smolorz watched attentively. Kitty stared at Mock, her eyes full of hatred. He walked up to her and whispered:

"Try to understand, Käthe, it's for your own good. You'll be put up in the best single, warm cell for a few days and then you'll be able to leave." He moved closer and whispered even more quietly: "Then later I'll make it up to you . . ."

The promise did not impress Kitty in the slightest. She spat at Mock, her spittle landing on the sleeve of his jacket. He looked round. All the policemen were smiling to themselves, banking on a violent reaction from the Criminal Assistant. They were disappointed. Mock approached Kitty, removed the wig from her head and smoothed her somewhat greasy hair.

"I'll visit you in your cell, Käthe," he said. "Everything's going to be alright."

The policemen had no trouble loading Kitty into the wagon. One of them joined her under the tarpaulin while the other took a seat on the box and cracked his whip.

"Commissioner, sir." Mock wiped his sleeve with a large leaf. "We can set a trap for the killer. He must be following me. Otherwise, how would he know who to kill? It should be enough for me to question someone and then for us to keep a close eye on that person. Kitty, for example. Let's free her. If we don't lose sight of her day or night we'll get hold of that swine in the end. And besides . . . I want to work for you. Of course, I don't have to lead this particular investigation, I could . . ."

"I'm not a street preacher. I don't repeat myself." Mühlhaus folded Smolorz's notes in four. "Besides, we don't have any other cases on apart from the Four Sailors. Every policeman in town is on the Four Sailors case or, to be precise, Six Sailors counting Ollenborg and Wohsedt. Wohsedt also held the honorary title of Rear Admiral. Goodbye, gentlemen."

Mühlhaus set off towards the Horch which was just drawing up outside the hotel. He climbed in and Ehlers the photographer, laden with his tripod, tumbled in after him. Doctor Lasarius' men heaved the stretcher bearing the corpse into their wagon. The engine of the Horch growled and shot a cloud of fumes from the exhaust. The car pulled away but did not go far, stopping beside Mock and Smolorz.

"Just explain one thing to me," Mühlhaus said, leaning his beard out of the window. "Why are there no signs of torture on Wohsedt's body when in the letter he wrote to you . . . I think he expressed it as 'the man in the executioner's hood tortured me'?"

"Maybe he meant mental torture." Lines appeared on Mock's face, mercilessly highlighted by the bright yellow sun. "Wohsedt wasn't difficult to break . . ."

"Are you sure?"

"Of course. One medical term was enough to get him to agree to work for me immediately. He nearly pissed himself in fright."

"And what term was that?"

"'Tuberculosis of the skin after being bitten by someone with tuberculosis'," Mock said, and at that moment he paled. Smolorz knew why. There was one other person Mock had condemned to death because he had questioned her on the Four Sailors case.

BRESLAU, THAT SAME SEPTEMBER 4TH, 1919, HALF PAST SEVEN IN THE MORNING

Thiemann & Co.'s cigar factory was located in the last of the inner yards on Reuscherstrasse. Since it was in full operation until all hours of the night, it gave out stinking fumes, and the clatter of its machinery disturbed the afternoon peace of everyone who lived in the tenements; they never stopped complaining, protesting, even demonstrating, and forming blockades at the gates of the establishment. Eventually the tenement landlords, descendants of Niepold, prevailed on the factory management to open up the establishment an hour later and shut it down an hour earlier. Having worked there for twenty years, even during the time of Mr Thiemann senior, Hildegard Wilck could not get used to the new working arrangements, and the clacking of her wooden clogs could invariably be heard in the inner yard before seven in the morning. And that day – as on every other day – fifty-year-old Miss Wilck stood outside the closed laundry gossiping with the concierge, Mrs Annemarie Zesche. Their interminable conversations drew facetious criticism from Siegfried

95

Franzkowiak, a carpenter living on the ground floor, who did not cease to be amazed at the eloquence of both women. "Those wenches can go on and on about nothing!" he would say to himself.

That day Franzkowiak was in no mood for jokes. He had not slept half the night because little Charlotte Voigten, who lived above him, had been crying. The child's wailing had been accompanied by the dog's howling. Franzkowiak had knocked several times on the door of the bedsit which Charlotte's mother, Johanna, had occupied with her daughter and dog for the past two months. The mother was not in, which did not surprise the carpenter since the entire tenement knew that the city at night was her natural place of work. Some kind person, however, would always look after the child – frequently it was Franzkowiak's wife – and the exceptionally trusting little girl had always allowed herself to be comforted by her carers. Finally, at about four o'clock that morning, the child had fallen asleep. Silence had descended on the lodgings and Franzkowiak had happily laid his weary head next to that of his spouse. It was hardly surprising that he was truly angry now when, after only a few hours' sleep, he heard the yapping of the two women.

"Just tell me, Mrs Zesche, what sort of times do we live in? The child lies asleep behind a screen while the mother and some stranger . . ."

"She's got to make a living somehow, my dear Miss Wilck. You do the laundry and she lives off men . . ."

"Animals, that's what those men are, Mrs Zesche, all they want to do is have it off . . ."

"And all you want to do is natter!" Franzkowiak yelled, leaning out of his window. "You can't let anyone sleep, can you, damn it!"

"What's up with him!" Hildegard Wilck had come to her own conclusions about men. "I've seen him going up to her room! An animal, he is! No better than the others!"

"You look after your own arse, not someone else's!" Now Mrs

Franzkowiak had leaned out too, coming to her husband's defence. "We're both helping that poor woman! One has to be human, not a swine!"

The shouting in the yard had obviously woken the child because little Charlotte's crying suddenly erupted again, followed by the rattling of a window being opened. The little girl's head appeared above the sill. Still sobbing, she shouted something which was drowned out by the dog's howling. People began to gather in the yard. Charlotte moved a chair closer to the window and stood on it. Tears had traced dirty furrows down her cheeks, and her nightdress was yellow with urine.

From the street came the drone of an automobile and a large Horch drove into the yard. The driver, a sturdy, dark-haired man, squeezed the horn and jumped out. An ear-piercing sound filled the well of the yard, this time occasioned by the passenger, a red-headed man with a moustache. The child fell silent, everyone fell silent, even the dog fell silent. As the two men ran through the gate, Miss Wilck's voice could clearly be heard in the silence:

"See, Mrs Zesche? That's one of her suitors. Just look what drink's done to his mug?"

The crash of a forced door resounded through the tenement, followed by the rustle of crumbling plaster and the shrill squealing of the dog. The dark-haired man ran to the windowsill and took the child in his arms. Charlotte looked at him in fright and tried to push him away with straight arms. Siegfried Franzkowiak, who was blessed with good hearing, detected sighs of relief in the child's crying. He also heard Mrs Zesche's commentary:

"See, my dear Miss Wilck, how the child has calmed down? That must be her father. See how alike they are? Tears are even running down that mug of his."

"Her father died in the war, you idiot!" Franzkowiak yelled.

Mock woke up in detention cell number 3 at the Police Praesidium on Schuhbrücke 49. He felt heavy and tired. He closed his eyes and tried to remember his dream, and succeeded without difficulty. The dream was hazy, unreal and melancholic. A meadow and a forest, grass criss-crossed by streams of water. There was a person there, too: beautiful, red-headed, with gentle eyes and dry, soft hands. Mock reached for the jug of unsweet-ened mint tea which the guard, Achim Buhrack, had prepared for him. He swallowed and established with some relief that he did not need the bever-age after all. His hangover had disappeared – and here Mock felt blood rush to his head – along with that morning's events. He remembered the drop of blood which had dripped from Wohsedt's head onto his cheek as he squatted by the pond in South Park; he recalled Commissioner Mühlhaus' words: "Now do you understand why I'm taking you off the case? Who else did you question, Mock? Who have you poisoned? Who else is going to die in this city?" He remembered all too well the little girl's despair as she first pushed him away, then snuggled into him; he remembered questioning the inhabitants of the dark inner yards on Reuscherstrasse: "Nobody knows anything, she often went out at night, but always came home – yesterday she came home at about four o'clock." He remembered Smolorz forcefully tearing the child away from him and saying: "We'll catch him. We'll catch him with or without Mühlhaus. It's too early now; we'll do it this afternoon." The last scenes he replayed were distorted and unclear – Smolorz pushing him into the car, saying: "You haven't slept all night. Get some sleep, the carpenter'll take care of the little one." Then the jug of mint tea and cell number three.

Mock got up from the bunk and performed several squats. He went to the cell door and knocked several times. The old guard, Achim Buhrack, opened up and said in his strong Silesian accent:

"It's the first time I've seen a police officer sleeping in cell number three when he's not drunk."

"Sometimes some people don't have anywhere to go to get enough sleep," Mock said as he ran his hand over the rough stubble on his cheeks. "I've one more favour to ask of you, Buhrack . . . Is there a razor around here anywhere . . ."

BRESLAU, THAT SAME SEPTEMBER 4TH, 1919
SIX O'CLOCK IN THE EVENING

As yet there were very few customers in the Hungarian King. Only one alcove had been occupied, and its heavy curtain was drawn. A few ladies, judging by the high pitch of their voices, could not make themselves comfortable. The curtain rippled and the rail separating the alcove from the rest of the restaurant kept ringing as if someone were striking it with a rod.

"They can't find anywhere to put their umbrellas," whispered Adolf Manzke, the young waiter who had helped Mock transport an unconscious Rühtgard to the car the previous night. Manzke was far from pleased that Mock had not ordered any alcohol that evening, but the first twenty-mark note with which this regular customer paid for his *Wiener Schnitzel* without asking for any change dispersed any concerns he may have had about his tip.

"What is your name, young man?" Mock asked, and on hearing his answer continued: "Explain something to me, Manzke. I asked for a fiacre yesterday and you called for the automobile which usually ferries drunken clients home. Isn't that so?"

"It is," Manzke said, and when he saw Mock fold another enormous twenty-mark note in four, he leaned in even closer.

"The fiacre's horses soil the pavement outside your establishment, isn't that what you said?"

99

"It is," – the waiter's neck was getting stiff – "Mr . . . Mr . . . I don't know your name – what should I call you?"

"Call me Periplectomenus," Mock said, remembering the sybarite from Plautus' comedy *Miles Gloriosus*. "So how would you explain the behaviour of your colleague when he was attending to the demands of one of the ladies? She called for a carter and he promised to fulfil her wish immediately. Explain that to me, Manzke."

"Maybe he needed to fetch the carter from far away and the lady was appropriately generous." The waiter kept glancing at the folded note Mock was weaving between his fingers. "Anyway, you should ask him . . ."

"Indeed, Manzke, you're right." Mock slipped the note into the waiter's waistcoat pocket. "But I don't know which waiter it was . . . Will you help me find him?"

Manzke nodded stiffly and moved away between the tables. The musicians bowed to the audience and blew on their trumpets. Several dance-hostesses – including a dark-haired woman who smiled broadly at Mock – began to sway to the music without leaving their tables. Three elderly men who, like Mock, had in the meantime taken their seats on the second tier overlooking the dance floor eyed the girls through coils of smoke. Eventually one of them made up his mind and approached the dark-haired hostess. She stood up slowly, and did not spare Mock a look of disappointment.

The Criminal Assistant settled down to his goose-liver pâté. He was interrupted in his consumption of this delicate cold meat by Manzke the waiter, who placed a napkin on the table and quickly disappeared. Beneath the napkin lay a clean strip of cash register ribbon on which was written: "Kiss my arse." Mock rubbed his eyes and lit a cigarette. He looked at the scrap of paper once more and heard a ringing in his ears. He stubbed out the cigarette, stood up and made his way through the tables. He entered the bar and, guided by his instinct for alcohol, soon found the serving counter. There stood Manzke, collecting slim, frothing glasses of beer from the barman. When he saw Mock he made towards the flapping kitchen door, but Mock was faster. The waiter did not manage to open the door of his own accord, but did so involuntarily when the weight of Mock's body shoved against his. He tumbled into the kitchen, but there, instead of running from the enraged man, he stood behind a table at which a bald waiter sat in his shirtsleeves counting his tips. Manzke glanced meaningfully at his colleague, who was surprised by the commotion, and apologized to Mock for not bringing him his bottle of gin in good time. Nobody said a word. The Criminal Assistant left the kitchen lobby and made towards the toilets. In the cubicle he tore off a scrap of toilet paper and wrote: "The bald, fat waiter." He went out, paid his bill and discreetly gave Manzke a considerable tip. He also handed him the piece of toilet paper and with his eyes indicated Smolorz, who was sitting in the bar. Manzke drifted over to Smolorz, and Mock towards the exit. "That Manzke ought to be employed by the police," he thought. "As an informer, for the time being; I liked the way he pointed out that waiter to me."

BRESLAU, THAT SAME SEPTEMBER 4TH, 1919
EIGHT O'CLOCK IN THE EVENING

Waiter Helmut Kohlisch finished work at eight o'clock that day. He was tired and angry. Crossing the kitchen, he climbed the narrow inner staircase which led to the stores and pantries. His mood was not improved either by the beer stain on his shirt or by the thought of what awaited him in his dank, one-room lodgings on Büttnerstrasse, squeezed between a delicatessen and a printers: Lisbeth, his heavily pregnant eighteen-year-old daughter, her unemployed husband Josef, a communist agitator who aroused the suspicions of every policeman, and his

101

own consumptive wife, Luise, ladling soup into their bowls. The meal would have been nutritious had it consisted of something more than water, a few pieces of potato and some pitiful strips of cabbage. All would sit there slurping the soup as their eyes bored into his pockets for the tips.

Kohlisch entered the staff room and undressed down to his vest and long johns. He carefully folded his uniform tailcoat and hung up his trousers only once the creases had been perfectly pressed together. He crumpled up the shirt stained by the copper and stuffed it into his bag. He opened the wardrobe, and inside it saw one of the customers he had served that day. Before he had time to be surprised, he had received his first blow. His assailant hit him on the jaw and he flew through the air towards some empty crates, trying to tense his muscles to soften the impact on his back. But this proved unnecessary. Someone grabbed him hard beneath his arms and wrapped him in a double Nelson. He felt the muscles in his neck weaken, the pressure making him bend his neck towards the floor. The red-headed customer clambered out of the wardrobe, pulled a handkerchief from his pocket and wiped his freckled and flushed face. Kohlisch thrashed this way and that, trying to tear himself away from his assailant. This only made the latter increase the pressure, forcing Kohlisch to contemplate his own darned socks. At that moment, Kohlisch remembered that there was a way of slipping out of a double Nelson, by raising your arms and falling to your knees. This he did, and it worked. For a moment he knelt on the floor. Then he received a second blow, this time from behind. A crate smashed on his head and he felt trickles of blood run down his bald skull. Only then did he feel pain. For a few moments, darkness enveloped him. The man behind him planted the crate, now without its base, on his head and pushed it down over his arms. Kohlisch was immobilized. He knelt in front of the red-headed customer, the crate pinning his arms at his waist. He tried to turn around, but his second attacker grabbed him by the ears and turned his face towards the man with the red hair.

"Listen, Kohlisch," he heard from behind. "We're not going to do anything to you if you answer politely."

Kohlisch screamed and immediately regretted it. The red-headed man's heel hit him in the mouth, shattering a lower tooth. Saliva mixed with blood stained the floor. Kohlisch rocked a while in the stocks formed by the old crate, and then collapsed. He heard a humming all around. Someone tied his shirt, which reeked strongly of beer, around his head.

"Are you going to scream again?"

"No." Air whistled through the gap in his teeth.

"Promise."

"Yes."

"Say 'I promise.'"

"I promise."

"Where do you get those male whores from for the ladies?"

"What whores?"

"The male ones. The ones who dress up. One as a carter, another one as a sailor, another a worker . . ."

"I don't know what you're . . ."

The next blow was very painful indeed. Kohlisch could almost hear whatever it was grind across his cheekbone. Someone was standing on his stomach with one heavy shoe. Blood and snot ran from his mouth and nose. The shirt around his head grew damp.

"That was a knuckle-duster. Do you want another taste of it, or are you going to talk?"

"The Baroness orders the boys . . ."

Someone carefully wiped his face with the shirt. A swelling on his cheek obscured the view from his left eye. With his right he saw the red-headed man throwing away the wet shirt in disgust. The strike of a match, smoke being exhaled.

"The Baroness' name!"

"I don't know," Kohlisch glanced at the red-headed man and yelled. "Don't hit me, you son of a whore! I'll tell you everything I know about her!"

The red-headed man slipped the knuckle-duster over his fingers and looked questioningly past Kohlisch's trembling body to where the smoke was coming from. He must have received an answer to his unspoken question because he removed the knuckle-duster. Kohlisch breathed a sigh of relief.

"So, what do you know about the Baroness?" said the man he could not see.

"I know she's a Baroness because that's what they call her."

"Who calls her that?"

"Her friends."

"What's the Baroness' name?"

"I've already told you . . . I don't know . . . I really don't know . . . Can't you understand," howled Kohlisch when he saw the knuckle-duster back on the red-headed man's hand. "The whore doesn't introduce herself to me when she wants a boy, does she?"

"I'm satisfied." The interrogator spat on the floor. The cigarette hissed. "But you've got to give me something to recognize her by."

"Her coat of arms," Kohlisch moaned. "The coat of arms on her carriage . . . An axe, a star and an arrow . . ."

"Good. Identify it in the Armorial of Silesian Nobility, in our archives." Kohlisch guessed that the instructions were directed at the red-headed man. "And now one more thing, Kohlisch. Explain what you mean by 'the Baroness orders boys'."

"The Baroness arrives and phones somewhere from here," Kohlisch practically whispered. "A droschka pulls up outside the restaurant, with some men in costume inside. The Baroness or one of her friends wishes, for example, for a carter . . . Then I go and get him from the droschka . . . As if I'd fetched him myself . . . It's a game . . ."

Kohlisch stopped talking. There were no more questions. The door to the staff room slammed. He flung his fat body around, taking in the room with crates thrown about all over the place. There stood two men Kohlisch had never seen before. One of them, a short man with a narrow, fox-like face, gestured to the other, a giant with bushy eyebrows. He seemed to be saying: "Take care of him!"

The giant emitted an inarticulate sound and then walked up to Kohlisch, slipped the temporary stocks from his arms and held under his nose a handkerchief permeated with a sweet and sickly, yet sharp smell. It reminded him of hospitals.

"It's for your own good. You're going to stay with us for a few days." That was the last thing Kohlisch heard that day.

BRESLAU, THAT SAME SEPTEMBER 4TH, 1919
NINE O'CLOCK IN THE EVENING

The villa belonging to Baron and Baroness von Bockenheim und Bielau stood at one end of Wagnerstrasse. Two cars drove up to the massive iron gates decorated with coats of arms on which ivy wound around a shield depicting an axe and a star pierced with a half-feathered arrow. From the garden at the back of the house came the shouts of children and the tinkling of a piano. The red-headed man climbing out of the first car listened intently to the sounds before he pressed the bell, holding it for some time. A butler in a tailcoat marched majestically from the villa. His face, framed by side-whiskers, radiated calm, and his long, stork-like legs in striped trousers advanced with a dancing step. He approached the gate and cast a contemptuous eye over the visitor – a travelling salesman, he presumed. He extended a silver tray to allow the intruder to slip his hand through the railing and deposit on it a business card with the name JOSEF BILKOWSKY, HUNGARIAN KING HOTEL, BISCHOFSTRASSE 13. On it was also written the word "Verte". The butler walked slowly towards the house, lifting his legs high. A few seconds later he disappeared behind the massive door.

The red-headed man got back into the automobile and drove off. After a short while, an elegantly dressed couple appeared on the drive. The woman, in her thirties, wore a black Chanel dress with extravagant wavy stripes, a hat with a white chrysanthemum and a stole, while the older man wore a tailcoat and a white waistcoat which reflected the light from the lanterns along the drive. They went to the gate and looked around. The man opened the gate and stepped out onto the pavement. Apart from a lone car parked at some distance, Wagnerstrasse was empty. The woman fixed her faintly amused eyes on the car. Her companion's gaze was none too friendly. Both noted the four men sitting inside. At the steering wheel sat a small individual with a hat pushed down over his nose. Next to him sprawled a well-built, dark-haired man. The smoke spiralling from his cigarette caused the two men in the back of the car to squint. One of the two had something wrapped around his face, as if he were suffering from toothache, while the other could barely fit in the back seat. The dark-haired man turned to them, caught the one with the bandage by the neck and pointed to the elegant woman.

He said something and the man with the toothache nodded. The dark-haired man touched the driver on the shoulder and the car abruptly pulled away. A moment later it had disappeared from view. The woman in the exquisite black dress and the man in the tailcoat returned to the villa. The butler looked at them in surprise. The man in the tailcoat was a little annoyed, the woman in the black dress indifferent.

The children's party being held at Baron von Bockenheim und Bielau's villa in celebration of the eighth birthday of Baron Rüdiger II's only daughter was coming to an end. Parents of those invited sat beneath canopies adorned with the Baron's coat of arms, moistening their lips and tongues with Philippe champagne. Ladies chattered about the success of Hauptmann's *Weavers* in Vienna, while men discussed Clemenceau's threats to call for changes to the German constitution. Puffed up with the grandeur of their master and mistress' *nouvelle noblesse*, the servants moved among them slowly and ceremoniously. The first of the trusted servants carried a tray of empty glasses, the second a tray of full ones. The children, wearing sailor suits or tweeds and caps *à la* Lord Norfolk, ran around the garden watched over by their governesses. A few girls stood around a piano singing Beethoven's "Ode to Joy" to the brisk rhythm hammered out on the keys by a long-haired musician. The lanterns, like the conversations, were slowly waning. The gentlemen had decided to smoke a farewell cigarette, the ladies to take one more sip of champagne "whose bubbles", as one of them expressed it, "added an interesting bitterness to the sweet Viennese pastry twists".

The lady of the house, Baroness Mathilde von Bockenheim und Bielau, placed her glass on the tray offered her by Friedrich the butler. She gazed lovingly at her daughter Louise, who was running across the garden trying not to lose sight of a small kite that was still just visible in the half-light of the lanterns. Out of the corner of her eye, the Baroness saw the empty glasses on the tray. She turned around in annoyance. Had the old man failed to notice that she had already replaced her glass? Didn't he realize that there were other guests to be seen to? Maybe something's wrong with him? He's so old . . . She looked at Friedrich with concern as he stood before her, his eyes revealing a readiness to lay down his life for his mistress.

"Did you want something from me, Frédéric?" she asked very gently.

"Yes, your Ladyship." Friedrich looked at little Louise von Bockenheim und Bielau as her governess chased her with open arms, calling with a strong English accent: "Don't run so fast, little Baroness, you'll get too hot!"

"I didn't dare disturb your moment of contemplation as you admired the little Baroness, like quicksilver . . ."

"Did you not hear my question, Frédéric?" the Baroness said even more gently.

"A telephone call for you, Baroness," Friedrich announced. "It's the man who handed your Ladyship that strange business card a few moments ago."

"You should spare yourself the word 'strange', my dear Frédéric," hissed the Baroness. "You're not here to make comments."

"Yes, of course, your Ladyship." Friedrich bowed, his eyes now revealing less readiness to sacrifice his life for his employer. "What am I to say to the gentleman?"

"I'll talk to him." She excused herself from the ladies for a few moments and floated across the garden, bestowing smiles all around. The warmest smile was for her husband, Baron Rüdiger II von Bockenheim und Bielau.

Climbing the steps to the villa, she looked once again at the business card and the word "Verte". On the reverse were the words: "Concerning cabbies and carters". The Baroness stopped smiling. She entered her boudoir and picked up the receiver.

"I'm not going to introduce myself," said a man's hoarse voice. "I'm going to ask you some questions and you're going to answer truthfully. Otherwise the Baron will have to find out about his wife's secret life . . . Why aren't you saying anything?"

"Because you haven't asked me anything." The Baroness took a cigarette from a crystal case and lit it.

"I want to know the addresses of the men you take as escorts after your visits to the Hungarian King. They dress up — one as a carter, another as a cabby. I'm only interested in the ones who dress up as sailors."

"You like sailors, do you?" The Baroness rippled with quiet laughter. "You want them to screw you, do you?" Obscenities excited her. She wanted to hear this man swear, in his voice hoarse with tobacco. She liked swearing and the smell of cheap tobacco.

"You'd know something about that, wouldn't you? Answer me, you old bag, or do I have to speak to the Baron?" The man's voice changed tone.

"You're through to him already," the Baroness replied. "Speak to this wretched blackmailer, darling!"

"Baron Rüdiger II von Bockenheim und Bielau speaking," said a deep voice. "Don't try to blackmail my wife, dear man. It's despicable and base."

Baron Rüdiger II von Bockenheim und Bielau replaced the receiver and left his study, kissing his wife on the forehead on the way.

"Let's say goodbye to our guests, my little dawn," he said.

BRESLAU, THAT SAME SEPTEMBER 4TH, 1919
ELEVEN O'CLOCK AT NIGHT

Baroness Mathilde von Bockenheim und Bielau sat at her escritoire writing a letter of warning to her friend Laura von Scheitler, a habitué of the Hungarian King whose noble title and coat of arms were brand new to her — just like her own. When she had finished the brief note, she sprayed the back of the paper with some perfume and put it into an envelope. She then tugged on the bell and, rubbing some cold cream bought at Hopp's House of Beauty for the astronomical sum of three hundred marks into her alabaster complexion, she sat down at her dressing table in front of the mirror. She waited for Friedrich and heard a knock at the door.

"*Entré!*" she called, and carried on rubbing the cream into her generous *décolleté*.

She looked into the mirror and saw two hands on her delicate skin. She felt one of them, rough and gnarled, over her mouth, while the other pulled her hair. The Baroness felt excruciating pain on her head and landed on the chaise longue. A man with red hair sat astride her, pinning her shoulders to the sofa with his knees. With one hand he again covered her mouth, and with the other slapped her sharply on the cheek.

"Are you going to be quiet, or shall I do it again?"

Baroness von Bockenheim und Bielau tried to nod. The red-headed man understood her gesture.

"The addresses of those sailors," he said, and the Baroness realized that this was not the man she had spoken to on the telephone. "Male whores dressed up as sailors. Immediately!"

"Alfred Sorg," she said quietly. "That's the name of my sailor. I'll give you his number. He brings other men too."

The red-headed man snorted and climbed off the Baroness with obvious regret. She stood up, wrote a telephone number on a piece of paper and sprayed the reverse side with perfume. Her assailant tore the paper from her hands, opened the window and jumped down onto the lawn. The Baroness watched as he climbed the railings. She heard the roar of an engine and the squeal of tires. She pulled the scarlet cord again and sat down at her mirror. She spread a thick layer of cream onto her hands.

"I know you let him in, Frédéric," she said gently as the butler appeared at her side. "As from tomorrow, I no longer want to see you in my house."

"I don't know what your Ladyship cares to mean." Friedrich's voice was full of solemnity and concern.

The Baroness turned to her servant and looked deeply into his eyes.

"There's only one way you can save your position, Frédéric." She turned back to the mirror and sighed. "I'm giving you one last chance."

Seconds passed, then minutes. The Baroness combed her hair while Friedrich stood there, stiff as a poker.

"I'm listening, your Ladyship." His voice betrayed unease.

"You'll lose your position" – she gazed at her reflection with satisfaction and tore up the letter to Baroness von Scheitler – "unless you bring me that red-headed monster before the night is out."

BRESLAU, THAT SAME SEPTEMBER 4TH, 1919
MIDNIGHT

In the Three Crowns beer cellar on Kupferschmiedestrasse 5–6 the air was heavy with tobacco smoke mixed with fried bacon, burned onions and human sweat. This odour drifted up towards the arched vault and enveloped the pseudo-Romanesque windows which gave on to the yard belonging to the White Eagle building. The fug was not alleviated by the few blasts of cold night air which blew in as the door opened to let in new customers. The traffic in the cellar was one way only. No-one was leaving; if someone left now, they would be considered a traitor by the others. In the Three Crowns, a meeting of the Breslau division of the *Freikorps* was under way.

Mock and Smolorz stopped at the back of the hall while their eyes adjusted to the stinging atmosphere. At the heavy tables sat men leaden with beer. They slammed their tankards on the oak tabletops swimming with white froth, clicked their fingers at the head waiter and hushed each other. To the eye of an experienced policeman their varied headgear was just as clear an indication of the men's social standing as any military

111

decoration. Workers sat at tables wearing canvas caps with patent peaks, or soft caps made of oilcloth. Their social class was further highlighted by their collarless shirts and rolled-up sleeves. A little to one side were tradesmen, restaurateurs and clerks. Their distinguishing attire was a bowler hat, with the additional attribute of a stiff collar – many of which were crying out for a visit to the laundry. These men drank less and did not slam their tankards down, but it was from their cigars and pipes that the heaviest smoke bombs wafted. The third and largest group was made up of youths in helmets, or round caps with no peaks known as *Einheits-feldmützen*, very familiar to Mock.

The Criminal Assistant paid keen attention to this last group. His watchful eye penetrated the smoke screen and inspected the grey uniforms with their medals pinned on here and there. Just then, a young, handsome man wearing one such uniform climbed onto a podium where usually – when the *Freikorps* were not meeting – a few musicians would beguile the beer cellar's guests as they ate their rissoles, a speciality of the house. The man now standing on the podium wore a medal which reminded Mock of the so-called Baltic Cross he himself had received for his service in Kurland.

"Brothers! Fellow companions in arms!" yelled the Knight of the Baltic Cross. "We must not allow the communists to poison our nation. We cannot let our proud Germanic peoples be defiled by the Bolshevik Asians and their lackeys!"

Mock switched off his sense of hearing. Otherwise he would have climbed onto the podium and slapped the young man whose ardour to fight was as inauthentic as his Baltic Cross. He knew the speaker well; he knew that, throughout the war, he had worked as a brave informer for the political police, which vehemently hunted down any sign of defeatism or lowering of morale among civilians. While Mock was delousing himself in the trenches; while, on the order of Captain Mantzelmann, he and

Cornelius Rühtgard were exposing their backsides to the icy north wind to crap; while they were pumping fountains of blood from the heads of Kalmucks; while they were looking into the sad eyes of dying Russian prisoners of war; while they were extracting fat larvae from infected wounds, this speaker, Alfred Sorg, was doing the rounds of taverns and listening bravely to embittered people; happily leading youngsters who were caught cursing the emperor to the nearest police station by the scruff of the neck; valiantly blackmailing young wives who abused the Reich's name, and then courageously presenting these wives who were so missing their husbands with a choice: either to face prison or to indulge in a moment of oblivion, forgetting everything and, above all, their faithfulness to their husbands.

Somebody nudged Mock and handed him a pile of pamphlets, saying "Pass them on". Mock studied them. They urged young men to join the Garde-Kavallerie-Schützen-Division. On one of them a member was pointing to a picture of a charming town above which a moulting, Polish white eagle with hideous talons and a foul, gaping beak spread its wings, while another *Freikorps* soldier aimed his bayonet at the beast. Beneath the cartoon was a quotation from Ernst von Salomon: "Germany burned darkly in daring minds. Germany was always there where it was being fought for, it showed itself where armed hands strove for its continued existence, it blazed where those possessed of its spirit dared to spill the last drops of their blood on its behalf."

"I wonder whether Germany was in the trenches at Dünaburg," thought Mock. "I wonder whether von Salomon, writing about 'last drops of blood', saw my comrades in arms dying of diphtheria, with bloody diarrhoea running down their trousers." The Criminal Assistant looked at another pamphlet with a picture of the American president blowing soap bubbles. One of the bubbles contained the caption: "President Wilson's pipe dreams".

"Do what you must!" thundered Alfred Sorg from the podium. "Be victorious, or die and leave the final decision to God!"

Still trying not to listen, Mock gazed in disbelief at the five-bullet Mauser 98 rifles leaning ostentatiously against the tables. He remembered a scout at Dünaburg who had informed von Thiede, the commander of the regiment, about a meeting of Russian spies at a Jewish inn. Mock and his scout platoon had burst through the inn door. A din erupted. Platoon Commander Corporal Heinz ordered them to shoot. Mock pulled the trigger of his Mauser 98, which belched thick smoke. There was a deathly silence. The smoke subsided. The communists were either female or at most ten years old. Later, Corporal Heinz laughed his head off, and he was still laughing when a bayonet ground into his guts. One of the men in the platoon which had arbitrated at the homes of the alleged spies had lost respect for his Führer. When Heinz had been found lying in the mud near his quarters with a ripped-up belly, Mock, as a police officer in civilian life, was given the task of conducting an investigation. The perpetrator was not found. Mock had been rather indolent, and a month later he was demoted by Regiment Commander von Thiede for not conducting the investigation skilfully enough. Since Mock had suffered some light wounds, von Thiede sent him to Königsberg in the hope that the police officer with the rebellious attitude would not return to his regiment. There Mock fell out of a window, and then as a convalescent he did indeed end up somewhere else: with Field Orderly Cornelius Rühtgard under the command of Captain Mantzelmann, who so loved the cold hygiene of the north.

The speaker sat down at a table at the front next to a young woman at whose sight Mock began to quiver. He knew her well; it was to her that his friend Rühtgard had dedicated his stories during the war. He bit his lip and once again suppressed the urge to slap Alfred Sorg across the face. The girl, unable to take her eyes off the inflamed speaker, was clapping

114

as enthusiastically as everyone else in the Three Crowns. Everyone, that is, apart from two police officers from Division IIIb who in their search for phony sailors had dropped into a nest of *Freikorps* supporters. Mock showed no enthusiasm because he was overcome by sad thoughts; Smolorz did not clap because his arm was being held down by two hands belonging to a man with butler's whiskers, who was whispering something in his ear. Smolorz had recognized him and was listening carefully.

BRESLAU, FRIDAY, SEPTEMBER 5TH, 1919
ONE O'CLOCK IN THE MORNING

Customers rolled out of the beer cellar after the *Freikorps* meeting, pumped up with equal measures of patriotism and beer. One man had drunk little, since his plans for the night would have been hindered by too much alcohol. With his arm around the slender waist of the girl next to him, Alfred Sorg felt the demon in his trousers petulantly demand an offering. He thought about his pockets – there was nothing with which to pay for a room by the hour – and about his miserable little room where two members of the so-called Erhardt brigade would shortly be snoring.

He scanned the street and noticed a shadowy opening between two buildings that led into a yard. That dark, damp cleft awoke in him a chain of associations which aroused him again. He stopped, put his arms around the girl and pressed a beery kiss onto her mouth. She parted her lips and her legs. He simultaneously slipped his tongue into her mouth and a knee between her thighs. He picked her up and they disappeared into the narrow opening. The damp draught did not surprise Sorg; the pungent smell of garlic, however, did.

A second later, as well as olfactory impressions, he experienced those of touch and sound. Chimes rang in his ear and the lobe began to swell from a hefty clout. Sorg was pushed along the alley and found himself in the yard behind Franz Krziwani's tobacco shop. The angry face that now confronted him was not entirely unfamiliar.

He was standing before a stocky, well-built man whose height constituted a medium between a much shorter man with a foxy face and a tall beanpole who was fanning his bowler hat to cool his red-moustachioed face. From the opening emerged a giant holding the struggling girl.

"Take it easy with her, Zupitza," said the stocky man. "Take the lady to the car and try to turn your breath away from her."

"You shit, you Jew! What do you want to do to her?" Sorg decided to show them all that he was a real man, and threw himself at Zupitza. "Leave her alone or I'll . . ."

Zupitza ignored his aggressor entirely. Sorg tumbled to the ground, having tripped over the foot of the man with the foxy face. He wanted to get up but received a hard punch on the other ear. Zupitza vanished with the girl. Sorg fell to the ground and for a moment pondered the difference between the two blows. He knew the second had been dealt with a shoe, and by somebody else. He sat on the cobblestones and stared at the stocky man who was now wiping the tip of his shining brogue with a handkerchief. Sorg knew the owner of these elegant shoes from somewhere, but could not think where.

"Listen to me, you war hero." The hoarse voice was familiar too. "Now you're going to tell me something. Give me some information. I'll pay you for it."

"Alright," Sorg said quickly, remembering when he had seen the man before. 1914. The beginning of the war. Sorg had been blackmailing a dimwitted married woman who had a poor grasp of historical events but associated the recently declared war with the absence of her husband, who had just been called up. Sorg had promised not to tell anyone what she had said against the state if she granted him that with which Nature had so generously equipped her. The woman had consented, and that very same day had gone to the Breslau Vice Department with a complaint. There she was met with complete understanding. The following day, at the time they had agreed, Sorg heard a knock at his door. He ran to it, his demon at the ready to accept the offering, opened the door and saw several men in black. One of them, a thickset man with dark hair, had attacked him with such fury that Sorg had practically lost his life beneath those shiny, polished shoes.

"Ask me."

"Do you dress up as a sailor and screw ladies of society?"

"Yes."

"And do you arrange for other young men to dress up for the ladies? Carters, cabbies, gladiators . . ."

"I don't, somebody else does."

"One lady told me she rings you and you arrange it."

"That's right. But I ring somebody else to organize other gigolos."

"Are you paid for it?"

"Yes, I get a commission."

The interrogator walked up to Sorg, who was still sitting on the cobbles, and grabbed him by the hair. Sorg picked up the the sour reek of a hangover.

"Who do you ring to get the boys?"

"Norbert Risse." Sorg did not want to smell the hangover any longer and threw the words out quickly. "That queer. He works from a ship, the *Wölsung*. It's a floating brothel."

"Here," said the interrogator, throwing Sorg some banknotes. "Rent a room at the Sieh Dich Für Hotel on Kleingroschenstrasse and get yourself a cheap whore. You can't afford the girl who was with you."

The men walked away and left Sorg sitting on the cobbles.

"You're to go to that ship now, Smolorz," Sorg overheard one of them say. "You're to find out everything about the four sailors. Take the photographs." From the corner of his eye, Sorg saw his aggressor hand Smolorz an envelope before striding off.

"Mr Mock!" Smolorz called, indicating Sorg. "What about him? You've just questioned him face to face . . . That swine might go and murder him . . ."

"Nothing's going to happen to him . . . Do you see any murderers around here, Smolorz?" Mock retraced his steps and approached his victim, then bent over and tore the Baltic Cross from his uniform. He went to the alleyway between the houses and leaned over a drain in the gutter. The subterranean waters of the city splashed quietly below.

"He'll buy himself a new one at the flea market," Smolorz concluded.

"Go and see Risse, Smolorz, and I'll take the girl," Mock said, ignoring his subordinate's remark. Sorg and Smolorz were left alone behind Krziwani's tobacco shop.

"How fair is that?" Smolorz said to himself, fingering the business card given to him in the tavern by the man with the sideburns and butler's manners. "He takes the girl and I get to go and see — a queer."

Sorg said nothing and with his finger inspected the hole in his uniform where the Baltic Cross had hung.

BRESLAU, THAT SAME SEPTEMBER 5TH, 1919
HALF PAST ONE IN THE MORNING

Wirth fired the engine, and Mock fell heavily onto the back seat next to the girl. His clothes were permeated with the smell of tobacco, and a hint of alcohol and expensive eau de cologne. The girl was intrigued by the man she had never spoken to but had frequently seen at home. Her interest was all the greater due to the circumstances of their meeting: a dark night, kisses in a back street, and men who looked like murderers.

Suddenly she was overcome with disgust. Her thoughts had been absorbed by the man who was Alfred's aggressor. And now Alfred, beaten up and humiliated, was trying to come to his senses in one of the seediest corners of the city! She turned away from Mock.

"I'm not going to say anything to your father, Christel." Mock wanted to put his hand on the girl's shoulder, but stopped himself in time.

"You can tell him whatever you want," Christel Rühtgard growled as she stared out at the military cemetery on the corner of Kirschallee and Lohestrasse. "I don't care what you or my father think of me . . ."

"I'm not saying it," Mock snorted, "to win you over or calm you down after that love scene in a stinking back street . . ."

"Then why *are* you saying it?" Christel's eyes were blazing.

"Because I don't know how to start the conversation." Mock glanced at her prominent bust and recoiled a little, frightened of his own thoughts.

"Don't even start one! I've got nothing to talk to you about . . ."

Silence descended. Mock was tired and would most happily have put the spoiled young madame across his knee and given her a thorough spanking. The thought which had frightened him a moment earlier was very innocent compared to what Mock now imagined might follow such a spanking. He plastered his cheek to the cold window and gaped dully at South Park as they approached. His eyes were closing of their own accord. Beneath his eyelids floated the lights of the Three Crowns beer cellar, then silent cemeteries. Trees rustled somewhere in the distance, a carpenter's plane swished, and a small child cried, pressing a face wet with tears against the tired man's face. She put her little arms around his neck and tried to say something, tugging at his arm, contorting her lips fretfully and then calling in a raised voice:

"Wake up, Mr Mock! The driver's asking where we want to go!"

Mock rubbed his eyes, extracted his watch from his pocket and glanced at Christel Rühtgard's angry face.

"I wanted to see you home," he muttered, "so that you're not accosted by any more drunks."

"Like you?"

Mock got out of the Horch and looked around. They were at the bottom of Hohenzollernstrasse. Wind blew through the treetops in South Park to his right. To his left, the satiated incumbents of the modern detached houses and stately villas slept the sleep of the righteous. None of them were getting ghastly notes from demented murderers; none of them had a child who had just been deserted – or maybe even orphaned – put her arms around their neck. They were not told to pay a gruesome penance for fabricated mistakes. Mock walked round the car, opened the door and offered his arm to the girl. She spurned his polite gesture and nimbly jumped onto the pavement of her own accord.

"Like me," he replied. "Those are especially dangerous."

"Don't make yourself out to be a demon," Miss Rühtgard said and she set off towards the park. "I haven't got far to go from here. I don't want you to walk me home."

"Today, not far from here," he called after her, "my men found a man hanging from a tree by his legs!"

Christel Rühtgard stopped and looked at Mock with distaste, as if he had been responsible for decorating trees with dead people. They stood for a while in silence.

"This park is not as safe as the promenade by the moat on Sunday mornings," Mock said, "where people go for an ice cream after church. It's haunted here at night, and corpses can be found hanging on trees or floating in the pond."

"You really won't say anything to my father about me and Fred?" Christel asked quietly.

"On the condition that I walk you home."

120

They walked in silence through the dark park, lit up here and there by islands of light from the few street lamps. Mock lit a cigarette.

"You don't know how to begin the conversation," laughed Miss Rühtgard quietly. She walked proud and upright. Irritation had given way to faint amusement.

"I know how to begin it, but I don't know whether you're going to want to talk about what interests me."

"I'm not going to talk to you about Alfred Sorg. Is there anything else you're interested in?"

"You're an intelligent young lady. I could talk to you about anything." Mock realized he had paid her a compliment and felt as embarrassed as a schoolboy. "But to touch on certain subjects we'll have to get to know each other better . . ."

"You want to get to know me better? Isn't what my father tells you enough?"

"I remember what your father said about you in the trenches at Dünaburg. You were his only chance of survival. You saved him, dear Christel." Mock stopped and rubbed the sole of his shoe hard against the pathway, swearing under his breath when he realized he had stepped into one of the mementoes Bert and other dogs leave in parks. He wiped it on the grass and returned to his broken train of thought. "And not only him, by the way. You saved quite a few Russian soldiers. If it hadn't been for you, your father would have thrown himself at the Russian trenches with his rifle and killed a lot of Russians, then he'd have died himself . . ."

"What makes you think he had suicidal thoughts?" In the dim light, Christel observed Mock as he pulled out a checked handkerchief and wiped the dust from the tip of his shoe.

"A lot of us had suicidal thoughts," he muttered. "A good many of us tried hard to imagine the end of the war, but couldn't. Your father did. You were the end of the war for him."

"He talked to you about me?"

"Constantly."

"And you listened? You sympathized with him? As far as I know, you don't have any children of your own . . . How long can one listen to somebody talking about their children, about boys exploding with energy and moody girls?"

"You weren't a moody girl in his eyes." This time Mock pulled out a starched white handkerchief and wiped his brow. The September night was almost sweltering. "You were the very idea of a beloved child. An idea in the Platonic sense. A paragon, an archetype . . . After those conversations I'd envy him. . . I wanted to have a child like that myself . . ."

"And after this evening?" Christel looked at Mock in despair. "Would you still like to have a daughter like that?"

"One evening doesn't cancel out a whole lifetime." Even though Mock said these words quickly, he hoped the girl had heard the negative in his reply. "I don't know what things are like between you on a day-to-day basis . . ."

Mock offered her his arm. After a moment's hesitation, Christel took him gently by the elbow. They circled the pond.

"You beat up my friend," she said quietly. "I ought to hate you for that. And yet I'm going to tell you how things are with my father on a day-to-day basis . . . He's possessive. Every boy I get friendly with, everyone who visits me, he considers a rival . . . Once he told me that after my mother's death — I was two at the time — I jumped for joy . . . I was happy my mother had died, my alleged rival . . . Note that . . . He always has books by Freud on his desk. In one of them he's boldly underlined the father of psychology's definition of the Electra complex. Entire pages scribbled on with horrible, smudged ink . . ."

"Try to understand your father." Mock felt uncomfortable to be so near the girl. "Young ladies ought to meet young men in the company of chaperones. They shouldn't be taking part in gatherings of drunken, fired-up commoners."

Christel let go of Mock's arm and looked around absent-mindedly.

"Please give me a cigarette," she said.

Mock offered her his cigarette-case and struck a match.

"Men always strike matches towards themselves, did you know that? You did too. You're one hundred percent male."

"Anyone would feel one hundred percent male, walking through a park on a fine night in the company of a young and beautiful lady." Mock suddenly realized he was courting his best friend's daughter again. "I apologize, Miss Rühtgard, I didn't want to say that. I'm supposed to be acting as your Cerberus now, not your Romeo."

"But the latter is decidedly nicer for any woman," laughed Miss Rühtgard.

"Is that right?" Mock asked, blessing the dark shadows for concealing his blushes. Feverishly he searched for an apt pun, a humorous retort, but his memory let him down. Minutes passed. Miss Rühtgard smoked her cigarette awkwardly and smiled at him, waiting for him to say something. He was seized by anger – anger at himself and at this chit of a girl who was wrapping him around her little finger. What was most infuriating was the fact that the role suited him.

"Stop it, my dear," he raised his voice a little, forsaking the formal "Miss Rühtgard". "You're not a woman. You're still a child."

"Is that so?" she asked playfully. "I stopped being a child in Hamburg. Perhaps you'd like to know the circumstances?"

"There's something else I'd like to know," Mock said, in spite of himself. "Are you aware of any of Alfred Sorg's friends dressing up and putting themselves at the disposal of rich ladies?"

"What does that mean, 'at the disposal'?" Miss Rühtgard asked. "I don't know what you're talking about. I'm still a child . . ."

Mock stood still and wiped the sweat from his brow. He moved away from his companion a little, aware that too many cigarettes did nothing to improve the smell of his breath. To his annoyance, Christel moved closer and her eyes grew enormous and naive.

"What does that mean, 'at the disposal'?" she asked again.

"Do you know of four young men" – Mock stepped away from the girl again and lost his self-control – "who dress up as sailors and pleasure rich ladies? They work with your friend Alfred Sorg. Maybe Alfred dresses up and screws ladies too? Does he dress up like that for you?"

Mock bit his tongue. It was too late. Silence. A chill wind blew from the pond. The lights in South Park Restaurant began to go out. The maid was waiting for the first glow of the pink-fingered maiden before going for a walk with Bert the dog. Corpses hung on trees and floated in the water. Mock felt terrible and did not look at Miss Rühtgard.

"You're just like my father. He's always asking who I've just screwed." Anger had turned her face to stone. "I'm going to tell him right now that you're interested too. I'll give him an account of our entire conversation. Then he'll understand that people don't stop being men and women just because they wear the words 'father' or 'daughter' on their chest. Even you, usually so self-controlled, got carried away and gloated over the word 'pleasure'. I thought you were completely different . . ."

"I'm sorry." Mock smoked the last of his cigarettes. "I've used inappropriate words when talking to you, Miss Rühtgard. Please forgive me. Don't tell your father about our conversation. It would put a strain on our friendship."

"You ought to put an announcement in the *Schlesiche Zeitung*," Christel said thoughtfully. "It would say: 'I dispel your illusions, Eberhard Mock'."

Mock sat on a bench and in an effort to control himself called to mind the first verses of Lucretius' poem "De rerum natura", about which he had once written an essay. When he arrived at the lines describing Mars' and Venus' amorous rapture, he was overcome with fury. Suddenly he became aware that he was not admiring Lucretius' hexameters at all, but imagining instead how the lovers were moving against each other, tangled up in Vulcan's net.

"Am I to feel guilty for exposing that creature Sorg to you?" His voice hissed with annoyance. "That I spared you from having to visit a doctor of venereal diseases? You don't have to worry about catching syphilis, do you? You've got one of the so-called bachelor disease's most eminent specialists close at hand! Am I to have scruples for having shown you that your knight in shining armour is, *de facto*, a slave in the bedroom?"

"How typical!" Miss Rühtgard shouted. "A knight in shining armour! What a stereotype! Can't you understand that not every woman is waiting for a fairy-tale prince, but for someone who will . . ."

"Give them a good screwing," Mock finished furiously.

"That's not what I had in mind," Miss Rühtgard countered in a low voice. "I wanted to say: 'who will love them'." She stubbed out her cigarette on a tree. "Fred is a nice boy, but I know he's a cad. You haven't shattered any of my illusions about *him*, but about *you*. I opened my heart to you, but you didn't want to listen. You gave me some beautiful lines about chaperones. You didn't want . . . All you wanted was to reprimand and warn me. A policeman through and through. When will you stop being a policeman? When you're dead? Goodnight, policeman, sir. Please don't see me home. I think I prefer the company of drowned and hanging bodies to yours."

Mock woke up in detention cell number three. Morning light edged through the small, barred window. Sounds of the usual bustle reached him from the Police Praesidium courtyard. A horse snorted, glass smashed against the cobblestones, one man swore a thousand curses at another. Mock pulled himself upright on his bunk and rubbed his eyes. He was thirsty. To his joy he spied a jug standing on the stool next to the bunk. A strong smell of mint wafted from it. The door opened and Achim Buhrack stood there. In his hand he wielded a towel and a razor.

"You're priceless, Buhrack," Mock said. "You remember everything. To wake me up on time, the razor, even the mint . . ."

"You don't need it today, I see." Buhrack's eyes expressed surprise. "Today, you're not . . ."

"I'm not going to need it," Mock took the jug from Buhrack, "not today nor ever again. I'm going to stop drinking and I'm not going to have any more hangovers." From another jug he poured some water into a basin, then took the towel and razor from the guard. "You don't believe me, do you, Buhrack? You've heard a lot of promises like that, haven't you?"

"Oh, many times over . . ." the guard muttered, and he left before Mock could thank him.

The Criminal Assistant took off his shirt, washed his armpits, sat on the bunk and reached into his pocket for a packet of talcum powder. He plunged his hand in it and rubbed the talc under his arms, then generously sprinkled some into his shoes. He spent the next ten minutes scraping the stubble from his face, which was no easy task seeing as the blade was blunt. Nor did it help that he had to use ordinary soap, which dried instantly and tightened his skin. Reluctantly he slipped on his shirt from the day before. "Father must be worried," he thought. He imagined his father hopping on one leg with a sock hanging off the other foot. "Always knocking it back," he heard his voice nag. All of a sudden Mock longed for a bottle and the mute, empty night that followed a drinking binge. He pulled on his shoes and left the cell. He shook Buhrack's hand warmly and made his way down the gloomy corridor through the morning hubbub coming from the cells: the groaning and the clanging of mess tins, the yawning and the passing of wind. He was glad to leave the detention wing and slowly climbed the stairs, wondering how the gunge which filled his lungs and head would react to the first cigarette of the day.

BRESLAU, THAT SAME SEPTEMBER 5TH, 1919 NINE O'CLOCK IN THE MORNING

Everyone had arrived at Mühlhaus' office punctually. Mühlhaus' secretary, von Gallasen, stood a pot of hot tea and nine glasses in high metal holders on the table. The September sun burned the necks of the detectives sitting with their backs to the window and illuminated the streams of tobacco smoke. Mock stood in the doorway with an unlit cigarette in his mouth, scrutinizing those present. He felt a sharp pain in his chest. Smolorz was missing.

"What are you doing here, Mock?" Mühlhaus freed his mouth of excess smoke. "You're supposed to be working for the Vice Department. Yesterday morning I terminated your transfer to the Murder Commission. Could it be that you've forgotten? Have you reported to Councillor Ilssheimer today?"

"Commissioner, sir," Mock said, sitting down uninvited between Reinert and Kleinfeld. "In this world of ours, people have killed in the name of God and the emperor. People commit murder with a sovereign's name on their lips. Over the past few days people have been murdered in this city in my name. The name Eberhard Mock has become this swine's trademark. He has murdered six people and perhaps made an orphan of a little child who wept in my arms last night. Forgive me, please, but today I don't want to book pimps or check the medical records of whores. I'm going to sit here with you and think about how to get rid of that bastard who is murdering in my name."

There was silence. Mock and Mühlhaus measured each other. The others stared over their steaming glasses of tea at the chief of the Murder Commission. Mühlhaus put his pipe aside, scattering shreds of blonde Virginia tobacco over his files.

"The person to decide who sits here," he said quietly, "is myself and myself alone. It is no secret that I consider you to be an excellent policeman. That I want to see you in my commission. But after the Four Sailors case. Only then."

Mühlhaus poked a cleaning skewer into his pipe and twisted it forcefully into the stem.

"Take a rest, go away somewhere." Unlike the expression in his eyes, the Commissioner's tone was exceptionally gentle. "Just for a while. Until this investigation is concluded. I don't want any more dead bodies, so you can't question anybody else . . . How do we know that the swine isn't going to think up something else? . . . Or start killing everyone you talk to? . . . When I've locked him up, I'll gladly welcome you amongst my men. I've spoken to Councillor Ilssheimer. He has willingly agreed to your transfer. But now you've got to go away. Don't think you won't be helping us in the investigation. Doctor Kaznicz is going to talk to you again, and you might remember some clue as to the identity of the murderer."

Mock studied his colleagues around the table. All were contemplating the colour of the hot drink in their glasses. They had been taught to obey their superiors. They were unfamiliar with words of dissent, and they felt no guilt; it was a long time since a child had wept into their starched collars. "Don't feel sorry for yourself, Mock. You don't deserve any pity."

Mock remained seated. "We all know that the murderer began with a spectacular crime, and then murdered two more people whom I had questioned. Listen to me, gentlemen! I propose . . ."

"We're not interested in what you propose, Mock," Mühlhaus interrupted him. "Are you going to let us get on with our work, or do I have to throw you out? Do I have to take disciplinary action?"

Mock stood up and approached Mühlhaus.

"First take action against your secretary, von Gallasen. He's made a mistake too. He brought two glasses too many. There are seven of you. Smolorz isn't here yet, and I'm no longer here." He went to the table and with a swipe knocked over the two empty glasses, which smashed on the stone floor. He bowed and left the office of the chief of the Murder Commission.

BRESLAU, THAT SAME SEPTEMBER 5TH, 1919
HALF PAST NINE IN THE MORNING

The windows of Criminal Councillor Josef Ilssheimer's large office looked out onto Ursulinenstrasse, or strictly speaking onto the gable roof of the Stadt Leipzig Hotel. Ilssheimer liked to observe one of the clerks working there who, in his spare moments, would arrange coloured pencils in a fixed and unchangeable order in his drawer, and then close his eyes, randomly pull one out, and draw a line on a piece of paper to see whether he had chosen the right one.

Ilssheimer was observing this spatial memory exercise now, but he tired of it more quickly than usual and remembered that Eberhard Mock had been sitting at his round table for a good few minutes, waiting in silence for orders or instructions.

Ilssheimer cast his eyes around his office, cluttered from floor to ceiling with files of cases which the Vice Department of Breslau's Police

Praesidium had conducted under him over the past twenty years. He was proud of the order which reigned there and, despite the suggestions of successive police presidents, he would not allow the material to be moved to the main archives located on the ground floor.

"I'm sorry," Ilssheimer began, "that you're not on the Four Sailors case any more, Mock. It can't be pleasant for you."

"Thank you for the words of consolation."

"But you won't be removed from the investigation altogether." Ilssheimer was somewhat offended that Mock had not addressed him as "Councillor sir". "You'll be talking to Doctor Kaznicz. He'll draw information out of you which will help Mühlhaus apprehend the murderer."

"I've already lived through one psychoanalytical session with Doctor Kaznicz and it didn't give us anything."

"You're a little impatient, Mock." Ilssheimer leaned over the man he was addressing and was disappointed; he did not detect the smell of alcohol. He began to stroll around the office, hands clasped behind his back. "And now listen to me carefully. These are your official instructions. Tomorrow you go to Bad Kudowa with Doctor Kaznicz. You'll stay there for as long as is necessary . . ."

"I don't want anything to do with Doctor Kaznicz." Mock sensed that a heated and painful argument was going to be inevitable. "I don't want to see him. Do you really believe, Councillor sir, that a man whom I neither trust nor like is going to draw anything out of me . . ."

"I understand you perfectly, Mock." Ilssheimer blushed on hearing his title. "The doctor is equally aware of your dislike for him. That's why he's decided to change his method . . ."

"Ah, that's interesting," muttered Mock. "So he's not going to talk to me about the time I stole apples from a stall any more, and he's not going to ask what I felt when I squirted people passing under my window with a water siphon when I was six?"

"No." Mock's words clearly amused the Criminal Councillor. "Doctor Kaznicz is going to subject you to hypnosis. He's a specialist in the field."

"I don't doubt it. But let him subject somebody else to his methods. I'm a police officer and I want to conduct a normal investigation," Mock grew more and more worked up with every word. "People I've come into contact with on the Four Sailors case are dying. But I don't have to talk to anyone personally; I don't have to question anyone at all. Somebody else can do that . . . I can do it over the telephone . . . I've got an excellent and simple idea . . ."

"Can't you understand, Mock, that nobody is intending to argue with you? I repeat, I've given you official instructions and I don't care if you're going to cry or stamp your feet in fury at the sight of Kaznicz."

Silence descended. Ilssheimer glanced out of the window at the clerk exercising his memory. He decided to continue.

"You drink a great deal, Mock." He rested his head on his hands and stared at his subordinate. There had been a time when criminals had writhed under Ilssheimer's glare. "Many policemen abuse alcohol and this is tolerated by their superiors. But not me!" he yelled. "I do not tolerate alcoholism, Mock! Alcoholism will lead to your dismissal! Do you understand, God damn it?"

Ilssheimer fixed his black eyes on Mock. In the past, his eyes had burned holes in the petrified consciences of bandits. Mock's faintly ironic expression told him that those times had long passed.

Mock stood up and allowed the wave of anger that gathered within him to settle. For the first time in many years he felt he had an advantage over Ilssheimer; one word from him could destroy the chief of the Vice Department. Mock clasped his hands behind his back and walked over to the window. "It's not going to work, it's not going to come off," he thought, adopting an attitude of defensive pessimism. He went to the hat-stand, took the chief's bowler and turned it around in his hands. Brand new, made by Hitz, as the inner ribbon informed him.

"You've bought yourself a new bowler," he said, purposely omitting Ilssheimer's title. "Where's the old one?"

"What's it to you, Mock? Are you mad? Stop trying to change the subject!" Ilssheimer did not move a muscle.

"I've got your old hat," Mock said, gloating over his advantage. "I found it in August's room at the South Park Hotel."

"I don't know what you're talking about." Ilssheimer's eyes grew pensive and distant. "As a police officer from the Vice Department I questioned August Strehl, a male prostitute. . . It's true . . . I must have left my hat there . . ."

"Not only your hat. You also left indelible memories in August's heart. Indelible to such a degree," Mock said, without believing that his bluff would work, "that August wrote them down. Very interesting reminiscences . . ." Mock rested his hands on Ilssheimer's desk and said very slowly: "Don't you think, Councillor sir, that Doctor Kaznicz is going to be a little short of time over the next few days? And besides, did you know, Councillor sir, that I'm not particularly susceptible to hypnosis?"

Ilssheimer glanced at the clerk who, having failed to pull out the right pencil this time, saw his mistake and threw a file at the wall in fury.

"Indeed," Ilssheimer said, without changing his expression one iota. "Doctor Kaznicz has been very busy of late . . ."

BRESLAU, THAT SAME SEPTEMBER 5TH, 1919
NOON

Wirth and Zupitza parked their Horch near a meringue shop not far from the university. They got out and set off towards the eighteenth-century Police Praesidium building, stopping on the way at the Opiela Inn so that

Zupitza could buy some Silano cigarettes. In the vestibule of the Praesidium, a solid barrier prevented anyone from climbing the stairs. Appended to it was an arrow which very clearly directed any visitors straight to the duty room, where the two caretakers, Handke and Bender, sat with grim expressions and bristly moustaches. One of them would telephone to announce any arrivals he was not personally familiar with, while the other would bore into visitors with suspicious eyes, as if X-rays radiated from his pupils. They did not stop Wirth and Zupitza, nor pierce them with X-ray eyes. They never did so when the arrival of an outsider had been announced by a high-ranking police official. Looking at the short dandy and the tall, gloomy bruiser, Bender and Handke ascertained that the descriptions Councillor Ilssheimer had give them an hour earlier were very fitting.

"I know those mugs from somewhere," Handke muttered, observing the duo as they disappeared behind the glazed doors of the main lobby.

"We know a lot of criminal mugs," Bender replied. "Goes with the job . . ."

Wirth and Zupitza crossed the courtyard and went through the gate, to where a police van had just arrived from Ursulinenstrasse. The guard opening the gate eyed them suspiciously. They climbed the winding stairs to the second floor and stood outside a heavy door with a plate that read:

DEPARTMENT IIIB

DIRECTOR: CRIMINAL COUNCILLOR DR JOSEPH ILSSHEIMER

POLICE OFFICERS: CRIMINAL ASSISTANT EBERHARD MOCK

CRIMINAL SECRETARIES: HERBERT DOMAGALLA AND HANS MARAUN

CRIMINAL SERGEANTS: FRANZ LEMBCKE AND KURT SMOLORZ

Zupitza knocked hard. A few seconds later the door was opened by a thirty-year-old with thinning hair who, without asking any questions, led them down a narrow corridor. Before long they found themselves in a large office with three desks. A sleepy Mock sprawled at one of them, another stood empty, and the man who had shown them in sat down at the third next to a door with the nameplate DR JOSEPH ILSSHEIMER, and carried on with his interrupted telephone conversation.

. Mock indicated two heavy chairs to the newcomers. They sat down in silence.

"Hot, isn't it?" Mock managed the unoriginal greeting. "I've a favour to ask, Domagalla," he then said to the balding man on the telephone. "Could you bring my guests some soda water?"

Domagalla nodded with no sign of surprise, replaced the receiver and left the room.

"Now listen to me carefully." Mock got up from his desk and angrily rubbed his poorly shaven cheek. "You're forming an investigative team with me. Apart from us, there's Smolorz. As from tomorrow our base will be your office, where you're holding the whore Kitty and that waiter from the Hungarian King. We'll meet there for a briefing every day at nine in the morning." Mock glared at Zupitza. "What are you laughing at? That you're going to play at being a policeman? Explain it to him, Wirth!"

Wirth made some movements with his hands, and Zupitza turned serious.

"When we've finished today's briefing," continued Mock, "we'll go and find Smolorz. When we've found him, we'll separate. Smolorz is going to get on with the tasks I've given him. I'm going to go for a stroll and you're to follow, watching carefully to see if anybody is tailing me. The minute you see someone suspicious, you pull his arse in. Understood?" When Wirth nodded, Mock began to bark instructions. "I'm going to Norbert Risse's floating brothel. You know the ship I mean? I'll question the boss there. Then you and your men are not to let him out of your sight. You're to tail him without fail, and discreetly protect him at the same time.

134

We're setting him up as bait. Somebody will want to kill him. You're to catch that person and then hold him at your place. And then I'm going to want to get to know him. Everything clear?"

Domagalla entered the room with a soda siphon and some glasses. He stood them on the empty desk, then sat down at his own and spread out the *Breslauer Zeitung* in front of him. The headlines on the front page shrieked: DISTURBANCES AND FIGHTING ON BRESLAU'S RING. Nobody felt like drinking anything.

"What did you tell your pal a moment ago?" Mock asked abruptly.

"Not to air his fangs needlessly," Wirth replied.

"And that's all?"

"No, there was something else . . ." Wirth hesitated.

"Well, go on!" Mock said impatiently.

"I said policeman, bandit, sometimes it's all the same."

"And that's God's own truth," Domagalla added from behind his newspaper.

BRESLAU, THAT SAME SEPTEMBER 5TH, 1919
HALF PAST TWELVE IN THE AFTERNOON

Caretakers Bender and Handke took their time deciding whether or not to allow the latest arrival in. It was not the man himself who made them doubtful – they knew him well – but the state he was in. Criminal Sergeant Kurt Smolorz did not stink of alcohol, but swayed on his legs and smiled like a moron. They detained Smolorz in their duty room, placed a steaming mug of tea in front of him and stood at the barrier deliberating quietly.

"He's fixed his hangover with a beer," Handke muttered to Bender. "But why doesn't he stink of booze?"

"Damned if I know," Bender replied. "Maybe he's eaten something. I've heard parsley can kill any smell."

"Yes." Handke was relieved. "He must have stuffed himself with parsley. Besides, we haven't disobeyed our instructions prohibiting drunken policemen. This one's not drunk, only a bit . . ."

"You're right," Bender's face brightened. "How are we to know whether a policeman's drunk or just in a good mood? Only by his breath. And his doesn't smell of booze . . ."

"Best phone for Mock," Handke said glumly. "Not Ilssheimer. That pain in the arse can't stand alcohol. But Mock's our man. He can decide what to do with his friend."

As they resolved, so they did. A moment later Mock tore his subordinate away from his mug of tea, discreetly led him by the arm out of the duty room, turning right and down the corridor to the toilets. One of the cubicles was occupied, as indicated by the sign. Mock and Smolorz went into another. They stood in silence, waiting for the neighbouring cubicle to become vacant. After a while they heard the grating of the cistern's handle and flushing water. The cubicle door clattered, the door to the toilets clattered, Mock's teeth grated in anger.

"Where were you, you shit?" he growled. "Where did you get so pissed?"

Smolorz sat on the toilet and stared at the brown wainscoting on the walls. He said nothing. Mock grabbed him by the lapels, dragged him to his feet and pinned him to the wall. He saw laughing, bloodshot eyes, damp nostrils and crooked teeth; it was the first time he had noticed that Smolorz was ugly. Very ugly.

"Where were you, you son of a whore?" roared Mock.

A smile stretched Smolorz's pink skin and his pale freckles receded. Grains of powder showed white against his moustache and there was a faint smell of a woman's expensive perfume. Smolorz was repulsive. Mock raised his hand but then lowered it a second later. He left the cubicle, slamming the door with such force that the sign above the door handle jumped to OCCUPIED. Smolorz tried to open the door but the lock was badly buckled and would not move. He hammered. Mock returned to the locked cubicle. His highly polished shoes rang out loudly. Smolorz's hand emerged from beneath the door and a business card appeared on the floor.

"That's where I've been," echoed the voice of the imprisoned man, and then he produced another business card. "And this is where the murdered sailors lived."

Mock gathered up the two cards. Besides the printed text, both bore a handwritten note. On the first, which was decorated with a coat of arms, were the words: BARONESS MATHILDE VON BROCKENHEIM UND BIELAU, WAGNERSTRASSE 13, and instructions had been written on the reverse in a woman's rounded writing: "Please visit me today in my boudoir, otherwise the person delivering this letter will lose his job here." On the back of the other card, which was printed: DR NORBERT RISSE, ENTERTAINMENT AND DANCING, THE WÖLSUNG, Mock recognized Smolorz's uneven hand: "Four sailors, Gartenstrasse 46". He left the toilets and lit a cigarette. He made off briskly, sensing that his lungs and head were reacting positively to his tenth nicotine hit of the day. As he passed the duty room, he said to the caretakers:

"Smolorz is going to stay in the lav for a while. He's not feeling too good."

"Goes with the job . . ." muttered Bender.

BRESLAU, THAT SAME SEPTEMBER 5TH, 1919
A QUARTER TO ONE IN THE AFTERNOON

Mock stepped into his office waving Norbert Risse's business card. Wirth and Zupitza were still sitting in their heavy chairs, and Zupitza was wielding the siphon and squirting soda water into the tall glasses. He handed one to Wirth and another to Mock, who downed the contents in one gulp and threw Risse's business card on the table.

"That's where we're going." He pointed a stubby finger at the address Smolorz had scribbled down. "You'll do exactly as I said, except for one thing: you're not going to tail Risse, you're going to tail whoever it is I question at this address, understood? The caretaker, for example, or one of the neighbours."

Angry invectives could be heard issuing from Ilssheimer's office. Mock approached the door and began to eavesdrop.

"What sort of order is this, damn it!" Ilssheimer's voice was harsh and swollen with anger. "You're a police pen-pusher, Domagalla. You ought to keep our archives in order!"

"Councillor sir, that whore could have had the tattoo done recently." Mock sensed determination in Domagalla's voice. "Our files are ordered alphabetically by surname, not according to distinguishing marks."

"You know nothing about our filing!" Ilssheimer yelled. "I drew up various sub-files myself, including one for distinguishing marks. At Mühlhaus' request. If there was a problem identifying the body of some prostitute we could always refer to the file. And now some whore has committed suicide, so Mühlhaus turns to me and says: 'Look into your excellent archive and find me a whore with the sun tattooed on her backside.' And what? I have to tell him: 'Unfortunately, Councillor sir, I don't have one like that amongst my files – my archive's a mess.'"

Domagalla said something so quietly Mock did not hear.

"Damn it!" Ilssheimer shouted. "Don't tell me the whore came here just to make a guest appearance during the war, and that's why she's not in our archive! I worked here in the war and I kept the register in good order!"

Domagalla mumbled something else.

"Domagalla . . ." Mock glued his ear to the door. Ilssheimer was hissing, a sign that he was at his wits' end. "I know for a fact that the prison archives have accurate descriptions of all tattoos . . ."

Mock heard nothing more. "No, it's impossible," he thought, "it definitely isn't Johanna, Wohsedt's mistress. She didn't make any 'guest appearances', she was a Penelope waiting for her Odysseus. And it was only when he didn't return from the war that she took to prostitution. She certainly wasn't in some prison getting a tattoo done on her backside."

He decided to adopt the method which had proved so effective during his talk with Ilssheimer that day. "That swine must have got at her," he thought. "He must have killed her, gouged her eyes out and hung her, gloating at the sight of her suffering; first he would have told her to write a letter to me saying it would save her, and then he would have broken her arms and legs, like he did the sailors'." Mock was invaded with such evocative images that they horrified him. He shuddered, thinking, "Death has looked me in the eye."

He knocked, and hearing a loud growl which he interpreted as "Come in", he entered his chief's office.

"*Nolens volens* I overheard your conversation, gentlemen," he said. "I apologize, Councillor sir, but would you mind telling me a bit more about this suicide?"

"Tell him, Domagalla," sighed Ilssheimer.

"Criminal Secretary von Gallasen phoned me," Domagalla said. "He'd been sent to a suicide. Probably a prostitute, judging by her clothes and make-up. On her backside was a prison tattoo of a sun with the writing: 'You'll get hot with me.' I'm just looking through our files to speed up identification of the body."

"Where did this happen?" Mock asked.

"On Marthastrasse. Probably jumped off a roof."

"How old was she?"

"Looking at her — well over thirty."

The sigh which issued from Mock's lips made the leaves of the palm in the corner of Ilssheimer's office tremble. A current of air set them moving again as Mock closed the door behind him.

"We're off," Mock told Wirth and Zupitza. "To Marthastrasse."

"Not Gartenstrasse, as on the business card?" Wirth asked.

"No," Mock said, irritated. "Von Gallasen is very young. A twenty-something-year-old prostitute, ravaged by life, could look forty to him."

Wirth understood nothing, but he asked no more questions.

BRESLAU, THAT SAME SEPTEMBER 5TH, 1919
ONE O'CLOCK IN THE AFTERNOON

Mock sat in the Horch next to Wirth, cursing the September heat. The dust rising from the cobblestones irritated him, as did the odour of the horses and their manure, and the threads of gossamer that stuck to his stubbly cheeks. When irritated or perturbed, he generally called to mind passages from writers of antiquity, which he had analysed years earlier as a schoolboy and student. He would recite the lofty and concise phrases of Seneca that he had once learned by heart, Homer's fleeting hexameters, and the sonorous endings of sentences by Cicerone.

He squeezed his eyes shut and saw himself in his uniform, sitting in the front row at secondary school, listening to the simple, crystalline sounds of ancient Roman speech. Into the din of the street broke his Latin teacher, Otton Moravjetz, his mighty voice reciting a painfully relevant passage from Seneca's *On Solace*: "*Quid est enim novi hominem mori, cuius tota vita nihil aliud, quam ad mortem iter est?*"†

Mock opened his eyes. He did not want to hear anything about death. At the newspaper kiosk on the corner of Feldstrasse and Am Ohlauufer,

---

† "What is so strange when a man dies? His life, after all, is no more than a journey towards death."

140

a little boy handed the vendor a small pile of banknotes and received in return a copy of *Die Woche* with its children's supplement.

Ten-year-old Eberhard Mock runs to the kiosk at Waldenburg railway station, a one-mark coin for Sunday's Die Woche *children's supplement clasped in his hand. Soon he'll be reading about Billy the Kid's adventures in the Wild West; soon he'll find out what happened to Doctor Volkmere, the explorer. Will he escape the cannibals' cauldron? The newsvendor shakes his head. "None left. Sold out. Go and look somewhere else." Little Ebi runs hopefully to the kiosk near his school; soon he'll buy it, read it — but again the apologetic smile, a shake of the head. Ebi drags his feet home. Now he has learned to think negatively. You have to keep repeating to yourself: it's not going to work, it'll all end in a fiasco, I'm not going to read about Billy the Kid's adventures, I'm not going to find out what's going to happen to Doctor Volkmere.*

Thirty-six-year-old Eberhard Mock found it difficult to breathe the Breslau dust and was amazed at the depth of his childhood reflections. "Defensive pessimism is the best attitude," he thought, "because the only disappointment you can suffer will be a pleasant one."

Comforted, Mock observed a horse-drawn wagon carrying barrels and crates marked: WILLY SIMSON. REAL FRANCISCAN BEER FROM BAVARIA, which was blocking the way into Marthastrasse. Two workers in soft caps and waistcoats were unloading the beer onto the platform of a three-wheeled cart. Mock imagined it to be a wagon belonging to the Forensic Medical Department, and instead of frothy drink in barrels it was Johanna's body beneath the tarpaulin. Her corpse's eyes are a sea of blood, a little girl and a howling dog are at her side. The girl tugs at one of her hands. If she could read she would learn from the piece of paper held tightly in the dead woman's fingers that she had died because of a certain Eberhard Mock, who should own up to some mistake but does not want to, which means that others will die.

They found themselves in Marthastrasse, a quiet little street lined with high tenements. Mock patted Wirth on the shoulder, indicating that he should stop the car. They were about a hundred yards from the crowd milling on the pavement outside number ten, near Just's Inn which, as Mock knew only too well, was accessed by way of the yard. The Criminal Assistant got out of the Horch while Wirth and Zupitza were instructed to stay inside. He went through the gate, showing one of the uniformed policemen his identification, and began to climb the stairs. On each side of the staircase were large rectangular alcoves from which three sets of double doors led to three apartments. The windows in these peculiar shared hallways, as well as all the kitchen windows, gave onto the ventilation pit. This was how apartments for less wealthy tenants were now being built – they were cheap, of poor quality and very cramped. Two men stood at the windows on the ground floor; one, a uniformed policeman on whose enormous head sat a shako adorned with a star, was answering the questions of the other, an elegantly dressed young man. Mock shook the hand of both. He knew them well, having seen the policeman in uniform several months earlier, and the civilian only that morning. Officer Robert Stieg was on the beat in that district, and Gerhard von Gallasen was Mühlhaus' assistant. Mock peered into the pit, at the bottom of which lay a small bundle covered with a sheet. "It was once a woman," he thought hard. "It had a young child and a boxer bitch."

"Do you know her name yet?" Mock asked (and then told himself, "She must have been called Johanna."). "Were her eyes gouged out?"

"We don't know her name," von Gallasen replied, surprised that Mock had shaken hands with an ordinary beat officer. "None of the gawpers knew her. Your colleague Domagalla has dug up the address of a pimp living in the vicinity . . ."

"They're just bringing him in," said Officer Stieg, pointing to two uniformed policemen and a short man with wispy blond hair and a top hat who was traipsing up the steep stairs between them.

"I asked you whether her eyes had been gouged out," Mock said, and his thoughts replied: "Yes, he stuck a bayonet into her eye socket and twisted it a couple of times."

"No . . . Of course not . . . The eyes are untouched," muttered Officer Stieg. "Tieske, tell the character in the top hat to have a good look at her, then bring him here! At the double!" he yelled to the uniformed policemen.

"Stieg, please tell me everything *ab ovo*!" Mock said, irritating von Gallasen who was higher than Stieg in rank, height and birth, and therefore believed that he ought to have been asked first.

"*Ab* what?" Stieg said, having no idea what was expected of him.

"From the beginning," Mock explained. "Didn't you learn Latin at school?"

"This morning, Christianne Seelow from number twenty-four on the fourth floor," Officer Stieg began, "was hanging out her washing on the roof. A gust of wind blew one of her sheets down into the ventilation pit. She went downstairs and discovered the body. The caretaker, Alfred Titz, ran to the police station. That's it. Do you want to see her?"

Mock shook his head and imagined Johanna's body covered by a sheet blown down from the roof by a merciful wind. The blond man in the top hat appeared next to them, evidently not pleased at the sight of Mock.

"Do you know her, Hoyer?" Mock asked, and in his mind he heard the pimp reply: 'Yes, her name is Johanna. I don't know her surname."

"No, Commissioner sir," Hoyer answered. "She wasn't from our district. I once saw her in the inn by the yard, but my girls soon drove her out. We don't like competition."

"What, was she so pretty?" asked Mock.

"She wasn't bad," Hoyer said, smiling at his lewd recollections. "To be honest, someone could have made quite a profit out of her . . . I wanted to

143

take her on, but my girls didn't like her. They teased her." Hoyer smiled again, this time at Mock. "I've got six girls to look after. Sometimes I give in. You can't argue with all six at once . . ."

"Fine," Mock muttered, and tipped his bowler hat in farewell. He was bursting with joy. It was not Johanna. "Defensive pessimism is the best possible attitude to have in the world," he thought, "because is there anything worse than unpleasant disappointment, than a painful surprise?"

"Teased her? How?"

Mock heard von Gallasen question Hoyer and thought: "The lad wants to ask at least one question. He likes interrogating people. One day it'll bore him."

"They called her names."

"Such as?" asked the novice detective. Mock paused on the stairs to hear the answer.

"Eczema," laughed Hoyer.

3.IX.1919

Recently my thoughts have been focussing on an anticipation of events. This evening as I passed a shop selling clocks, I caught sight of a painting advertising a timepiece on a strap which you fasten around your wrist. These watches are still a novelty, and one often sees them advertised in the windows of department stores. The black strap in the painting encircled a man's suntanned wrist. It immediately reminded me of a woman's leg sheathed in a stocking. The black watch strap reminded me of a suspender. A short while later I went into a restaurant and ordered dinner. The waiter discreetly placed the business card of a brothel on my table. On it was a drawing of a young woman wearing a tight dress and displaying legs in stockings with suspenders. I ate my supper and approached the tenements into which the prostitute I was tailing the day before yesterday had disappeared. I waited. She emerged at about midnight and winked meaningfully at me. A moment later we were in a droschka, and a quarter of an hour after that at the place where we bring offerings to the souls of our ancestors. She undressed, and for a generous sum allowed me to tie her up. She did not protest even when I gagged her. She had terrible eczema on her neck. This constituted the fulfilment of anticipation. After all, yesterday I offered up to science Director W., aged sixty, who had identical eczema. And his was on the neck too!

After a while I began my lecture. She listened, and suddenly she began to reek of fear. I moved away from her and continued my subtle interpretation of two passages from Augsteiner. I'll summarize what I told her here:

Incarnations of the soul, writes Augsteiner, appear in a space that is hostile to them. The soul, which in itself is good because it is identical to the concept of man, because he himself is *eo ipso* the effluence of the element of the soul, which *ex definitione* cannot be evil because *ex definitione* it is opposed to that which pertains to substance, *ergo* bodily, *ergo* bad; and so the soul becomes incarnate where the bad element finds expression, in order to balance out the attributes of evil which dwell within it. In this way, the emanation of the soul brings about a natural harmony, namely deity. And now for a partial, empirical confirmation of Augsteiner's theses. The soul of that vile Director W., aged sixty, appeared in the place where he became a victim of torment – in this very house, on the ground floor. And it is this soul which indicated where Director W. had hidden the letter to his wife, deceitful yet protesting his innocence. This does not tally with Augsteiner's views because the soul remained deceitful – just as it had done in this man during his lifetime, so the soul continued to do evil because it convinced the wife that her husband was no shameless adulterer, but an angel. But the soul destroys the evil in

145

the otherwise correct suspicions of Director W.'s wife, allowing her to be steeped in blissful ignorance. Blissful ignorance is the absence of evil, *ergo* – is good.

Using the prostitute as an example, I wanted to check whether the soul is more intelligent than I who direct it, or whether – according to Augsteiner – the *elementum spirituale* can become independent of its conjurer. And here is the experiment I carried out. Once I had induced a sense of horror and dread in the woman, I broke her arms and legs one at a time, and each time I said that her suffering was due to Eberhard Mock who lives in Klein Tschansch, at Plesserstrasse 24. I didn't gouge out her eyes because I wanted to see the fear in them, and the desire for revenge. Besides I had another reason not to do so: I wanted her soul to remember me well. To whom would it come? To me, who tortured her, or to the man who is the main cause of her death? I'm interested to know whether I have power over her soul, and whether I can direct it to the house of the man who is our greatest evil. If manifestations of spiritual energy occur at this address, it will be proof that I have power over the *elementum spirituale*. I will be the creator of a new theory of materialization. A theory which, we must add, is true because it has been proven.

BRESLAU, THAT SAME SEPTEMBER 5TH, 1919
HALF PAST ONE IN THE AFTERNOON

The cocaine had already ceased to have an effect on Kurt Smolorz's nervous system. The jester, who a moment earlier had been in fits of laughter at being imprisoned in a toilet, was now trying to think of a way to get himself out. First he resolved to let anyone entering the toilets know of his predicament. Minutes passed, then a quarter of an hour, half an hour, but all the policemen who needed to answer a call of nature stubbornly avoided using the toilets on the ground floor. Smolorz closed the toilet seat and cursed the two people responsible for his pitiful state: Mock, and the person who had designed the toilets. By making the distance between the floor and the bottom of the cubicle door only ten centimetres, and by installing a partition made up of eight small panes of glass between the top of the door and ceiling, the latter had immobilized Smolorz for longer.

Smolorz looked at his watch and realized he had been sitting in his prison for over an hour. This meant that Mock had not informed the caretakers about the door being stuck, which in turn meant that he had decided to punish his subordinate. The thought made blood rush to his head. At that moment his wife, Ursula, was no doubt dishing out lunch to the two little Smolorzes, not knowing whether their father was alive or whether he was lying in some dark side street, or on his deathbed in a hospital . . . He could have gone home in the early hours of the morning, slipped beneath the warm duvet and cuddled up to his wife's back. Instead he had snorted white powder up his nose. Cocaine had robbed him of all feelings for his family and changed him into a laughing fool, who wallowed in the Baroness von Bockenheim und Bielau's silk sheets. He remembered the tension his chief was living under, bringing death to innocent victims; and then he remembered his own nocturnal antics and felt disgusted at himself.

He took off his jacket, wrapped it around his hand and stood on the toilet seat. With a mighty blow he knocked out two panes. The sound of glass shattering on the floor was horrendous. Smolorz waited for someone to come into the toilet and listened hopefully to the sounds coming from the courtyard and corridor. Nothing. He thought of his chief's attitude to life. He knew the gist well. If he persuaded himself that nobody would hear him, a swarm of people would appear immediately. Smolorz took another swing at the piece of wood that separated the now-shattered panes. After the fifth blow the wood split with a crack and a moment later

Smolorz's heels were grinding into the glass scattered across the floor. He ran out of the toilets and up the stairs to the offices of the Vice Commission. He opened the door with a key. Mock was not there. The only person was Domagalla, barely visible amidst stacks of files and binders. He looked up hopefully.

"Help me, will you, Smolorz," he said. "We've got to identify that whore by her tattoo. A sun on her arse with the words: 'You'll get hot with me.' We've got to go through all the files."

Smolorz glanced at Mock's desk. On it was a brown envelope.

"How long has this letter been here?" he asked.

"Bender just brought it up," Domagalla said.

Smolorz reached for the envelope.

"But it's not for you!" Domagalla was outraged.

Smolorz opened the envelope, telling himself: "It's bound to be from the murderer. That Johanna with the eczema is bound to have been murdered."

"Do you know the meaning of 'Confidential'?" Domagalla insisted.

"'Blessed are those who have not seen and yet have believed. I'm dying because of you, Mock. Mock, admit your mistake, admit you have come to believe. Unless you want to see more little children crying. Johanna Voigten,'" read Smolorz quietly.

The term "defensive optimism" came to mind, and at that moment he stopped believing in Eberhard Mock's psychological theories.

BRESLAU, THAT SAME SEPTEMBER 5TH, 1919
THREE O'CLOCK IN THE AFTERNOON

At Mock's command, Wirth stopped the Horch near the Red Tavern on Karl-Marx-Strasse.

"You can go back to your business." Mock climbed out of the car. "The investigation's over."

He wandered slowly along the dusty pavement. The September sun warmed his neck and shoulders. He removed his bowler hat and slung his jacket over his arm. His feet slid around in their hard shoes. He sniffed and realized that he smelled, a discovery which made him change his plans and bypass the Red Tavern in a wide arc. He dragged his feet and stared at the tall tenements to his left. Beyond them stretched allotment gardens. A boy on a bicycle rode out of the gate holding a bucket of apples with one hand. "That's the end of the investigation, the end of sleepless nights, the end of alcohol. Nobody else is going to die because of me." Workers were leaving Kelling's dyeworks after the first shift. They shook hands with each other and dispersed into smaller groups. "I'll change my job, go away from here." Pastor Gerds greeted him as he emerged from the evangelical school. Dust, sweltering heat, gossamer, and Johanna lying in the ventilation pit. "I wonder if the rats scurrying along the pit walls in search of food kept on windowsills have had a go at her yet."

He was glad to leave Karl-Marx-Strasse behind and made towards Plesserstrasse, an empty, cobbled street lined with acacias. His was the first building on the left. He went up the stairs to Uncle Eduard's old butcher's shop, then on up to his room on the first floor. Nobody was at home. On the kitchen table stood the leftovers of lunch: cucumber soup and potatoes seasoned with crackling. He opened the window and heard Dosche's dog growling. Mock's father was sitting on a bench in the shade and playing with Rot, teasing him with his walking stick. Mock waved to him and tried to smile. The elderly man got to his feet and came towards the house, looking furious. Mock carried the washbasin into his alcove and filled it with cold water from the bucket. He hung his clothes on the bedstead, threw his underwear and socks under the bed and stood naked over the basin, listening to the sounds coming from below: the creaking of the stairs, the crash of the hatch, the wheezing of paternal lungs.

"You're pissed again!" he heard his father say.

He soaped his neck and armpits, mumbled something in reply and sat down in the basin, feeling his testicles contract with cold. Rot burst in from behind the curtain and stood up on his hind legs, wagging his tail. Mock stroked him on the head with wet hands and returned to his ablutions.

"What is this, damn it? What's this supposed to mean?" his father shouted, clattering the lids on the stove. "Where were you last night?"

Mock washed his feet and rinsed off the soap with water from the jug. The floor was soaked. He wrapped an old dressing gown around himself and emerged from the alcove. His father's grey hair stuck out alarmingly in all directions, and behind his pince-nez his eyes flashed with anger. Mock took no notice. He fetched a rag from under the stove, wiped the water off the floor, then lay down on his bed and stared at the ceiling. The damp patches on the wall formed the features of a face. Mock strained his imagination, but the face did not appear familiar. "After today, I ought to be seeing Johanna's face everywhere," he thought. He felt pangs of guilt that it was not so.

"Come and get some soup!" called his father.

Mock sat at the table and reached for a spoon. The first mouthful flowed down to a stomach of stone. The second stopped somewhere on the way. Mock set down the spoon.

"I'll eat in a minute."

"In a minute it'll be cold. Am I supposed to heat it up for you again? Do you think I'm your cook or something?"

Little Ebi is sitting in the kitchen eating dumplings. "Eat up or they'll get cold" says his father, lighting his pipe. Ebi washes them down with soured milk and feels the doughy balls expand. They fill his gullet and mouth, the grey dough swells, sticks to his palate, he cannot breathe. "Daddy, I can't have any more." "You're not leaving the table until you've eaten. The dumplings are delicious, you little brat, and we haven't got

150

any pigs! Everything's got to be eaten! Look at Franz, he's polishing it off!" . . .

"I'm not eating." Mock pushed the plate of soup aside. "Don't cook anything for me, Father. I've told you so many times."

He went to his alcove, opened the wardrobe and laid out a clean shirt and long johns on the bed.

"Pushing his plate away like that, the little rat." The wheezing in his father's lungs turned to rasping. "And you, old man, you wash up, you do everything for him . . ."

Mock dressed carefully and raised the hatch; his heels rang out against the steps. He went outside and stood in the sunlight. He no longer felt like a visit to the Red Tavern. He sat down on a bench beneath an acacia and lit a cigarette. He heard Rot barking and his father's footsteps on the stairs; a moment later Willibald Mock appeared in the small porch to which his brother Eduard's clients had once swarmed on slaughter days. In his hand was a tin plate heaped with steaming potatoes.

"Maybe you'll eat this?" he asked.

Eberhard Mock stood up and walked away. He turned and looked at his father standing in the porch. Short. Helpless. Mashed potatoes steaming in his hands.

BRESLAU, SATURDAY SEPTEMBER 6TH, 1919
THREE O'CLOCK IN THE MORNING

The red-headed nurse stroked Mock's hand. Her skin was so fair and smooth he thought the tear now falling from her lashes would slide down her cheek in one hundredth of a second. The nurse removed her bonnet and let down her hair. The thick copper locks fell with a gentle rustle onto the starched collar of her housecoat. She leaned over Mock. He caught the scent of her breath. Gently, he touched the fabric stretched across her large breasts. The girl stepped back abruptly, knocking over the bedside table. Mock had expected a sharp, metallic sound, but it was dull and somewhat muffled. All of a sudden the sound exploded, as if someone were thumping their fist against a wooden door. Mock sat up in bed and pulled aside the curtain. A penetrating cold shudder ran through him. "Must be hunger," he thought. "I didn't have anything to eat yesterday." It was pitch black. He lit a candle and looked around the room. His father was snoring quietly, and Dosche's dog was looking at him attentively, his eyes glowing amicably in the dark. Mock reached under his pillow where he kept his Mauser, a wartime habit, and stood in the middle of the room. He could have sworn that the noise which had woken him had come from the hatch leading down to the old butcher's shop. He lay flat on the floor, opened the hatch a little and peeped through the smallest gap by the hinges. He knew any intruder would attack where the gap was widest. He yanked open the hatch and jumped back. Nobody attacked. With shivers still running down his spine, Mock held the candle to the opening. He could not see further than the first few steps. He glanced at the dog; it was resting its head peacefully on its outstretched front paws, blinking sleepily. The animal's behaviour vouched there was no danger. Mock went down the stairs, holding the candle high.

The butcher's shop was empty. He directed the light to the grille on the drain, and finding nothing went out on to the porch. The September night was fair but cool. He made sure the door to the shop was locked securely and went back upstairs. He yawned, stood the lighted candle on the table and got into bed without drawing the curtain. Images drifted before his eyes: a discussion in the street, scraps of conversation, a lame horse pulling a droschka, a porter pulling the shafts of a two-wheeled cart. Something falls from the cart and lands with a loud noise on the cobbles.

Mock leaped to his feet and looked at his father and the dog. His father was snoring, but the dog was growling. He shuddered – the animal was staring at the hatch and baring its teeth. He sat down on his bed, the Mauser in his hand, and felt sweat trickling from his armpits. Suddenly Rot jumped up and started wagging his tail. Standing on his hind legs he went round in circles, just as he had done when he had greeted Mock some hours earlier as he was washing behind the curtain. The dog then lay down to sleep in his usual place. For a long time Mock heard nothing but the dull thumping in his chest; unlike the dog, he did not sleep a wink that night.

BRESLAU, THAT SAME SEPTEMBER 6TH, 1919
SEVEN O'CLOCK IN THE MORNING

Birdsong could be heard through the open window of Doctor Cornelius Rühtgard's office. Mock stood next to the sill, breathing in the cool mist formed by sunlight on damp grass. Doctor Rühtgard himself could be heard singing in the bathroom adjacent to the office, a sure sign that a well-honed razor was making fine work of his morning stubble. The doctor's servant knocked on the office door and entered silently to place a tray with a coffee service on a small table by the desk. Mock turned away from the fresh scent of the awakening park, thanked the servant with a nod and sat in the armchair next to the small table. He noticed that his hands were shaking as he clumsily knocked the spouts of both the coffee pot and the milk jug against the rim of his cup. To alleviate this classic ailment suffered by insomniacs, he concentrated instead on admiring the Waldenburg porcelain, the provenance of which was disclosed by the letters T.P.M. As he inhaled the aroma of Kainz coffee he heard an unsettling sound, like a muffled moan. He set down his coffee on the marble tabletop, rested his stubby hands on the edge of the table and listened. The singing in the bathroom grew by turns louder and quieter as Doctor Rühtgard gargled to rinse out the tooth powder. During a moment of

153

silence Mock went out into the hall. He heard another moan from behind a closed door next to the kitchen. As he approached it he sharpened all his senses. His hearing told him that someone was crying behind the door, tossing and turning in their sheets and thrashing their pillow with every moan. His nostrils caught a faint whiff of perfume and the stuffiness of a bedroom.

"I hope you're not intending to visit my daughter in her room." Doctor Rühtgard was glaring at Mock from where he stood at the other end of the corridor in a dark-crimson quilted dressing gown with velvet lapels. He did not look like a man who only a moment earlier had been humming a couplet from Ascher's operetta, *What Young Girls Dream Of*. He marched into his office and slammed the door.

Mock could not explain his friend's behaviour. The thought of his walk two nights earlier with the rebellious young madame who had provoked such an improper response in him now entered his tired and aching head. His ears, which a moment earlier had listened so attentively to the sound of a girl's muffled despair, rang with the various forms of the verbs "to pleasure" and "to screw", with which he had tried to shock the young woman torn between her love for a sensitive good-for-nothing and her possessive father. He realized that it had been two days since he had questioned that good-for-nothing, leaving him at the mercy of a murderer. He pictured Christel Rühtgard behind the closed door of her bedroom, burying her face in her pillow so as to muffle the sobs that were tearing her apart. He reached for the telephone receiver in the hall and dialled Wirth's private number. Ignoring the maid who had just entered the apartment with a basket of hot bread rolls, Mock croaked into the receiver:

"I know it's early, Wirth. Don't say anything, just listen. You're to lock Alfred Sorg up in the 'storeroom'. He's the man I questioned in the yard behind the Three Crowns. He'll either be there or at the Four Seasons."

He replaced the receiver and became aware of Christel Rühtgard standing in the doorway of her bedroom. The anger in her swollen eyes made her resemble her father.

"Why do you want to lock Alfred up? What's he done to you?" Mock heard her say as he made towards her father's office. "You're a foul monster! A miserable, drunken beast!" she yelled as he closed the door behind him.

Doctor Rühtgard was leaning out of the window, pouring the hot coffee from Mock's cup onto the lawn. He turned towards Mock.

"You've had your coffee, Mock. And now leave!"

"Don't behave like some offended countess." Mock was clearly pleased with his comparison. He felt perfidiously exhilarated and a faint smile appeared on his face. "Spare yourself the melodramatic gestures and tell me what's happened! And without any preludes such as 'You're asking *me*?'"

"The day before yesterday my daughter returned from a concert at night. She was shaking all over." Rühtgard stood holding an empty cup with tracks of aromatic Kainz coffee running down its sides. "She said she bumped into you during the walk she decided to take after the concert. You were drunk and insisted on seeing her home. On the way you were vulgar towards her. By this you're to understand that you're forbidden from entering this house again."

Mock strained his memory, but no Latin verse, no passage of prose came to mind which might calm him. He stared at a print on the wall showing a scene from the Gospels – the healing of the man possessed. At the bottom was written the year 1756. It dawned on Mock how he might quell his anger. He recalled an episode from school: Professor Moravjetz had thrown dates from German history at his pupils, who quickly translated them into Latin.

"*Anno Domini millesimo septingentesimo quinquagesimo sexto*," Mock said, and flopped into the armchair.

"Are you out of your mind, Mock?" Rühtgard gaped in amazement and the cup twisted on its handle spilling a few drops of coffee on his desk.

"If you believe your daughter, there's no point in us talking." Mock got to his feet and leaned over the desk. He looked into Rühtgard's eyes without blinking. "Shall I go on, or am I to obey your order and leave?"

"Go on," Rühtgard sighed, and he placed his hand on the head of a stork standing on a small, mahogany grand piano. The piano opened, the stork bent over and in its beak caught a cigarette which had appeared in place of the keyboard. Rühtgard took the cigarette from the bird's beak and closed the lid of the cigarette case.

"Only one thing in what your daughter says is true: the fact that I used inappropriate language towards a young lady from a good home. I won't say any more. And not because I gave her my word of honour that I'd be discreet. I could quite easily grant myself dispensation . . . No, that's not the reason . . . Someone once said that at times, truth is like a sentence. You don't deserve a sentence."

Rühtgard pulled greedily on his cigarette for a minute and exhaled the smoke through his nostrils. A blue fog hung over the surface of the desk.

"Pour yourself some coffee," he said quietly. "I'm not interested in what my daughter has been up to . . . Probably the same thing her mother liked so much . . . I never told you . . ."

"About her mother? Never. Only that she died of cholera in Cameroon. Before the war, when you had a well-paid job there."

"I've told you too much then." Rühtgard did not look at Mock, but squinted at a point somewhere in the corner of the room. "May she be swallowed by eternal silence."

Mock fell heavily into the expansive armchair. Silence. Rühtgard quickly stood up and went to the Waldenburg service to pour Mock some coffee. He pressed the stork's head and stuck the cigarette offered by the bird into Mock's mouth. He walked out of his office, leaving his guest with an unlit cigarette between his lips.

BRESLAU, THAT SAME SEPTEMBER 6TH, 1919
HALF PAST SEVEN IN THE MORNING

Mock and Rühtgard sat in the dining room and buried their spoons in a mixture of soft-boiled eggs, butter and several leaves of parsley which filled two tall glasses delicately etched with slender lilies.

"Tell me, Ebbo." Rühtgard poured a stream of honey onto a crispy roll. "Why have you come to see me?"

"The diet didn't help." Mock sucked up the eggy concoction with gusto and helped himself to two fat veal sausages. "I still had nightmares. I'm going to tell you something you might not believe, or might even laugh at." Mock broke off and fell silent.

"Go on, then." Rühtgard attacked a soft pear with his fruit knife.

"Remember how we used to entertain ourselves at night on the front with weird stories?" When Rühtgard murmured his affirmation, Mock went on: "Remember Corporal Neymann's stories about his haunted house? Well, my house is haunted. Understand, Rühtgard? It's haunted."

"I could ask what you by mean haunted," Rühtgard said. "But first of all I know you don't like that kind of question and, secondly, I've got to go to the hospital in a minute. But that doesn't mean I'm not going to hear you out. We can talk on the way. So, how does this 'haunting' manifest itself?"

"Noises . . ." Mock swallowed a mouthful of sausage. "I'm woken up by noises in the night. I dream about people with their eyes gouged out, and then a thumping on the floor wakes me up."

"That's all?" Rühtgard allowed Mock to pass at the dining-room door.

"Yes." Mock accepted his bowler hat from the servant. "That's all."

157

"Listen to me carefully, Eberhard," said Rühtgard slowly once they were on the stairs. "I'm not a psychiatrist but, like everyone else these days, I am interested in the theories of Freud and Jung. There are some very good passages in them." They stepped out onto sun-drenched Landsbergstrasse and set off alongside the park. "Especially where they write about the relationship between parents and children. Both scholars write about paranormal phenomena. Jung apparently experienced them in his own house in Vienna . . . Both he and Freud advise hypnosis in such situations . . . Perhaps you could try it?"

"I don't see why." They turned left into Kleinburgstrasse. Mock stopped to let a young woman with a child in a huge wicker pram go by before they briskly walked on, passing the Communal School building with its garden and playground. After a lengthy silence he said: "This is happening in my house, not in my head!"

"I read several of Hippocrates' tracts in Greek during my medical studies." Rühtgard smiled and led Mock to the right into Kirschallee, towards the enormous water tower. "That's your field . . . I suffered like hell over that Greek text . . . I don't remember now which of them has a description of the brain of an epileptic goat. Of course we can't be sure if it really did have epilepsy. Hippocrates dissected the brain and concluded that there was too much moisture in it. The poor animal might have had hallucinations, but it would have been enough to drain some water from its brain. The same applies to you. A part of your brain is responsible for your nightmares and for the noises in your house. All we have to do is work on it – perhaps with the help of hypnosis – and it'll be over and done with. You'll never dream of those dead, blinded people whose murderer you're after ever again."

"Are you trying to say" – Mock stopped, removed his bowler and wiped his brow with a handkerchief – "that those terrifying phantoms are in my brain? That they don't actually exist?"

"Of course they don't," Rühtgard exclaimed with joy. "Can your father hear them? Can that dog hear them?"

"My father can't hear them because he's deaf." Mock stood stock still. "But the dog can. He growls at someone, jumps up at someone . . ."

"Look, the dog is reacting to you." Rühtgard was flushed with the ardour of his argument. They passed the water tower and made their way along the narrow path between the sports ground and the Lutheran community cemetery. He took Mock by the arm and accelerated his step. "Come on, let's walk faster or I'll be late for the hospital. And now listen. Something wakes you, something that's in your head, and you wake the dog. The dog sees his master on his feet and greets you. Understand? He's not fawning on a ghost, he's fawning on you . . ."

For a long while they did not say anything. Mock tried to choose his words carefully.

"If you saw what I saw, you'd think differently." They were nearing the imposing Wenzel-Hancke Hospital building, where Doctor Rühtgard worked in the Department of Contagious Diseases. "The dog was on the other side of the room, standing by the hatch in the floor wagging its tail."

"You know what?" Rühtgard stopped on the steps leading up to the hospital and looked intently at Mock's ravaged countenance. Every wrinkle and every bit of puffiness caused by his sleepless nights was accentuated by the merciless September sun. "I'll prove to you that I'm right. I'll stay at your place tonight. I sleep very lightly, the slightest sound wakes me up. Today I'll find out whether phantoms actually exist. See you this evening! I'll come to your place after supper, before the 'phantom's hour', meaning midnight!"

Rühtgard opened the hospital's huge double door and was about to reply to the old porter's greeting when he heard Mock's voice and saw his friend's massive frame coming up the steps. The Criminal Assistant caught him by the sleeve, his face hard and his eyes fixed.

"You mentioned some dead blinded men a moment ago. Tell me, how do you know about the investigation I'm conducting?" Fear rang in Mock's voice. "I must have blurted something out on Wednesday, when I was drunk. Is that it?"

"No. It's not." Rühtgard squeezed Mock's hand tightly. "You do far worse things when you're drunk, things you push out of your conscious mind. I know about the murders from little Elfriede on Reuscherstrasse."

"From *who*? What the bloody hell are you talking about?" Mock tried to tear his hand away from the iron grip.

"You know those buildings on Reuscherstrasse." Rühtgard would not let go of Mock's hand. "The ones enclosing all those courtyards. If you were to go into one of the yards at midday, what would you hear, Ebbo?"

"I don't know . . . children screaming and playing certainly, on their way home from school . . . noise from several factories and taverns . . ."

"What else? Think!"

"The crooning of organ grinders, that's for sure."

"Right." Rühtgard let go of his friend's hand. "One of the organ grinders is called Bruno. He's blind. Lost his eyes in the war, in an explosion. He plays and his daughter, Little Elfriede, sings. When Elfriede sings, tears flow from Bruno's eye sockets. Go there today and see what Elfriede is singing about."

BRESLAU, THAT SAME SEPTEMBER 6TH, 1919
NOON

Mock sat in his office in the Police Praesidium trying to stifle the incessant musical rondo which had been going around in his head for over an hour, ever since he had returned from his gloomy walk through the labyrinth of inner yards between Reuscherstrasse and Antonienstrasse. In the dark side streets, from which not even the sweltering September sun

160

could burn away the musty dampness, pan vendors had set up temporary stalls; grindstones whistled in a hiss of sparks and organ grinders set down their boxes and played picaresque and romantic urban ballads. The yard's morality play, sung by Bruno the organ grinder's ten-year-old daughter, did not belong in either of those categories:

> In the city of Breslau after the war
> No longer safely can you all live.
> For a vampire prowls, a terrible brute,
> Like a spider, a bloody web does he weave.

Mock looked up at his colleague, Herbert Domagalla, who was clattering on the platen of a Torpedo typewriter, transforming the statements given by the prostitute sitting opposite him into the rhythmic scansion of well-oiled machinery. Mock grabbed a pencil and snapped it in two. A small splinter of wood hit the prostitute on the cheek, and she glared at Mock. He was looking at her too, but he did not see her. Instead he saw himself the day before: an energetic police officer who blackmails his chief, gets carte blanche to do what he likes and then, his head brimming with ideas, follows in the murderer's footsteps with his loyal helpers from the criminal underworld. After the death of a prostitute covered in rashes, that same police officer turns into a dried-up, moaning little soul who renounces everything he is doing and at night shakes with terror at imaginary ghosts. The following day that weepy and meek anima overdramatizes his experiences in the presence of a friend from the front.

> The vampire kills in our dark city streets.
> Our officers strive to track the fiend down.
> Led by our brave Commissioner Mock,
> A hunt for the vampire runs through the town.

161

Soon I will tell you why Mock leads this case,
I'll tell you what gives him this admirable knack
But now, for the moment, I must be still
For a grim shudder runs down my back.

Mock rested his chin on one fist and thumped his desk with the other. The inkwell and chewed bone penholder jumped, the antique sand shaker with Breslau's coat of arms rocked, the rolled-up newspaper with its headline PRISONERS OF WAR RETURN rustled. The prostitute glared at Mock again.

"If only you had seen me yesterday," he said to her and broke off.

"Pardon?" Domagalla and the prostitute said at the same time.

Mock ignored them and continued in his head: ". . . you'd have seen a moron, fluctuating between contradictory decisions. One minute he abandons Alfred Sorg to the mercy of the murderer, then he locks him up in Wirth's 'storeroom'. One minute he wants to attack the perpetrator, the next he practically drowns in tears for fear that somebody he has questioned is going to die. I've got the address of the four sailors. Why haven't I gone there? Because I'm afraid of killing somebody. I'm like Medusa: I kill with my eyes. I drill holes in stomachs and pierce lungs with my eyes alone. So how am I supposed to conduct this investigation, damn it? Not look at people? Not question them? Write letters?" After this last question, an answer occurred to him.

"Use the telephone," he said, and this time neither Domagalla nor the woman were surprised.

With eyes gouged out whole, and hearts pierced with pins,
This violent vampire's offering's grim
O, dear Commissioner, when is it ending,
The vampire's fearful and terrible hymn?

162

Only Mock knows the truth, only he understands
In all of the world it is only he,
O, dear Commissioner, when can you stop this?
Why all this killing? Pray tell this to me.

Mock dialled the number of Smolorz's neighbour, the lawyer Max Grötzschl, and asked him to let the Criminal Sergeant know that he had called. Ten minutes later a polite voice, polished by appearances at tribunals, informed him that a tearful Mrs Ursula Smolorz did not have the slightest idea where her inebriated husband had gone the previous day. Mock thanked Mr Grötzschl and hung up in a fury, almost over-turning the telephone. Unlike Mrs Smolorz, he knew perfectly well that for the past two days her husband had been mingling with Breslau's aristocracy.

The vampire sends notes to Commissioner Mock,
In which he reveals those motives of his.
Read these aloud to the folk of your city
Tell the people of Breslau the horror that is.

Another thought silenced the nagging of the little organ grinder's daughter in Mock's head. Smolorz was not the only member of his infor-mal investigative team. There were others he could trust absolutely. He dialled the number of Bimkraut & Eberstein, the forwarding agency. After two rings he heard a voice which did not belong to either Bimkraut or Eberstein; nor could it, since both had died long since and their names, carefully copied from gravestones in the old St Bernard's cemetery, had been used as a front to register a business whose boss was somebody completely different, and whose undertakings had little to do with the forwarding of goods.

163

"Listen, Wirth," Mock said, but his eyes followed the prostitute who, with a charming smile, whispered something in Domagalla's ear as she left. "What? What's that you said?" Mock continued. "Don't be vulgar . . . Sorg and Kohlisch are forcing themselves on Miss Käthe, you say! . . . Yes, keep her away from them! And now stop bothering me with your nonsense and listen! We're making a move . . ." Mock glanced at Domagalla as he left with his charge and immediately issued instructions. In his head, Elfriede the organ grinder's daughter was singing her last verse:

> *When will my organ stop grinding so sadly*
> *This terrible story, this tearful song?*
> *How long, Commissioner, must our torment endure?*
> *Please tell us, dear Mock, oh for how long?*

BRESLAU, THAT SAME SEPTEMBER 6TH, 1919
TWO O'CLOCK IN THE AFTERNOON

Erich Frenzel, the caretaker of a block of houses between Gartenstrasse, Agnesstrasse, Tauentzienstrasse and Schweidnitzerstrasse, was sitting in the yard he administered, straining his uncomplicated brain to its limits over an equally uncomplicated problem: whether to spend Saturday night there, in Bartsch's Inn, with a tankard and bowl of black pudding, peas and bacon, or in the back rooms of Café Orlich, with walnut schnapps and cabbage with crackling. The first possibility was tempting because of the new accordionist in Bartsch's who came from Swabia, like Frenzel, and played beautiful tunes from the fatherland; the second possibility, on the other hand, appealed to Frenzel's love of gambling. In a secret room at the back of Café Orlich at Gartenstrasse 51, brawny men gathered for arm-wrestling contests across the tables, flexing their muscles and entirely ignoring gamblers like Frenzel as they looked on and cheered. Remembering one strongman who was coming to Breslau from Poland, and his own substantial loss the previous week, he was gradually inclining towards the latter option.

He did not make a final decision, however, because his entire attention was drawn to a huge wagon which had rolled through the gates and into the yard from Agnesstrasse. The wagon was empty. Being short-sighted, Frenzel could not decipher the company name on the tarpaulin, which fluttered freely in the wind and revealed the empty interior. He got to his feet, buttoned up his jacket, adjusted his cap with its broken peak and, feeling like a soldier, clattered loudly across the cobbles in his tall, highly polished boots. He was fuming with rage at the audacious carter who had the cheek to drive into the yard, despite the clear NO ENTRY sign hanging above the gate. His presence – which was, after all, forbidden in his yard – could not in any way be justified since there was no business in that block of tenements to which any sort of goods could be delivered. Frenzel snorted in anger as he passed three little girls, two of whom were turning a thick piece of rope while the third skipped over it, performing all kinds of acrobatics. He grew red with fury when he saw a short man jump from the box, stand with his legs apart facing the old linden tree planted by Frenzel's father, and unfasten his trousers.

"Hey, you undertaker!" shouted Frenzel as he charged towards the wagon. "You don't piss here, you little shit! Children play here!"

The shorter carter looked up in surprise at the approaching caretaker, fastened his flies and clasped his hands together pleadingly. His gesture made no impression on Frenzel. He was now drawing near, his moustache bristling. Once more he was Frenzel, the bombardier who had lived through so much and had sent many a man packing. He took a swing of his broom. The short man did not turn a hair, quite unabashed by the caretaker's threatening gesture. Frenzel took another swing, this time aiming at the intruder's head. But the broom was stopped in mid-air. The caretaker stared at his implement, which now looked tiny in the hands of a powerfully built man dressed much like Frenzel himself: peaked cap, waistcoat and high boots. This image was the last Frenzel would recall of that sleepy afternoon. After that came darkness.

BRESLAU, THAT SAME SEPTEMBER 6TH, 1919
THREE O'CLOCK IN THE AFTERNOON

Eberhard Mock walked slowly out onto Schuhbrücke, which was drenched in blistering sunshine. He looked about him and strolled along the pavement towards the vast mass of Matthiasgymnasium. The chestnut trees by the statue of St John Nepomuk were taking on new autumn colours. Contemplating nature's changing ways, Mock stepped into the Matthiasgymnasium church. A minute later, a tall man appeared at the door through which Mock had disappeared and watched with suspicion anyone who approached the church. An elderly matron dressed in black walked up to the door of God's house. The man barred her way.

"The church is closed today," he said politely.

The woman's eyes bulged in surprise. She soon collected herself and said in a condescending tone:

"My good man, this is not a shop that can be closed. The church is always open and you'll find room for yourself in there too, I assure you."

"Are you going to make yourself scarce, Madame, or do I have to kick you up the arse?" the church's Cerberus asked in the same polite tone.

"You lout!" shouted the lady, looking around. As she did not see anybody who could help her, she turned and marched off towards Ursulinenstrasse, angrily tossing her considerable rump.

Another guard stood at the church's sacristy door, which gave on to the school garden. The door opened abruptly and the guard watched as Mock and the parish priest shook hands. A moment later, Mock was beside him.

"Nobody?" he asked.

"Nobody," was the answer.

"Duksch is at the main entrance. Tell him he's free to go. You can go too."

Mock took the small, narrow street and out onto Burgstrasse. The school warden locked the church door behind him. At Mock's back stood the Matthiasgymnasium building, in front of him a low wall beyond which the murky Oder flowed sluggishly by. He watched the traffic on Burgstrasse for a while, then dashed across the road and walked alongside the wall, observing the river's current and the people walking down the street. He stopped at the beginning of Sandbrücke, leaned against a pillar plastered with posters informing people about Lo Kittay's seances of non-tactile telepathy, and stood motionless for about twenty minutes. Everyone he had seen on Burgstrasse had disappeared, yet Mock still stood surveying the busy street. All at once, he briskly crossed Sandbrücke. He passed several houses and the Phönix watermill before ending up on Hinterbleiche. Ignoring a swarm of schoolboys who were releasing the stress brought on by their poor knowledge of elliptical equations and Latin conjunctions in clouds of cigarette smoke, he passed Hennig's distillery and ran on to the footbridge leading to Matthiasstrasse. As he set foot on the wooden planks, two uniformed policemen appeared behind him. With their massive shoulders they barricaded access to the footbridge to anyone who might have wished to cross to the opposite bank. Mock ran across the bridge, making it sway gently, and found himself on a wide riverside boulevard. A large Horch stood at the curb. Mock jumped into the car and fired the engine. He immediately accelerated and made towards Schultheiss brewery, which was smoking in the distance. Now he could be sure nobody was tailing him.

BRESLAU, THAT SAME SEPTEMBER 6TH, 1919
FIVE O'CLOCK IN THE AFTERNOON

Someone removed the hood from Frenzel's head. He gasped for air and looked around. He was in a semi-circular room whose bare brick walls were illuminated by two small windows. The stool he sat on was the only piece of furniture. His eyes, at first unaccustomed to the darkness, could make out only two other objects, one of which he supposed to be a wardrobe, the other a small nematode. A moment later, he recognized the wardrobe as the man who had blocked his broom, and the nematode as the short carter who had tried to answer Nature's little call in his yard. He pulled a watch from his pocket. Its hands – as well as his aching neck – were irrefutable proof that he had spent three hours in a jolting wagon before trekking up countless stairs. He got to his feet and stretched his shoulders, then made his way hesitantly towards one of the windows. The wardrobe moved fast. Frenzel stood still, terrified.

"Let him look at the view of the city," the other man said quietly and gestured enigmatically with his hand.

Frenzel walked to the window and was spellbound. The orange autumn sun enhanced the squat building of the church of St John the Baptist on Hohenzollernstrasse and slid along the elaborate cornices of the Post Office building and Juventus manor, leaving the magnificent art-nouveau tenements which circled Kaiser-Wilhelm-Platz in soft shadow. Further afield he identified the church of Carolus Boromeo and the modest tenements of the working-class district of Gabitz. He was about to look eastwards, towards the wooded cemeteries beyond Lohestrasse, but stopped short as he heard a new sound. Someone was issuing halting instructions in a hoarse voice and muttering something in approval. Frenzel turned and in the dim light saw a well-built man in a pale frock coat and bowler hat. Beneath the folded wings of his gleaming white collar was the fat knot of a black silk tie, cut through with crimson zigzags. The picture was rounded off with a pair of carefully polished, patent-leather shoes. "Either a pastor, out whoring secretly, or a gangster," thought Frenzel.

"I'm from the police." The dandy's hoarse voice dispersed Frenzel's doubts. "Don't ask me why I'm interrogating you here – I'll only say it's none of your business. Don't ask me any questions at all. I want answers, O.K.?"

"Yes, sir," retorted Frenzel dutifully.

"Stand in the light so I can see you." The police officer sat on the stool, exhaled, unbuttoned his jacket, removed his bowler hat and placed it on one knee. His ribcage and belly constituted one unified mass. His face suggested future corpulence.

"Name?"

"Erich Frenzel."

"Profession?"

"Caretaker."

"Place of work?"

"I look after the yard on Gartenstrasse, behind Hirsch's furniture shop."

"Do you know these men?" The dandy shoved a photograph under Frenzel's nose.

"Yes, yes," Frenzel said as he studied the stiffened features of the four sailors. "Oh hell, so that's why I haven't seen them for a week . . . I knew they'd end up like this . . ."

"Who were they? Give me their names."

"I don't know their real names. They lived in an annexe on

Gartenstrasse. Gartenstrasse 46, apartment 20, to be precise. At the very top. The cheapest there is . . ."

"What do you mean you don't know their names? They must have registered somehow. Who did they register with? The tenement's landlord? Who owns it?" Frenzel was inundated with questions.

"A man called Mr Rosenthal, Karlsstrasse 28. I'm his right-hand man at the tenement. The apartment was standing empty, and that worried Mr Rosenthal. These four came along in June. A bunch of wastrels – like so many others discharged from the army after the war. They were a bit tipsy and, by the look of things, they hadn't a pfennig to their names. I told them there weren't any vacancies, but they asked politely. One of them showed me some money and said: 'This is a good spot, old man. We'll conduct our business here and pay you regularly.' Somehow he managed to talk me round. I get a commission from Mr Rosenthal for every new lodger."

"You didn't ask for their names?"

"I did. And they said: Johann Schmidt, Friedrich Schmidt, Alois Schmidt and Helmut Schmidt. That's what I noted down. They said they were brothers. But they didn't look like each other somehow. I know what life's like, Commissioner sir. No shortage of chaps like that after the war. They loiter, steal, haven't got anything to do . . . They prefer to conceal their real identities . . ."

"And you took the risk for a few measly pfennigs and registered who knows who, bandits maybe?"

"If I had a suit like you, sir, I wouldn't be registering anyone . . ." Frenzel said quietly, and was immediately alarmed by his impudence.

"And they paid up regularly?" His comment left no impression on his interrogator's face.

"Yes. Very regularly. The one who called me 'old man' always came with the rent towards the end of the month. I gave it to Mr Rosenthal and he was perfectly happy."

"What sort of business were they in?"

"They were visited by ladies."

"What sort of ladies, and what for?"

"Rich ladies, judging by the way they dressed. They wore hats with veils. And what for? What do you think, Commissioner sir?"

The police officer lit a cigarette and stared at Frenzel for a long time.

"Remember what I said at the beginning of our talk? The rules of our conversation?"

With difficulty Frenzel breathed in the dust that swirled in the light falling from the window. He racked his brains and had no idea how to answer the question. All he knew was that in two hours the strongman from Poland was going to be sitting at a table in Café Orlich.

"I'm the one asking the questions here, Frenzel, not you. Understand?"

"Sorry," Frenzel said. "I've forgotten what you asked me."

"What did the ladies visit them for? Answer quickly, don't pick your words."

"They visited them" – a toothless grin brightened Frenzel's face – "for hanky-panky."

"How do you know?" There was not a trace of amusement on the face of the interrogator.

"I eavesdropped at the door."

"How many rooms in the apartment?"

"One room and a kitchen."

"The lady would be in the room with one of the boys and the others stayed in the kitchen?"

"I don't know, I didn't go in. The ladies came alone, sometimes in pairs. Sometimes one of the Schmidts would go out during these visits. Sometimes all of them were there. It varied . . ."

"And this didn't disturb the neighbours?"

171

"There were only two complaints, about the ladies shrieking and shouting . . . Because there weren't all that many ladies. Barely more than a handful."

"Did you ever see these men dressed up?"

"Dressed up?" Frenzel did not understand. "What do you mean? How?"

"Have you ever been to the theatre, Frenzel?"

"A few times."

"Did the Schmidts ever wear costumes like actors in a theatre? Zorro, for example, knights and so on?"

"Yes, sometimes, when that fat man came for them."

"What fat man?"

"I don't know. Fat, spruced up. He drove a car with 'Entertainment' or something written on it . . . I'm not sure, my eyesight isn't that good."

"How often did the fat man come?"

"Several times."

"Did he go up to their apartment?"

"Yes, and then they'd all climb into his car and go off somewhere. He must have paid them well because they'd drink twice as much afterwards and go and have a good time at Orlich's, not far from here."

"Did any other men visit the Schmidts?"

"There was one other. But he never came alone. There were always two women with him, one in a wheelchair. He'd lug the wheelchair with the invalid up the stairs himself."

"Would you recognize the man?"

"I'd recognize the man and the other woman. They didn't hide their faces."

"And the one in the wheelchair?"

"The cripple always wore a hat with a veil."

172

"What did the man look like, and the other woman, the one who wasn't an invalid?"

"I don't know . . . He was tall, she had red hair. A pretty woman."

"How old?"

"He was about fifty, she about twenty."

"Weren't you surprised when those four men disappeared? Why didn't you report it to the police?"

"Surprised? Yes, I was surprised. Sometimes they'd drink for two days at Orlich's before coming home, but now a whole week . . . As for the police . . . Sorry, I don't much care for the police . . . But I would have reported it today anyway . . ."

"Why today?"

"The Schmidts were always here on Saturdays because that man with the girl and the invalid came on Saturdays."

"Are you saying they came regularly, every Saturday?"

"Yes, every Saturday. At the same time. But not together. First the man with the invalid, then a few minutes later the red-head."

"At what time did they come?"

"They'll be there in about half an hour." Frenzel pulled out his watch. "Always at six."

"Were they there last Saturday?"

"Yes. But without the red-head."

"Was that the last time you saw the Schmidts?"

"No, it was the previous day. The fat man came for them in his car. They went off somewhere."

"How do you know they were at home on Saturday if you saw them for the last time on Friday?"

"I didn't see them, but I heard them in their apartment."

"You eavesdropped?"

"Yes."

"And what did you hear?"

"Their voices, and the moans of the invalid woman."

"Did you hear the man too?"

"The man? No."

"You're free to go." The police officer took out his watch and showed Frenzel the door. "Here's for a cab." He tossed him two ten-mark notes. "You can go home. But remember, this giant here" – he indicated the man-wardrobe – "is going to keep a discreet eye on you for the next few days. Wait, just one more thing . . . Tell me, why don't you like the police?"

"Because they're too mistrustful, even when you go to them of your own accord and want to report something." Again, he was frightened by his own impudence. "But that doesn't apply to you, sirs . . . I really . . . Besides, you don't look like a policeman . . ."

"So what do I look like?"

"A pastor," Frenzel replied, and thought "out whoring."

He went to the winding staircase and ran down as fast as his legs could carry him. Once he reached the ground floor and was out of the building, all his tiredness left him. He ran to the nearest crossroads and whistled with two fingers to passing droschkas, showing no interest whatsoever in the enormous, multi-storied building from which he had just emerged. Frenzel could only think of how to get home as quickly as possible, fetch his money, and go to watch the strongmen arm-wrestling across a beer-soaked table in a back room at Café Orlich.

BRESLAU, THAT SAME SEPTEMBER 6TH, 1919
A QUARTER TO SIX IN THE EVENING

The stairs groaned under the heavy footsteps of the three men. Mock, Wirth and Zupitza finally made it to the fourth floor of the tenement at

Gartenstrasse 46. They stood panting outside the door of apartment 20 and sniffed the air in disgust. The rank odour came from the toilet on the landing.

"The lav's probably blocked," muttered Wirth as his gloved hand unlocked the apartment door with a picklock.

Mock kicked the half-open double door with a patent brogue — very gently, so as not to scuff the toe. Fetid air surged from the room. He screwed up his nose at a stench he abhorred, one which reminded him of a changing room at a sports gymnasium. He pulled out his Mauser and nodded to Zupitza to do likewise. Once in the dark hallway, he groped for the light switch and turned it on, drenching the hall in a dirty yellow glow. He leaped at once to the side to avoid a possible attack. None came. The brown, painted floorboards in the hallway creaked beneath their shoes. Zupitza wrenched open a huge wardrobe. It was empty save for some coats and suits. The dim light of a bulb covered with newspaper made it impossible to examine the clothes properly. Mock gestured to Wirth and Zupitza to search the main room while he turned on the light in the kitchen. The lighting proved as miserable as that in the hallway. He could, however, discern the mess one might expect to find in an apartment devoid of the female touch: stacks of plates covered in congealed tongues of sauce, cups with sooty traces of black coffee, rock-hard remnants of bread rolls and chipped glasses streaked with a tar-like liquid. This was everywhere: in the deep, semi-circular sink; on the table; on stools, and even on the floor. Mock was not at all surprised to see several glistening blowflies which lifted off at the sight of him to settle on the flaking wainscoting and on an embroidered picture bearing the words "The Early Bird Catches the Worm". Despite the open window, there was an overwhelming smell of wet rags.

"No-one here!" he heard Wirth call from the main room. He left the kitchen and entered quarters which he thought would be far cleaner, as

175

befits a place of work where hygiene plays rather an important role. He was not mistaken. The room had a window which gave on to the main road, and it looked like any other room that had not been cleaned for a week. Two huge iron beds were neatly covered with bedspreads embroidered with red roses. Between them was a bedside table on which stood a lamp with an intricately twisted shade. There were no pictures on the walls. It was a room with no soul, like in a miserable hotel where all one could do was lie on the bed, stare at the lamp, and try to banish suicidal thoughts. Mock sat on one of the beds and looked at his men.

"Zupitza, go and keep an eye on the caretaker for the rest of the evening and the whole of tomorrow." He waited for Wirth to pass on his instructions in hand signals, then turned to the interpreter. "Wirth, you go and see Smolorz at Opitzstrasse 37, and bring him here. If he's not at home, go to Baron von Bockenheim und Bielau's villa at Wagnerstrasse 13 and give him this note."

Mock took out his notebook, tore a page from it and wrote in an even, slanted script, far smaller than the classic Sütterlin handwriting: "Kurt, come to Gartenstrasse 46, apartment 20, as soon as possible."

"And I," Mock said slowly in answer to Wirth's mute question, "am going to wait here for the red-headed girl."

BRESLAU, THAT SAME SEPTEMBER 6TH, 1919
A QUARTER PAST SIX IN THE EVENING

Mock had realized long ago that, since leaving the hospital in Königsberg, he was highly susceptible to women with red hair. Not wishing to believe that the red-headed nurse taking care of him was merely a figment of his imagination, a phantom brought to life by morphine, he would carefully scrutinize every *pyrrhokomes* (as he called them) he met. Walking down a street he would often see loose red locks escaping from beneath a hat in front of him, or fiery, thick plaits bouncing on spry shoulder-blades in time with their owner's brisk footsteps. He would rush after these women, overtake them and look them in the face. He would raise his hat, whisper "I beg your pardon, I mistook you for somebody else," and walk away as they looked after him with eyes full of fear, disdain or disappointment, depending on whether they were inexperienced virgins, happily married women or debauched maids. As for Mock, he was usually deeply disappointed, not to say frustrated. Because when these red-headed women revealed their faces to him, not one of them resembled the face of the nurse in his dreams.

He was not frustrated now, even though he could not be at all sure that the girl standing on the threshold was not the one he had told Rühtgard about during those frosty nights in Kurland. So little light came from the four sailors' room that any woman standing in the doorway would have looked like a vision from a dream.

"Sorry I'm late, but . . ." Seeing a stranger, the girl broke off.

"Please, come in." Mock moved away from the door on which he had heard a gentle knock a moment earlier.

The girl entered hesitantly. She looked around the empty apartment with unease and wrinkled her slightly upturned, powdered nose in disgust at the sight of the filthy kitchen. Mock closed the door with his foot, took her by the arm and led her into the main room. She removed her hat with its veil and tossed her summer coat onto one of the beds. She was wearing a red dress which reached down to her calves and stretched teasingly across her considerable breasts. The dress was old-fashioned, giving nothing away, and to Mock's irritation it ended in a pleated frill. The girl sat on the bed next to her discarded coat and crossed one leg over the other, revealing high, laced boots.

"What now?" she asked with feigned fear. "What are you going to do to me?"

"Criminal Assistant Eberhard Mock," he replied, squinting at her. He said nothing more. He could not.

The girl gazed at him with a smile. Mock did not smile. Mock did not breathe. Mock's skin was on fire. Mock was sweating. Mock was by no means sure if the girl sitting in front of him resembled the nurse in his dreams. At that moment the image of the red-headed angel from Königsberg was blurred, indistinct, unreal. All that was real was the girl who was smiling at him now – charmingly, disdainfully and flirtatiously.

"And what of it, Criminal Assistant, sir?" She rested the elbow of her right arm in her left palm and gestured mutely with her middle and index finger that she wanted a cigarette.

"You want a cigarette?" Mock croaked, and seeing the amusement in her eyes he began to search his jacket pockets for his cigarette case. He opened it right in front of her nose and was taken aback when he realized that its lid had almost grazed her delicate nostrils. She deftly plucked out a cigarette from under the ribbon and accepted a light, holding Mock's trembling hand in her slim fingers.

Mock lit a cigarette too and remembered old Commissioner Otton Vyhlidal's advice. He was the one who had assigned him to work in Department IIIb, in a two-man team which, after the eruption of prostitution during the war, had become the official Vice Department. Vyhlidal, knowing that the young policeman could be vulnerable to a woman's charms, used to say: "Imagine, Mock, that the woman was once a child who cuddled a fluffy teddy to her breast. Imagine she once bounced up and down on a rocking horse. Then imagine that once-small child cuddling to its breast a prick consumed by syphilis or bouncing up and down on greasy, wet, lice-ridden pubic hair."

Vyhlidal's drastic words acted as a warning now as Mock fixed his eyes on the red-headed girl. He set his imagination to work and saw only the first image: a sweet, red-headed child nuzzling her head into an ingratiating boxer. He could not envisage the child dirty, corrupted or destroyed by the pox. Mock's imagination refused to obey him. He looked at the girl and decided not to overstretch his imagination. He sat on the bed opposite her.

"I've told you who I am," he said, trying to make his voice as gentle as possible. "Now please reciprocate."

"Erika Kiesewalter, Assistant Orgiast," she said in a melodious, almost childish voice.

"You're witty." Mock, because of the contrast between her voice and the licentious nature of her words, remembered old Vyhlidal's warning and slowly regained his self-control. "You like to play with words?"

"Yes." She inhaled deeply. "I like games of the tongue . . ."

Mock did not register this innuendo because he was seized by a terrible thought: that his interrogation was sentencing this girl to death, to having her eyes gouged out, to having a metal needle stuck in her lungs. "To save her," he thought, "I'll have to isolate her in the 'storeroom'. And what if I never catch the murderer? Will she have to sit in Wirth's old counting-room for years while her velvety skin wrinkles and withers? I can still save her! I won't ask her any questions. But if the murderer's following me, how can he know whether I've questioned her or not? He'll kill her anyway. Yet without her evidence I might not catch him, and I'll be forcing her to stay in that old counting-room, with blemishes and wrinkles creeping over her withered skin. Besides, if we don't catch the murderer, everyone stored away at Wirth's place is going to get old, not only the girl."

"Stop staring at me like an idiot and don't talk nonsense," he snarled – and forced himself to think, "What do I care about some whore and her alabaster skin!" – "Answer my questions! Nothing more."

"Yes, Officer sir." Erika stood up, opened the window and flicked a column of ash into the warm, autumnal evening. The air resounded with the grating of trams and the clip-clopping of horses' hooves. The waist of her dress was dark and sat on her hips, accentuating their roundness. Mock felt that strong tension which awakens teenage boys from the deepest sleep, and which for ageing men is a sign that not everything in life has yet been lost. "I'll ask her a question," he thought, "and she'll answer me. I'll ask her another and be calm."

"Answer my questions," he repeated hoarsely. "Quickly. First question, what's your profession?"

"Hetaera,"† said the girl, making way towards the bed. This time she sat modestly, and her face displayed nothing but concentration.

"How do you know that word?" Mock's surprise diminished the tightness he felt.

"I read this and that." A smile appeared on her face which Mock thought impudent. "I'm especially interested in antiquity. I even played Medea in an amateur production. I'm trying my hand at acting."

"Why did you come here? To this apartment?" Mock closed his eyes to conceal the contradictory feelings that were preying on him.

"I've been coming here every Saturday. For several weeks."

"And you plied your . . . profession here?" Mock took his time picking the right words.

"The one I ply, but not the one I dream of."

"And what do you dream of?"

"Acting," she whispered and a blush suffused her cheeks. She clenched her teeth as if trying to stop herself crying. Then she laughed derisively.

"You're to describe accurately what you did here last Saturday," said Mock, and thought, "She's probably mentally ill."

"Same as every other."

"Tell me everything."

† A courtesan in Ancient Greece.

180

"It excites you, does it, sir?" she asked, lowering her childlike voice.

"You don't have to give me the details. Tell me broadly."

"I don't know what that means, broadly . . ." Another smile.

"Go on, damn it!" Mock yelled. "The four men who used to live here are dead. Do you understand?"

"I'm sorry." Mock wanted to believe that the fear in her face resulted from his shouting and not her acting abilities. "Right, I'll tell you. I was hired by a wealthy man. I don't know his name. I met him in the Eldorado, where I'm a dance-hostess. He had a beard. He danced with me, then we went to my room. He proposed a regular commission. To partake in debauchery. I agreed, on condition that I could back out after the first time if I didn't like it."

The girl fell silent and picked at the bedspread with her slender fingers.

"Go on," Mock said quietly, so as to hide his hoarseness. "It's not the first time I've met somebody like you. I'm not aroused by stories of hetaeras . . . Gone are the days when I was excited by the works of Alciphron."

"Shame," she said gravely.

"Shame? Why?" Anger surged in Mock. He felt himself being manipulated by this crafty whore.

"I'm ashamed to talk about it," she said in the same serious tone of voice. "If I aroused you, I'd simply be doing my job, which is arousing men. But otherwise, I don't know how to say . . ."

"Use the term 'to look after' to describe the act you abandon yourself to when you're doing your job."

"Fine," she whispered, and told him everything. "The man accepted my condition and gave me this address. I was to come here every Saturday after six. He was quite insistent about the time. So I came. I didn't do anything perverted. There were six people in the room. The man who hired

181

me, a young girl in a wheelchair and four young sailors. The sailors lived here. I suspect they weren't sailors at all, but dressed up. Sailors live on ships, they don't rent themselves out as . . . On my client's instructions I'd get undressed. One of the sailors would look after me. My client would transfer the girl from the wheelchair to the bed and then the three other sailors took care of her. The girl would watch me and my . . . the one who was with me, and it obviously had a great effect on her because when she'd had enough of watching she very willingly looked after the three sailors all at once. It was like that every time."

"And your client never looked after you?" Mock gulped. "Or the girl in the wheelchair?"

"God forbid!" Erika shouted.

"Why weren't you with them last Saturday?"

"I was indisposed."

"So the four sailors took care of the invalid?"

"Probably. I don't know. I wasn't there."

Somebody knocked energetically. Mock pulled out his Mauser and made towards the door. Through the peep-hole he saw Smolorz. He let him into the hallway and breathed in the smell of alcohol. Smolorz was swaying slightly.

"Listen, Smolorz, you're to keep an eye on the girl," he said, nodding towards Erika, "until we transport her to the 'storeroom'. You're even to accompany her to the toilet. And one other thing. You're not to lay a finger on her! Come back in one hour. I don't know how you're going to do it, but you have to be sober. Do you understand?"

Smolorz nodded and left. He did not argue or protest. He knew his chief well enough, and knew what it meant when his chief addressed him informally, as he had done in the note delivered by Wirth: it certainly did not bode well. Mock closed the door behind him, went back into the room and looked at Erika. Her expression had changed.

"Sir," she whispered. "What storeroom? Where do you want to lock me up? I've got to work. This job is finished. I've got to dance at the Eldorado."

"No," Mock whispered back. "You're not going to work at the Eldorado. You're going to work here."

BRESLAU, THAT SAME SEPTEMBER 6TH, 1919
A QUARTER PAST SEVEN IN THE EVENING

Mock lay next to Erika straining his memory to count the women he had had in his life. But this was not in order to add another trophy to his collection. They were no trophies. Most were prostitutes, usually when he was drunk, and usually without much satisfaction. Mock counted all the women he had had and could not fully square his accounting. Not because there had been a vast multitude of them, but because during intercourse he had often been in a stupor or a fever, and could not remember whether these encounters could be called what is commonly termed *finis coronat opus*. Touching Erika's warm thigh, he decided to include only those times that could in all certainly be summed up by the Latin maxim. Erika put an arm around his neck and mumbled something. She was falling asleep. Mock stopped counting, he stopped thinking of anything at all. But he was sure of one thing: up until now, til this day, til this evening spent with a red-headed prostitute in a room belonging to murdered male whores, he had never really known what teenage boys dream of, and what makes ageing men start believing in themselves again. This evening Erika had revealed the secret to him. Without saying a word.

He got up and covered the girl's slim body with his jacket. He could not resist running his hand over her white skin speckled here and there with islands of freckles; he could not resist slipping his hand beneath her

183

arm to touch her sleeping breasts, which only a moment earlier had been full of life and urgently demanding their due.

He stood wearing nothing but his long johns and observed her shallow sleep. A scene from Lucretius' poem "De rerum natura" unexpectedly came to his mind: a man is drenched in sweat, his voice and tongue falter, a hum fills his ears. This was precisely the state he was in. He had been struck down dead. His school professor, Moravjetz, had described the scene as "pathographical" when they had discussed it in the optional Classics group. He had compared it with Sappho and Catullus' famous verses on how the human body reacts to violent emotions. Mock had been struck dumb, not by his recollection of Professor Moravjetz, but by the words his teacher had used to describe the scene in the poetry.

"The pathography of love," he said out loud. "But there's no love here. I don't love this crafty whore."

He walked up to Erika and tore his jacket from her. She woke up.

"I don't love this crafty whore," he said resolutely.

She smiled at him.

"Crafty, are you?" Mock felt the flame of anger rise in him. "Why are you laughing, you crafty whore? Are you trying to annoy me?"

"God forbid!" said Erika barely audibly.

She looked away. Mock sensed her fear. His anger branched and crackled in his breast. "She's frightened, the crafty whore!" he thought and clenched his fist. At that moment there was a knocking at the door. Slow-slow-slow, pause, slow-slow-slow-slow-quick-quick. Recognizing the code to be the rhythm of "Schlesierlied", Mock opened the door to Smolorz, who no longer reeked of alcohol but instead gave off a scent of soap. To all intents and purposes he was sober.

"Have you been eating soap?" Mock said as he dressed, not in the least embarrassed by Smolorz's presence. Erika wrapped herself in her dress.

"Water and suds," said Smolorz. "To spew it all up and get sober."

Mock donned his hat and left the apartment. He paused on the stairs. As the stench from the blocked toilet reached him, he was overcome with nausea and took the stairs two at a time. When he got to the gate he stopped and took a few very deep breaths. The nausea left him, but his mouth was still filled with saliva. He was only too familiar with these feelings of self-disgust. He heard his own voice: "Are you trying to annoy me, you crafty whore?", and was struck again by Erika's fearful gaze – the gaze of a child who does not understand why it will soon be beaten, of a red-headed little girl who likes to snuggle her face into a happy boxer's fur. He heard her reply: "God forbid!" He slapped his forehead and ran back upstairs. He tapped the rhythm of "Schlesierlied" on the door. Smolorz opened it. He had been sitting on a chair in the hallway. The stench of wet rags wafted from the kitchen and he could hear the buzzing of blowflies.

"Get the caretaker, Smolorz." Mock screwed up his nose and handed his subordinate a wad of notes. "Pay him to clean the kitchen. And tell him to bring the girl some fresh sheets. Well, go on, what are you waiting for?"

Smolorz left. The door to the main room was closed. Mock opened it and found Erika sitting on the bed in her summer coat, shivering with cold.

"Why did you say 'God forbid'?" He went to her and rested his hands on her fragile shoulders.

"I didn't want to annoy you, sir."

"Not now, before. When I asked you if your client took care of you or the girl in the wheelchair you shouted 'God forbid'. Why?"

"It wouldn't have been so awful if he had taken care of me. But the girl in the wheelchair called him 'Papa'."

"Why do you need my dog for the night?" Dosche the postman looked at Mock in surprise. They were sitting on a bench in the yard at Plesserstrasse, staring at the light shining in the window of the Mocks' apartment. They could distinctly make out two heads bent over a table: Willibald Mock's rugged grey mane and Cornelius Rühtgard's parting, laboriously perfected over the years.

"What are they doing?" Dosche asked, momentarily forgetting Mock's strange request.

"The same as you do with my father every day," Mock answered. "Playing chess. But going back to my request . . ."

"Exactly. What do you need my dog for?"

"See that?" Mock pointed to the sky where a swollen moon hung suspended, its soft light gliding across the dark windows of the building, the privy door and the stoop of the pump. "It's full, isn't it?"

"Correct." Dosche decided to have his last smoke of the day and extracted his tobacco pouch from his pocket.

"I'm going to tell you something." Mock glanced meaningfully at the man to whom he was speaking. "But it must remain absolutely confidential, understood? It's to do with the investigation I'm conducting . . ."

"Ah, the one everybody's going on about?"

"Shhh . . ." Mock put a finger to his lips.

"Yes, sir." Dosche struck his breast and a cloud of smoke escaped through his lips. "I swear I won't say a word to anybody!"

"The first murder was committed a month ago . . ."

"I thought it was a week ago . . ."

"Shhh . . ." Mock cast his eyes around and, noticing Dosche's perplexed expression, went on. "Well, the first murder was committed at full moon, like tonight. I've got a suspect who hasn't got an alibi. If he *did* commit the murder, he would have had to keep the corpse in his room for a few days. Please don't ask why! I can't tell you, my dear Dosche." He lit a cigarette and blew the smoke in the direction of the chess players, who were noisily putting away the chess pieces. "The suspect has a dog and says he couldn't have kept the corpse at his place because the dog's howling would have alerted the neighbours. Howling, you understand, my dear Dosche? Dogs howl in the presence of a corpse, or so the suspect claims. I've got to verify that tonight! Using your dog!"

"But, Mock," Dosche wheezed through his old pipe, "are you going to take my Rot off somewhere? To some corpse? Where?"

"Shhh . . . If my experiment is successful, I'll take you there, too. Would you like that?"

Sparks erupted from Dosche's pipe. He passed the leash to Mock.

"Fine, fine, take him. But shhh . . ."

Mock took the leash and tugged the sleepy Rot out from under the bench. He shook Dosche's hand and went home.

Rühtgard stood on the threshold of the old butcher's shop smoking a cigarette.

"Is this our gauge for measuring the strength of the spiritual event?" With the glowing stick he indicated the dog, which was looking at him distrustfully.

Mock winced when he heard Rühtgard's joke and said, "Who won?"

"Three to one."

"To you?"

"No, to Mock senior. Your father plays very well."

Mock felt himself flush with pride.

"Are we going to go to sleep now?" he asked.

"We are. I think your father's already made up the beds." Rühtgard looked around uncertainly. "Where can I throw my cigarette away? I don't want to leave rubbish outside the house . . ."

187

"This way." Mock opened the door. "There's a drain in Uncle Eduard's old shop. I even thought the noises might have been made by rats getting into the shop that way."

Rühtgard went behind the counter, lifted the grille and disposed of his cigarette butt. He went up the stairs. Mock carefully bolted the door, blacked out the shop windows with wooden shutters, filled the lamp to the brim with paraffin and hung it from the ceiling. The place was now well lit. He then went upstairs to their quarters, pulling the somewhat reluctant dog behind him. The hatch door lay open; he did not shut it. He unhooked the dog's leash, lowered the wick in the lamp and only then cast his eye around the semi-darkness of the room. Rühtgard lay covered with a blanket on his father's wooden bed, with eyes closed. Carefully folded trousers, jacket, shirt and tie hung over the headboard. Mock's father was asleep in the alcove, turned towards the wall. Mock undressed down to his long johns, placed his clothes on the chair, just as neatly as his friend had and stood his shoes to attention next to the bed. He slid his Mauser under the pillow and lay down next to his father. He closed his eyes. Sleep did not come. Erika Kiesewalter came several times, however. She leaned over Mock and, contrary to a prostitute's principles, kissed him on the lips. As tenderly as she had done that evening.

BRESLAU, THAT SAME SEPTEMBER 6TH, 1919
MIDNIGHT

Mock was woken by the sound of laughter from below. Malicious laughter, as if someone were playing a practical joke. Mock reached for his Mauser and sat up in bed. His father was asleep. From his sunken, toothless mouth came an asthmatic whistle. Rühtgard was snoring, but the dog was trembling, its tail between its legs. The hatch was open, just as he had left it before going to sleep. He shook his head. He could not believe the laughter. Releasing the safety catch of his gun, he approached the hatch and lay down on the floor beside it. The dog howled and ran under the table; Mock caught a glimpse of a shadow gliding beneath the ceiling of the old shop; the dog squealed; something ran past Mock as he lay there, something larger than a rat, something larger than a dog. It slipped past his hand and under the bed, avoiding Mock's blow. He grabbed the paraffin lamp and pulled up the sheet, damp with his own sweat, which covered the gap between the bed and the floor. A child was sitting there. It flared its nostrils and smiled. Out of its nose slid a blowfly, green and glistening. More malicious laughter came from below. Mock leaped up, wiped the sweat from his chest and neck and threw himself towards the open hatch. He knocked into the chair laden with clothes. It toppled over and hit the basin. Hearing the clanging of metal above him, he slid down the stairs on his buttocks, ripping his long johns. There was nobody there. He heard a rustling from the drain. He quickly jumped over the counter and lifted the grille. Something was moving down below. Mock aimed the muzzle of his Mauser. He waited. From the grille loomed Johanna's head. The scales on her neck rattled quietly. Two needles were lodged in her eyes. He fired. The house shook with the noise. Then Mock woke up for real.

BRESLAU, SUNDAY, SEPTEMBER 7TH, 1919
A QUARTER PAST MIDNIGHT

Mock stood beside Rühtgard's bed, gun in hand, and stared down at his closed eyes. The doctor twitched his eyelids sleepily.

"Did you hear that?" asked Mock.

"I didn't hear a thing," Rühtgard slurred, his tongue stiff with sleep.

"Then why aren't you asleep?"

"Because you're leaning over me and staring at my eyes." He wiped

189

his pince-nez and pressed it onto his nose. "I assure you, when you stare at someone so intensely when they're asleep, they're bound to wake up. That's how we sometimes wake patients from a hypnotic trance."

"You really didn't hear anything? But the chair fell over onto the basin and made a racket, I fired at Eczema's head . . ." Mock sniffed. "Can't you smell the gunpowder?"

"It was only a dream, Ebbo." Rühtgard sat up in bed and lowered the thin legs that protruded from his nightshirt to the floor. He took the gun from Mock's hand and held it under his large nose. "There's no smell of gunpowder. Take a sniff. There was no shot, or it would have woken your father up. See how fast he's asleep? The chair is still standing where it was too."

"But look." There was a note of satisfaction in Mock's voice. "The dog's behaving strangely . . ."

"True enough." The doctor studied the animal which was sitting under the table with its tail curled under, growling quietly. "But who's to know what the dog was dreaming? They have nightmares too. Like you do."

"Alright. But you've noticed that my father's a little deaf, haven't you?" Mock would not give in. "Besides, even when he was young he was a heavy sleeper. No shot would've woken him up! So I fired, and he's carried on sleeping."

"Smell your gun," Rühtgard repeated in a bored tone. "And now let's do an experiment." He stood up, approached the open hatch and slammed it shut. Mock's father sighed in his sleep and then opened his eyes.

"What the hell is going on!" For a man who had just woken up he had a powerful voice. "What are you doing, Eberhard? Thumping around at night? Are you pissed again or what? What a bastard . . ." The bed creaked as Mock's father expressed his disdain for the night's din with a resounding fart. Mock felt nauseated at the thought of having to lie next to him.

"Sorry," Rühtgard could not help laughing. "You've been undeservedly

190

rebuked. But you can see for yourself, the shot would have woken him . . ."

"I'm getting out of here." Mock started getting dressed.

"Listen, Ebbo." The doctor reached into the pocket of his jacket and pulled out a cigarette case and notebook. "There are no ghosts . . ." Mock froze, all ears. "They only exist in your head . . . After we talked this morning, I asked my assistant at the hospital to research what are known as paranormal phenomena. This what he found." Rühtgard lit a cigarette and opened his notebook. "I didn't want to tell you before . . . I wanted to keep it as a strong argument to the very end . . ."

"Go on then."

"Ghosts exist in the disturbed cerebral cortex, the so-called visual cortex of the right hemisphere of the brain. Problems in this part of the cerebral cortex influence vision. They appear as phantoms, hallucinations . . . The aural cortex, on the other hand, is responsible for sound. If I were to open up your head and touch this cortex you'd hear voices, or music perhaps . . . One composer would tilt his head and note down the music he then heard. If, in addition to this, there are disturbances in the right cerebral lobe, you have real pandemonium. Because this lobe is responsible for distinguishing between the objective and the subjective. Where it has been damaged, 'people,' as somebody once said, 'take their thoughts to be real people and things'. Most likely your brain is slightly damaged, Ebbo. But it can be righted . . . I can help you . . . I'll call on the best specialist in the field, Professor Bumke from the university . . ."

"I'm not convinced by your scientific explanations," Mock said thoughtfully. "Because how does your neurology explain that I experience this anxiety, these nightmares, only in this house and nowhere else . . . Damn it!" He raised his voice. "I've got to leave this place . . ."

"Well then go! Move to another apartment with your father. A better apartment, one with a bathroom!"

191

"Father won't agree to it. He only wants to live here, and he wants to die here too. He told me once . . ."

"Well then you leave for a while!" Rühtgard extinguished his cigarette in the ashtray, stood up from the table and rested his hands on the bulky mass of Mock's shoulders. "Listen to me! Get away from here for two or three weeks. Take a holiday and get away. Take a break from everything — corpses and ghosts . . . You'll build up your strength, catch up on sleep . . . Go to the seaside. Nothing calms like the sound of shifting sand and the monotonous murmur of the sea. I'll go with you, if you like. We could go to Königsberg and eat flounder. I'll put you under hypnosis. You can trust me. We'll get to the root of all your problems . . ."

Mock buttoned up his shirt in silence. As he slipped in a cufflink he pricked himself. He hissed and glanced at Rühtgard with animosity, as if he were to blame.

"Come on, get dressed and let's get going . . ."

"Where on earth?" There was resentment in Rühtgard's voice.

"Get dressed, please, and let's go . . . to your hospital . . ."

"What for?"

Mock smiled to himself.

"For the housecoat and nurse's hat . . ."

"I beg your pardon?" The doctor barely controlled himself.

Mock smiled again.

"I've met her at last . . ."

BRESLAU, THAT SAME SEPTEMBER 7TH, 1919
TWO O'CLOCK IN THE MORNING

Mock stood outside the door of apartment 20 and tapped out the rhythm to the "Schlesierlied" for the second time.

"Who's there?" came the voice of a sleepy child.

192

"Eberhard Mock."

The door opened a little. Erika was wearing a long and rather too large nightdress. She let the door swing open and went back into the room. Mock closed the door behind him and sniffed. He could no longer detect that unpleasant odour. The kitchen table was now covered with a cloth on which stood upturned plates and glasses, their rims leaving wet rings on the material. The floor was still wet. He entered the room and placed a large package on the chair. Erika sat on the bed and stared at him fearfully. Mock was sure neither of his emotions nor his words.

"Did my man bring you the bedlinen?" he asked, to break the silence.

"He did."

"Who washed the dishes?"

"Kurt." Fear gradually disappeared from Erika's eyes. "He did it very comprehensively. He doesn't like dirt . . ."

"So you're on first-name terms?" He reacted irritably, unable to bring to mind anything to substantiate Smolorz's preference for excessive tidiness. "Just how well have you got to know each other?"

"So-so." The trace of a smile appeared on Erika's lips. "I just like the sound of the name Kurt. Why are you so annoyed? I'm only a whore. What was it you called me? 'A crafty whore.' Why shouldn't I get to know sweet little Kurty very well indeed?"

"Where is he?" Mock ignored the question.

"About an hour after you left," Erika said more seriously, "a large man came round. He was huge. He didn't say anything, just wrote something on a piece of paper. Kurt read it and rushed out with him. He told me not to open the door to anyone."

Silence descended. The headlamps and shadows of passing cars drifted across the ceiling. Coloured illumination from the neon sign of Gramophon-Spezial-Haus on the opposite side of the street seeped

193

through the net curtain. Erika sat shrouded in red and green speckles of light and studied Mock without the hint of a smile.

"Why don't you come and sit next to me, sir?" she asked in a low, serious voice.

Mock sat down and watched with astonishment as his hand glided across her white arm. Never before had he seen such white skin, never before had his diaphragm deprived him of air for so long, never until now had he felt such pain in his thighs. *Fiat coitus et pereat mundus.*† With great disbelief he felt his chapped lips part to allow her tiny tongue to enter; he could not believe that his gnarled fingers were pulling up her nightdress.

"Why don't you take me, sir?" she asked just as seriously. She moved up the clean bedclothes and opened herself before him.

Mock sighed, got to his feet and went to the chair. He unwrapped the rustling package and hung a nurse's hat and starched housecoat over the back of the chair.

"Put this on," he said hoarsely.

"With pleasure." Erika leaped out of bed and freed herself from the nightdress. As she raised her arms, flickers of neon blazed across her prominent breasts. She tied her hair into a loose bun and put on the hat. Mock unfastened his trousers. At that moment Smolorz, Wirth and Zupitza stepped into the apartment. Erika quickly jumped into bed as Mock kicked the door shut. He approached the bed and pulled the eiderdown off the girl. A moment later somebody's knuckles were tapping out the rhythm of the "Schlesierlied". Mock sighed, walked over to the window and gazed for a while at the street lamp which illuminated the hairdresser's salon. He approached the girl and stroked her hair. She

---

† "Let there be intercourse, then may the world perish" (Latin) – a travesty of the well-known *Fiat iustitia et pereat mundus*, generally translated as "Justice must be done, even were the world to perish".

clung on to his hand with both of hers. He bent and kissed her on the lips.

"Wait a moment," he muttered, and went into the hall.

Smolorz was at the door, about to knock again. Wirth and Zupitza were sitting at the kitchen table surrounded by wet dishes.

"Why are you rapping out our signal, Smolorz?" Mock scarcely managed to suppress the irritation in his voice. "I saw you come in. And now hop it, all of you! From now on I'm going to keep an eye on the girl myself."

"Caretaker Frenzel . . ." Smolorz said, giving off the scent of soap. "He's not there."

"Tell me what happened, Zupitza," Mock hissed through clenched teeth.

"I was at the caretaker's" — Zupitza set his hands to work while Wirth translated into his characteristic German with its Austrian lilt — "and was keeping my eye on him all the time. He was uneasy. He kept looking around as if he wanted to go somewhere. All the more reason for me to keep an eye on him. I took him to the toilet. Stood outside the door. For a long time. In the end I knocked. Several times and — nothing. I forced the door. The window was open. The caretaker had escaped through the window. Mr Smolorz can take it from there."

"Didn't you hear what Wirth said?" Mock growled at Smolorz. "Out with it!"

"This is what Zupitza wrote." Smolorz handed Mock a piece of paper with large scribblings. "Then we questioned the neighours. Nobody knows where Frenzel is. One said that he was a gambler. We've combed the local gambling dens. Nothing."

Yet another corpse. The following day, or in a few days time, the murderer would send Mock a letter. They would go to a given address and find Frenzel with his eyes torn out. The organ grinder's little girl would

195

sing yet another verse. And you, Mock, you are to go home and talk to your father, and repair all the damage you've done. Admit you're defeated, Mock. You've lost. Hand over the investigation to others. To those who haven't made any mistakes that will be punished by people having their eyes gouged out or their lungs pierced.

Mock walked slowly to the table and grasped its edge. The surface shuddered and bounced, and then a moment later it was up in the air. Wirth and Zupitza fled to the wall, dishes crashed to the floor, glass shattered, plates gave an ear-piercing wail and cups screeched. The noise was terrible, and became intolerable when eighty-five kilograms of Mock jumped on to the upturned table. Fragments of crockery gave out their last strains, a shattered complaint, a grating *requiem*.

Panting, Mock stepped off the table and immersed his head in the iron sink. Cold water rushed around his neck and burning ears.

"Towel!" he yelled from the sink's cool interior.

Somebody put a sheet round his shoulders. Mock stood upright and covered his head with it. Streams of water flowed down inside his collar. He felt as if he were in a tent; he would have liked to be in a tent at that moment, far from everything. After a while he uncovered his head and took stock of the anxious faces.

"We're ending this investigation, gentlemen," he spoke very slowly. "Criminal Commissioner Heinrich Mühlhaus will take over. I'll just take down Erika Kiesewalter's statement and you, Smolorz, are going to hand it to the Commissioner. He'll know that they've got to find a man with a daughter in a wheelchair. Well, what are you staring at? Read the statement, then you'll know what it's all about."

"And what about the people in the storeroom? Are we going to let them go?" Wirth asked nervously.

"You take them to a detention cell. Tomorrow night Guard Buhrack will be waiting for you. He'll look after them. Any other questions?"

196

"Criminal Assistant, sir," Smolorz mumbled. "What about her? The storeroom, or straight to Buhrack?"

There was silence. Mock looked at Erika as she stood in the doorway. Her nurse's hat was now askew. Her lips were trembling and her vocal organs were positioning themselves to ask a question. But the bellows of her lungs could not expel the air. She stood breathless.

"What happens" — Smolorz had become exceptionally talkative — "if Mühlhaus wants to question her himself?"

Mock was staring at Erika. She shivered as the clock in the hall struck three times. The shivering did not subside, even though she was wrapped in an eiderdown. He looked at the nurse's starched housecoat, at Smolorz, who was unhealthily excited, and then came to a decision.

"If Criminal Commissioner Mühlhaus wants to question the witness, Miss Erika Kiesewalter, he's going to have to put himself to the trouble of going to the seaside."

RÜGENWALDERMÜNDE, TUESDAY, SEPTEMBER 9TH, 1919
NOON

Erika clenched her teeth. A moment later she sank slowly down onto Mock and snuggled her face between his neck and collarbone. She was breathing heavily. Mock swept the damp hair from her temple. Gradually her numbness passed and she slid from the man onto the tangle of sheets.

"It's a good thing you didn't cry out," he said, barely able to control the shaking in his voice.

"Why?" she asked in a whisper.

"The receptionist didn't believe we were married. He didn't see any wedding rings. If you had yelled out that would have just confirmed his suspicions."

"Why?" she repeated drowsily, and closed her eyes.

197

"Have you ever seen a married couple not leave their bed for fifteen hours?"

There was no reply. He got out of bed, pulled on his long johns and trousers, then stretched his braces and let them go. They slapped loudly against his naked torso. He whistled the well-known song "Frau Luna", opened the window that gave onto the sea and breathed smells which transported him to the Königsberg of his past, when nobody demanded he admit to some nameless offences or blackmailed him with eyeless corpses. The waves beat hard against the sun-baked sand and the two piers built on mounds of vast boulders. As he gazed at these constructions which embraced the port like a pair of arms, Mock tasted microscopic salty drops on his lips. From the nearest smokehouse wafted an aroma which set this fanatical lover of fish quivering nervously. He swallowed and turned towards Erika. She was no longer asleep. The slap of his braces had evidently woken her and she was resting her head on her knees, staring at him. Above her head hung a model of a sailing yacht which swayed in the salty breeze.

"Would you like some smoked fish?" he asked.

"Yes, very much," she smiled timidly.

"Well, let's go then," Mock said as he buttoned up his shirt and tried on the new tie Erika had chosen for him in Köslin the previous day.

"I don't feel like going anywhere." She got out of bed and, stretching after her short nap, ran several paces across the room. She put her arms around Mock's neck and with slender fingers stroked his muscular, broad shoulders. "I'm going to eat here . . ."

"Shall I bring you some?" Mock could not resist kissing her and gliding his hand over her naked back and buttocks. "What would you like? Eel? Plaice? Salmon, perhaps?"

"Don't go anywhere." She moved her lips towards his. "I want eel. But I want yours."

She clung to him and kissed him on the ear.

"I'm afraid," Mock whispered into her small, soft lobe tangled in a net of red hair, "that I might not be able . . . I'm not twenty any more . . ."

"Stop talking," she rebuked him in a stern voice. "Everything's going to be fine . . ."

She was right. Everything was fine.

RÜGENWALDERMÜNDE, THAT SAME SEPTEMBER 9TH, 1919 TWO O'CLOCK IN THE AFTERNOON

They left the Friedrichsbad Spa House Hotel holding hands. Two droschkas and a huge double-decker omnibus with a metal sign announcing its route between Rügenwalde and Rügenwaldermünde were parked in front of the porch of this massive building. Not far from the hotel stood a group of primary-school children and a bald, stout teacher who, as he fanned himself with his hat, was telling his charges that during the Napoleonic wars Prince Hohenzollern himself had taken the waters at this spa; the corpulent preceptor made use of his finger and pointed to a name plaque attached to the wall. Mock also noticed a pretty girl sitting alone on a bench outside the spa house, smoking a cigarette. He had worked long enough in the Vice Department to be able to indentify her profession.

They passed several houses on Georg-Büttner-Strasse and stopped at an ice-cream parlour. Erika attacked her icy column of raspberry scoops like a child and, much to Mock's surprise, even bit into it, the very idea of which made his own teeth ache. The rasping of a barrier announced that the raised bridge had now been lowered. They crossed it and found themselves on Skagerrak Strasse. They followed the left side of the street and entered the first house on the corner, a tavern. Mock asked the innkeeper, a Mr Robert Pastewski — this was the name that appeared above the entrance – for a dozen Reichsadler cigarettes for himself, and the same number of English Gold Flakes for Erika.

The strength of the burning September sun was tempered by a wind coming from the sea, which entangled Erika's hair as she stood on the narrow pavement.

"I'm hungry," she complained, and looked meaningfully at Mock.

"But . . ." – Mock was troubled – "we'd have to go back to the hotel . . ."

"I'm not speaking in metaphors now." The wind tossed a strand of hair into her eyes. "I really do want to eat."

"Then we're going for some real smoked eel," he said. "But I'll buy you a roll first. Let's go . . ."

He stepped into a nearby bakery and was enveloped by the smell of warm bread. The only customers in the place were two sailors, who were leaning on a counter decorated with starched tapestries and talking to the fat baker. They were speaking so fast in a Pomeranian dialect that Mock could hardly understand what they were saying. But one thing he did know: neither of them was buying anything, and the baker was not paying the slightest attention to him. Mock felt a vague unease, but could not get to the root of it. "It's the two sailors, no doubt," he thought to himself, "not four but two."

"And what would the esteemed gentleman like?" the baker asked in a strong Pomeranian accent.

"Two doughnuts, please. What's the filling?"

"Wild rose jam."

"Fine. Two please."

The baker took his money, handed him a paper cone of doughnuts and went back to his conversation with the sailors.

"Listen, Zach," Mock heard one of them say as he was on his way out. "Who was that?"

In response he tinkled the bell above the door and glanced at Erika, who seemed bored. With the tip of her shoe she was drawing some figures in heaps of sand scattered across the uneven pavement. Mock handed her the cone and absentmindedly erased the mysterious annotations with his shoe.

"*Noli turbare circulos meos,*"† Erika said, pretending to take a swing at him; instead she stroked his clean-shaven cheek. At that moment he recognized the source of his anger.

"What am I supposed to say," he thought as he walked beside her in silence. "I'm supposed to ask her where she knows that sentence from, and whether she went to secondary school, but every idiot knows it, after all. It doesn't prove she's educated or well read. 'I'm a hetaera,' she said to me when I asked about her profession; she uses the concept of a 'metaphor' correctly and quotes Cicero. Who is this whore, this crafty little whore? Maybe she wants me to start asking her about her past, her parents and her siblings; maybe she wants me to feel sorry for her and hug her. And she's putting me to the test. Delicately and subtly. First she ruts like a she-cat in heat, then she quotes sentences in Latin which must be rattling around somewhere in that head of hers, which must be as good as empty with all this debauchery. 'I partake in debauchery,' she said. I wonder if she did the same way as that cripple – with three at a time."

They walked on. Erika ate the second doughnut with relish. As they passed a large square house with huge green doors carrying a sign which read SOCIETY FOR THE AID OF THE SHIPWRECKED, Erika crushed the empty cone and asked casually:

"I wonder if there's a society for the aid of the life-wrecked?"

Crafty whore. She wants me to feel sorry for her; she wants me to see her as a child snuggling into the fur of a fawning boxer.

Mock stopped outside the smokehouse and said something he later long regretted.

† "Don't destroy my circles." (Latin)

"Listen to me, Erika" – he controlled the tone of his voice but not what he said – "you're not a whore with a heart of gold. There's no such thing. You're simply a whore. And that's all. Don't confide in me; don't tell me about your miserable childhood; don't tell me about your monster of a step-father and your mother whom he raped. Don't tell me about your sister who gave herself an abortion at the age of fifteen. Don't try and squeeze any tears out of me. Do what you're best at, and don't say anything."

"Alright, I'll watch myself," she said with no suggestion of tears. "Are we going to that smokehouse or not?"

She walked past Mock and made her way towards a temporary counter on which a fishmonger in a rubber apron and sailor's hat had arranged lightly smoked eels. He watched her slim back, which was shaking. He ran to her, turned her round and made to kiss away her tears. He did not do so, however, as Erika was not crying, she was shaking with laughter.

"My childhood was normal and nobody raped me," she spluttered. "And talking of life's wrecks, I wasn't thinking about myself at all, but about a certain man . . ."

"A man who goes by the name of Kurt, no doubt? Go on, say it!" Mock was shouting, heedless of the fishmonger's knowing eyes which said "that's what young wives are like". "That's why you like the name Kurt so much, eh? You told me that the day before yesterday! Kurty, eh? Who was Kurty? Go on, tell me, damn it!"

"No." Erika became serious. "The man's name is Eberhard."

8.IX.1919

It was remarkable, the occultists' conference organized by Professor Schmikale, the representative of the Thule order in Breslau. The whole world and their father were invited! Ludwig Klages himself, Lanz von Liebenfels and even Walter Friedrich Otto! They did not, however, trouble themselves to come to this out-of-the-way Silesian province. Instead, the first of these sent his assistant, some lisping lad who gave a completely incomprehensible lecture on the cult of the Pelasgians' Great Mother goddess. Furthermore he kept on suggesting that Klages' master, Friedrich Nietzsche, was in constant spiritual contact with the Magna Mater. It was she who allegedly gave him the idea to call Jahwe and Jesus "usurpers of divinity". At the same time he mercilessly criticized the young Englishman Robert Graves, who in a lecture had dared to claim that it was he who had come up with this term for the Jewish gods. It's ridiculous! A paper on who was the first to think up some trivial formulation!

From the order of the new Templars it was not von Liebenfels who came, but a Doctor Fritzjörg Neumann, who foretold the return of Wotan. His lecture was rewarded with applause, not because of his searing anti-Semitic and anti-Christian attacks, but for the lecture's constant reiteration of the support of Erich von Ludendorff – chief quartermaster of the Emperor's Armies – for the concept of Wotan's Second Coming.

It is not surprising that after Neumann's utterances the next lecturer, an intelligent, young Jewish woman, Dora Lorkin, was met with iciness and contempt. Oh, you profane people! Oh, you idiots with "von" before your names! Oh, you quarrelling chieftains who see nothing beyond your own dull tribes! You're unable to appreciate true wisdom! Because through this young woman spoke Athena! Dora Lorkin was the representative of W.F. Otto's polytheistic spiritualism. It transpired from the insightful theories of the Master she was representing that the human soul is a playing field for the ceaseless action of the Greek gods, who are the only true beings, while all other gods are mere myth. I will pass over her onto-logical reasoning. It is not vital. What made the greatest impression on me was the not new — as, after the lecture, some people accused it of being — but very apt notion of the Erinyes as the workings of a bad conscience.

Several sentences on the subject led me to ponder deeply, and allowed me to modify the piece on which I was working. Because as yet our bitter enemy has not admitted to his guilt, has not confessed his mistake. First I set free the spiritual energy of four young men. This energy was to guide him to a rightful way of thinking. The gouged eyes and the quotation from the Bible were supposed to make things evident to him. Our enemy, in his stubbornness, has not admitted to anything. In his house, some former butcher's shop, I forced the evil spirit of an old libertine to return and torment the inhabitants. Still no confession of any guilt. Finally, for our cause, I offered up a harlot covered in scales. Admittedly I did not tear out her eyes. He is bound to know by now what we want of him! It should not take the rheumy eyes of an adulteress to make him realize! But he persists in his silence.

Only now, after Dora Lorkin's lecture, have I understood that I must bring down true evil — the Erinyes — upon him. Then his torments will reach their zenith and he will admit to everything. At home I had a look at my shelf of books by writers of antiquity and took down Aeschylus' tragedies. After reading for several hours I understood. I will bring down the Erinyes upon our enemy, and sacrifice his father as an offering to him. The Erinyes persecuted Orestes because he killed his mother. Aeschylus writes that they did not listen to Orestes' reasonings or his pleas for mercy. Only one thing was important to them: to punish him and avenge his mother's blood. At that point I had doubts. Our bitter enemy would not, after all, be guilty of patricide because I would be the one offering his father in sacrifice. Will then the Erinyes come down upon him? After all it is he who, *de facto*, has exposed his father to death by abandoning him and going off with a harlot. He has abandoned his father to his fate because now his father has to face the demons I have set loose in their house. When his father is left entirely alone and learns from me that his son has gone away to have it off with some courtesan, he will be jealous. He will be jealous of the whore, the basest scum in the bourgeois hierarchy.

When this thought came to mind, I remembered that I had once read about one of the Erinyes, probably Megaera or Tisiphone, being the personification of wild jealousy. I now knew what to do. The worst I can do is fail. True wisdom is not the garbled analysis of some baroque mystic! True wisdom is not to be found in Daniel von Czepko or Angelus Silesius! True wisdom is achieved only through experience. And it is precisely my next experiment which will show whether Aristotle was right when he wrote: "The soul in a way is all that exists." We will see whether, as Otto claims, the Erinyes really do exist.

RÜGENWALDERMÜNDE, TUESDAY, SEPTEMBER 16TH, 1919 FIVE O'CLOCK IN THE AFTERNOON

Erika and Mock passed the lighthouse and turned right towards the eastern beach. Erika rested her head on Mock's shoulder and turned away for a moment to let her eyes glide indifferently over the houses on the other side of the canal. Mock followed her gaze. Although his interest in maritime architecture was equal to his interest in the question of civilizing Slavs and Kasubians, frequently blared out in newspaper headlines, he nevertheless unexpectedly took in a large number of technical details: on the whole the houses were built with timber-and-stone walls and generally covered with tarred roofing sheets, which somewhat surprised Mock, accustomed as he was to the Silesian craft of roof slating. Once in a tavern, where Bornholm salmon sizzled on a spit, he had asked about this maritime roofing and had been told by an old sailor how incredibly strong the sea wind could be, and that flying slates would smash against the walls of the houses or on the heads of passers-by.

"Do you remember, Erika, that old sailor who told us about how roofing is done in Pomerania?" He felt her nod on his shoulder. "When you left to go out for a walk he told me about another effect of the sea wind . . ."

"What effect?" Erika took her head off his shoulder and looked at him with interest.

"When the wind howls for a long time it drives people insane. Makes them commit suicide."

"Then it's a good thing it's not howling now," she said gravely and huddled against him.

The eye of the lighthouse lit up behind them. Its built-in horn monotonously announced a fog which was to descend on the port after the hot autumnal day. Seagulls screeched in warning.

At a seafront café they turned down to the beach. Erika was full of energy. She ran across the sand below the café terrace and raced towards the ladies' changing room. For a moment Mock lost sight of her. Carrying a wicker basket filled with bread, wine, fried marinated herring and half a roast chicken, he could barely keep up with her. He panted and gasped, his lungs damaged by nicotine.

Finally he staggered onto the eastern beach. A few strollers were building up an appetite for supper with a brisk walk. Some daredevil in a tight tricot bathing suit was cutting through the gentle waves with his solid knots of muscle. On the footbridge leading to the splendid ladies' changing room, supported by several metre-long wooden stumps sunk into the beach, Erika stood talking to a young woman. Mock wiped the sweat from his forehead with the back of his hand and looked carefully at the girl. He recognized her. It was the prostitute who was staying at the Spa House Hotel where, as Mock had already managed to discover, a four-woman team of Corinthian professionals was at work.

"She's met her match," he thought, and walked on westwards,

ignoring Erika who bade her friend-by-trade goodbye and ran gaily after him. They sat down on a dune. Erika turned her face to the salty sea breeze; Mock turned his mind to an all-consuming fury: "She's met her match — surely I'm mad to associate with this whore." Erika paid no heed to the man lying next to her with his hands behind his head, watching the girl step off the footbridge which connected the changing room to the beach. When she found herself past the broken teeth of the groyne, the girl lifted her dress a little and progressed more slowly, digging holes in the sand with her crooked heels. Mock's fury began to abate. "She wanders around like that all day — I've never seen her with a client. A darned dress, twisted heels, a parasol with prongs sticking out, eyes of a heifer, bleary and vacuous. A cheap whore." All of a sudden he felt sorry for her, twisting her ankles on cobblestones in an empty seaside spa, pursued by the screeching of angry seagulls. He turned to look at Erika. He wanted to put his arms around her in gratitude that she was no cheap, downtrodden whore, grinding down the pavements. He controlled the urge, however, and looked at the long fingers which held on to what once had been his strong biceps.

"Do you know, I come from a seaside village just like this," Erika said, her eyes closed. "When I was a girl . . ." She baulked and glanced anxiously at Mock, anticipating an acerbic reaction.

"See to the supper, Erika," he muttered and closed his eyes. He pictured her laying out the blanket on the white sand and, struggling against the slight wind, spreading over it the clean tablecloth with its embroidered fish. Then she would take the herring, chicken and wine out of the basket. He opened his eyes and saw everything as he had imagined it. He waved a hand invitingly. She snuggled up to him and felt him place a kiss first on one eye, then the other.

"I can anticipate everything you're going to do and say," she heard him murmur. "So, tell me about your seaside village."

207

Erika smiled and freed herself from Mock's embrace. She grasped a chicken thigh with the tips of her fingers and not without difficulty pulled it away from the rest of the meat. She gave it to Mock. He thanked her and tore off the crisp, golden skin with his teeth, then dug into the juicy fibres covered with a slippery veneer of fat.

"When I was little, I fell in love with our neighbour." With the very tips of her fingers Erika lifted a thin slice of herring to her lips. "He was a musician, like my parents. I used to sit on his knee and he'd play Saint-Saëns' *The Carnival of the Animals* on the piano. Do you know it?"

"Yes," Mock muttered and sucked in air as he detached the last strips of meat from the bone.

"He would play and I'd guess what animal the piece was supposed to be about. Our neighbour had a greying, evenly trimmed and well-groomed beard. I loved him with all my burning, eight-year-old heart . . . Don't worry," she briefly changed the subject, detecting a glimmer of unease in Mock's eyes. "He didn't do anything bad to me. He sometimes kissed me on the cheek and I would pick up the smell of good tobacco from his beard . . . From time to time he played cards with my parents. I'd sit on my father's knee this time, staring in bewilderment at the figures on the cards and not understanding anything of the game, but wishing with my whole heart that my father would be the loser . . . I wanted our neighbour, Herr Manfred Nagler, to win . . . I've always liked older men . . ."

"Glad to hear it." Mock passed the wine to her and watched as she drank straight from the bottle.

"I studied at the Music Conservatory in Riga, you know?" She was breathing quickly; the wine had momentarily taken her breath away. "Most of all I liked to play *The Carnival of the Animals*, even though my professor railed against Saint-Saëns. He said it was primitive, illustrative music . . . He was wrong. All music illustrates something, doesn't it? Debussy, for instance, illustrates a sea warmed by the sun, Dvořák the vigour and power of America, and Chopin the states of a human soul . . . Do you want some more chicken?"

"Yes, please." He watched her slender fingers, rested his head on his arm and moved closer to her. The sun dappled the sea before his eyes.

He was torn from his nap by Erika's voice. She was asking him something insistently.

"You agree, really?" she whispered delightedly. "Well, go on then! Tell me when you were born! Exactly, including the time!"

"What do you want to know that for?" Mock rubbed his eyes and glanced at his watch. He had not slept for more than a quarter of an hour.

"But you nodded, you agreed with everything I said," Erika said, disappointed. "You were asleep all along — you've had it up to here with my babbling . . ."

"Alright, alright . . ." Mock lit a cigarette. "I can give you the exact time I was born . . . What's it to me? The eighteenth of September, 1883. At about midday . . ."

"Ah, so it's your birthday the day after tomorrow. I've got to get you a present . . ." Erika traced the date in the wet sand. "And your place of birth?"

"Waldenburg, Silesia. Are you trying to work out my horoscope?"

"No, not me." She rested her head on his knee. "My sister . . . she's an astrologer. But I told you . . ."

"Alright, alright . . ." he muttered.

"Why are you being so kind to me?" She was not looking him in the eye; she was looking lower. At his nose? Lips? "You haven't called me a whore for a whole week . . . You've been calling me by my name . . . You even listen when I tell you about my childhood, even though it bores you . . . Why?"

Mock struggled with himself for a while. He pondered his reply, weighing all its consequences.

"The wind isn't howling." He avoided an honest answer. "And there's no aggression or insanity in me."

17.IX.1919

I could not put my plan into effect because I had to seek approval from the Great Assembly. When I presented him with my plan to awaken the Erinyes a few days ago, the Master wrote to me to say that further sacrificial offerings could prove dangerous. Apart from that, the Master voiced other reservations and summoned the Council. The meeting took place this past night at my house. The Master quite rightly pointed out my inconsistency. It lies in the lack of a precise definition of the notion of the "Erinyes". According to my plan, the spiritual energy which will escape when the body of our bitter enemy's father is offered in sacrifice will become an "Erinye". How can we be certain that this will be the case? the Master asked. How do we know that the "Erinye" is not going to be some part of our bitter enemy's soul, or some spiritual being independent of our bitter enemy and his father? Some demon we have awakened? And that demon we are not going to be able to control. It is too dangerous. What should we do therefore? There was a discussion. One of our brothers rightly pointed out that the ancients believed in three Erinyes. One of them, Megaera, was the Erinye of jealousy. So, with the help of Augsteiner's formulae, we could transform the spiritual energy slipping from the body of our enemy's father into either Megaera or Tisiphone. The second Erinye, Tisiphone, being the "avenger of murder", while the third, Allecto, is "unremitting in her vengeance". We have to offer two further sacrifices, three in all – our bitter enemy's father, and two others whom he loves to be Tisiphone and Allecto. Everybody agreed with this reasoning. When three Erinyes descend on our greatest enemy, he will turn to an

210

occultist. There can be no doubt that we have a hold on every occultist in the city. Then we will bore into his mind and make him aware of his terrible guilt. It will be the final blow. We cannot blatantly spell out to him where this guilt lies — he has to be deeply convinced of it himself. That is why our plan of self-knowledge is the best one possible. There remains the problem of the two other Erinyes — Tisiphone and Allecto. Who can they be? Whom does he love apart from his father? Does he love anyone at all? Because surely he does not love the prostitute with whom he went away — he who knows all the hideous secrets of the prostituted soul? We resolved to examine this carefully in the light of ancient writings, and we will meet in three days to settle everything.

RÜGENWALDERMÜNDE, FRIDAY, SEPTEMBER 26TH, 1919 NOON

Erika and Mock sat in silence on the covered terrace of a café on the eastern side of the canal, staring out at the stormy sea through small, rectangular windowpanes lashed with fine rain. Both were preoccupied, Erika with her coffee and apple strudel, Mock with his cigar and balloon of cognac. The silence which had come over them heralded imminent chaos, foreshadowed changes, relentlessly signalled the end.

"We've been here for more than two weeks," Mock began, and fell silent again.

"I'd say we've been here for almost three weeks." Erika smoothed her napkin on the marble table.

"This cognac would be a lot of alcohol for you." Mock swirled his glass and watched as the amber liquid ran down its inner sides. "There's still quite a bit left, but for me it's no more than a gulp. I'll knock it back and it'll be gone."

"Yes. In that we differ," Erika said, and she closed her eyes. Two streams of tears trickled from beneath her long lashes down towards the corners of her lips.

Mock riveted his eyes to the windowpanes streaming with rain and listened to the howling of the gale above the sound of the waves. Another gale tore at his chest and forced words into his head that he did not want to utter. He looked about him and shuddered. On the terrace besides them was the prostitute with the broken parasol, whom he knew by sight. She was gazing at the streaming window, grating a spoon in her cup. And now there appeared one other person: the hotel bell-boy. He swiftly ran up to the table occupied by Mock and Erika.

"Registered delivery for Frau Erika Mock," he said, clicking his heels loudly.

Erika accepted the letter, the boy some coins and Mock a few moments of respite. The girl tore open the envelope with a fruit knife and began to read. A faint smile appeared on her lips.

"What is it?" Mock could not resist asking.

"Listen to this." She put the letter on the table and weighted down an unruly corner of the page with the ashtray. "'The man born on September 18th, 1883, in Waldenburg is a typical Virgo, full of inhibitions and unconscious longings. Sad events experienced not long ago – perhaps an unfortunate love affair? – weigh heavily on his mind.'" Erika glanced at Mock with interest. "Tell me, Eberhard, what was this unfortunate love affair . . . You never talk about yourself. You don't want to confide in a crafty whore . . . But now, after three wonderful weeks together . . . Tell me something about yourself . . ."

"There was no unfortunate love affair." Clumsily Mock held Erika's chin in one hand and with his thumb roughly wiped away her tears. "It was the war. I was called up in 1916. I fought on the Eastern front at Dünaburg. I was injured on leave in Königsberg. I fell out of a first-floor window. I was drunk and I can't remember anything. Do you understand,

212

girl?" Mock could not tear his fingers away from her cheeks. "I wasn't hit by Russian shrapnel – I fell out of a window. It's ridiculous and embarrassing. Then I went back to Dünaburg and lived through some hard times there . . . Who compiled this horoscope?"

"My sister sent it to me from Riga. And what, does it fit?"

"From what you've read so far it's so general it has to fit. Every human being has a complicated personality and many strange longings. Keep reading!"

"'In his youth somebody disappointed him badly. Robbed him of his dreams . . .'" Erika continued. "What did you dream of when you were young, Ebi?"

"A career in academia. I even wrote a few papers in Latin." Mock recalled his student years, when five of them had lived in a leaking garret. "But nobody disappointed me in any way. I gave up my studies quite early on. I took a job with the police because I didn't want to live in poverty in some small dark room, with one of my colleagues spitting blood on his translations of the works of Theognis of Megara, and another fishing out bacon rind from behind the stove, where he had chucked it a few weeks earlier, then dusting it off, cooking it over a candle and cutting it into tiny pieces to fill his stomach . . ."

"'He is characterized by irritating punctiliousness and an exaggerated love of detail. When in charge he will point out to his subordinates their untidy clothing as readily as, for example, neglecting to water the flowers . . .'"

"Rubbish," Mock interrupted her. "I don't have a single flower in my office or at home."

"It's not about flowers," Erika explained. "It's about you finding fault with your subordinates for the smallest of things . . . Besides, there's a wonderful *à propos* here . . . 'The example of flowers is inadequate. As a thoroughly practical person he will hold that potatoes should rather be

213

grown in flower pots because at least they would prove useful. He is a man with the heart of a dove, clasping to his breast every lost and frightened creature, a man who could become involved in charity or missionary work. His warm heart experiences a great love once every seven years. And here is a warning to the ladies of his heart . . .'"

Mock was no longer listening because the sea wind had started to howl in his head once more. "What a crafty whore!" he thought. "She's written the horoscope herself. She wants Mock, the dove, to take care of her and clasp her troubled heart to his breast. This man, with his magnanimous and warm heart, is supposed to pick up a piece of rubbish from the gutter that has been thrashed about by the wind, dry it with his kisses and wrap it in an eiderdown of love! Best if we married, we'd have four sweet children – they would inherit her good looks – and I would walk the streets of Breslau with a heavy head, seeing my 'brother-in-law' in each man I met. There I am at a ball and someone introduces her to some creep: 'This is Criminal Councillor Mock's wife.' 'Surely we know each other from somewhere?' There we are at the races in Hartlieb, and the gambler sitting next to me slips the furled tip of his tongue out at my wife . . ."

The wind gave a savage howl and Mock thumped his open palm on the table. The plates jumped; the prostitute sitting a few tables away squinted over her cup.

"Don't read any more of that nonsense," he said quietly. "Let's have a goodbye party. A threesome."

"And who is the other man to be?" Erika folded Mock's horoscope in four and adjusted her hat.

"Not man, woman," Mock hissed. "Your friend sitting over there."

"Please, no. I can't do that," she said softly and began to cry.

Mock lit another cigar and gazed at the prostitute. She looked up from her cup and smiled at him timidly.

"I haven't shared you with anyone over these three weeks." Erika soon pulled herself together, took out a lace handkerchief and wiped her dainty nose. "And I want it to stay that way."

"Two weeks," Mock corrected her. "If you don't want to, then go and pack your bags." He pulled his wallet from his pocket. "Here's some money for your ticket. I'll pay you for everything. How much do you charge?"

"I love you," Erika said calmly, then got up and approached the girl sitting nearby. They spoke for a moment and she returned to Mock.

"We'll wait for you in the ladies' changing room. That's her chamber of ill repute." She turned, put her arm around the girl's waist and they went down to the beach. The wind howled and tugged at the stem of her parasol. A moment later they were on the footbridge leading to the changing room. The prostitute opened the door to the first cabin and they disappeared inside.

Mock paid the waiter and he too went out to the beach. The wind and fine rain had scared off the strollers, setting Mock's bourgeois conscience at rest. He stood still for a while looking about, then furtively ran across the beach, up the steps above the groynes and, sprayed with sea froth, cleared the footbridge and entered the cabin. The two women sat naked on the bench, shivering with cold. As soon as they saw the man they began to caress and embrace each other. Goose pimples appeared on their thighs and arms. Erika kissed the other girl without taking her eyes off Mock. The cold wind rushed in through gaps in the floorboards. The seagulls rent the air with their screeching, and still Erika looked at him. The prostitute beckoned him to join them, and Mock felt everything but sexual arousal. He reached into his trousers and pulled out a hundred-mark note. He handed it to the prostitute.

"This is for you. Get dressed and leave us alone for a moment," he said quietly.

"Thank you, kind sir," she said with a strong Pomeranian accent and pulled on her underwear, then adjusted the folds of her dress. A moment later they were alone.

"Why did you send her away, Ebi?" Erika was still sitting there naked, her dress wrapped around her. "Now that our month is coming to an end, tell me . . . Our honeymoon and the past month . . . Tell me why you sent her away . . . Say that you don't want to share me with anyone during these happy days in Rügenwaldermünde. Lie and tell me you love me . . ."

Mock opened his mouth to tell her the truth, and at that very moment there was a loud knocking on the changing-room door. He sighed with relief and opened it. There stood the hotel bell-boy. A little way off stood the prostitute in her crooked shoes, hunched from the cold.

"A telegram for the good gentleman," said the boy, peeking inquisitively into the depths of the cabin.

Mock gave him some more coins and loudly slammed the door in his face. He sat down next to Erika, opened the telegram and read:

YOUR FATHER HAD ACCIDENT STOP FELL DOWNSTAIRS AT HOME STOP SERIOUS CONDITION STOP IN HOSPITAL STOP AM WAITING BY MAX GRÖTZSCHL'S TELEPHONE STOP SMOLORZ.

20.IX.1919

Everyone arrived punctually. In fact, punctuality is one of our brotherhood's principles, which stems from our respect for the passage of time, for the unchanging laws of nature. *Deus sive natura*,[†] wrote Spinoza and he was absolutely – *par excellence!* – right. But to the point.

From the erudite performance of some of our brothers (and this erudition was gleaned from Roscher's mythological lexicon) we learned a great

† "God or Nature" (i.e. "God is not distinguishable from Nature").

216

deal about the ancient avengers the Erinyes, black-skinned and wrapped in black clothing. These goddesses of vengeance, as we learned from Brother Eckhard of Prague, hid in morning mists or glided in dark, stormy clouds, and their hair and cloaks were charged with electricity because, as Plutarch writes, "fire flickered in their cloaks and viperous knots of hair". These "bitches of Styx" rendered people mad with their ominous barking, infected germinating grains with their poisonous breath, lashed those who transgressed the laws of nature with their whip. (How well this fits in with our doctrine of Natura Magna Mater!) And how can one most keenly violate the laws of Nature? By killing her who gives life, by matricide, concluded Brother Eckhard. These natural ethics became the basis of the popular ancient notion of the Erinyes as goddesses of vengeance.

A heated discussion broke out after Brother Eckhart's lecture. The first question concerned the universality of the Erinyes. Brother Hermann of Marburg asked whether the Erinyes are independent beings or whether they are allocated to one murdered person in particular? After all, argued Brother Hermann, Homer writes that following the suicide of Jocasta, mother of Oedipus, Oedipus was tormented not by Erinyes "in general" or "Erinyes as such", but by his mother's particular Erinyes. In Aeschylus we read that Orestes was tormented first by the Erinyes of his father, who had been hacked to death by his mother, and only later, after Orestes had taken vengeance for the death of his father in the same way on his mother, Clytemnestra, the murderess of her husband, only then did the Erinyes of Clytemnestra appear. The first, Agamemnon's Erinyes, forced his son Orestes to avenge his father's death, the second, Clytemnestra's Erinyes, tormented the matricide. So the Erinyes, as Brother Hermann argues, belong to a particular, given soul: they are not independent or universal beings. Brother Hermann's reasoning was convincing, and nobody disagreed with him.

I took the voice and agreed that after offering up the father of our bitter enemy in sacrifice, we will unleash specific Erinyes, those appropriate to the old man's soul. I also said that the appearance of Jocasta's Erinyes, those which tormented Oedipus, clearly demonstrates that the haunted person does not have to have killed with his own hands (after all, Jocasta committed suicide!) but he has to be the one to blame (and Oedipus is certainly to blame!). This is the basic principle of the Erinyes' materializing!

I received applause and those assembled raised the other issue which had come up after the lecture given by Brother Eckhard of Prague. Namely, can the Erinyes take vengeance for patricide, or only for matricide? The Master argued the legitimacy of the former view, quoting the appropriate passages from Homer and Aeschylus. It was clear from these that the Erinyes of Laius, killed by his son Oedipus, haunt the murderer, proving that patricide, too, is a violation of nature's laws. After the Master's declaration, everything became clear: it would be right to offer the father of our sworn enemy in sacrifice. This father must be convinced, however, that he is dying because of his son. I told the assembly that we would make this known to him before his death, just as we made it known to that scabby harlot.

After that it was Johann of Munich who took the voice. He went back to the issue which had initially brought us together, and which we were supposed to be clarifying with the help of ancient literature, namely, since there were three Erinyes – Allecto, Megaera and Tisiphone – then is it necessary to make three offerings, each corresponding to the "essential" characteristics of a given Erinyes? The majority responded in the negative. First of all, reasoned Brother Johann, the triple and individualized Erinyes appear only in Euripides, and are therefore already removed in time from the primeval notion, from the most primitive (and therefore the most authentic!) beliefs; secondly, in later literature (mainly Roman!), they become confused and take each other's places. For example, to one author

Megaera is the personification of "relentless jealousy", to another it is Tisiphone. It is evident from this that our second and possibly third sacrifices would be sacrifices offered in the dark, without any firm grounds – in other words, unnecessary sacrifices. The last word belonged to the Master. He supported Johann of Munich's view and gave me instructions to offer in sacrifice only the father of our sworn enemy.

When they had all left, a feeling of irritation swept over me. The Master had not let me take the voice! I had not managed to say that the Erinyes do not have to be particles of a parent's soul alone. In Sophocles' *Women of Trachis*, the Erinyes are invoked against Deianira, who unwittingly killed her lover Heracles! And in the same author's *Electra*, the Erinyes are called upon to avenge matrimonial infidelity! I have made a decision: I am going to kill the one who loves our greatest enemy, and I will make it known to her before she dies that she is dying through his fault and because of him! I will be releasing not only his father's Erinyes, but also the Erinyes of the woman who is in love with him! In this way I will put an end to everything. I will bring down upon him a twofold attack of the Erinyes. Then they will sing out their dismal hymn inside his head, a song which, like the songs of the Tyrolean snow maidens, will drive him insane. And only then will he turn to an occultist for help. And only then will he get to know the truth and become aware of his mistake!

BRESLAU, THAT SAME SEPTEMBER 26TH, 1919
A QUARTER PAST TWELVE IN THE AFTERNOON

Kurt Smolorz sat at the marble table in the waiting room of his neighbour, the solicitor Doctor Max Grötzschl, lazily leafing through the *Ostdeutsche Sport Zeitung*. The articles did not particularly interest him. Only one thing interested Smolorz: how the instructions Mock was going to give him that day would complicate his evening rendez-vous with

Baroness von Bockenheim und Bielau. He was soon to find out: the telephone on the marble table jumped and rang loudly. Smolorz lifted the round receiver from its cradle and held it to his ear. With his other hand he grasped the mouthpiece and brought it to his lips. He tilted back his chair with an expression of a man of the world.

"May I speak to Doctor Grötzschl?" said a woman's quiet voice. He did not know how to react. Usually at moments like this, when he was at a loss as to know what to do, he scaled down his reactions and did nothing. So it was now. He simply looked at the receiver and replaced it on the cradle. The telephone rang again. This time Smolorz was not in such a predicament as a few seconds earlier.

"Go on, Smolorz." He heard Mock's hoarse bass. "Tell me what's happened to my father!"

"There were noises in the house last night," Smolorz mumbled. "He went to check and fell down the stairs. Fractured his leg and injured his head. The dog barked and woke the neighbours. A certain Mr Dosche took him to St Elisabeth Hospital. He's in good care. Unconscious. On a drip."

"Call Doctor Cornelius Rühtgard immediately on seventeen sixty-three. If he's not at home, call the Wenzel-Hancke Hospital. Tell him I want him to take care of my father." Mock fell silent. Smolorz did not say anything either and, staring at the tube into which he had just spoken, wondered at the fundamental nature of telephone communications. "How's our investigation going?" Smolorz heard Mock say.

"Twenty young female invalids in wheelchairs in the whole of Breslau. We visited them with Frenzel . . ."

"Frenzel has turned up?" Smolorz could hear the hoarse bass voice tremble with joy at the other end of the receiver.

"Yes. He's a gambler. He was betting at Orlich's. Arm-wrestling. He lost, and two days later went home broke."

"And what? You showed Frenzel those women? Discreetly, I hope?"

"Yes. Discreetly. From a distance. Frenzel in a car, the women in the wheelchairs on the street. He recognized one of them. Louise Rossdeutscher, daughter of the physician Doctor Horst Rossdeutscher. The father is a big fish. Commissioner Mühlhaus knows him."

"This Rossdeutscher, was he questioned?"

"No. Mühlhaus is prevaricating. Big fish."

"What's that supposed to mean, damn it, 'big fish'?" growled the voice in the receiver. "Explain, Smolorz!"

"Commissioner Mühlhaus said he's 'an important person'." Smolorz could not help being amazed by the fact that here he was, grasping all of Mock's emotions over the telephone, even though the latter was hundreds of kilometres away from Breslau. "'We have to proceed carefully. I know him.' That's what he said."

"Is Rossdeutscher being watched?"

"Yes. All the time."

"Good, Smolorz." The crack of a match resounded in the receiver. "Now listen. I'm arriving in Breslau tomorrow, at 7.14 in the evening. At that very hour you're to be waiting for me at Main Station. Wirth, Zupitza and ten of their men are to be with you. You're going to show the girl I'm with — you know, it's that red-headed Erika — a photograph of Louise Rossdeutscher . . . If you don't have a photograph of her, get in touch with Helmut Ehlers and pass my request on to him: he's to take a photograph of Louise Rossdeutscher's face by tomorrow. Remember — tomorrow, 7.14 at the station. And don't plan anything else . . . For the whole evening and night you're to be at my disposition. By tomorrow you're to have gathered every scrap of information you can about this doctor. I know it might be difficult, officially we've been removed from the investigation and Mühlhaus is treating the suspect like a rotten egg, but do whatever is in your power. Any questions?"

"Yes. Is Rossdeutscher suspected of all these murders?"

"Think, Smolorz." Cigarette smoke expelled from Mock's lungs hit the telephone membrane. "The four sailors were stuffed with morphine before they died. Who has access to a lot of morphine? A physician. I don't know whether Rossdeutscher is a suspect, but I do know that he and his daughter were probably the last people to see those dressed-up men. I want Rossdeutscher with his back up against the wall."

"One more question. Why Wirth and Zupitza?"

"How would you describe Mühlhaus' behaviour as regards Ross-deutscher?" This time Smolorz heard the voice of a kind-hearted teacher examining a dull-witted pupil. "He's afraid to interrogate him, he speaks of him as 'an important person' and so on . . . How would you describe such behaviour?"

"I'd say he's fluffing about."

"Good, Smolorz." Mock had stopped sounding kind-hearted. "Mühlhaus is fluffing about. We're not going to fluff about. That's why I want Wirth and Zupitza."

BRESLAU, SATURDAY, SEPTEMBER 27TH, 1919
7.14 IN THE EVENING

The train from Stettin pulled into Breslau's Main Station. Erika Kiesewalter held her head out of the window. Through tears forced from her eyes by the rush of air she watched the fleeing platforms, the flower kiosks, the mighty iron columns holding up the glass vault, and the tobacco and newspaper kiosks. White columns of steam blew onto the platforms and enveloped the people waiting there in a warm cloud. On the whole they stood alone, most of them elegantly attired gentlemen wearing velvet gloves and holding bunches of flowers wrapped in coarse parchment. There would also generally be a few dignified ladies amongst them who, at the sight of much-missed and long-awaited faces at the carriage windows, would suddenly open their parasols or tear their hands away from their lips to send kisses into the distance. There was no shortage of similar types on the platform now. But the group of thirteen glum-looking men, most with peaked or soft caps pulled down to their ears, formed a clear contrast. The sleeper carriage stopped practically in front of them. The men looked like bandits and Erika watched them anxiously, but she was soon reassured by the sight of the familiar face framed by wiry red hair that belonged to Mock's subordinate. Mock himself, entrusting their suitcases to a porter, stepped off the train and – much to his colleague's surprise – slipped his hands beneath Erika's arms, spun her like a child and stood her on the platform. He shook the hands of the red-headed man and of two other men who, though diametrically opposite in height, had one characteristic in common: both were repulsive.

"You have the photograph, Smolorz?" Mock asked.

Smolorz looked drunk. He was swaying on his legs and grinning inanely. Without a word he pulled a large photograph from his briefcase and handed it to Erika. She looked at the girl in the photograph and said without prompting:

"Yes, I recognize her. She's the one who came with her father to the apartment on Gartenstrasse."

"Good," Mock muttered, casting a critical eye at Smolorz. "And now to business. Are Mühlhaus' men tailing Rossdeutscher? And where is my father?"

"At Wenzel-Hancke Hospital in the care of Doctor Rühtgard," Smolorz said, answering Mock's questions in the order of their importance. "I don't know how it stands with Rossdeutscher. There's nothing about him in our archives. Nothing at all. Only his address. Carlowitz, Korsoallee 52. Here's what I found out about him." He handed Mock a piece of paper covered in even writing.

"Good, Smolorz," Mock said, and his expression changed as he read on. "It appears our Rossdeutscher was accused by the Breslau Chamber of Medicine of practising the occult on his patients . . . He successfully defended himself against the accusations . . . And he is extremely well connected . . ."

Mock looked about him. Their party had drawn attention to itself. A newspaper vendor was staring at them, a beggar was pleading for a few marks.

"Get rid of them, Wirth." Mock glanced at the short man in the bowler hat who with one gesture passed on the instructions to the giant standing next to him. The latter lurched towards the gawpers and they dispersed in clouds of steam.

"Smolorz," Mock said, nodding towards Erika, "take Miss Kiese-walter to the apartment on Gartenstrasse. You're to keep an eye on her until I send somebody to relieve you. And not a drop more today, under-stood? The rest of us" – he looked at Wirth – "are off. First to the hospital, and then to Carlowitz to pay Doctor Rossdeutscher a visit."

He approached Erika and kissed her on the lips.

"Thank you for saying 'Miss Kiesewalter'," she whispered, returning the kiss, "and not simply 'take her, Smolorz'. Thank you for not saying 'her' . . ."

"Did I really say that?" Mock smiled, and ran his rough hand across her pale cheek.

BRESLAU, THAT SAME SEPTEMBER 27TH, 1919
EIGHT O'CLOCK IN THE EVENING

Smolorz unlocked the door to the sailors' apartment, stepped inside first and slammed the door in Erika's face. He switched on all the lights and carefully inspected the rooms, and only then did he re-open the door. He

224

took Erika by the elbow and led her in, bolting the door behind them, and sat down heavily at the kitchen table. He produced a bottle of Danzig Łosoś liqueur from his briefcase and poured a sizeable shot into a clean glass. As he sipped the burning liquid he watched Erika hang up her coat in the hall and then, dressed in a hat and a tight, cherry-red dress, enter the main room, bend over the bed and straighten the tangled sheets which nobody had changed for three weeks. Erika's hips and the crumpled sheets from which, Smolorz presumed, her scent still emanated fuddled his thoughts for a moment. He remembered the Baroness writhing among the damp sheets and her husband standing next to the bed with an expression of curiosity, and then Baron von Bockenheim und Bielau sniffing some white powder and scattering acrid clouds all around himself with his coughing.

His next sip of Łosoś liqueur did not taste as good. He blamed this on the image of the polite, haughty Baron before his eyes. To make the drink taste better he turned his thoughts to the people who stirred warm feelings in him. What was his little Arthur doing now? Was he playing with his toy car? The liqueur was excellent. Was he kneeling on the kitchen floor in his thick trousers, reinforced on the backside with a leather patch, and pushing the little model Daimler along one of the well-polished floorboards? Cleanliness in the kitchen made him think of his wife, Ursula Smolorz. There she was, kneeling on the kitchen floor scrubbing the smooth floorboards with Ergon powder. Her strong arms, her gently swaying breasts, her tearful, freckled face, her rending sobs as Smolorz, pushing her aside, slammed the door and made his way blind drunk towards the stately villa on Wagnerstrasse, where the Baroness was waiting for him in velvet sheets, clammy with sweat. Little Arthur had cried when his furious mother explained to him in a lowered voice that Papa didn't love him any more, that he loved some trollop instead. "What's a trollop, Mama?" "An evil viper, the devil in human flesh," she had explained. Arthur Smolorz had run from his father when he wanted to pick him up, and had yelled to high heaven: "I don't want you, go to the trollop!" The Criminal Sergeant reached for his bottle. He knew what worked best on a guilty conscience.

BRESLAU, THAT SAME SEPTEMBER 27TH, 1919
EIGHT O'CLOCK IN THE EVENING

Sister Hermina, on duty in the surgical ward at Wenzel-Hancke Hospital, replaced the telephone receiver. She was as aggravated as an angry wasp. Yet again that day she had received instructions from Doctor Rühtgard, and yet again, in the confines of her heart, she expressed her disapproval. What was it supposed to mean? Since when was she receiving instructions from a doctor in another department? She decided to complain to her immediate superior, Doctor Karl Heintze, Head of Surgery. What impudence! This Rühtgard, as a dermatologist, ought to restrict himself to his rotting prostitutes and his lustful middle-class men devoured by tertiary syphilis! Sister Hermina chased away these bad thoughts, incompatible as they were with her gentle, understanding nature consolidated by years in the service of others. Through the glazed panel of the duty room, she watched as two orderlies pushed a wheelchair in which pot-bellied Herr Karl Hadamitzky, dazed with morphine, travelled towards the operating theatre, to encounter the drainage tube and scalpel that were destined to cut away the cancerous growth from his kidney.

The wheelchair was followed by a man who was running. His jacket was unbuttoned and he was fanning himself with a bowler hat. Sister Hermina stared at him for a while, her attention drawn to his sallow skin darkened by a considerable five-o'clock shadow, his broad shoulders and his black, wavy hair. He passed her duty room without a word of explanation as to who he was or what he was doing there. That was too much.

226

"Hey, my good man!" she shouted in a loud, almost masculine voice. "Are you visiting one of our patients? You have to report to me first!"

"Eberhard Mock," the man said in a deep, hoarse voice. "I am indeed. I'm going to visit my father, Willibald Mock."

Saying this he donned his bowler hat and then removed it, bowing to Sister Hermina. This greeting was as ironic as it was courteous. Without waiting for her permission, and disregarding any reaction she may have had, he walked briskly down the corridor.

"Mock Willibald, Mock Willibald," the irate nurse repeated, running her finger down the column of names. A moment later her finger stopped short. "Ah, he's the one who found himself on our ward on Doctor Rühtgard's instructions. He's the patient requiring special care! What's that supposed to mean, 'special care'? They all require special care! Not only the elderly Willibald Mock! I'll soon put a stop to this!"

Sister Hermina reached for the telephone and dialled Professor Heintze's home number.

"Doctor Heintze's residence," said a well-spoken male voice at the other end of the receiver.

"It's Sister Hermina from Wenzel-Hancke Municipal Hospital. May I speak to the doctor, please?"

The butler did not deign to reply and placed the receiver next to the telephone. She knew he always behaved like this when he heard someone introduce themselves with a name not preceded by a scholarly title. She heard the strains of a piano, merry voices and the tinkling of glasses. The usual sounds of a party being held at the professor's on a Saturday evening.

"Yes, sister," Doctor Heintze's voice was none too friendly.

"That Doctor Rühtgard from the Department of Contagious Diseases, Professor, is bossing everyone around and giving me instructions as to that . . ."

"Ah, I know what this is about, Sister," Doctor Heintze interrupted her snappily. "Please listen to me carefully. You may regard all of Doctor Rühtgard's instructions as if they were my own. Do you understand me, Sister?" The receiver crashed onto its cradle.

Sister Hermina was no longer annoyed, but curious. Who was this old man with concussion and a double fracture of the leg? Most certainly someone important. That's why Rühtgard had told them to transfer him to a private room and look after him night and day, despite the shortage of staff. And now this son of his . . . Elegant and arrogant.

Sister Hermina made her way down the corridor towards the private room where the older Herr Mock lay. The rustle of her starched housecoat and the sight of the broken wings on her bonnet animated the patients and filled them with hope. They propped themselves up in bed and paid no heed to their pain, certain that in a short while, with a single injection and an understanding glance, Sister Hermina would take them to a land of gentleness and peace. Their hopes, however, were in vain. Sister Hermina knocked on the door of the private room and, getting no reply, entered. It was hardly surprising no-one had invited her in: the older Herr Mock was lying unconscious while his son was pressing his father's hand, riddled with needle marks, to his lips. She looked at the younger Herr Mock and was disgusted. She was always disgusted at the sight of a grown man crying.

BRESLAU, THAT SAME SEPTEMBER 27TH, 1919
ELEVEN O'CLOCK AT NIGHT

Sister Hermina, urine bottle in hand, approached the door to the private room and opened it wide, certain she would see the two men asleep again. One of them, as Sister Hermina told herself somewhat bombastically, had been lulled by physical pain, the other by spiritual. This time Sister

Hermina's otherwise faultless intuition had let her down. Neither of them was asleep. The older Herr Mock interrupted some lengthy utterance when he saw her and took the bottle with visible relief. The younger Herr Mock, obviously not wishing to disturb his father, went into the corridor and lit a cigarette. Sister Hermina carried out the embarrassing object and, remembering Doctor Heintze's harsh words, restrained herself from pointing out to the smoker the unsuitability of surrendering to such a pernicious addiction in a place like this. The younger Herr Mock, as if reading her thoughts, extinguished the cigarette with his shoe, wrapped it in a scrap of paper and went back into the room. The sister slid the urine bottle onto the lower part of her trolley that was stacked with clean sheets, removed her impressively large bonnet and pressed her ear to a gap in the door.

"If you'd been at home at the time," she heard the sick man's muffled moan, "you'd have scared off that burglar who made such a racket in the night . . ."

"It wasn't a burglar, Father," the hoarse, bass voice interrupted him. "Burglars don't make a noise . . . If you'd agreed to move out of the house, if you weren't so stubborn, this accident wouldn't have happened . . ."

"If, if . . ." The older man must have been regaining his strength since he was aping his son so well. "What a louse . . . Telling me it's all my fault . . . Is that it? My fault? Who was it who went off with some whore to God knows where, and left the old man alone without any help? Who? Father Christmas? No, my own son, Eberhard . . . No-one else but he . . . And you, old man, you can snuff it, it's time for you to go . . . That's how grateful he is to his father . . ."

"And what, in truth, should I be grateful to you for, Father?" Sister Hermina had heard that tone many times before, that suppressed timbre. This was the way people spoke who, on learning of the death of someone close to them, were trying desperately not to show their weakness.

229

Intonation through the whole range of notes, like in an adolescent boy.

Silence. Steam hissed in the sterilising units, patients groaned in their sleep, the kidney-shaped metal dish containing Herr Hadamitzky's cancerous tissues clattered against the flagstones of the operating theatre; the hospital was falling asleep; the cockroaches under the sinks and in the damp crannies beneath the sewer pipes were waking.

In the gap of the door left ajar appeared the eye as well as the ear of Sister Hermina. The sick man was gripping his son's hand tightly. The two hands with their short, fat fingers were identical.

"You're right." The older man's voice wheezed like that of a dying man. Pain crossed his face in waves. "Any ass can have it off and spawn. You're right . . . That's all you have to be grateful to me for . . ."

The son squeezed his father's hand so hard that Sister Hermina could have sworn it made the old man's leg jump, even though it was encased in stiff wooden splints.

"I'll never leave you again," the son said.

He stood up and rushed to the door. Sister Hermina sprang away. The departing visitor had a strange glint in his eyes as he passed her. "He must have noticed my embarrassment," she thought as she adjusted her bonnet. Her dry, downy cheeks glowed. "And he's going to think I'm knocked out at the sight of him."

Sister Hermina was wrong. She was the last person Criminal Assistant Eberhard Mock was thinking about at that moment.

BRESLAU, THAT SAME SEPTEMBER 27TH, 1919
A QUARTER PAST ELEVEN AT NIGHT

A new Adler stood on Korsoallee opposite Doctor Rossdeutscher's grand villa. Four glowing cigarettes betrayed the presence of the passengers inside. Similar lights glowed beneath two large linden trees next to the villa's railings, spiked like flames. The windows of the house were lit up, and through the partially lowered blinds came the sound of raised voices, as if someone were arguing or taking a ceremonial oath.

A solitary man appeared in the silent street. There was a cigarette glowing in the corner of his mouth too. He approached the car and pulled open the back door on the driver's side.

"Move up, Reinert," he said hoarsely. "I'm not slim enough to squeeze in next to you any more."

"It's Mock," Reinert said, and obediently moved across the seat.

Mock looked around the interior of the dark car and recognized other police officers from the Murder Commission: behind the steering wheel sat Ehlers, and the back seat was occupied by the inseparable Reinert and Kleinfeld. Next to the driver was a man in a top hat with his fat thighs spread across the seat. Mock did not recognize him.

"Tell me, gentlemen," Mock whispered, "what are you doing here? And what about those clever investigators by the trees? Their cigarettes are visible from the banks of the Oder. Everyone leaving the Am Alten Oder tavern is asking himself: who are those two lurking beneath the trees? Don't you think Doctor Rossdeutscher's servants might be asking themselves the same question?"

"The servants aren't home," Ehlers said. "The cook and butler left the house at about six."

"Who's this?" said the stranger in the top hat. A monocle gleamed in one angry eye. "And what right has he got to be asking such questions?"

"Criminal Assistant Eberhard Mock, Doctor Pyttlik," Ehlers said coldly. "He has more right than anybody to be asking such questions. And it's our duty to answer them."

"Don't lecture me on my duties, Ehlers." The monocle fell onto the lapel of the infuriated Doctor Pyttlik. "I, as the representative of the

231

municipal authorities, am your superior here. I know who Mock is and I know the pitiful role he is playing in this case. I also know that Mock has been removed from the investigation and is on leave." Doctor Pyttlik suddenly swivelled his hundred-kilogram body in his seat and the Adler rocked on its suspension. "What are you doing here, damn it, Mock? You ought to be mushroom-picking, or fishing . . ."

On his face Mock felt breath permeated with the smoke of a cheap cigar. In his head he counted to twenty in Latin and stared at the enraged Doctor Pyttlik.

"Herr Pyttlik, you said . . ." Mock was still whispering.

"*Doctor* Pyttlik," corrected the owner of the scholarly title.

"Herr Pyttlik, you said you know the pitiful role I'm playing in this whole affair. And what role are you playing? Is it not equally pitiful?"

"How dare he!" Pyttlik choked on self-righteous indignation. "Tell him, Kleinfeld, who I am in all this . . ."

"You can tell him yourself," Kleinfeld smiled. "You're not some taciturn Moses for whom the eloquent Aaron has to speak."

"I am here as the Mayor's plenipotentiary." Pyttlik raised his voice. "And I'm to see to it that the apprehension of Doctor Rossdeutscher takes place according to the law. Besides, I'm in charge of the operation and I'll give the order when to start."

"He's in charge? He's the boss here?" Mock gave himself a light slap on the cheek as if to sober up. "This is the new police president?"

"Without Herr Pyttlik's decision . . ." Ehlers said.

"*Doctor* Pyttlik." The plenipotentiary was fuming.

"Herr Pyttlik decides." Ehlers did not pay the slightest attention to the man. "Those are Commissioner Mühlhaus' orders."

"Where is Mühlhaus?" Mock rubbed his eyes.

"What business is that of yours?" Pyttlik lowered his voice to a whisper. "Go somewhere else, take a break . . . Go and pick some mushrooms . . ."

"Where is Mühlhaus?" Mock looked Reinert in the eyes.

"Negotiating," Reinert muttered. "He's asking the Mayor for permission to detain and question Doctor Rossdeutscher."

"Now? He's negotiating at night?" This time Mock looked at Pyttlik.

"Not now," sighed the plenipotentiary, resigned. "Unfortunately, no. Just now the Mayor's at a reception and won't be receiving Commissioner Mühlhaus until tomorrow. And we have to sit here until the morning to wait for the Mayor's decision. Because we can't leave this house . . ." He threw a longing glance at the nearby tavern.

Mock climbed out of the car and slammed the door. He stood on the pavement for a moment and stared at one of the windows of the villa. Suddenly a woman's voice rose above all the others. A high-pitched incantation reached the ears of the police officers. The song of the sirens. This association helped Mock regain peace of mind after his exchange with Pyttlik. He was back in the classroom in his secondary school, in a classics lesson. Amidst maps of Italia and Hellas, amidst plaster busts on which pupils had left the marks of their schoolboy woes, amidst Greek and Latin conjugations, young Eberhard Mock gives his answers. He recites a fragment of *The Odyssey*, and with the help of pacy hexameters reveals the image of Odysseus tied to the mast, summoned by the siren song of the temptresses. Homer's verses rang out in the quietness of Korsoallee.

"They're happy. Singing away," Pyttlik said, indicating the bright windows of Rossdeutscher's villa. "But what's with him?" He pointed at Mock. "Has he gone mad? What's he gabbling about?"

Mock walked around the car and up to the passenger window from which poked a top hat.

"Thank you for your explanation, Doctor Pyttlik," said Mock. "I have one more question. I wanted to make sure. I don't know whether you are aware . . . Doctor Rossdeutscher made use of the services of the four

233

murdered male prostitutes, so he is most likely the last person to have seen them. He has to be questioned. Nobody is doing so. Instead the Mayor sends you, Doctor, makes you responsible for the entire operation — in other words entrusts you with Commissioner Mühlhaus' duties, but has no time for Commissioner Mühlhaus himself. Is that it, Doctor Pyttlik?"

"I won't take this," Pyttlik said and flounced in his seat, making the car sink once more on its new, beautifully balanced suspension. "Your insinuations regarding the Mayor are highly . . ."

Mock whistled three times. He then spread his fingers across Pyttlik's bloated face and gave it a hard push towards Ehlers. He heard the crunch of a top hat being crushed. Six men rushed into the street from the tavern side, and seven more from the park. The two detectives beneath the trees left their posts and walked up to the Adler in bewilderment. Pyttlik tried to clamber out of the car in his squashed hat.

"Now I'm in command," Mock said to the face of the raging boor, and he jammed the door with his foot.

"This is an act of violence!" Pyttlik yelled, unable to climb out of the car. "An assault on a representative of the Mayor! I'll make you pay for this, Mock. You're finished! Seize him!" he shouted to the two detectives who had left their posts beneath the linden trees and were now watching the whole incident with expressions of indifference. "Arrest him!"

"Don't move," Ehlers barked at them from the car. "This is an assault, Doctor Pyttlik. You said so yourself. We've been terrorized."

"He assaulted me! Attacked me!" Pyttlik hollered, and again the Adler rocked from side to side. "You are my witnesses!"

"Did you see anything, Kleinfeld?" Reinert asked languidly as he watched Mock force open the dangerously spiky railings with the help of a towering strongman.

Mock's men easily cleared the fence and dispersed around Doctor

Rossdeutscher's villa at a run. The giant opened the kitchen door with what Reinert surmised was a pick-lock. Mock said something in a low voice to a short man in a bowler hat and the latter passed this on to the strongman with a few hand movements. Mock entered the house and his men slipped in after him.

"Did you see anything, Kleinfeld?" Reinert asked again. "Did anyone attack anyone?"

"No, nothing at all," Kleinfeld muttered. "All I see is that Herr Pyttlik can't make himself comfortable in the car. He keeps on wriggling like Jonah in the belly of the whale."

27.IX.1919

In the evening there was to be a meeting at which we had to gain the acceptance of the deities. The summoning of the Erinyes did not in itself seem a difficult task, but to do this contrary to the will of the Highest would have been a terrible sacrilege. My duty as chronicler of our brotherhood is to describe accurately these rites of acceptance.

Present at the meeting were: the Master, the Brothers Eckhard of Prague, Hermann of Marburg and Johann of Munich. Also there were all the brothers from Breslau. After prayers to Natura Magna Mater we commenced the initiation rites. The hymn to Cybele followed by the ancient Indian mantras in honour of Gauri sent our medium into a trance. After a while, the deity spoke in the medium's high-pitched voice. Brother Johann of Munich translated, while brother Hermann of Marburg noted down the deity's message. Our medium has great power. The daughter has all her father's strength, certainly. This power has only to be freed. The medium was able to free all the beings circulating around her. Was able to pick up mighty clusters of spiritual energy from supersensory reality. We heard whispers and voices all around and within the house, and . . . [the rest is illegible zigzags].

BRESLAU, SUNDAY, SEPTEMBER 28TH, 1919
A QUARTER PAST MIDNIGHT

Mock stood in the doorway of a vast room and studied the people assembled there. He could do so quite openly and without inhibition, because everybody was completely and utterly focussed on a woman in a wheelchair; all eyes were glued to her lips. The woman was shouting something in a shrill voice, and as she did so her veil billowed about her large head. It looked as though her hair had either been shaved or plastered down. Mock's brain, geared towards philology as always, registered the hissing sibilants in the invalid's cries, which constructed entire sentences fused by a clearly stressed rhythm.

In this enormous room with panelled walls blackened with age, empty but for seven leather armchairs and piles of ancient publications on a three-metre-long desk, sat seven men. All were in evening attire, with snow-white shirt-fronts shining from the lapels of their tailcoats. The eldest of those assembled was translating the invalid's ecstatic groans and a fifty-year-old bearded man who looked like an office worker was noting down the translation, while the rest fixed their anxious eyes on the crippled prophetess.

It sounded to Mock as if the woman was reciting some poem in a language unknown to him. He felt genuine admiration for the elderly man who was interpreting these utterances *ex abrupto*, and indeed slowly and clearly enough for the bearded secretary sitting next to him to note everything down accurately. Every now and again the secretary tossed the page on which he had written onto a pile of others held together with a steel paper clip.

236

Mock stepped into the room and clapped loudly.

"Take a break, good gentlemen," he shouted.

Nobody took anything. The invalid continued to spit out dark tautologies, the veil sticking to the saliva on her lips. The assembly did not take their eyes off her. The man leading the meeting made a mistake in his interpretation, and the bearded secretary crossed out something in his notes. Nobody so much as glanced at Mock.

"Which of you gentlemen is Doctor Rossdeutscher?" asked Mock.

He was answered by the cries of the lame Sybil. She choked and spluttered over the agglomerations of consonants which no vowel severed, no anaptyxis disjoined. Mock walked around those gathered there and approached the secretary. He reached for the pile of papers, unfastened the clip and pulled out a few sheets from the very middle. He began to read.

"It is he," the leader translated, and his secretary noted everything in cursive script. "He is here. Our greatest enemy. He is here!"

"I have conducted an experiment; time will verify its results. How did I do it? I isolated the man and forced him to confess to his adultery in writing. It was a terrible confession for him to have to make since he was permeated to the bone with middle-class morality. I brought this man to a certain place late at night. He was bound and gagged. I freed his right hand, tied him to a chair and then asked him once again to deny what he had written previously, promising him that if he obeyed I would give this second letter to his wife. Feverishly he scribbled something down. I took the second letter, the denial, and slipped it down the drain. I witnessed his fury and his pain. 'I'm going to come back here,' his eyes told me. Then I took the man out to the carriage and drove away. Later I killed him, leaving him where he was sure to be found. His ghost will return and draw the attention of the inhabitants of that place to the drain," Mock read.

The medium began to wail. She rubbed her twisted knees, dribbled saliva and thrashed her head about. The veil slid slowly down her smooth skull. A gloved hand slipped through the folds of her dress. Her screams, which sounded like the howling of an enraged bitch, infected the translator.

"It's him! It's him!" translated the man. "Kill him! Kill!"

"I ate my supper and approached the tenements into which the prostitute I was tailing the day before yesterday had disappeared. I waited. She emerged at about midnight and winked meaningfully at me. A moment later we were in a droschka, and a quarter of an hour after that at the place where we bring offerings to the souls of our ancestors. She undressed, and for a generous sum allowed me to tie her up. She did not protest even when I gagged her. She had terrible eczema on her neck. This constituted the fulfilment of anticipation. After all, yesterday I offered up to science Director W., aged sixty, who had identical eczema. And his was on the neck, too!,'" Mock read.

He put down the pile of papers and looked at the bearded secretary. Police cars could be heard entering Korsoallee. Mock was assailed by piercing sounds from all sides: the wailing of sirens, the high-pitched yowls of the bitch, the howling of the sea wind. He grabbed the scribe by the throat and forced him to the back of the armchair, so that his balding head thudded dully against the wood at the top of the backrest.

"Did you write this, you son of a whore?" Mock's lower jaw jutted out as he covered the secretary's beard with thick gobbets of saliva. All of a sudden he felt a blow on his thigh. He spun around and turned to stone. The creature in the wheelchair had wispy, plastered-down hair. Through it he could see white patches of skin with dark blotches here and there; sparse clumps grew over the horny edges. The tip of her tongue vibrated in her open, gabbling mouth. Her egg-shaped head thrashed from side to side, with first one temple then the other thumping against the back of the wheelchair.

238

"Slaughter him! Slaughter him! Tear him apart!"

Mock drew back his arm as if to take a swing.

"Don't hit her!" he heard the secretary shout. "She'll tell you everything! You'll realize your mistake, Mock! You were wrong that time in Königsberg! Admit your mistake!"

Mock's head found itself momentarily in the harbour of his elbow and arm. He struck. He felt pain in his wrist. The cripple opened her eyes wide and, falling backwards with the wheelchair, spat out the tongue she had just bitten off. She was no longer choking on the indigestible groups of consonants, she was choking on her own blood.

The secretary ran to her, kneeled down and turned her on her side. The invalid kicked out her twisted legs in agony. The secretary tore his bloodied cheek away from her head and stared at Mock. A swollen weal cut across his face; one eye glistened, circumscribed by a band of gore.

"My name is Doctor Horst Rossdeutscher," he said, wiping the blood from his face. He pointed to the prostrate being. "And that's my daughter, Louise Rossdeutscher. You've killed her, Mock. The strongest medium that ever lived. I satisfied all her whims, fulfilled all her needs, and you, a shoemaker's son, killed her with one blow of your hoof."

The sound of metal-capped shoes resounded on the stairs. Doctor Pyttlik and Commissioner Mühlhaus were on their way up to the first floor.

"But vengeance will come, Mock," yelled Rossdeutscher as he slipped his hand into the inside pocket of his tailcoat. "The Erinyes born of the corpses of those closest to you will find you." Rossdeutscher pulled out a gun and put it in his mouth. "Those whom you love, Mock . . ." – the barrel of the gun made him lisp – "tell us, where are they now? . . ." He pulled the trigger. The sirens were silenced.

Mock ran up to the fourth floor of the tenement on Gartenstrasse, taking three stairs at a time. The loud pounding of his brogues on the wooden steps woke the residents and their dogs. He conquered floor after floor chased by barking, swearing and the stench that erupted from dirty kitchens and draughty toilets.

At last he found himself outside the door to number 20. He rapped out the rhythm of "Schlesierlied": slow-slow-slow, pause, slow-slow-slow-slow-quick-quick. Silence. In a low voice he sang *"Kehr ich einst zur Heimat wieder"*.† Pausing to check that he had remembered the rhythm correctly, he tapped it out again. He was answered by abuse from a neighbour on the floor below who had opened his door and was spouting gutter obscenities.

Mock went down one flight of stairs to watch the man raging in the corridor and allowed the stream of abuse to flow on. But when the neighbour — who was clearly drunk and dressed in one-piece long-johns — became fully awake and came at him with a coal scuttle, Mock lost his patience. He felt a whoosh of air by his head, dodged the scuttle at the last moment and with the point of his polished brogue kicked the assailant in the shin. The blow was not hard, but it was painful enough for the scuttle's owner to need to rub the spot. For a moment both his hands were occupied, one rubbing his smarting leg, the other holding his warlike scuttle at the ready. Mock took a swing very like the one he had aimed at the invalid during the seance, and the outer side of his palm came down hard on his assailant's collarbone. His hand, sprained once already that day, burned with a raging fire as he felt the crunch of tiny bones in his wrist. Mock's assailant let go of his scuttle and clutched his neck. Then all he heard was material ripping and shirt buttons hitting the wall of the

† "Should I ever return home" – from the "Schlesierlied".

corridor. He plunged down the stairs, his head struck the door to the toilet on the half-landing, and he heard nothing more.

Mock ran back up to the top floor. He pressed his entire weight against the rickety banister and threw himself at the door to apartment 20, aiming his shoulder at a point just above the handle. There was a terrible crash, but the door did not give way. Other doors did open, however, and on every floor. The tenement residents and their four-legged friends edged out into the stairwell. Mock gathered speed once more, charged at the door and tumbled into the apartment. Bits of rubble pattered against his bowler hat and dust poured down his shirt collar.

He lay on the floor in the hallway, on top of the door, and took stock of the apartment. Smolorz was lying down too, but on the kitchen floor. He was smiling in his sleep, misting the empty stoneware bottle of liqueur at his lips with his breath. Mock turned his head, got to his feet and went into the main room. It was empty; only Erika's hat hung on the back of a chair. He picked it up with two fingers. On the bed sat Rossdeutscher, shouting: "Vengeance will come, Mock. The Erinyes born of the corpses of those closest to you will find you. Those whom you love, Mock . . . Tell us, where are they now . . ." Mock collapsed onto the bed and tried to catch the scent of Erika in the clean sheets which had been there for three weeks, and had not yet lost their starchy smell. Try as he may, he could detect nothing other than the sterile smell of cleanliness. There was no Rossdeutscher, no Erika.

The neighbours of the four sailors stood uncertainly in the doorway watching the two men, one of whom was trying to clamber to his feet, while the other did not want to get off the bed. Suddenly a dog howled and barked at the threshold, and Mock got up and glared at the small crowd gathered at the door.

"Get the fuck out of here!" he roared, and grabbed the chair in the hall and spun it as if throwing a discus.

241

"We're going, we're going." said Frenzel the caretaker, urging his neighbours to leave. "I know him. He's a police officer. It's best not to stand in his way . . ."

The neighbours jumped away from the door and the chair hit Smolorz on the head. Mock's red-headed subordinate clutched his forehead and red trickles ran through his fingers. Mock raised the chair once more and brought it down with a crash. He watched as a sizeable haematoma swelled and split on the bald patch at the back of Smolorz's head. He kicked the chair into a corner of the kitchen and grabbed the poker from a bucket on top of a small pile of coal. He took a swing and struck. The cartilage in Smolorz's ear crunched beneath the spiralled end of the poker. He lay in a foetal position with both hands over his head. Mock grabbed him by the arms and dragged him to the kitchen door, positioning his head against the doorframe. He grasped the door handle and swung the door shut as hard as he could. He thought he heard Smolorz's skull crack.

It was not Smolorz's skull but the kitchen door he had heard as the bottom of it rammed over the poker. Splinters flew off it and Smolorz looked up with drunken eyes.

"Sorry," he croaked in a schnapps-baritone. "I was supposed to keep an eye on her . . . I don't remember a thing . . ."

Mock knelt on the floor and took several deep breaths, allowing his fury to subside. Streams of sweat ran down his neck and seeped into the pale layer of dust that covered the collar of his best shirt. His cuffs were red with Smolorz's blood, his shoes scuffed from the kicks, his jacket torn from breaking down the door, his hands black with soot from the poker.

"I'm sorry," Smolorz said as he cowered by the doorframe. Something had happened to his eye: it was open, bloodshot, and so big that the eyelid could not cover it. "For the love of God, I swear on my Arthur's soul . . ."

"You son of a whore," hissed Mock. "Never swear on a child!"

"On my soul, then" Smolorz groaned. "I'll never touch alcohol . . ."

"You son of a whore," Mock repeated, tossing his head to the side. Drops of sweat darkened the newly polished floorboards. "Get up, pour some soap down your throat and get to work. I'll tell you what you have to do . . ."

As Mock spoke, so Smolorz sobered; with every word Mock uttered he grew more and more amazed.

BRESLAU, THAT SAME SEPTEMBER 28TH, 1919 THREE O'CLOCK IN THE MORNING

It was the second time Sister Hermina had seen the younger Herr Mock that day, and this time he made a far worse impression on her. His suit was covered in dust and torn at the sleeve, his shirt was bloodied and his brogues scuffed at the toe. Small pieces of stone, like bits of rubble, were lodged in the brim of his bowler hat. Herr Mock ran into the corridor of the Surgical Ward repeating something under his breath, something Sister Hermina could not quite make out. It was as if he were saying: "Those closest . . . Where are they now . . . ?"

"Herr Mock!" she called after him as he passed the duty room, muttering to himself. "Where do you think you're going?"

He paid no attention to her and ran towards his father's private room. Sister Hermina set her thin, tall body into motion and her heels clicked loudly down the hospital corridor. Her bonnet with its four folds flapped in all directions like a sailing boat finding its course. Hearing the sound of her heels, patients woke from their painful torpor which none could call sleep, pulled themselves up in bed and waited for a merciful injection, for the gentle touch of her dry, bony hand, for a sympathetic, comforting smile. Sister Hermina's telepathic receptors did not pick up the patients' mute complaints and requests this time, however; they were more sensitive to the anxiety and unease of the dark-haired man who was stumbling

243

from wall to wall, heading for the empty private room. Herr Mock tumbled in and slammed the door. Sister Hermina heard a stifled cry. Perhaps one of her patients was sharing his pain with the others?

But it was not a patient. The younger Herr Mock was lying on his stomach with his arms spread across the clean, freshly made bed, moaning. She rushed over and shook him.

"Doctor Rühtgard came to collect your father an hour ago," she said. "The gentleman felt much better and Doctor Rühtgard took him home with him . . ."

Mock had stopped thinking, stopped feeling anything. He took a few banknotes from his pocket.

"Could you ask somebody, Sister," he whispered, and his bloodshot eyes flashed, "to clean my suit?" He collapsed onto the pillow and fell asleep.

Sister Hermina stroked his cheek, through which the pinpoints of a five o'clock shadow were beginning to protrude, and left the private room.

BRESLAU, THAT SAME SEPTEMBER 28TH, 1919
TEN O'CLOCK IN THE MORNING

Mock walked out of Wenzel-Hancke Hospital and stood deep in thought on the street corner next to a newspaper kiosk. Small children jostled past him in their Sunday best. Entire families hurrying to the evangelical church of St John the Baptist for morning Mass marched along the pavement. Industrious fathers strode by, their gastric juices dissolving fat Sunday sausages; next to them tripped mothers, flushed and sweating in the sun, chasing small herds of unruly children with their parasols. Mock smiled and stepped behind the kiosk to allow four young citizens to pass as they walked in a row holding hands, singing the miners' song:

244

Glück auf! Glück auf!
Der Steiger kommt!
Und er hat sein helles Licht
Bei der Nacht
Schon angezündt.†

A girl of about twelve wearing a pair of thick, darned stockings was making her way behind the children, carrying a bouquet of roses and pushing it under the noses of those standing at the hospital entrance.

Mock glanced down at his cleaned suit and his brogues; a thick layer of polish concealed the scuff marks. The sleeve of his jacket had been well repaired and he could tell from the exceptional softness of its felt that his bowler hat had been cleaned over steam. He beckoned to the girl. She ran to him with her bouquet of roses, apparently limping. Mock inspected the flowers critically.

"Take the flowers into the hospital, to the nurse who was on night duty." He handed the girl ten marks and a small card printed with the words EBERHARD MOCK, POLICE PRAESIDIUM. "And attach my business card."

The girl hobbled to the hospital and Mock was reminded of the cripple he had killed the previous day. He thought of Erika's empty bed. His diaphragm heaved, and his gullet filled with burning bile. He felt faint and held on to the railings surrounding the hospital. Everything seemed to be at a slant. The elegant Neudorfstrasse grew distorted in yellow-black reflections. The mighty buildings with their elaborate decoration rolled and pressed down on one other. He rested his head against the railings and closed his eyes. His head was bursting, as if he had a hangover. The worst hangover was better than a bad conscience, than the invalid's

† "Luck up! Luck up!/Here comes the foreman!/His bright light/Has already been lit." Traditional German song to welcome miners up from the mine.

contorted legs thrashing against the floor and the empty bed where there was no longer even a trace of Erika's scent. Mock wanted a hangover, wanted to suffer, anything so as not to hear the baying of the Erinyes. He looked up and saw the sun-drenched street in its proper perspective. Among the shop signs, one stood out: M. HORN — COLONIAL GOODS. Mock knew the owner and knew he could persuade him to sell him a bottle of liqueur, even on a day of rest.

He set off in the direction of the shop, but stopped at the kerb. The street was very busy. Carriages and cars carrying citizens to church wound their way towards the town centre; in the opposite direction strolled those intending to enjoy an autumnal walk in South Park. All of a sudden there was a commotion. A cab had almost hit a speeding motor with its shaft. The horse yanked at its harness and the cabby swore at the driver, aiming his whip at the elegant gentleman sitting in the open-topped car. Making the most of the confusion, Mock leaped into the street and ran towards the shop and its shelves of bottles filled with colourful sweetness.

But before he could reach them he was accosted outside the shop by a newspaper vendor.

"Special edition of the *Breslauer Neueste Nachrichten*!" yelled the boy in the cap. "Vampire of Breslau commits suicide!"

When Mock saw the article on the front page, he forgot all about alcohol:

VAMPIRE NO LONGER THREATENS CITIZENS OF BRESLAU

Last night, during a spiritual seance, the well-known Breslau doctor, Horst Rossdeutscher, committed suicide. Notes were found in the suicide's house, a singular diary in which he admits to the cruel murder of four men, unidentified to this day, of Julius Wohsedt, director of the Wollheim river port, and of a young prostitute identified as Johanna Voigten. The diary claims that the murders committed during the first four days of September were of a ritualistic nature. According to the Chief of the Murder Commission of the Police Praesidium, Criminal Commissioner Heinrich Mühlhaus, Rossdeutscher had summoned the souls of those he had killed during spiritual seances and, using occult practices, had channeled them to harm an employee of the Vice Department. Neither Criminal Commissioner Mühlhaus nor the aforementioned employee himself, Criminal Assistant Eberhard Mock – we give his name here for the organ grinders of Breslau sing of him! – can explain why Rossdeutscher harboured such a burning hatred for Mock.

Yesterday at midnight, during a successful operation by the police under Criminal Commissioner Mühlhaus and the Mayor's plenipotentiary, Doctor Richard Pyttlik, all those taking part in the seance were arrested. They were, according to the notes, members of a secret occult brotherhood that worshipped ancient Greek deities. Among those arrested were eminent representatives of learning, such as a prominent Hittite linguist at one of the oldest and most renowned German universities. They have been apprehended in order to investigate the matter, but there are unofficial reports that Rossdeutscher's notes – which consist of obscure and garbled notions on mythological subjects – cannot form the basis of a charge.

An unfortunate incident occurred during the seance. Rossdeutscher's handicapped and wheelchair-bound daughter, Louise (twenty), used by her father as a medium to enable the brotherhood to communicate with the dead, suffered a fatal accident as she fell from her wheelchair. On witnessing the death of his beloved daughter, Rossdeutscher shot himself.

The grisly investigation known by the police as the "Four

247

Sailors" case has come to an end. Certain individuals allegedly at risk of death at the hands of the vampire, and for that reason held in isolation by the police, have now been released. The city breathes a sigh of relief. But one question arises: what is happening to our society when one of its foremost representatives, a well-respected surgeon, yields to superstitions which lead him to commit such monstrous crimes? It would be understandable for some eccentric aristocrat, or a shopkeeper tormented by rampaging inflation, to find solace in supernatural powers, but an enlightened representative of science? *Sic transit Gloria mundi.*†

At the bottom of the page there was a large photograph of a young woman with the caption "Erika Kiesewalter", and beneath it the following text:

Twenty-three-year-old Erika Kiesewalter, actress and dance-hostess at the Eldorado Restaurant, disappeared on the night of 27th to 28th September. Dark-red hair, medium height, slim build. No distinguishing features. Anyone with information regarding the missing person is requested to contact the Police Praesidium. Information resulting in Erika Kiesewalter's discovery will be rewarded with the sum of fifteen thousand marks.

BRESLAU, THAT SAME SEPTEMBER 28TH, 1919
ELEVEN O'CLOCK IN THE MORNING

Mock climbed to the first floor of the imposing, detached tenement near South Park and knocked energetically at the door to one of the apartments.

† Thus passes the glory of the world.

It was opened by the owner himself, Doctor Cornelius Rühtgard, who was wearing a crimson dressing gown with velvet lapels and embossed brown-leather slippers. From beneath the velvet lapels peeped the knot of a black necktie.

"Come in, come in, Ebbo," he said, opening the door wide. "Your father feels much better."

"Is he with you?" Mock asked, hanging his bowler hat on the clothes stand.

"He's at my hospital," the doctor said, taking Mock's walking stick.

"The nurse told me he was with you." Mock made his way along the familiar corridor towards the doctor's study.

"Because he is with me." Rühtgard sat down at a small coffee table and gestured for Mock to sit down opposite him. "At my hospital."

"Maybe that's what she said." Mock clipped the end of the Hacif cigar Rühtgard had offered him. "That's probably what she said . . . I was so tired and devastated I didn't take anything in."

"I know, I read about it in the *Breslauer*." Rühtgard stood up. "It's all over. You shouldn't be devastated. It's finished. Nobody's ever going to sing another mournful ballad about the vampire of Breslau. I'll make you some coffee. It's the servants' day off, and Christel's not here either. She's gone on an excursion with the Frisch Auf gymnastics society." He studied his friend. "Tell me, Ebbo, how did that handicapped girl die?"

"I killed her." Mock gazed out at the rustling chestnut tree as it generously bestowing the earth with its yellow leaves. "Unintentionally." The wind murmured, the yellow leaves drifted. "No doubt there's a storm and gales by the sea," he thought, then said out loud: "I hit her when she attacked me. She bit her tongue off and choked on her own blood. Is that possible, Corni?"

"Of course." Rühtgard forgot about the coffee, opened the sideboard and took out a carafe of Edelbranntwein and two small glasses. "In the state you're in, this will do you more good than coffee and cake." He poured with an experienced hand. "Of course it's possible. She drowned in her own blood. If you were to open somebody's mouth and pour a glass of water into it in one go, they would choke and could drown in that small amount. And there would certainly be more blood if you bit your tongue off than one glass."

"I killed her." Mock felt a burning sensation under his eyelids. "And I killed another woman too, though indirectly." He ran his fingers over his eyelids and felt the sand that had built up through lack of sleep. "A woman I fell in love with . . . She was a prostitute and a dance-hostess . . . I'd spent three weeks with her in Rügenwaldermünde . . ."

"Is it that Kiesewalter?" Rühtgard asked, reaching for the *Breslauer Neueste Nachrichten*. He looked very tense, his face like a petrified mask of pain. The doctor leaned towards Mock and grabbed him by the biceps. His fingers were as strong as they had been when he picked up his shattered friend in a Königsberg street.

"What's happened, Corni?" Mock said, putting down his full glass.

"Brother," Rühtgard stammered, "how sorry I feel for you . . . That girl" – he sprang out of his armchair and slammed his palm down on the photograph on the front page of the newspaper – "is your dream. It's the girl of your dreams, your nurse from Königsberg who doesn't exist . . ."

Mock stood up and wiped his damp forehead with the back of his hand. Doctor Rühtgard's study grew longer and narrower. The window appeared to be a far off, bright point. The pictures on the walls distorted into rhomboids, Rühtgard's head sank into his shoulders. Mock stumbled into the bathroom adjacent to the study, tripped and fell to the floor, hitting his forehead against the edge of the porcelain toilet bowl. The blow was so hard that tears filled his eyes. He closed them and felt the warm bump on his forehead pulsate. He opened his eyes again and waited for the veil of tears to disperse. Objects returned to their rightful proportions.

Rühtgard was standing in the doorway, his head once again its rightful size. Mock pushed himself up on his knees and pulled his Mauser from his pocket. He checked that it was loaded and slurred:

"Either I kill myself, or I kill that son of a whore who was supposed to keep an eye on her . . ."

"Wait a moment," Rühtgard said, grasping Mock's wrists in his iron grip. "Don't kill anyone. Sit down on the sofa and tell me everything, calmly . . . We'll find a solution, you'll see . . . After all, that girl has only disappeared, she might still be alive . . ."

He pulled Mock forcibly to the study sofa. The velvet-upholstered piece was too short for Mock to lie on comfortably, so Rühtgard laid his friend's head on a large pillow and his feet on the armrest at the other end. He removed his shoes and applied a cold letter-knife to the bump.

"I'm not going to tell you anything." Rühtgard's nursing clearly brought Mock relief. "I can't talk about it, Corni . . . I just can't . . ."

"You have no idea how much it can help to talk to someone who sympathizes with you . . ." The doctor was very serious. His grey, evenly trimmed beard bristled with kindness, and his pince-nez flashed wisely. "Listen to me, I know a form of therapy which can work extremely well when patients have a block, when they don't want to or can't fully trust their psychologist . . ."

"You're not a psychologist, Rühtgard." Mock sensed drowsiness creep over him. "And I'm not your patient . . . I haven't, as yet, caught syphilis . . ."

"But you are my friend." Now it seemed that Rühtgard was the one with the block; umpteen seconds passed before he blurted: "And the only one at that, the only one I've ever had, or have . . ."

"And what method is that?" Mock appeared not to have heard the confession.

"A method which allows one to get into your subconscious . . . which

251

reveals what is unconscious and negated in an individual. What you may have experienced only once, what you may be ashamed of . . . This method might, for example, make you realize that it is your father you love most, and that the girl who has disappeared is no more than a passing infatuation . . . When you understand yourself, nothing will make you angry . . . You will live and act true to your innermost being. *Gnothi seauton!*† This method is called hypnosis . . . Don't worry, I'm an expert hypnotist. I've mastered the art. I won't harm you, just as I didn't harm my daughter when I put her into a trance. How could I ever harm the person dearest to me?"

Mock did not hear Rühtgard's last words. The autumn wind sending flurries of yellow leaves into flight in Breslau's South Park became a sea wind, and the river whose dark and turbulent waters flowed not far from Rühtgard's house ceased to be the lazy Oder, and became the Pregel, stirred by the salty breeze.

Mock found himself in Königsberg.

KÖNIGSBERG, SATURDAY, NOVEMBER 28TH, 1916
MIDNIGHT

Private Eberhard Mock could not climb the stairs in the tenement at Kniprodestrasse 8, but not because they were exceptionally steep or slippery. The reason was quite different: pumped up with six tall shots of Trishdivinis, a Lithuanian herbal schnapps, he was not in a state even to give the date of his birth. Slumped against the banister he tried to recite the first twenty lines of *The Aeneid* without making any mistakes, in order to convince himself that he was sober. But he could only get as far as the bit about Carthage before the epic's first lines – "*Arma*

† Know thyself.

virumque cano"† — would come back at him like an echo. The regularity of the Latin hexameters introduced a certain order to his brain, which on that winter evening was swimming in schnapps as bitter as absinthe rather than in cerebrospinal fluid.

A signal from his brain reached his extremities and Mock finally made it to the first floor, his spurs ringing out proudly. Even though he had been demoted to private as a former soldier of a reconnoitring platoon, he retained the right to wear spurs. Outside his apartment he felt a huge wave of shame at not being able to get beyond the twelfth verse. He clicked his heels, making an ear-splitting racket with his spurs, and yelled:

"I'm extremely sorry, Professor Moravjetz! I've not learned it for today, but I'll know it all by tomorrow! All fifty verses!"

His diaphragm surged and a mighty hiccough forced its way through Mock's gullet. He pulled a key from his pocket and pushed it into the hole. There was a grating, and he felt the metal resist. Swaying, he produced a metal pipe-cleaning brush from his pocket and slipped that into the keyhole. He pressed his whole weight down on the primitive lever and heard a crack as the cleaning brush snapped. A Mauser 98 appeared in his hand. He aimed at the lock and pulled the trigger.

The noise shook the tenement. Doors to the other apartments opened. Someone shouted at Mock from above:

"What are you doing, you drunken pig? You live one floor up!"

Mock kicked the lock with his heel and forced his way into the hallway. "Did you hear that noise, like a gunshot?" somebody was shouting. "It's him! He's here already!" Mock stood unsteadily in the middle of the hallway before proceeding slowly, his spurs clanking. He came to a velvet curtain and drew it aside. He entered another hallway. It was a waiting room, with doors giving on to several rooms. One of them was ajar, but

† "I sing of arms and of a man."

another heavy curtain hung from its lintel. One of the walls had no door but a window. It gave on to the ventilation pit. Outside on the window sill stood a paraffin lamp whose feeble glow barely penetrated the dusty pane. In the meagre twilight, Mock saw a number of people sitting in the waiting room. He did not manage to get a good look at them as his attention was drawn to the curtain hanging over the door. It moved suddenly. A cold draught and a sigh drifted from beyond it. Mock began to walk towards it, but a tall man in a top hat stood in his way. When Mock tried to move him aside the latter took off his headwear. In the pale semi-darkness he saw a knot of scar tissue as it refracted the dim light; the scars criss-crossed and interweaved in the man's eye sockets. Instead of eyes he had a tangle of scars.

Mock stepped back but was not afraid. He shoved the blind man against the wall, laughed out loud and grabbed the edge of the curtain. From behind it two voices, those of a man and a woman, were uttering inarticulate sounds. Mock yanked at the fabric and caught his spur on an unevenness in the floor. He tumbled onto the sandstone flags and, with a rattle of fastening hooks, the thick green plush tore away and flowed down over him like a shroud. He pulled himself up and advanced on all fours towards an elderly woman who was sitting in the small room beyond the curtain, wheezing. She wore a trailing dark robe. The lamp on the windowsill illuminated her toothless mouth, and from it poured a white swathe which fell in tangles and folds at her feet.

"Ectoplasm!" shrieked a woman's high-pitched voice. "She's materialized it!"

Mock shook with a suppressed hiccough, which was all the stronger for being accompanied by drunken, uncontrollable laughter. The patter of the feet of curious neighbours resounded in the apartment.

"What ectoplasm!" Mock was in convulsions of laughter. He got up, tripped and made towards the medium, who was frozen in a trance.

Without the slightest disgust he began to extract long white strips from the old woman's mouth. "It's an ordinary bandage!"

"Bandage! It's an ordinary bandage!" said a man's stifled voice. "A bunch of frauds, not psychics! And you wanted to make me believe it! I'm going to write everything in the *Königsberger Allgemeine Zeitung*."

"He's wrong, the drunk," a loud voice answered. "'Blessed are those who have not seen and yet have believed!' I have no eyes, but I do believe . . ."

Mock was still unravelling the bandage when he felt a blow to his midriff. He clasped his stomach, amazed at the strength of the toothless woman's punch. Her eyes were still closed as she aimed another blow, this time at his chin. His boots and spurs skidded apart on the bandage, which was sodden with mucus and saliva. He hurtled towards the window. It was not quite shut. He felt the sill beneath his buttocks, and then nothing.

BRESLAU, THAT SAME SEPTEMBER 28TH, 1919
NOON

"And now get up and sit at the desk," said Rühtgard.

Mock obeyed. He got up, sat at the desk and joined his hands. He stared down at the green desk leather as Rühtgard placed a sheet of stiff, decorated wove paper and a Colonia fountain pen in front of him. Then he extracted a wallet adorned with the Königsberg coat of arms from the inside pocket of his jacket and held it open in front of him.

"Write down what I dictate to you," Rühtgard spoke loudly and clearly. "I, Eberhard Mock, the undersigned, being of sound body and mind, declare that on 28th November, 1916, in the city of Königsberg on Pregolya, I was witness to a spiritual seance. Prompted by ill-will and under the influence of alcohol, I attempted to catch hold of the ectoplasm issuing through the mouth of the medium, Frau Natasha Vorobiev. Failing

255

to do so, I assured those assembled that I had caught hold of a bandage, and that the entire seance was a sham. My behaviour prompted Herr Harry Hempflich, a journalist from the *Königsberger Allgemeine Zeitung*, to publish in his newspaper on 31st November a slanderous article aimed against spiritualism. I hereby declare that all the information presented by H. Hempflich and based on my so-called experiences are false and spring from my materialist and scientific outlook on life. I also ardently declare that I firmly believe in the existence of spirits and phantoms, having experienced their activity in my house on Plesserstrasse. At the same time I vouch to assume responsibility for the deaths of six people, namely, Julius Wohsedt, Johanna Voigten and four sailors. They suffered death for a great cause — to prove to me that spirits do exist. If I had not disbelieved, those persons would still be alive. Blessed are those who have not seen and yet have believed. Eberhard Mock."

Mock finished writing. Rühtgard put the wallet back into his jacket. He folded the letter Mock had written into four and slipped it into an envelope. Then he placed the envelope in front of the police officer sitting at his desk and said in a loud voice:

"Address it to Herr Harry Hempflich, Chief Editor, *Königsberger Allgemeine Zeitung*. And now get up and go to the door!"

Mock stopped in the doorway, his eyes still closed.

"Walk down the corridor and through the first door on the left!"

Mock walked into the games room, with Rühtgard following him.

"Walk over to the balcony door, open it and walk out on to the balcony!"

Mock knocked into the piano in the middle of the room, but soon found his way to the balcony. He opened the balcony door and stepped onto the small terrace.

"Climb onto the balcony ledge and jump!"

Mock clambered onto the ledge with difficulty. He held onto the balustrade with one hand, and with the other grabbed an enormous flowerpot that was secured to the ledge with a metal hoop. The flowerpot broke away and smashed onto the pavement between the spiked railings and the tenement wall. Mock lost his balance and fell back heavily onto the balcony floor.

"Stand on the ledge!"

Mock lifted his leg and placed it once again on the stone balustrade, holding on to the wall with one hand with such ease as if walking the tightrope was his daily bread.

"And now jump, impale yourself on those railings!"

Mock jumped.

BRESLAU, THAT SAME SEPTEMBER 28TH, 1919
ONE O'CLOCK IN THE AFTERNOON

Mock jumped. His torso was not impaled on the railings, however; his legs did not hang from its arrow-shaped spikes or thrash at the metal in agony. Mock turned his shoulders and jumped . . . from the balustrade onto the balcony. But not by choice. As he was bending his knees to launch himself off the balustrade and soar in a wide arch onto the spiked railings, a tall figure who had been squatting in the corner of the balcony sprang to his feet. A strong, freckled hand covered with thick red hair grabbed him by the tails of his jacket and pulled him forcefully to itself.

"What's this, Herr Mock!" growled Smolorz. "What's all this about?"

Mock's subordinate had a raging hangover. His gullet was burning; his stomach was aflame; his ear — enormously swollen and blue-black from the blow dealt by the poker — radiated heat to his cheeks; the haematoma at the top of his head and the bump on his forehead boiled beneath a thin film of skin. Smolorz was angry. At Mock and at the whole world. He grabbed his boss by the collar and lugged him back into the

257

room. He placed the sole of his shoe on Mock's pale jacket and shoved him under the piano.

"Lie there, fuck it," he muttered and hurled himself after Rühtgard who had disappeared into the hall, slamming the door to the games room behind him.

Smolorz was exploding with fury. He opened the door so energetically it almost came off its hinges. He heard the sound of a body falling in the hall, and was there a second later to see that the rug had been moved and the small table with the telephone overturned. The figure of Rühtgard flashed through the front door. Smolorz ran into the corridor and saw the fleeing man already halfway down the stairs. His brain, overcooked with alcohol, now began to function. Why had the rug in the hall been moved, and why were the table and telephone lying on the floor? "Because Rühtgard slipped," Smolorz answered his own question, and instantly formed his plan of action. He caught hold of the stair carpet held in place with metal rods and tugged hard. The rods rang out in the silence of the corridor, rolled down the stairs, and Cornelius Rühtgard's feet lost contact with the floor. The doctor tumbled down to the half-landing, protecting his head from hitting the wall. A moment later he was also having to shield it from the blows of a rod. Smolorz was truly furious, and Rühtgard was feeling his fury.

BRESLAU, MONDAY, SEPTEMBER 29TH, 1919
ONE O'CLOCK IN THE MORNING

Doctor Cornelius Rühtgard sat in the middle of a large room encircled by a mezzanine floor. A fibrous rope cut into his swollen wrists when he moved his hands, and his eyes were struggling to adjust themselves to the bright electric light beaming from a lamp on the table. A moment earlier a sack had been removed from his head, reeking of something that reminded him of detestable mornings spent in the mortuary at Königsberg University – formaldehyde, and an even worse odour which he preferred not to identify.

"It's strange, Rühtgard," came Mock's voice from the darkness, "that you, a doctor, after all, should loathe corpses . . ."

"I'm a doctor of venereology, Mock, not a pathologist." Rühtgard cursed the hour when, lying in the trenches surrounded by gleaming snow and the glimmering of the stars, he had once confided in Mock and told him about the terrible moments he had experienced during his classes in the mortuary: his colleagues had made a show of eating their sausage rolls while he, in spasms, had clasped his stomach and vomited trails of bile into the old sink.

"Take a look around our museum of pathology," Mock said quietly, "while I read something to you . . ." He opened out the denial he himself had written. "Let's see whether handwriting changes under hypnosis."

Rühtgard cast his eye at the glass display cases and turned pale. A foetus turned its film-covered eye towards him from a jar of formaldehyde. Next to it was a stretched, rectangular piece of skin, and above a tangle of pubic hair loomed a bold tattoo: "For beautiful women only"; below this, an arrow pointed downwards to indicate what had been reserved for the fair sex.

"Tell me, Rühtgard" – Mock's voice was very calm – "where are my father and Erika Kiesewalter? I gather no-one at your hospital has even heard of them . . ."

"Before I tell you" – Rühtgard's eyes wandered to a severed hand which had been arranged in a jar in such a way that students could study its tendons and muscles – "tell me how you found out about me."

"I'm the one asking the questions here, you swine" Mock's voice did not change one iota. His stocky form was obscured in the shadow cast by the lamp.

"I have to know, Mock." Rühtgard's eyes paused at a glass shelf on which lay a row of skulls with bullet holes. "I have to know whether I was betrayed by a member of my brotherhood. I'll give you an address and you can send your men there. But what are we going to do while your brave boys search the cellar where I keep the prisoners? We'll talk, won't we, Mock? We'll carry on our conversation to shorten the wait. And each of us will both answer and ask questions. No-one's going to say: 'I'm the one asking the questions here'. It's going to be a quiet conversation between two old friends, alright Mock? You choose. On one side of the scales my silence and your pitiful copper's pride shouting 'I'm the one asking the questions here', on the other the address and a quiet conversation. Are you a reasonable man, Mock, or are you so full of anger that all you want to do is hit your square head against the wall? It's your choice, Mock."

"And why shouldn't I go to the cellar with my men? I want to see my father and Erika. There'll always be time to listen to you . . ."

"Oh dear . . ." Rühtgard closed his eyes to the grotesque exhibits. "I've forgotten the address. It'll come back to me when you promise to stay here . . . What's it to you, Mock? I can tell you about Königsberg and many other things besides. . . You listen to me, I listen to you . . ."

For a long while Mock did not say anything, then finally he uttered a single word:

"Address."

"Common sense has prevailed over fury. Löschstrasse 18, cellar number ten." Rühtgard felt his throat constrict as he studied a vast aquarium of formaldehyde in which stood a two-metre-tall albino with Negroid features. "So tell me, how did you track me down."

Mock got up, left the room and shouted: "Löschstrasse 18, cellar number ten. At the double! And take a nurse!" A clatter of shoes rang out on the stairs.

260

"How did you track me down?" Rühtgard felt a peculiar satisfaction in manipulating Mock. "Go on, divulge your famous, impeccable logic!"

"Remember when I confided in you about my night terrors?" The crack of a match, and a blaze of light cut through a column of smoke. "You broke the whole thing down to areas of the brain, with one area being responsible for one thing, another for something else. You asked me then whether my father and the dog heard the noises. I never told you anything about a dog. Never mentioned I had one, because I don't. How could you have known? Because you'd been to my place one night. I asked myself: what could Rühtgard have been doing at my place? I couldn't answer this." Mock lit a cigarette with trembling hands. "When you spent the night with me, you smoked a cigarette before going to sleep. You threw the butt into the grille in the drain. How did you know it was there, in the corner behind the old counter? Because you'd already been there once, I answered. I couldn't believe you were a murderer, that you'd put Director Wohsedt's letter down the drain. There was only one thing for me to do: keep an eye on you. Unfortunately, I only thought of this rather late — yesterday, in fact. I got out of the habit of thinking during my three weeks at the seaside. Smolorz has been tailing you since yesterday. He got into your apartment on the quiet and hid on the balcony. I told him not to let you out of his sight. Smolorz is a simple lad and takes everything literally. That's why he wasn't standing outside, but he kept an eye on you anyway."

Mock got up and strolled over to a skeleton in a show-case.

"Now I have a question for you," he said. "Who did the killing? Who tailed me? Who knew whom I was questioning?"

"Rossdeutscher and his men tailed you." Rühtgard was gradually getting used to his ghastly surroundings. "You have no idea how many of them there are . . ."

"No, I don't." Mock sat down at the desk again. "But you're going to tell me everything. You're going to give me their names and addresses . . ."

"Don't forget the friendly form this conversation is supposed to be taking. You can't force me to do anything!"

"You're no longer my friend, Rühtgard. You appeared at my side as far back as Königsberg . . . Was that to . . ."

"Yes . . . Offer me a cigarette! You don't want to? Too bad. You know I was told to take a job at the Hospital of Divine Mercy soon after you got there . . . The brothers instructed me to persuade you to write this denial. Unfortunately, that wasn't possible in the hospital. You didn't want to know about anything other than that nurse who'd appeared in your dreams. I had to go with you to the front, and then here to this accursed city, where there's not even the slightest breeze to disperse this malarial air. The brothers rented me an apartment and set me up with a medical practice. You have no idea how many of us are doctors . . . But I'm gabbling away, not letting you get a word in edgeways . . . A question for a question, Mock. Tell me, have you really fallen in love with this . . . Erika Kiesewalter?"

Mock retreated into the shadow cast by the lamp. Rühtgard closed his eyes and counted the purple patches beneath his eyelids, caused by the bright light beaming on his face.

"Yes," came the reply.

"So why didn't you tell her that on the beach in Rügenwaldermünde?" Rühtgard would have given a great deal to see Mock's face. "She even asked you after your failed attempt to arrange a threesome."

Rühtgard stood up and took a swing at the burning-hot lampshade. The lamp fell off the table and cast a shaft of light on some nooses suspended from a stand, which in the past had bound the necks of humans. Mock sat quite still, his Mauser aimed at Rühtgard's chest.

"You're an idiot, Mock!" Rühtgard yelled, and then, looking into the dark hole of the barrel, he drawled, "Rossdeutscher and I once considered how we might use your obsessions and phobias to the advantage of our cause . . . The cause of salvaging the honour of the brotherhood . . . I told Rossdeutscher that you were mad about a red-headed nurse from Königsberg. He then introduced me to Erika at the Eldorado. It didn't take long to persuade her . . . She was the ideal bait – red-headed, slim but with a big bust, well versed in ancient classical writers . . ."

"What a mistake, what a terrible mistake . . ." Mock was still aiming at the chest of his captive. "A crafty whore, a crafty whore . . ."

"You made an enormous mistake. Not in trusting her . . . but in not telling her that you loved her. She tried to drag it out of you on the beach, but you wouldn't say anything . . . No doubt you considered it unworthy of yourself to declare your love to a whore . . . But by that you lost her . . . I asked her: 'Has Mock told you that he loved you?' 'No,' she replied. So I didn't need her any more. If you had declared your true feelings for her she would be where your father is right now, rather than at the bottom of the Oder . . ."

Mock fired. Rühtgard threw himself to one side and avoided the shot, but the albino did not. The slabs of glass shattered, the formaldehyde sluiced over Rühtgard as he lay curled up on the floor and the huge, pale faced Negro broke apart at the knees and fell from the display case. Mock leaped onto the table to avoid being sent sprawling by the formaldehyde and aimed his gun once more, but then decided this was unnecessary. Rühtgard was lying on the floor, his mouth gaping and sheer terror in his eyes. Lumps of the albino's body had attached themselves to his jacket. He looked like a man who had suffered a heart attack.

"He's alive," Doctor Lasarius said, touching Rühtgard's neck. "He's in shock, but he's alive."

"Thank you, Doctor." Mock breathed a deep sigh of relief. "We'll do as I said earlier."

Doctor Lasarius made towards his office and shouted into the depths of the dark corridor: "Gawlitzek and Lehnig! Come here!"

Two stalwart men wearing rubber aprons entered the museum of pathology. Their heads were split into two equal halves by wide partings, and moustaches sat proudly above their lips. One of them efficiently cleaned away the remnants of formaldehyde and flaccid human tissue from Rühtgard's face; the other sat him on a chair and gave him a sound slap across the cheek. The stricken man opened his eyes and looked around the room full of macabre exhibits with disbelief.

"Get him undressed!" Lasarius ordered curtly. "And into the pool!"

Mock and Lasarius descended the stairs from the first to the ground floor and made their way down cold corridors decorated with pale-green wainscoting. Along the walls stood trolleys on which the dead made their last journey to the doctor. Mock could not keep count of the turns they both took, but eventually they found themselves in a tiled area where the floor dropped away into a two-metre-deep pool. In it stood Doctor Rühtgard, shivering with cold. Lasarius' subordinates were in the process of opening the sluice gate and filling the pool with water that smelled of formaldehyde.

"Thank you, gentlemen!" Lasarius said to his subordinates, handing them a few banknotes. "And now home, take a droschka on me! Keep the change!"

Lehnig and Gawlitzek nodded and disappeared down the cavernous corridors. Lasarius followed in their footsteps, leaving Mock alone. He looked at Rühtgard standing up to his waist in water, and turned the wheel of the sluice gate as if it were a helm. The hairs on Rühtgard's shivering body fell in wet strips.

"Frightened of corpses, eh, Rühtgard?" Mock called as he put on a rubber apron. "See this gate?" He indicated the sluice above the edge of the pool. "I'm going to let some fat fish into the pool through it . . . In no time at all there'll be masses of them. Then I'm going to pour in some more water mixed with formaldehyde until the pool's full to the brim. You like the smell of formaldehyde, eh, Rühtgard? Remember how you ate cucumber soup after your first pathology classes in Königsberg? You raised the spoon to your lips and smelled that unmistakeable odour under your fingernails. You told me all about it and gave me your portion of cucumber soup at Dünaburg. Answer my questions, or you'll be swimming in formaldehyde with fat, disintegrating fish."

"If you torture me," called Rühtgard from the pool, "sooner or later you're going to kill me. The first dead thing that floats into this pool is going to give me a heart attack. Idiot!" he yelled. "Don't kill me until you've freed them from the cellar . . ."

"You just said 'them'." Mock squatted at the edge of the pool. "You've only got my father, so why do you say 'them'?" – he felt a wave of hope – "You said Erika was at the bottom of the Oder. Are you bluffing?"

"You ignorant fool." Rühtgard's bloodshot eyes flashed with amusement. "The Erinyes of two people are more powerful than the Erinyes of one . . . It's obvious . . . Simple arithmetics . . . I had to find one other person you love . . . Apart from your father, and instead of the whore to whom you would not declare your love . . ."

"And who did you find?" Mock felt deeply uneasy.

"There is such a person." Rühtgard laughed as if demented and leaped up and down, slapping his pale, bruised thighs. "You walked through the park with her that night, you courted her, paid her compliments . . . She says you've fallen in love with her . . ."

"You crazy swine!" Mock grasped his head, unable to hide his horror. "You've killed your own daughter? Your own beloved daughter?"

"I haven't killed her yet," Rühtgard shouted through cupped hands from the bottom of the pool: "For the time being I've merely imprisoned my Christel . . . My daughter . . . She proved useful in my hypnosis experiments, as best she could. And now she's out there somewhere, together with your father . . . She and your old man are a guarantee of my immunity."

"That's why you looked so strange when I told you I'd fallen in love with Erika Kiesewalter, before the hypnosis . . ." Mock said quietly. "You realized you had imprisoned your own daughter unnecessarily . . . You could have locked Erika away, and you wouldn't have felt her death as acutely as that of your own child . . ."

"Correct." Rühtgard grabbed hold of the pool's edge and hauled himself up. His face found itself at a level with Mock's. He looked the police officer deep in the eye. "But I stopped loving Christel . . . She betrayed me once too often. Besides, she's no use to me any more. . . She won't undergo any more hypnosis . . . She said it hurts afterwards. . . She hates me . . . She'll soon leave me for some stinker . . ."

Mock recoiled in disgust. Rühtgard made a rapid move, straightened his arms on the pool's edge and managed to lean against them. One more move and his knee was over the edge too. Mock hit him in the face. There was a loud splash.

"Don't try to get out of there," he said calmly. "And answer my questions. Who was it, then, who wrote the murderer's diary? And who scribbled 'Have to run for it' at the seance?"

"That 'diary', as you call it" – Rühtgard was standing at the bottom of the pool, rubbing one cheek, red from the blow, and the injuries inflicted by Smolorz looked like boils on his white skin – "was written by me. Rossdeutscher took minutes during the rites. I was the brotherhood's chronicler but only Rossdeutscher could take down the Master's translations. When I heard you, I scribbled something and hid under the desk. My notes fell into your hands. You assumed Rossdeutscher had written them. You don't know my handwriting. Our German secondary schools are fortunately very strict about Sütterline handwriting, apart from for Greek and Latin. Our writing looks much the same: yours, mine and Rossdeutscher's. No court is going to believe a handwriting expert."

Firm, resolute steps resounded in the subterranean corridors of the Institute of Forensic Medicine. Kurt Smolorz entered the pool room.

"There's nobody in that cellar," he said, out of breath. "Only a sign on the door." He reached into his pocket and handed Mock a scrap of paper.

"'*Gnothi seauton*,'" Mock read the Greek words. "'Know thyself.'"

Mock looked at Rühtgard dispassionately and instructed Smolorz:

"Turn the wheel, open the sluice! Tell me, you son of a whore, where is my father?"

Smolorz turned the wheel, and water mixed with formaldehyde spurted straight into Rühtgard's open mouth. The Criminal Sergeant then opened the sluice gate, resting the end of it against the pool's edge to form a kind of platform, and moved away in revulsion. Beneath the sluice gate was a swollen, green corpse.

"Listen to me, Mock . . ." Rühtgard again hauled himself up on his hands, but this time only his chin appeared above the pool's edge. "You've got nothing on me. Rossdeutscher committed suicide. He was your murderer . . . And I'm untouchable. But that's not all. You're in my hands. Send your denial to the *Breslauer* and the *Königsberg Allgemeine Zeitung*, and let me go. The worse that can happen is that you'll lose your job in the police force. But you'll save your own father and my daughter. What's the girl done to you? Don't forget the impression you made on her that night. You can have her, you can screw her as much as you like . . ."

Mock stepped away from the pool and reached for a thick rubber hose.

"Don't try to climb out, or you'll get a jet of water in your mug," he said calmly. "What guarantee do I have that you'll let them go? Maybe you'll take revenge on me and kill them after all . . ."

"I'm not going to murder my own daughter, much as I may despise her." Rühtgard stared with disgust at the green corpse lodged in the sluice. "Let me go, Mock, and everything will be alright. All you'll do is lose your job, while the denial will reap such fruit. The denial, Mock. I can make you do things – like I did during hypnosis. I'm untouchable. Even if I were to screw that whore Kiesewalter in front of your very eyes, you wouldn't do anything to me because I've got you in my hands . . . I must have given you the wrong address for the cellar – I'll give you the right one now . . ."

Mock gave Smolorz a signal. The Criminal Sergeant tugged the corpse by its hair with disgust and the greenish body slid into the water with a gentle splash. The face of the deceased was blackened by fire, his hair thick and brown. His pubic hair reached as high as his navel. Mock squirted water into Rühtgard's face and the doctor found himself back in the pool. The bloated body spun slowly in the stream of water and formaldehyde. Rühtgard yelled at the top of his voice. Only his head remained above the surface.

"Where is my father?" asked Mock.

Once again, Rühtgard clambered up the pool's edge. He put his forearms on the tiles and rested his chin on his hands. His bloodshot eyes were fixed on Mock.

"It's stalemate, Mock," he said. "It only takes four days for a man to die of dehydration. Send that denial to the press."

"Tell me one more thing," Mock said, as if he had not heard the ultimatum. "Where did my dreams, my nightmares come from?"

"They weren't dreams, they were the Erinyes. Real beings which exist

268

objectively. Ghosts, phantoms, spectres if you like." Rühtgard's chin was still resting on his hands, while the stout railwayman who had urinated from a viaduct onto a high-voltage cable a few days earlier turned in the eddies below.

"Then why did you try to prove to me that ghosts are only subjective?"

"I was playing devil's advocate, to strengthen your belief . . . To make you confess to your mistake with utter conviction . . . So that you'd say: it must have been real ectoplasm after all!"

"Why did you gouge out their eyes and stick needles into their lungs?"

"Are you really so stupid, or are you just pretending?" Rühtgard's pupils dilated and contracted like a shutter in a camera. "Strain your drunken brain a little! 'If your eye causes you to sin, gouge it out.' It's from St Matthew.† And listen to St John, that great visionary, who wrote: 'Blessed are those who have not seen and yet have believed.'"‡

"And the needles in their lungs?"

"I was taking away their breath, taking their spirit!"

Mock thought back to his university lectures in comparative literature and could hear Professor Rossbach's voice: "Marcus Terentius Varro was right in saying that the Latin *animus* (spirit) is related to the Greek *anemos* (wind)," the professor had explained. "A living person breathes and from his lips, *ergo*, comes wind, but a corpse does not breathe. In a living person there is a spirit; a dead man has no spirit. Hence the simple – we could almost say 'commonsensical' – identification of spirit with breath. It is the same in the Slavic languages, where *dusza* (spirit) is etymologically related to *zdech* (died), and *oddech* (breath). It is the same even in the Hebrew language. There, *ruach* means both spirit and wind, although – and here I must castigate myself – the concept of 'breath' is rendered by an entirely different word, namely *nefesh*. So you see,

† St Matthew 5:29, *Holy Bible*, New International Version (2001)
‡ St John 20:29, ibid.

gentlemen, the study of etymology is one way of learning about spiritual culture, a culture, let us add, that is common to both Indo-Germans and Semites." Professor Rossbach's voice fell silent in Mock's head. In its place he heard his own father's nagging: "Chamomile and hot milk".

"Where's my father?" Mock said, then nodded to Smolorz who allowed the cadaver of a thin man covered in contusions through the sluice. The two bodies danced in the stream of water and formaldehyde. Mock swung the hosepipe. The rubber slapped against Rühtgard's body. The doctor fell into the pool again. The surface of the water was now half a metre below the pool's edge.

"Remember, Mock?" — Rühtgard resurfaced by the sluice gate and tried to shout above the roar of the water — "You always dreamed about the corpses of those who died because of you. Those were your Erinyes. Don't fall asleep now, or the Erinyes of your father and my daughter will fly to you. Now you'll never fall asleep. As long as you stay awake, they'll still be alive. Beware of sleep, Mock, choose benevolent insomnia . . ." Once more he scrambled over the edge of the pool and hoisted himself up on outstretched arms. "Blessed are the meek!" he yelled. "I'm not going to tell you where your father is. I may die, but my brothers are here in Breslau. When your denial has been printed, they'll set the prisoners free. Remember — don't sleep. Your sleep is their death. Now look what I learned at the seance . . ."

Rühtgard slipped his tongue between his teeth and pulled his hands away from the pool's edge. His legs, arms and torso slid into the churning water as his chin hit the tiles. Rühtgard's severed tongue danced like a living creature at Mock's feet as the doctor choked.

The following day, Doctor Lasarius stated that it was impossible to diagnose unequivocally whether Rühtgard had choked on his own blood, or on a mixture of water and formaldehyde.

Heymann's Coffee House was open for business. Among its regular customers — chiefly employees of the German Fisheries Company who had nipped out for a coffee and strudel with whipped cream before it became too busy — sat two men raising steaming cups to their lips. One of them smoked one cigarette after another, while the other, his teeth clenched around the ivory mouthpiece of a pipe, expelled small columns of smoke from the corners of his lips. The dark-haired man took a few folded sheets of paper from the inside pocket of his jacket and handed them to the bearded man, who puffed out squat mushrooms of smoke as he read. His companion brought a small phial to his nose. The pungent odour of urine drifted over the table. Several customers screwed up their noses in obvious disgust. The older man was red with agitation and high blood pressure.

"Now I know where this absurd declaration to the press comes from, Mock. I also know" — Mühlhaus gripped Mock's face — "much more than that. Yes, much, much more . . . You don't have to publish it any more. . ."

From his briefcase Mühlhaus pulled two pieces of paper headed "Post-mortem Report" and handed them to Mock. Mock tried to focus on Lasarius' wobbly writing. "'Male, aged about seventy-five; height: one metre sixty centimetres; weight: sixty-two kilograms. Clear fracture in two places of lower left limb. Female, aged about twenty, height: one metre fifty-nine centimetres; weight: fifty-eight kilograms. Both found in the cellar at Paulinenstrasse 18. Cause of death: dehydration.'"

Mock shook his head and rested his elbows on the table. He was staring at the headings on both pieces of paper where Lasarius had written in a spidery hand "Alfred Salomon and Catarina Beyer."

"It's not them," whispered Mock. "They're the wrong names . . ."

Mühlhaus put his arm around Mock's neck and rested his head on his shoulder.

"Sleep, Mock," he said. "And don't have any dreams, no more dreams . . ."

ACKNOWLEDGEMENTS

This book would have been very difficult to write had it not been for the expertise and kindness of many people.

Above all I thank Dr Jerzy Kawecki of the Centre of Forensic Medicine at the Piastów Śląskich Medical Academy in Wrocław for his medical knowledge and for his advice on pathological morphology; Professor Jerzy Maron, Deputy Vice-Chancellor of the University of Wrocław, for his historical advice; Małgorzata Nawotka, curator at the National Museum in Wrocław, for her advice on costumes; Marek Burak, curator at the History Museum in Wrocław, and Piotr Dudziak for their advice on topography; Zbigniew Kowerczyk and Przemysław Szczurk for their literary advice; my editor Anna Rudnicka for her valuable comments and Bogda Balicka for granting me access to the riches of her library and archives.

At the same time I would like to stress that any eventual errors are mine alone.

M.K.
Wrocław